Not Fade Away

JIM DODGE is the author of four books: *Fup*, *Not Fade Away*, *Stone Junction* and *Rain on the River: Selected Poetry and Short Prose*. He lives on an isolated ranch in California's Western Sonoma County.

Praise for Jim Dodge

NOT FADE AWAY

'the best road novel never to be adapted for the big screen ... *Vanishing Point* with a point, *Easy Rider* with no hippies and a sense of historical depth' *Guardian*

'the writing pulses with heavy abandon' *Sunday Times*

'a book which screams off the starting blocks and just keeps accelerating' *Uncut*

'a potent mix of bawdy folk-tale, philosophy and principled techno-awareness. Strong threads of humanism work within a fabric of vibrant characters, hillbilly landscapes and cathartic wit' *Dazed and Confused*

'snappier dialogue than anyone this side of Elmore Leonard' *Scotland on Sunday*

'expect your brain cells to be frazzled by the funk and fervour of his prose' *Herald*

'an extraordinary little book ... a piece of American grotesque
that ends with an epiphany as unexpected as it is beautiful. The
writing is often as good as writing gets ... I expect anyone
glancing at this review to make a respectable effort to read this
book' *Literary Review*

'[a] witty and sprightly modern allegory ... you'll love it'
Independent on Sunday

'this novel is fupped uck' *The Times*

'there is a moment of real horror and loss, and then a quite
beautiful resolution. The story twists and turns between Twain
and Steinbeck but has a fairytale ending worthy of Oscar Wilde.
By the way, Fup is the name of the duck, and apart from anything
else, this book is very funny' *Sunday Telegraph*

STONE JUNCTION

'an irresistible kaleidoscope of manic, tragic and exquisitely funny
Americana' *Time Out*

'an often glorious narrative, peopled by characters of genuine
imaginative force' *Herald*

'the kind of book that should make the John Grishams of this
world weep into their overstuffed pillows' *Evening Standard*

Not Fade Away

Jim Dodge

First published in Great Britain in 1998 by
Canongate Books Ltd, 14 High Street,
Edinburgh EH1 1TE. Reprinted in 2000.

This edition published in 2004

First published in the United States in 1987
by the Atlantic Monthly Press

10 9 8 7 6 5 4 3 2 1

British Library Cataloguing-in-Publication Data
A catalogue record for this book is available on
request from the British Library

ISBN 1 84195 486 1

Typeset by Palimpsest Book Production Limited,
Polmont, Stirlingshire
Printed and bound in Germany
by Bercker, Kevelaer

www.canongate.net

This one's going out for Mom, brother Bob, and Victoria (that's right: dedicated to the one I love); for Jacoba, Leonard, and Lynn; for Sylvia, Boney Maroni, and Peggy Sue; for Jeremiah, Jerry, and Jack; Freeman and Nina; Gary, Allen, Lew, and John; for Boots, Annie, Dick, Joe, and all the cats and kitties down at the Tastee-Freeze on a hot summer night; for all the players and dancers and pilgrims of the faith; in memory of Ed O'Conner and Darrell Gray; and to the great spirits of Buddy Holly, Ritchie Valens, and the Big Bopper, R.I.P.

Acknowledgments

I wish to thank the following people for their gracious assistance in the preparation of this manuscript:

Charles Walk, now publisher of the *Helena Independent Record*, who was the first reporter at the scene of the February 3, 1959, plane crash, and whose story was picked up by the major wire services;

Jean Wallace of the Beaumont Library for her unstinting professional aid and encouragement in the course of my laggardly research;

Eric Gerber of the *Houston Post* for little details that were a big help;

Dr Alfonso Rodriguez Lopez for medical care and understanding;

Gary Snyder, for background and foreground and a lot of ground in between;

a number of friends whose early readings of the manuscript were uniformly marked by acumen and uncommon tact – Leonard Charles, Richard Cortez Day, Morgan Entrekin, Bob Funt, Jeremiah Gorsline, Michael Helm, Jack Hitt, Freeman House and Nina, Jerry Martien, Lynn Milliman, and Victoria Stockley;

Anne Rumsey, for coordinating permissions and envelopes within envelopes;

Gary Fisketjon, for his sweet heart and sharp pencil;

and Melanie Jackson, for keeping together what tends to fly apart.

My gratitude.

Introduction

KEVIN SAMPSON

Jim Dodge lives on a remote ranch in Northern California. His is a community of potions, ghosts, myths and legends and his writing – the most imaginative of any living author – reflects the best traditions of the yarner. Magic, music and the hills and forests of deepest darkest California inform all his books. *Fup*, an enchanting tale of immortality and fence-posts occupies a world of whiskey stills where the lawman turns a blind eye to justifiable criminality. It's only the dog-savaging, fence-chewing, duck-rutting wild hogs that have him stumped. *Stone Junction* deals with a network of philanthropic anarchists and alchemists who can do *anything they want*. And they do. They make themselves invisible and steal the biggest diamond in the whole world. They can beat anyone in a fair fight if they need to, and they sometimes make love to seven maidens under one full moon. Strange things are afoot in the forests of Sonoma County, we can only hope.

Potions figure strongly in both books and it's under the influence of another mystical 'flu remedy that the vessel of *Not Fade Away* receives the testimony of Floorboard George Gastin, retired hippie car thief. *Not Fade Away* is a rattling good yarn about a chap who's paid to steal and destroy a perfect white Cadillac. Before steering us through the whacked-out cut and thrust of a pan-American car chase, however

– and it's one heck of a weird taxi-ride – Jim Dodge gives a precise and loving portrait of the fledgling San Francisco Beat movement.

It's easy to think of the San Francisco scene revolving around Haight-Ashbury, flower power and love-ins. It's easy to think '69. But the seeds of the hippie scene were scattered fifteen years earlier with the free thinkers, jazz musicians and dodgy poets of the North Beach community. Café Trieste and Bar Vesuvio became the hangout for every philosopher and drifter in town. It was a great time for ugly guys to get laid. You turned up, read poems and copped off. It's a magical time magically captured at the start of *Not Fade Away*. Jim Dodge manages to mock the scene and celebrate it, brilliantly, both at once. In one episode a youthful Floorboard George meets Kacy, a rich, beautiful dropout at a jazz bar. His description of Big Red the saxophone player bending and sustaining his notes in a way that drains the listener's soul is stunning. Kacy makes George take his clothes off outside the club and walk naked with her to his apartment. It's a superbly erotic scene, neither salacious nor sentimental. He barely described the sex yet you read it with a soaring bonk-on. His evocation of high times and loose living is spellbinding – truly rock 'n' roll writing at its best.

That spell is cast over the rest of the story, too. It's a fabulous fable, rich with exotic, deranged, hopeless characters. It's rare to find yourself rooting for such a fantastic array of losers, but this is the essence of Jim Dodge's writing. It is wonderfully humane. There can't be a writer so besotted with his own creatures. He made them and he adores them, one and all – even Scumball, the baddie. So we meet and fall in love with Donna Walsh, trailer-trash single mom, unlucky in love, barely keeping it together. There's the shamanistic inventor, Joshua Springfield who traverses the land, experimenting with light and sound and drugs. The Reverend Double Gone Johnson is looking for a few dollars to start his own church – the only other thing stopping him is his search for the appropriate name for his new love sect. Should it be The Comedown Tabernacle Of the Grim View? Or The Rock Solid Gospel Light Church Of The Holy Release? Whatever, it sounds like a church you'd cheerfully don your Sunday best for.

All of this splendid battiness is underscored by a rock 'n' roll soundtrack that as good as jives off the page at you. Buddy Holly, Little Richard, Elvis, The Everlys, Fats Domino, Chuck Berry, Jerry Lee Lewis and so many more are written up with a relish you can taste. If the story were not so grippingly told you'd have no choice but to drop the book and wrench your dorsals doing back-drops to 'Chantilly Lace'. George's mission is to deliver this Caddy to the grave of The Big Bopper himself and pay the final tribute by setting the rockmobile ablaze. As he sets off on this incredible picaresque, the bump and grind of the music, music, music is never far away.

As Floorboard George charges through the city limits and interstate highways, day and night, mile after mile sustained mainly by the 1,000-pill jar of uppers he bought at the outset, you start to get a sense of his immortality. Perhaps the drugs take their toll on the reader, too, because a pervading atmosphere of sub-reality starts to infuse the characters and places and scenarios. Towards the end of his journey George encounters crazies like Phillip Lewis Kerr, The Greatest Travelling Salesman In The World, who have a distinctly spectral feel. George starts having visions and hearing voices. You can feel his paranoia as the big world closes in on him. But above all you feel that no amount of road blocks, helicopters, FBI gooks or clueless gangsters will ever get close to George. You know he's an Untouchable – he won't fade away.

With his amphetamines mine reduced to a sticky residue, George arrives at his spiritual destiny. Ghosts and legends and tragedies rend the skies. The boundaries between the real and the unreal, between myth and truth, between substance and vapour have been blurred forever. The narrator comes out of his potion-induced stupor, unsure whether he even met Floorboard George Gastin at all. Was his story told to him or did he dream the whole thing up? We don't know. We don't need to know. We ourselves have just come out of the trip of our lives, a hallucinatory ride through the motels and madhouses of rock 'n' roll America. That's about as good as you can get from words on pages.

This is *Not Fade Away*. A classic, indeed.

Kevin Sampson
September 1999

'... music, sweet music ...'

—*Martha and the Vandellas*,
'Dancing in the Street'

PROLOGUE

'To the understanding of such days and events this additional narrative becomes necessary, like a real figure to walk beside a ghost.'

—Haniel Long,
Interlinear to Cabeza de Vaca

THE DAY DIDN'T begin well. I woke up at first light with a throbbing brain-core headache, fever and chills, dull pains in all bodily tissues, gagging flashes of nausea, a taste in my mouth like I'd eaten a pound of potato bugs, aching eye sockets, and a general feeling of basic despair. This deepened with the realization that I had to get out of bed, drive a long way on bad roads, negotiate a firewood deal, and then drive back home to the ranch, where I still had my own winter's wood to get in. If I'd had a phone I would've instantly canceled the meeting, but since the ranch was too far out in the hills for the phone company to bother with, and because it had taken me a week to set up the meeting with Jack Strauss, who was driving all the way over from Napa, there was no choice. Besides, Strauss was going to front me $1000 on twenty-five cords, which was $993 more than I had, but about $4000 short of what would've satisfied my creditors. At the mere thought of my finances, despair collapsed into doom. Compelled by circumstance, I arose, dressed, stepped outside, and greeted the day by lurching over behind the empty woodshed and throwing up.

The dawning sky was black with roiling nimbus, wind gusting from the south: rain any minute. I let out the chickens, threw them some scratch, split kindling, and moaned through the rest of the morning chores. Back in the house, I started a fire in the woodstove and put on the tea kettle, then scrabbled through a cupboard till I found my first-aid kit, in which, against all temptation, I'd stashed a single Percodan. Though it looked small and forlorn in the bottom of the vial, I swallowed it with gratitude. I was sending a sowbug against Godzilla, but anything would be an improvement.

I hurt. Since I had taken neither drink nor drug for a week – another depressing realization – I assumed I'd fallen victim to the virus sweeping our rural community. People were calling this one the Smorgasbord Flu, because that's how the bug regarded the body; in some cases the feast had gone on for weeks. The thought of weeks made my stomach start to twist again, but I bore down, fighting it back. To lose the Percodan would've killed me.

Feeling slightly more in command after my show of will, I choked down some tea and dry toast, damped the stove, and then oozed out to my '66 Ford pick-up to begin the long drive to the meeting with Strauss in Monte Rio.

The truck wouldn't start.

I took the long-bladed screwdriver off the dash and got out. Hunched down under the left fender-well, I beat on the electric fuel pump till it began clicking.

The truck started at the same moment as the rain. I switched on the wipers. They didn't work. I got out again and pried up the hood and used the screwdriver to beat on the wiper motor till the blades jerked into motion like the wings of a pelican goosed into flight. I was on my way.

My way, I should explain, is always long. I live deep in the coastal hills of Sonoma County, out where the hoot owls court the chickens, on a nine-hundred-acre ranch that's been in the family for five generations. The house was built in 1859 and still lacks all those new-fangled modern amenities like indoor plumbing and electricity. You can reach the ranch on eight miles of mean dirt road that runs along the ridgetop, or by a two-hour pack from the coast on a steep, overgrown trail. The nearest neighbor is seven miles away. Where the dirt road hits the county road, it's another six miles of twisty one-lane blacktop to the mailbox, and nine more to the nearest store. I live in the country because I like it, but bouncing down the dirt road that morning, my brain shrieking at every jolt, I would have rented a townhouse condo in a hot second, faster if it was near a hospital.

To distract myself from misery, I tuned in a San Francisco station and listened to the early morning traffic report – already snarled up on the Bay Bridge, a stalled car blocking the Army Street on-ramp – but for once it didn't console me. The Percodan, however, was getting there, or at least the pain seemed to be moving away.

By the time I hit the paved county road just past the Chuckstons' place, I was feeling like I might make it. The rain continued, a determined drizzle. Lulled by the smoothness of pavement, mesmerized by the metronomic slap of the wipers, perhaps a bit lost in my appreciation of the Percodan, I didn't see the deer until I was almost on top of him, a big three-point buck with a rut-swollen neck. He leapt clear in a burst of terrified grace as I simultaneously hit the brakes and a slick spot on the road, snapped sideways, fishtailed once, twice, and slammed into a redwood stump on the righthand shoulder. My head smacked off the steering wheel and recoiled backwards just in time to meet my .20-gauge flying off the gunrack. The twin blows knocked me goofier than a woodrat on ether. I dimly remember feeling lost in some pulsating forest, looking for my mind, tormented by the knowledge I needed my mind to find my mind and that's why nothing seemed to make the tiniest bit of sense. Then a blessed rush of adrenalin burned the murk away. I opened the truck door and slid out, jelly-legged but standing, hurting but still alive.

The drizzle on my face was refreshing. I paused a moment, then started walking toward town, holding my thumb out even though there was no sign of a car in either direction. I'd gone a half-mile before I realized my best move was to walk back to the Chuckstons' place. They had a CB I could use to call for help. I needed help.

The rain thickened from drizzle to drops. As I walked, I absently kept touching my head, thinking the rainwater was blood, brain leakage, or something equally vital seeping from my skull.

I stopped when I got back to my truck. I hadn't checked for damage, and was suddenly taken by the wild hope it might be driveable, a hope horribly dashed by a closer look: the right-front fender, mashed against the wheel; the tie-rod badly bent; steering knuckle broken. I trudged on.

Nobody was home at the Chuckstons' place – they'd probably left early to gather sheep – but the spare key was still where it had been when I'd taken care of their house the summer before. I wiped my muddy boots on the welcome mat and let myself in. I turned on the CB and tried to think who to call, somebody with both a CB and a phone. Donnie. Donnie Schatzburg. He came right back like he'd been waiting for me all morning.

I explained what had happened, gave him the location of the truck, and asked him to call Itchman's Garage in Guerneville to send out a tow – if not Itchman's, Bailey's on the coast.

Donnie was back in five minutes with ugly news: both of Itchman's trucks were already out and had calls backed up, so it was liable to be a couple of hours at best, and there was no answer at Bailey's.

Donnie kept asking if I was all right, and offering to come over and lend a hand, but I assured him I was broken but unbent, which was much more jaunty than I felt now that the adrenalin was wearing off. I asked him if he'd call the Kozy Korner Kitchen in Monte Rio and leave a message for Jack Strauss that I'd crashed and would call him at home as soon as possible. Donnie said he'd be glad to, and I signed off with heartfelt thanks.

I walked back to my wreck to wait for the tow truck. Why I didn't arrange to wait at the house I still lack the wit to explain. The rain had turned hard and relentless, a three-day storm settling in. I hunched up in the damp cab and considered my situation.

In the brightest light I could imagine, it was bleak. I wondered if I could possibly risk using my Visa card. I was pretty certain I'd violated my credit limit long ago, and was sure I hadn't paid them in five months, but this was an emergency. I could ride into Guerneville with the tow truck, rent a car, go to a motel, call Strauss for new arrangements, sleep, meet him the next day and pick up the $1000 in front, buy flu drugs, drive the renter home, stay in bed recovering till the truck was fixed, cut wood like a maniac, sweat profusely, spend most of the money I'd make just to pay for the truck repairs, but without the truck I couldn't cut wood, and no wood, no money. Money. I checked my wallet. One piece of bad plastic and seven bucks in cash. I leaned my head against the steering wheel and whimpered. I wanted my mommy.

That's when I heard the roar. My head snapped up, instantly alert, senses flared. Through the rain-blurred windshield a grey hulk took form, grew larger, denser, the roar taking on a mass of its own, all of it coming right at my face. Without thinking I hit the door and rolled across the road. I came up on all fours in the drainage ditch, poised to flee, fight, shit, or go blind.

A large truck was hurtling down the straight stretch of road. I threw myself against the embankment, pressing myself into the root-clotted clay. At the moment I moved, the truck's rear end locked up; it shimmied for a heartbeat, then the rear end came around in a slow arc, 180°, rubber squealing on the wet pavement, water squeegee'd into a thin roostertail. The whole mass of the truck shuddered against the brakes and slid to a smooth stop, direction reversed, its back end no more than two feet from the twisted front bumper of my truck. I stared, flash-frozen in the moment. It was a tow truck, a big tow truck, all painted a pearly metal-flake grey. Within a thin-line oval on the driver's door, written in a flowing ivory script, it read: THE GHOST.

I felt like I was filling with helium, hovering at the threshold between gravity and ascent. I heard voices chanting in the rain, women's voices, but no words came clear.

There was vague movement behind the fogged side-window of the tow truck, then the door flew open and a ghost leaped out.

I died.

Death laughed and sent me back.

I felt rain on my eyelids. It didn't feel baptismal, holy, or otherwise spiritually endowed; just wet. I felt a warm hand clamped firmly to my wrist. Another touched my cheek. I opened my eyes. Instead of a ghost, it was the tow truck driver, his face and form obscured in a hooded, wind-billowed poncho, the grey oilcloth lustred with rain.

'Well, well: life goes on.' That was the first thing George Gastin said to me. He seemed genuinely pleased.

I groaned.

'Yes indeed,' he continued, 'it *does* go on, don't it now, moment to moment and breath to breath. Looks like Death shot at you and missed and shit at you and didn't, but you'll likely live. Your pulse is outstanding and your color's coming back. Just take it slow and easy. You're in the good hands of the Ghost and the situation is under control . . . or as much control as usual, which – truth be told – is hardly at all, just barely any, one wet thread. But it's certainly enough for our purposes this glorious morning, so hang on here and we'll see if your feet still reach the ground.'

He eased me to my feet, a steadying hand on my shoulder. I was soaked, shivering, weak, confused. Everything but his voice and touch seemed blurred. I took a deep, trembling breath. 'I'm sick,' I told him. 'Flu. Wasn't hurt in the wreck.'

'That lump on your forehead? That the flu, or just your third eye coming out for a peek?'

'I've seen enough,' I said.

He chuckled and patted me on the back, a gesture at once consoling and oddly jovial. 'That's the spirit,' he said. 'You're a mess now, but you'll be laughing about it in fifty years.'

'I'll make it,' I said bravely. I actually did feel better with my feet back under me.

'Yup,' George agreed, 'nothing stronger than the will to live. We'll get that truck hooked on and hauled down the line, but let's get you fixed up first.' And in a voice calm, direct, and decisive, the shapeless figure swept me gladly into his command. 'Start off, we get your ass dry from flopping around in mud puddles.' He measured me with a glance. 'I pack spare duds, but you look a little on the stubby side of my frame. 'Course this ain't Wilkes-Bashford either, so fuck fashion in the face of need, and fuck it anyway just on good general principles.'

He opened a tool bay on the side of his truck and took out a small duffel bag, then reached back inside and removed what looked like a floppy green plastic envelope. 'Okay, listen up: strip outside and throw your wet clothes in the bag' – he gave the green envelope a shake and it billowed into a large plastic trash sack – 'and leave it outside for me to take care of. When you're stripped down, climb in the cab there where I got the heater humming and put on some dry clothes from the duffel. Should be a towel in there, too. While you're making yourself presentable, I'll survey the damage here.'

I appreciated his crisp, step-by-step instructions. I needed them. I was not thinking in an orderly fashion. However, as I stripped off my soggy clothes and stuffed them in the plastic sack as instructed, the cold rain pelting my goose-pimpled flesh seemed to draw me together and steady my wobbling attention.

The cab was a rush of warmth, and strong odors of orange peel and coffee, and a more subtle fragrance, faintly rank, like rotting seaweed or old axle grease. I unzipped the duffel bag. The towel was neatly folded on top. I unfurled it: a huge beach towel, fluffy white, HOTEL HAVANA in maroon block letters emblazoned down the center. I dried off, then wrestled myself into the clothes. The legs of the black Can't-Bust-'Ems and the sleeves of the green-plaid flannel shirt were a little long, but not bad. The grey down vest and sheepskin slippers fit perfectly.

I leaned back, letting the warmth soak toward my bones. Chains rattled behind me, followed by the clank and clunk of couplings, a hydraulic hiss. The truck shuddered slightly as the cable wound up. I turned and watched through the rear window as the mangled front end of my truck rose into view. This wasn't something I wanted to look at, so I turned around and shut my eyes. In a minute or so we'd be on our way. In a couple of hours I'd be asleep in a motel room. Tomorrow there might be money to pay for all of it. The chickens would have to look out for themselves. I wondered if there was a doctor in Geurneville who would prescribe Percodan for the flu.

I was drifting away when a tool bay opened and then slammed shut along the driver's side. George, quick, smooth, slid in behind the wheel, his poncho gone. He glanced at me and recoiled, feigning surprise: 'My God, it *was* human. What say we haul in that mess you made – I'd guess you're looking at six bills in fix-it-up.'

No ghost at all. Flesh and blood. He was maybe 5'10', 165, angular and lean, but a shade too compact to qualify as gangly. His poncho gone, I saw we were dressed almost exactly alike, except his pants were so faded the grease spots were darker than the fabric, and his grey down vest was scabbed with patches of silver duct tape. The only true difference was our footwear: he was wearing a pair of black high-top Converse All-Stars, a classic I hadn't seen since my last high school gym class.

When I didn't speak, he gave me a frank, appraising look – the first time I'd really noticed his eyes. They were a remarkable blue, the color of the sky on a scorching summer afternoon, almost translucent; and when they took on a sweet, maniacal glitter, a wild flash that faded to reappear as a slow, delighted grin, his eyes for a moment were colorless.

'How's the noggin? Want to swing by a sawbones to check for any extra brain damage?'

'No, really,' I blurted, 'it's this damn flu. The Smorgasbord Flu. Hope you don't catch it.'

'Sure it ain't the Water Buffalo flu?'

'What's that?' I should've known by the gleam in his eyes.

'Feels like you been gang-stomped by a herd of water buffalo.'

'Naw, that's just one of the symptoms.'

'Sweet Jesus,' he laughed, 'that does sound bad. But if you don't want to see a doc, how about some medicinal relief? Simple pain is a job for drugs.'

I heartily concurred, but tentatively said, 'It's a long way to a pharmacy.'

'Glovebox.' He nodded in its direction. 'I think there's some codeine in the first-aid kit. Number fours. Don't know what the four means, but help yourself.'

I was. The first-aid kit was already open on my lap, and that despite a conscious effort to mask my eagerness. 'The four,' I explained, 'means you're supposed to take four at a time, otherwise they don't reach the right level of chemical effectiveness.'

'Hey, I never thought of that,' George said. 'I tell ya, that's one of the great things about getting out and meeting the public – get all sorts of new angles and information.'

He reached under the seat. Since I was grossly munching the codeine, I thought he'd just turned away to be polite. But when he straightened back up I saw he was holding a black baseball cap, which he slapped on his head and adjusted down over his eyes. In white letters fanned across the crown it read: *Gay Nazis for Jesus*.

'Kwide a had,' my powder-thickened tongue managed, even though my brain had stopped. Suddenly it was crowded in the cab.

'Last guy I towed gave it to me. Name was Wayne. Took him from Anchor Bay up to Albion. He said it was a real conversation starter.'

'Grabbed me,' I admitted, slipping the first-aid kit back into the glovebox.

George tapped the gas impatiently.

'I want to thank you for the dry clothes and the codeine,' I told him. 'Sure improved a shitty day.'

'Been there myself,' George said. He tapped the gas again. 'So my man, what's the plan? Where to and how soon?'

I leaned back in the seat, overcome by weariness. Sleep, bad plastic, firewood, sweat, loss, cash – somewhere along the line I'd made a plan, but could only remember the pieces. 'Take me to Itchman's in Guerneville. If I'm still alive in the morning, I'll figure the rest out then.'

'You're on your way,' he said, reaching for the emergency brake.

Despite my effort to contain it, my conscience broke through. He'd been kind to me, thoughtful, humane, and I had to pay him in bad plastic. Not even my desperation could justify fucking him over. 'Wait a minute,' I sighed. 'Let me tell you how it is. All I've got to pay you with is a Visa card the bank demanded I return about three months ago. I was on my way into town to pick up a thousand-dollar front on a firewood order. I think I can get it tomorrow, and I could leave the cash with Itchman. How much do you figure it'll be?'

He reached in a vest pocket and handed me what I assumed was a rate card. In a way, it was:

> ## TOWED BY THE GHOST
> *One of the few free rides in life*
>
> *George Gastin*
> *No Phone*
> *No Fixed Address*

'What are the other free rides?' I asked.

He gave me a sharp look, surprised, appreciative, then an odd little bow of his head. 'To tell the truth, I don't know. First love, maybe, though I've heard some hard arguments the other way. I was just allowing for my ignorance, changes, and the possibilities of imagination.'

I was suddenly very curious about George Gastin, tow-truck driver. He wasn't with Itchman's or Bailey's. 'Where you from?' I said. 'You sure seemed to get here fast.'

'Twenty-one minutes,' George said. 'I was just turning up Sea View when I picked up the call from Itchman's. His boys were stacked up, so I got on the horn and told 'em I was damn near on your bumper, and they gave me the go. They couldn't get to you for a couple of hours soonest, and Bailey over on the coast is down with a busted crank. Itchman don't give a shit. Best money is in short tows, and his garage is getting the work, anyway, as it turns out.'

'So what are you doing driving around at dawn in this neck of the woods?'

'My good sir,' George huffed with mock offense, 'a gentleman never tells.' That maniacal glitter; the slow, delighted grin.

'So you love around here, but don't live around here, right?'

He shrugged. 'Sometimes. I bum around the Northwest. Visit friends. Do some fishing. Look around. Mostly I live out of this truck here. Got a tent and a propane stove and a whole shitload of gear stashed in the tool bays. I had the truck built to my own specs by Roger Armature over in Redding. And in my travels, if I can be of help to folks, I'm glad to do it. Always interesting to meet new people, hear their stories, shoot the shit. No reason to hurry.'

'And you tow these people for free?' I felt unsettled; he sounded reasonable, but something wasn't meshing.

'Yeah, if they need it. Sometimes they're just out of gas or got a flat or are down with some piddly-ass mechanical problem. I'm not too shabby at twisting wrenches.'

'And no charge, right?'

'Well, if they turn out to be *outlandish* assholes, I charge them for parts.'

'Been in business long?' I thought this was tactful enough, but George started laughing so hard he had to re-set the emergency brake. His laughter seemed so disproportionate to my unintentional wit that I was disconcerted, my confusion quickly giving way to a space-collapsing sense of claustrophobia. It struck me that maybe even a free ride with the Ghost was no bargain.

'Hey,' George recovered, still chuckling, 'I'll be in business forever. I'm not *filthy* rich, but I made a few sound investments in my youth and I'm pretty much free to do what pleases me, and this is what it pleases me to do.'

A cuckoo, I thought to myself. *I should've known.* Not that I'm prejudiced against strange kicks or weird behavior – often, in fact, I enjoy them myself – but I wasn't in the mood. Why couldn't he be excessively normal, wholly competent, eminently sane? I didn't want an adventure in consciousness or character; I wanted a savior.

George released the emergency brake again, checked the mirrors, eased slowly off the shoulder onto the pavement, then stood on the gas. Slammed back in the seat, I twisted my head around to check my truck, certain it had torn loose and was tumbling down the road behind us. It hadn't yet, but given the way it was whipping around, we wouldn't be attached for long. Just when I thought his transmission would explode, George slammed into second. The big rear duals squealed for an instant, then bit, hurtling us forward. I glanced at the speedometer, convinced we must be doing 50 already, but the needle was resting on zero. I refused to believe it. My eyes frantically scanned the other gauges: tach, oil pressure, fuel, water: nothing, nada, zip. We might as well have been standing still. With an eerie, spine-freezing jolt of pure dread, for a moment I thought we *were* standing still, that reality had somehow inverted and left us stationary while the landscape blurred by. I felt my brain attempting to curl into a fetal position as a scream dug for traction in my lungs.

George nailed third. Expending my last bit of control, I squelched the scream and gathered my voice. I knew I'd sound foolish, but I didn't care: 'Excuse me, but are we standing still?'

George's eyes never left the road. 'Nope,' he replied matter-of-factly, 'we're doing about forty-seven miles per.' He flicked it into fourth. 'About fifty-two now.'

I pointed out as casually as I could manage – no point in alarming him – that none of the dash gauges appeared to be functioning.

'You got that right,' he nodded. 'Disconnected them. Too distracting. I listen to the engine, feel the road. Been doing it about thirty years. You get dialed-in after a bit, know what I mean? I can damn near calculate the fuel down to the last wisp of fumes and read the oil pressure with my fingertips. Not suggesting I'm *perfect*, understand, but when it comes to whipping it down the road I'm right up there with the best. Never been in a wreck that wasn't on purpose, and I've probably made more long-distance runs in my life than you've whacked-off in yours.'

'I doubt that,' I said in all sincerity, remembering that unappeasable ache that had wracked me at puberty. The memory deflected whatever my point could've been, and I ended up half-blurting, 'I thought you said you refused to live life in a hurry?'

He glanced over at me, smiling. 'This ain't in a hurry. This is my normal cruising groove.'

I got earnest. 'Listen George, I'm amazed and impressed with your abilities, but I drive these roads *all the time*, and seventy miles an hour is about forty too fast. *Slow down.*' I'd hoped to make it sound like a calm, well-reasoned request, but too much pleading quavered into my voice.

'Well,' George said, 'what you got to understand is that you probably drive like Lawrence Welk, and I drive like John Coltrane. Don't mean that as a put-down at all. I was born with it, had it on the natch; and I've had time to refine it. You can probably lay a tree down a foot either way from where you want it, while I'd be bucking it up in someone's living room. Or maybe you got that nice green touch in the garden. I sure don't. What I'm trying to tell you is *relax*. Just ease back, shake your cares, let it roll. I've been turning wheels since my feet could reach the pedals and I've always brought it in with the shiny side up and the dirty side down. So don't give it a piss-ant worry. The Ghost'll get you there.' *His* tone was completely reasonable, without a trace of pleading or terror.

Streaks of ochre and crimson, the maples along Tolan Flat ripped past. George's assurance actually seemed to relax me, or perhaps it was the exhaustion of the day in combination with the four #4's, sweet little 16, coming on strong about then. He *did* seem to hit every gear slick and clean, held the road like a shadow, and generally displayed consummate skill. I gave it a moment of dull contemplation and took the best philosophical position available: *Fuck it. Whatever.*

'How old are you anyway?' George interrupted my metaphysical reverie, 'Twenty-seven, twenty-eight?'

I had to think about it a minute. 'I'll be twenty-eight a month from today.'

George nodded as if the information confirmed some inner conviction. 'Yup, that's about how old I was when I went crazy and made *my* pilgrimage.'

Pilgrimage. The word wouldn't grab hold on my smooth brain. Caravans across the relentless Sahara. Dust and deprivation. Maybe he really was some twisted religious zealot. *It doesn't matter*, I told myself, truly beginning to relax. If I was going crazy, I was so far gone that all I could really do in my weakened condition was wave goodbye. Even the suicidal speed at which we were hurtling took on a strange comfort — if he wrapped it up, at least we wouldn't suffer. Everything was beyond control. I was fading fast, functioning on my autonomic nervous system and a piece of brain about the size of well-chewed Chiclet. I was no longer capable of the intricacies of conversation, the immense effort necessary to assemble and speak words. All I truly wanted to do was vanish into a warm oblivion and come back at some other time, when everything was better. So I asked him about his pilgrimage, and then slumped back and closed my eyes to listen.

Part One

FLOORBOARD GEORGE:
COAST TO COAST
& GONE AGAIN

'It is good to know
that glasses are to drink from.
The bad thing is not knowing
what thirst is for.'

—Antonio Machado

I'M GLAD YOU want to hear about my pilgrimage, but I should warn you it's a real ear-bender. Thing is, it doesn't make much sense unless you understand what got me crazy enough to make it, and even then I'm not sure it'll make any sense to you. I'm not sure – what is it now, twenty years later? – that it makes that much sense to me. But let me play you some background and we'll see where we go.

I was born and raised in Florida, near Miami, the youngest of three kids and the only boy. My sisters were married by the time I was eight so we were never really close. My dad was a long-haul trucker, mainly citrus to the Midwest. He was a union man all the way, solid as they come. Driving big rigs was just a job to him, a skill – no romance. What he really loved were his roses. He and Mom grew these miniature roses, and every hour he wasn't on the road he was in the rose garden. By the time he made retirement, the garden was a nursery. He died out in his rose garden one bright summer afternoon about two years after he retired. A stroke. Mom still tends the garden – got a couple of young girls to help her because she's in her late seventies now and getting slowed down a bit, but the nursery actually makes pretty good money. People will pay serious bucks for fine roses.

When I was a kid I'd ride with my dad when school was out in summer. I loved every minute of it. The power of the diesels. Roaring through the night, imagining all the people asleep in their houses and dreaming all those dreams as the moon burned across the sky. Iowa sweltering in August and the little fan on the dash of the Kenworth barely drying the sweat. Guys waving howdy in the truck-stop cafes and kidding me whether I'd finally taken over for the old man or was still riding shotgun. Free ice cream from the waitresses and that hard-edged wiggle they used to move through the men, laughing and kidding and yelling orders to the cook.

I started learning to drive when my feet could reach the pedals at the same time my eyes cleared the wheel. I was driving relief for dad when I was sixteen, and by eighteen I was on my own. I wasn't like dad. I had a bad case of the romance, sitting way up there above the road balling it down the pike, eaten up with white line fever. Bad enough to have the romance, but I was good at the work. Natural hand-eye coordination. The other truckers started calling me Floorboard George, 'cause that's where I kept my right foot. Say what you want about good sense, one thing was for certain: I could cover ground. I took great pride in the fact the only tickets I ever got were *moving* violations, and that's only when they could catch me. Unfortunately, they caught me over thirty times in twenty months, and when the judges in three states have jerked your license, work is hard to find. When you're hauling perishables, it ain't easy to justify driving *around* a state just because they'll bust you for driving through it; trucking companies like you to take the shortest route, even if I could drive around Georgia and still make reasonable time.

Besides, early on I got into the methamphetamine version of speed. The heat wasn't on then, and you could buy a handful of pharmaceutically pure benzedrine from any truck-stop waitress between Tallahassee and LA. That's why truck-stop waitresses were so good humored and sassy back then: they had a lock on the bennie concession. Just about all the drivers used them, and I sure held up my end. For two years there I thought White Cross was the trucker's health plan. Dad never used them, though, said they'd rot your reflexes and make you try to do things you couldn't do. What I found out was even worse: they helped me do things I shouldn't have.

What Dad used was coffee – one-gallon stainless-steel thermos – and he'd put maybe three shots of peach brandy in it. Hardly taste the brandy. And Dad knew how to sleep. He'd sleep four and drive twenty. Thing was, he *slept* those four hours. Shut his eyes and straight to deep sleep without a quiver. And four hours later, right to the tock, no alarm, he was fresh and ready to roll. He claimed he never dreamed on the road, or no dreams he remembered. Me, I dreamed all the time. But I never slept.

Dad dreamed at home, though. I heard him down in the kitchen one morning telling Mom he'd dreamed his brain had turned into a huge white rose. Mom just burst right out crying. Dad was saying, 'Hey, hold on, it was a *great* dream – I loved it.' And Mom, really sobbing then, said, 'Yes. Yes it is, Harry. I know it is.' Dad says, 'So why the waterworks?' And I could hear Mom sniffling, trying to gather herself, saying, 'No, it's a *fine* dream,' and then they must've been holding each other because all I could hear was their muffled voices and the coffee glubbing in the percolator. But I understood why Mom was crying: some dreams are just too beautiful to have.

That's probably part of the reason I was hitting those ol' white cross benzedrines so hard – sometimes twenty a day. They fed my natural inclination to go fast, which I'm sure was also partly the baffled frenzy of being eighteen years old and suddenly cut loose of school. Jamming like a cannonball cross-country, riding it as fast as you could make it go, getting paid to eat the horizon was a magnificent feeling, but pretty soon it got so I didn't want to stop. I was young, restless, and dumb, but I somehow knew deep down in my gut that when it gets so you don't ever want to stop, that's when you *have* to stop, or you're gonna be long gone for good. I'd lost my license in two more states, had a nasty bennie habit, and was spending far too much time getting fried in the short-order hearts of truck-stop waitresses. The life was collapsing on me and I knew I had to make a move. So in October of '56 I headed to San Francisco, mainly because hitchhikers I'd been picking up agreed it was about the only place in the country with a pulse. It's odd, looking back: 1956, and I wanted *off* the road. And I really, truly, cross-my-heart wanted to get away from those little white pills that made you go fast and feel good. Well, to be honest, I didn't *want* to, but I understood that I was going to make a bad and unhappy mess out of myself if I didn't. Even if I wasn't exactly sure what I wanted to be, I knew it wasn't a shit-heap wreck. Maybe the bare minimum, but I had *some* sense.

Soon as I hit Frisco, things started running my way. I found a sweet little apartment, clean and cheap, above an Italian bakery in North Beach, and took a job driving tow truck at Cravetti's garage. After a tough month, I'd cut the bennies back to two a day, which for me, you understand, was virtual abstinence.

Towing was different back then. Any call, whether a bad wreck or just somebody parked in a red zone, went out on an open line to every towing service in the city, and the first truck there got the job. Hell, after 18-wheelers, driving a tow truck was like driving a Maserati. I snagged a lot of work. It took me a while to learn the streets and the best routes, but it never took me long to get there.

The competition was intense. I remember the first call I took. Mainly because I didn't know the turf and innocently went the wrong way up a one-way street, I aced in about three seconds in front of this insane fool, Johnny Strafe, who drove for Pardoo Brothers. I was chortling as I hooked up, but when I got back in the cab and hit the ignition, damn engine wouldn't grab. Like it wasn't getting spark. I look up puzzled, and there's Johnny Strafe holding my plug wires like some greasy bouquet at a marriage of rubber freaks, and before I can even scream he starts stuffing them down the grating on a corner storm drain. I'd have gone after him if the cops hadn't been on the scene. I complained to them, but they had other problems. Finally this older sergeant took me aside and told me, 'Hey, if you can't tow him, the other guy gets to. It's called "eat shit, rookie," and that's how it is. We've got enough to do without dealing with you crazy assholes. You're new, okay, you didn't know. But don't bother us again.'

So I developed a few chops of my own. Turnip up the tailpipe, that's one I introduced. One time around the Fourth of July I slipped under Bill Frobisher's rig and taped a box of sparklers to his manifold. When the heat set 'em off, you should've seen Bill hit the pavement running. I got Johnny Strafe back, too – squirted Charcoal-Lite all over his front seat and set it off. He was hooking on at the time and didn't even notice the flames, but fortunately I'd brought the biggest damn fire extinguisher from Cravetti's shop and I filled his cab up with foam till it was running out both windows and the radio was gurgling like a drowning rat. The second one was even better: I took a can of quick-dry aluminum spray paint and did his windshield.

Anyway, there I was, just a nudge short of twenty, driving tow like a werewolf at top dollar for my trade and generally enjoying myself. I was still holding the bennies steady at two a day – one *after* breakfast and one for lunch, and that was it. It helped that I was living fairly regular, clocking 8 to 5 on the day shift, weekends free, two squares a day, and logging six hours of solid Z's most nights. Health – nothing like it.

The job was great, even if it was work, but the true joy was living in North Beach. The place was alive. This is the late 1950s I'm talking about, and the Beats were going strong. Lots of people will tell you the best time was '54, '55, before all the publicity hit, but for a wet-eared kid who'd been stringing his nerves between Miami and St Lou, this looked like a good time to me. The Beats were the people I'd been looking for. They had a passionate willingness to be moved. It was a little artsy-fartsy, sure, lots of bad pretenders, but it was a whole helluva lot better than Sunday School, which is what the 50's were generally like – a national

Sunday School for the soul, smug with dull virtues, mean with smothered desires. But the thing is, you can't live in fear of life. You do and you're dead in the water.

The Beats at least had the courage of their appetites and visions. They *wanted* to be moved by love, truth, beauty, freedom – what my poet friend John Seasons called 'the four great illusions' – while my passion, at the time, was the firing stroke in a large-bored internal combustion engine transmitting its power through the drive-train and out to the wheels – four small illusions. Because of the explosive qualities inherent in the liquified remains of dinosaurs, I could roar through the day and the dark at speeds no one even marginally sane could consider reasonable. And if I happened to mention what that felt like in any North Beach bar, more than likely the woman on my left had just written a poem that tried to capture that same abandoned moment and the guy on my right had finished that very afternoon a painting he hoped touched the same soaring spirit, and we'd be yakking drunk and laughing till the bar closed at two in the morning and I was walking down Broadway in the fog, shivering and elated. That was North Beach. An eruption of people hungry for their souls. And for all the poses and silliness, it was splendid.

I did my share of posing, I must admit, most of it prompted by raw teenaged insecurity and a sense of intellectual inadequacy. This I hid with the usual ration of brass and bravado, but bald ignorance is a lot harder to cover. Since I could authentically claim – as few others could – an honest working-class life, I hid at first behind a fairly nasty anti-intellectualism. Fuck big words, I drive a truck. Fortunately, most people were gracious enough to ignore my bullshit, and generous enough to include me in conversations and lend me books. You could pick up a couple of Liberal Arts degrees just sitting in the bars and listening. Gradually I changed from an anti-intellectual to an unbearably eager one. I wanted to know everything – an appetite I've had many subsequent occasions to regret.

It's usually the happy case that you learn best from your friends. My tightest buddy in the early years was this huge horn player everybody called Big Red Loco, a mulatto cat with rusty red hair. He was about 6'7", and every inch of him was music. I heard him play with all the best, and he cut them into fish bait. Big Red could go out there and bring it back alive. Everybody and their aunt wanted to record him, but he'd had this vision when he was seven years old that his gift was for the moment alone, and that if his music was ever recorded, ever duplicated in time outside memory, he would lose his gift. At least this is what he told me, and I don't doubt it at all.

Lou Jones – Loose Lou, they called him – adored Big Red's sound so much that one night he crawled under the bandstand before a gig and hooked up a tape machine through the microphone. He was still shaking when he told me about it the next day: every instrument came through clean on the tape, except Big Red's sax. Not a trace. I never mentioned it to Big Red. No reason to mess with a man's music.

Except for his music, Big Red hardly ever spoke. Ten sentences a day left him hoarse. And when he did say something, it wasn't much. 'Let's grab a beer,' or 'Can you lay a five on me till the weekend?' If you asked him a direct question, he'd just nod, shake his head, or shrug – or, maybe two percent of the time, he'd answer with a few words. It drove me ape-shit when I first knew him, so finally I asked him point-blank why he never said diddley. He shrugged and said, 'I'd rather listen.'

With all that practice he was an incredible listener. He ate at the Jackson Cafe because he liked the *sound* of their dishes, if you can feature that. I remember one time we were eating lunch and this busboy came by with a big clattering cart of dirty dishes and Big Red slipped right out of the booth, dropped to all fours, and followed it right into the kitchen, ears locked, listening. However strange, it was fortunate for our friendship that he was such a listener, since it's plain I'm a rapper.

Hanging out with Big Red meant making the local jazz scene. Up till then I'd never given much of an ear to anything besides the singing of tires on asphalt and the throb of a big diesel drilling the dark, but jazz, heard live and close and smoky, with the taste of whiskey in your mouth and a high-stepping woman in the corner of your eye, just took me away. Lifted me right out of myself. I don't know anything about art, but I do know when I'm gone.

It might've been Big Red's influence – he never owned a record – but I only really loved jazz live, right *now*, straight to the spine. I bought some records, which I enjoyed and appreciated and all that, but they weren't the same. I guess I'm one of those people who can't really grasp something if it's more than a foot from the source. I mention this as a way of explaining I really didn't know anything about rock-and-roll, even though it was coming on strong at the time. Blasting from about every jukebox in every bar, it was there in the background, but it never made it through my ears to grab hold of my brain. Besides, people on the jazz scene were constantly putting it down as bubblegum for the soul. But it was interesting that Big Red didn't bad-mouth it. 'It's all music,' he said. 'The rest is taste, culture, style, times.' For Big Red, that was a speech. A lot later, about the time the Beatles were taking off, I remember sitting in Gino and Carlo's with John Seasons and Big Red, and John saying, more with sadness than disgust, 'The Beatles are the end of North Beach.' Big Red, unsolicited, said, 'You're right. You can hear it.'

John Seasons was, in a strange way, more mentor than friend, and we really didn't get close till late '63, early '64. John was a poet, and through him I met Snyder, Ginsberg, Whalen, Corso, Kerouac, Cassady, and the rest of that crew – though I don't think they were ever all around at once. John was *always* there, it seemed. He'd been living in North Beach before it was hip, and was still there after the fashion had passed. He was a devoted poet with an aversion to the limelight – certainly a notable trait at the time – and a strong academic background. On his living room walls were about two dozen honorary doctorates in about half that many fields – I remember one from Harvard in physics, another from the Sorbonne in linguistics. They were all excellent forgeries. As John was fond of pointing out, he supported his poetry, which he claimed was a true attempt to forge the real, by creating facsimiles of the fraudulently real. John could find absolutely no good reason why people needed documents and licenses to partake of American culture, and it especially pissed him off that you had to *pay* to obtain them. John wasn't one to favor undue social regulation in the human community. Art, sports, and the Laws of Nature, he argued, were all the regulation necessary for an enjoyable life. As an advocate of personal authority, he thought it was stupid to award *real* power to abstractions like nations, senators, and Departments of Motor Vehicles.

John had a darkroom, two printing presses, a complete assortment of paper stocks, and a collection of official seals that would have shamed the Smithsonian. John was also gay, and it helped that he seemed to prefer highly placed civil servants for lovers. John felt that if your sexual preferences were going to brand you a security risk, you might as well risk some security, and he was convincing enough that his boyfriends helped him expand his collection of official seals, often providing the authentic forms on which to affix them. For John, a bogus California driver's license was little more than a snapshot and a short typing assignment. He claimed he could fake anything on paper except money and a good poem, and that he could do the money with the right plates and proper stock.

So, after about eighteen months in North Beach, closing in on twenty-one and legal American adulthood, I had a job I enjoyed by day and high friends and wild company at night; and through reading, and by talking to people who knew what they were talking about, I was accumulating enough good information to make a run at knowledge. I was beginning to know my own mind, or at least understand I had a mind to know. Or so I thought.

It was February 1, 1959, two days before my twenty-first birthday, when I came in off-shift and Freddie Cravetti – old man Cravetti's son, the swing-shift garage manager – motioned me over and introduced me to this runty guy sporting a blue seersucker suit so filthy you could have cleaned it with dog shit. Freddie introduced him as Scumball Johnson, then discreetly remembered some paperwork. When I shook Scumball's hand, it was like lifting a decayed lamprey out of a slough. He spoke in a low monotone mumble, head down, eyes constantly moving. I made him immediately as an ex-con.

I only liked one thing about Scumball Johnson: the money. Two hundred cash, back when a dollar bought dinner; and that was only the half in front. There was another two yards on delivery. All I had to do was wreck a car without wrecking myself – total it and walk away. Since I'd been making a living either by avoiding wrecks or picking them up, it sounded interesting. First, however, I had to *steal* the car, which reduced my interest considerably until Scumball explained that the car's owner *wanted* it stolen and wrecked so he could collect the insurance. I was completely covered, Scumball assured me. I'd be given a key, a handwritten note from the owner explaining I was checking out the transmission or something, the owner would stay by the phone in case anyone checked, and he wouldn't report it stolen till I'd called in safe and clear. Scumball said I could use a tail to watch my back and pick me up, but I'd have to pay for that out of my cut. Scumball didn't care how or where the car was wrecked as long as it was totaled for insurance purposes. If I got myself hurt or didn't phone within eight hours, I was on my own and nobody knew me. And if I even so much as murmured his name to the law, I would likely be visited by large men who'd had twisted childhoods and would undoubtedly take great delight in tearing off my fingers and feeding them to me.

A sleazy proposition, sure, but not without some provocative attractions, especially if you're young, restless, bored, and stupid. Looking back, I'm more astounded than ashamed that I agreed to the deal, though I must admit the $400 pay-off didn't improve my judgment.

Scumball Johnson. I'll tell you where he was at: he *liked* his name. 'That's me all right,' he'd chuckle, 'a real scumball.' As if it confirmed his essence. Those are the people I can't understand: cold rotten to the fucking quick, and quick to brag about it. Maybe that acceptance is close to enlightenment, but to enjoy it so much seems slimy. I can still see his grin. And here's the weird thing: Scumball was a walking compost heap, but his teeth were perfect – strong, straight, brushed to an immaculate luster. And since he showed them only when someone called him Scumball or otherwise confirmed his sleaziness, the grin always carried this shy, pleased, strangely *intimate* acknowledgment, as if you were praising him, or he was trying to seduce your loathing.

From what I gathered, Scumball was running a fairly complex scam. If I was cutting $400, you could bet Scumball was clearing *at least* a grand, with the rest going to the owner. But that arrangement begged an obvious question: if the owner needed the bucks, why didn't he simply *sell* the car and pocket *all* the money? I figured either the insurance value was tremendously inflated – maybe an agent in cahoots – or there was something funny about the cars.

Now I don't know this for a dead mortal cinch, but I'd bet the cars were stolen out of state and probably bought at quarter-price by Scumball, who in turn did a plate and paper job on them, let people use them for six months or so for the cost of full insurance coverage, and then Scumball collected close to full value when they were wrecked. Maybe the 'owner' got a small piece of the action, but a guy like Scumball doesn't like to see the pie sliced up too much. I don't know what Scumball did with his loot, but he sure as hell didn't piss it away on clothes.

I trashed my first car for him the very next night, February 2, and I'll admit I had more than a few whiskeys in me when I turned the key on the new Merc conveniently parked just off Folsom. I'd also awarded myself three bonus bennies for bad behavior, preferring a little extra focus for the tight work.

Big Red was my tail and pick-up man, and perfect for the job. He had his own car, an anonymous '54 Chevy sedan, and had proven himself invariably reliable in the hundred small favors of friendship. Plus he needed the money. I'd cut him in for $100, probably too much, but I had a steady job going in and could write it off as a contribution to the arts if I ever paid taxes. Big Red also offered his imposing height, that wild tangle of copper-colored hair, and a nose that looked like it had been broken twice in each direction. Should anyone object to your behavior, he was a good man to have on your side.

Nobody objected as I let the Merc idle while the defroster cleared the glass. The car was close to mint condition, just over 9000 on the odometer, and no visible dings. When the glass cleared I pulled out onto Folsom, Big Red swinging in behind me, and headed for the Golden Gate.

I'd only had a day to think it over, but I'd come up with what seemed a solid plan. I'd go out Highway 1 up above Jenner where the road hugs the ocean bluffs, find a likely turnout, and shove it over into the Pacific. I'd brought along a bag full of empty beer cans and couple of dead pints of cheap vodka to scatter around the interior – make it look like a snorting herd of adolescent males, frenzied on some giant squirt of young warrior hormones, had swiped the short for a joyride and crashed it for fun.

I cruised north on 101 at a legal 65, took 116 through Sebastopol to Guerneville, then followed the Russian River to its mouth at Jenner, where I caught Highway 1. There was hardly any traffic. I checked the rearview to make sure Big Red made the turn, and saw the bobbing lights of his Chevy about a quarter-mile behind.

I found a good spot about twenty minutes up the coast, a wide turnout along the edge of a high cliff. I pulled over to check it out. The ocean air was powerful, a cauldron broth of salty protein and tidal decay. There were no guardrails, so it was an easy roll over the edge and a long way down to the waves bashing the rocks. I looked carefully for lights along the beach, any flashlights or campfires. I didn't want to drop two tons of metal on a couple of lovers fucking their romantic brains out on the narrow beach below. No reason to encourage absurdity. Of course, on the other hand, nobody with a brain more complex than a mollusc's would consider mating on a rocky, wave-wracked beach on a raw winter night, so I might've been doing evolution a favor.

Still wearing the gloves I'd put on before touching the car, I scattered the empties over the floorboards while Big Red wheeled his Chevy around to screen the Merc. I put the Merc in Neutral and cramped the wheels to the left. Big Red and I put our shoulders to it, a few good grunts at first, and then she was rolling on her own weight. When the front tires dropped over the edge, the back end flipped up, but rather than nosing straight down it dragged on the frame and tilted sideways slow enough for us to hear all the cans sluicing toward the driver's side, and then she cleared the edge and was gone. The earth suddenly seemed lighter. It was silent so long I figured we hadn't heard it hit, that the sound of impact had been muffled by the surge and batter of the waves below, and I was just about to peer over the edge when it smashed on the rocks KAAABBBBLLLLAAAAAAM.

Big Red stood there, rooted, eyes closed and head thrown back, swaying slightly from side to side. He was obviously lost in something, but, though I hated to interrupt, it didn't seem wise to hang around appreciating the sonic clarity of a new Mercury meeting ancient stone in the middle of a felony.

I touched his arm. 'Let's hit it.'

'You drive,' Big Red replied – a command, not a request.

Silent, eyes closed, Big Red didn't twitch from his reverie

until we were coming back across the Golden Gate. I was half-depressed with spoiled adrenalin, half-pissed that he'd withdrawn when I felt like yammering, so when he finally opened his eyes and asked 'Did you hear it,' I was a little cross. 'Hear what? The waves? The wind? The wreck?'

'No man, the *silence*. The gravitational *mass* of that silence. And *then* that great, brief, twisted cry of metal.'

'That sound isn't high on my hit parade, Red. I *like* cars, trucks, four-bys, six-bys, eight-bys, and them great big motherfuckers that bend in the middle and go shoooooosh shoooooosh when you pump the brakes. It'd be like throwing your horn off the cliff.'

'*Yes!*' He grabbed my shoulder, '*Exactly!*'

He was so pleased that it seemed cruel to admit my understanding was the accidental result of petulant exaggeration, if not outright deceit. In fact, only one thing had bothered me about wrecking the Merc: it was too easy.

I reminded Big Red that we still had to check in with the man, and soon as we hit Lombard I called Scumball from a Shell station pay phone. He answered on the third ring. After that first night, I had occasion to call him lots of times, and he *always* answered on the third ring. We used a simple code. I'd say, 'The chrome's on the road,' and he'd reply, nasty, 'Who is this?' Then I'd hang up.

When I slipped back behind the wheel of Big Red's Chevy, Red wasn't interested in what Scumball had said. He wanted to explore that silence. 'Let's fall by my place and pick up my horn and see who's out jamming.'

North Beach. Where else at 3:00 A.M. could you find some small club that was supposed to be closed and jam and yak and drink because the people who owned it understood better than the law that you can get lonely and thirsty and in need of music at all hours, especially the late hours of the night?

Right before dawn Big Red took the bandstand alone and

announced he was going to play a new composition he called 'Mercury Falling,' and that he wanted to dedicate it to me on my birthday. I'd forgotten that at midnight I'd officially turned twenty-one, but Big Red hadn't, and I felt like a shithook for my impatience with him earlier. But as soon as Big Red's breath shaped that first note, my little puff of shame was blown away.

For the twenty minutes Big Red played, there wasn't a heartbeat in that room. Cigarets went out. Ice melted in drinks. I know it's hopeless to try to describe music, but he *played* that silence he'd heard, heard so clearly, brought every note *through* it and *to* it, pushed them over the edge into the massive suck of gravity, hung them in the wind and hurled them gladly to the surging bash and wash of water wearing down stone, and every note smashing on the claim of silence was a newborn crying at the light. When he finished there wasn't a sound and there wasn't a silence and we all took our first breath together.

Big Red nodded shyly and walked offstage. Applause wasn't necessary. Everyone just sat there breathing again, feeling air curling into lungs, afraid to break the spell, the room silent except for the shifting of weight in chairs, the scuff of shoes on the littered floor. Finally a woman sitting alone at a corner table stood up, and that snapped it. A black bass player named Bottom sitting next to me at the bar groaned, '*Yeeess*. Yes, yes, yes,' and then reached over, put his skinny arm around my shoulder, and hugged me, whispering with sweet citric breath, 'Happy birthday, man – you got yourself a present there you can unwrap for the rest of yo life.'

Then everyone was nodding, smiling; a sweet, low babble filled the room. Everyone except the woman who'd stood up. She was taking off her clothes. Her back was to me, so I hadn't realized what she was doing till the green knit dress slipped from her bare shoulders. She wasn't wearing anything underneath. Tall, lean, with long hair the color of half-weathered pine, she stepped out of the dress around her ankles and made her way, composed and magnificent, between the crowded tables toward the back door. Everyone stopped breathing again. I was in love. She closed the door softly behind her without looking back. 'Sweet Leaping God o' Mercy,' Bottom moaned beside me, his arm dropping from my shoulders.

I caught up with her at the end of the alley. Thick fog swirling in the first pale light of morning; cold; the odor of garbage. She heard me and turned around. I was trembling too wildly to speak. She brushed her hair back from her face, her fine blue eyes, fierce and amused, looking right into mine.

'Let me walk you home,' I said in what can be kindly described as a blurt.

She tilted her head, a playful flicker of a smile, waiting. I immediately understood and began shedding my clothes, hopping around on one foot to take off the opposite shoe – taking forever, it seemed to me, while she stood and waited, hip shot, arms folded across her breasts, watching me frantically trying to pretend I wasn't frantic. And then, somehow, I was standing naked in front of her, my cock hard as a jack handle, shivering, foolish, hopeful. She laughed and took me in her arms. I started laughing, too, relaxing against her fine, long warmth. And then, hand in hand, as natural as night and day, we strolled the seven blocks to my apartment. There was some early morning traffic, first stirrings of the city, but we were invisible in our splendor.

Her name was Katherine Celeste Jonasrad, Kacy Jones to those who loved her, and there were many, definitely including me. When I met her she'd just turned nineteen and, to the relentless dismay of her parents, had recently dropped out of Smith to see what the West Coast had to offer in the way of an education. Her father owned the largest medical supply company in Pennsylvania, and her mother was a frustrated novelist who seemingly regretted her every act and omission since her own graduation from Smith. Kacy phoned them one night from my place – her father's birthday – and I remember her eyes flashing as she repeated her mother's question: '"What am I going to do?" Well, I'm going to *do* whatever I feel like, whatever I need, whatever it takes, and whatever else I can get away with.' That was Kacy in her uncontainable essence: a free force, a true spirit on earth. She did fairly much as she pleased, and if she wasn't sure what pleased her, she was never afraid to go find out.

That birthday morning when we walked naked through the early morning streets to my apartment, she turned to me as the door closed and said, 'I'm not interested in a performance. The quality of the permissions, that's what I'm after.' I must have shown my confusion because she put it more plainly: 'I don't want to be fucked; I want us to feel something.'

'I'll try,' was all I could think to say.

She slipped her arms around my bare waist and drew me to her. 'Let's try together.'

I've never known a woman with the range and originality of Kacy's erotic imagination. I don't mean positions and all that sexual gymnastics, or the wilder fantasies and obsessions – those were just the entrances to other realms of possibility. Kacy was interested in the *feelings*, their clarity and nuance and depth, what could be shared and what couldn't. With Kacy there was no casual sex. I told her that much later. With that tone of playful cynicism people use to keep their dreams honest, Kacy said, 'Well, a sweet quickie now and then sure never hurt anything.'

I don't want to bog you down in the voluptuous details, so suffice it to say that on that birthday morning with Kacy I shoot through Heaven on my way to the Realm of Unimaginable Pleasure Indefinitely Prolonged. We tried together, heart and soul, and there is nothing like those first permissions to make you believe in magic, and without that belief in magic there's no heart for the rest. In the late afternoon, when Kacy went out for supplies, I just laid there grinning like a fool. She was back in half an hour with a whole bag of groceries. Sourdough bread from the bakery downstairs, a carton of antipasto from the deli around the corner, two cold quarts of steam beer, a jar of pepperoncini, a half-pound of dry jack cheese, candles, a Sara Lee chocolate cake, and the afternoon *Examiner*. That was one thing about Kacy: she loved to pull surprises from the bag. According to Kacy, there were only seven things human beings required for a happy life on this planet: food, water, shelter, love, truth, surprises, and secrets. Sounded good to me.

I remember how happy she looked as she unpacked our feast, explaining that there were only eight candles in a package but if I wasn't *too* traditional we could just make the figure of 21 instead of actually using that many candles. Suddenly she stopped in midsentence, obviously arrested, staring down at the table.

I sat up in bed. 'Kacy, what's the matter?'

Without turning, she made an impatient gesture with her hand as she looked down at the front page of the newspaper. I saw her shoulders rise as she took a deep breath, then fall; when they remained slumped I knew the news was bad. She turned around, tears in her eyes, and lay down on the bed beside me. 'Buddy Holly, Ritchie Valens, and the Big Bopper were all killed in a plane crash last night. That's a *lot* of music to lose all at once.'

I held her without saying anything. Fact was, I wasn't really sure who Buddy Holly, Ritchie Valens, and the Big Bopper were, an ignorance I was afraid would only make her sadder. You need the same knowledge to share another's grief, but not to comfort it. I held her till the tears were dry, then we ate my birthday feast and, later that night, opened some more presents.

The party actually lasted another four years. I can't truly say I lived with her those four years, since she came and went as she pleased. Kacy would not be possessed. On Valentine's Day, about a week and a half after we'd met, I came home after work to find a giant red heart pinned to my door, the words BE MINE in great white letters printed across it, the word MINE neatly crossed out. Her life belonged to her; mine to me. Where they touched, the terms were mutual regard, honor, and love without possession, dependency, or greed. I tried to explain it to John Seasons one night after Kacy had been gone a couple of weeks, and I was trying hard to convince myself that that was fine. John said, 'Sounds like one of them modern relationships to me.' He finished his Johnny Walker and looked at the bottom of the glass. 'Actually,' he continued, his voice suddenly serious, a bitter trace to his tone, 'it sounds like Saint Augustine's definition of love: 'I want you to be.' I've always liked that notion of love, but I've sure as hell never come close to making it real.'

I found it difficult myself. Doubt, jealousy, particularly the anxious stabs of inadequacy, all jerked me around at one time or another. Kacy lived out of a battered backpack, and when she left – sometimes for a few days, sometimes for weeks – she took everything with her except the promise she'd be back. When she returned, she'd always call to ask if I was in the mood for company. I always was, but once I said no just to see what she'd say. 'Fine,' she said. 'I'll call again.' After a couple years my doubts and dreads fell away, for finally they only compromised the pleasure of her company. Besides, when she was there, she was *really* there, and that's all I could fairly ask if I wanted to love her, not own her.

I don't want to give the impression that all we did was screw ourselves stupid while gazing deeply into each other's eyes. When we were together we were like any other couple. We'd hit the bars and coffeehouses and jazz clubs, visit friends, go to the movies . . . the usual. Kacy loved good food and enjoyed cooking, and was appalled to discover I was a can opener – a can of chili, another of corn, and a six-pack of beer was my idea of an eight-course dinner. Kacy taught me to cook some simple dishes, like pasta and stir-fry. Bought me a wok on *her* birthday. She also introduced me to backpacking. In the time we were together we took eight or nine long trips in the Sierras. Kacy loved high mountain lakes, and after the first trip I shared her appreciation. Air, water, granite, the campfire – Kacy liked the elemental.

She was also partial to marijuana, peyote, the natural highs – 'real drugs,' she called them. Speed was the only thing she ever ragged me about, and she was remarkably free of judgments. She claimed speed tore holes in the soul. So, ready to give it up anyway, I finally kicked, though I did allow myself a couple when I had a car to wreck for Scumball. I smoked weed with her now and then, but never developed her fondness for it; it softened the focus, distracted concentration, seemed to make my brain mushy. Peyote was more interesting – legal then, too – but I got the bad pukes every time, and that takes the fun out of anything.

Baseball was one thing Kacy and I did hold delightedly in common. For years her father had been part owner of a Class A team in Philly, and Kacy grew up going to every home game they played. We both liked baseball the way we liked jazz, live and close up. Since this was before the Giants moved to San Francisco, that left us the Triple A Seals, though as long as it was baseball, we hardly cared if it was the majors or minors. I always thought it was a sad indictment of the North Beach crowd that you couldn't lure them near anything as American as a baseball game even if you bought them season tickets and sprung for the beer. The only exception was John Seasons, who actually had a season ticket and was honestly offended when I jokingly suggested he print up a couple of extras for me and Kacy.

The three of us truly had a ball at the ballpark. John and Kacy were always drooling over some first-baseman's forearms or the center-fielder's butt, but they enjoyed the drama and strategy as much as the physical grace. And nobody ever rode an umpire like John Seasons. John was sort of gangly and diffident looking, but he had a voice like a meat cleaver. 'May you be buggered by a caveful of Corsican thugs! May Zeus fill your loins with curdled goat's milk! May Poe's raven pluck your infirm eyeballs and every being in Rilke's angelic order piss in the empty sockets!' John really worked out.

If it sounds like I was having a good time, a life of high spirit and the pedal pretty much to the metal, I was indeed. Maybe too much so. Because when you're running with a remarkable woman and large-hearted friends, bathing in the fountain of fresh possibilities, pulling forty hours a week gets tremendously boring, even when it's work you like. There just wasn't that much left to learn about tow-truck driving, and nothing's more heartless than mastery without challenge. When you start losing satisfaction with your work, that's the first sign of slippage at the center.

Despite the outlaw thrill, wrecking the occasional car for Scumball was also becoming routine. Maybe, if there'd been one or two jobs a month instead of one every three months, I might've hung it up at Cravetti's. Granted, coming up with new ways to wreck cars without establishing a pattern stretched the imagination. But the fact is, it doesn't take much to total a car for insurance purposes – only has to be more expensive to repair than the car is worth. Your granny could do it in an easy two minutes with an eight-ounce hammer and a handful of sand.

Anyway, this was boring enough that Big Red and I started getting fancy in our destructions. He found a place up on Mount Tam where there was a loose boulder above the road, and after we got everything lined up good we used a couple of pry bars to roll that stone straight down on a new '61 Impala, bullseye. We torched a Chrysler out by Stinson Beach, but the most fun we had destroying a car was probably this Olds 88 we took way the hell and gone up Fort Ross Road, pretending we were deranged service-station attendants. Big Red had bought a couple of red stars at the five-and-dime to give us that official look. We pinned them on and got right to it, humming 'You can trust your car, to the man that sports a star,' as we bent to the task.

'Fill it up this evening, sir? Would you like mortar mix or regular cement?'

'I'll get that windshield, George,' Big Red called cheerfully, putting an eight-pound sledge right through it. 'Clean, huh? Just like the glass wasn't there.' Red liked this so much he was damn near babbling with enthusiasm.

'Hey, Red! While I'm checking things out here under the hood, why don't you grab that pair of sidecutters and snip off them valve stems and make sure air comes out of those tires. Look overinflated to me.'

'You got it, Chief. How's it look under the hood?'

'No damn good: bad oil leak from the valve cover. Toss me that number-eight sledge and I'll see if I can get that gasket *flat*. Maybe reseat the valves a little deeper while I'm at it.'

By that time I was really *enjoying* the gig – and remember, I was a long-time faithful at the altar of internal combustion. Another sign that things were coming apart. Of course, I didn't see it then, or not clearly. But what difference does it make to understand you're hungry when there is nothing to eat?

I might not have known the cause, but I could feel something was wrong. I had a good woman, honest work, fine friends, and some illicit thrills to keep me sharp, but I wasn't happy. Had no idea why, and I'm still not dead certain. John's diagnosis was a severe case of late-adolescent spiritual edema, the strange disease of drowning in your own juices. His prescription was to let the affliction run its torpid course, hopefully washing away the more negligible parts of the psyche in the purging process.

Big Red Loco thought it was the air. He didn't elaborate except to add, upon my harshest questioning, 'You know, man: the *air*.' He even provided a visual aid by sweeping his hand vaguely above his head.

And Kacy, sweet Kacy, I never found out what she thought, because she was suddenly gone, off to Mexico and eventually South America with two gay Jungian psychologists, brothers named Orville and Lydell Wight. The purpose of the trip was to investigate first-hand the shamanistic use of various drugs employed by native tribes. They had a new Chevy van, some independent financing, and no time limit, although Kacy was talking about at least two years, or about twenty-two months longer than I had in mind.

But what I wanted was at odds with what I knew was going to be. This was an adventure she couldn't pass up and remain true to herself, so against my true sadness and wounded sulking I mustered the dubious grace to let go of what I couldn't hold anyway.

Our last night together is committed to cellular memory. I don't think I've ever held anyone as tightly. In the morning, wishing her off, I had no regrets. None at all. But that didn't stop it from tearing me up.

A month later, the same day I received Kacy's first letter, I heard that Scumball had gotten busted. Young Cravetti let me know it had nothing to do with me, that the arrest was for loan-sharking and conspiracy to commit assault. Evidently Scumball had employed some agents from the Contusion Collection Service, a company of goons who stood completely behind their motto, 'Pay or Hurt.' The wife of a damaged debtor had gone to the cops, who probably would've filed it in the wastebasket if she and the Police Commissioner's wife hadn't been cheerleaders together in high school. I was out a steady chunk of fun money, but felt worse for Big Red. He'd come to depend on this income, and now had to go back to work for Mort Abberman who, when he was sober enough to pour the molds, had a little cottage industry making latex dildoes in his basement.

According to Kacy's letter they were in Mexico, near Tepic, going to a language school for a crash course in both Spanish and Indian dialects. Orville and Lydell were great company, loose and intelligent and serious scholars, and once they had enough language to proceed, they planned to stop in Mexico City for research before leaving for Peru. She missed me, she said, and thought of me often and fondly, but even as I read the letter I felt her slipping away.

North Beach itself was no longer a consolation. Grey Line

had scheduled tours to look at the Beatniks, even though the germinal core were long gone to other parts, leaving young and awkward heirs who seemed more enchanted by the style than the substance, and leaving behind as well the low-life despoilers and cut-and-suck criminals who seem to thrive on exploiting freedoms they're incapable of creating. Jazz clubs closed to become topless joints, silicon tits swinging on the same stages that had once featured music so amazingly real you didn't want it ever to stop. Now you just wanted to leave.

When Scumball finally came to trial in late September, leaving seemed like a good idea – just in case he was more nervous than I was and started talking deals with the DA, I decided to take a month's vacation, maybe wander down Mexico way. There was no hassle with work; I had plenty of vacation time coming. Old man Cravetti understood my anxiety, but he assured me not to burden my trip with worry since Scumball, though not without his faults, was a stand-up guy, and moved in circles where snitches were often sent on long walks off short piers, usually in cement shoes. Since I'd been introduced to Scumball through the Cravettis, where I usually picked up my delivery money, I understood the garage was involved – maybe some of the mechanics did ID changes – but I'd never asked, figuring it was wiser not to know. If they weren't worried, maybe I was overdoing it, though a month in Mexico City was still an attractive idea.

I hardly remember the vacation, most of which I spent pretending I wasn't looking for Kacy. No regrets, like I said, but many, many second thoughts, most of them washed down with tequila. On Gary Snyder's sage advice that it was the most likely place to find the face I sought, and that there was much else of interest and beauty to look at in case she didn't show, I haunted the Museum of Anthropology, maybe the best in the world. I saw wonder upon wonder, but the only glimpse I got of Kacy was in the lines of a gold jaguar, Mayan, seventh century. A letter from Kacy, postmarked Oaxaca, was waiting when I returned to San Francisco, explaining they'd decided to skip Mexico City and head straight for Peru.

A week later, Kennedy was assassinated. I was cleaning up a fender-bender on Gough when a cop came over and said in that stunned, vacant voice you heard all day, 'They shot the President. They fucking *shot* the goddamn *President*.' The immediate understanding that it was a conspiracy even if Oswald had acted alone joined the forces of shock, chaos, pain, and grief in that single moment of national violation.

A lot has been made of Kennedy's assassination as some turning point in the 60's, the beginning of a profound disillusionment. And it was, in the sense that it cracked some illusions, but in a strange way. You've got to remember that we were the most privileged children in history, and probably among the most brainwashed. We had been taught history as the inevitable triumph of American ideals: those wonderful, powerful ideals of equality, freedom, justice, and dedication to the God-fearing truth. We believed. And we knew, because we were endlessly told so from kindergarten through high school, that to achieve those ideals required the unstinting application of celebrated American virtues like hard work, gumption, enterprise, courage, sacrifice, and faith. Our teachers pointed to postwar America, the mightiest, most affluent nation on the planet, as inarguable proof of the pudding.

We believed so deeply that Kennedy's death, rather than shattering our ideals served, as only a martyrdom can, to refresh them. We believed those ideals because they were beautiful, spirited, and true. If the realities didn't always agree, realities could be changed – were *made* to be changed – both by the collective will of the people and a single heroic leader with grit and stick-to-itiveness. If Negroes were being denied the right to vote – the *right* – we would go register them. If people in India were starving, we would sustain them with our surplus while we taught them how to farm. If the wretched rose up in a desperate rage of dignity and took arms against their oppressors, they could count on our freedom-loving support. And the more we tried to bring those ideals to reality, the more we understood how deeply the corruption reached. We believed so profoundly that even when we finally realized what hopeless, deluding, bullshit rhetoric those ideals had become, what a seething of maggots they masked, we *still* believed.

Once the shock of Kennedy's assassination was absorbed, you could feel a new energy on the street, a strangely exhilarated seriousness, like that first pull of the current before you hear the whitewater roaring downriver. This quickening seemed most apparent in people my age and younger, the war babies, victims more of the victory than the pain of the effort. The older generation seemed to take Kennedy's death as a defeat, a shocked return to the vulnerability and chaos World War II and Korea were supposed to end. They seemed tired with the knowledge that bad times weren't going to end. But not my generation, reared on the notion that you had to dare to dream, and dream large. But we were never truthfully warned that dreams die hard.

I say 'we,' my generation, but I don't know how much I can honestly include myself. As things quickened, I was beginning a slow fade into myself. I'd lost some essential connection. I logged my forty a week driving tow, which still retained some pleasure, but no sustaining joy. Nights and weekends I hit the streets, hungry for that old excitement, but for me it was gone.

My friends were sweet and understanding. John Seasons pronounced it a classical case of ennui and recommended a change of life as soon as I could gather my forces. Until then, he suggested strong drink and great poetry, offering to buy me one and lend me the other.

Big Red Loco just shook his head. He was feeling it too, as it turned out, finding less and less that moved him to pick up his horn. Spiders were nesting in the bell, he said, and I knew what he meant. They were nesting in my head. When I finally started boring myself, I went on a brain-cracking rampage. Got shit-faced crazy drunk every night for about a month straight and abused enough drugs to singlehandedly raise the standard of living in Guadalajara. I screwed everything that moved, or at least those who held still for it. The binge ended when I made a desperate play for John, who shocked me with the cold anger of his refusal: 'I don't want anything to do with you. You're just thrashing around, and you don't have enough forgiveness in your soul to expiate me if I take advantage of it. This would destroy the true feelings we have for each other, and I won't risk that. Slow down for once, George.' I ended up crying on his shoulder right beside the Golden Rocket pinball machine in Gino and Carlo's.

In response to John's admonition and the obvious fact that I was stuck in the mud right up to my frame, I changed my ways – perhaps the most decisively conscious change I'd ever made. I became austere. Not monkish, mind you, but seriously determined to eliminate the reckless waste. No booze, no drugs, no heartless sex. If I was mired in my own mud, there was no reason to blow up the engine in frustration.

Austerity is a good way to fight those bad blues, the ones that turn your soul into sewage. For one thing, *you* assume control, though it is, in all likelihood, sheer delusion. But if nothing else, it helps minimize the damage, if not so much to yourself, at least to others.

In a way, I actually enjoyed myself. I spent a lot of time reading, mainly poetry (taking John's advice) and history, a subject that hadn't much interested me before. I also took long walks around the city, looking at it without the insulation of a moving vehicle. Besides opening my eyes to a wealth of cultural diversity, the sheer exercise helped burn off that free-floating energy that comes of restless boredom. I did my job at Cravetti's diligently, alertly, with a new eye to the fine details. That's yet another benefit of the strict approach: you're forced outside into the whip and welter, which in turn forces you to take refuge in the moment, which is perhaps the only refuge anyway.

Once in a while I went out just to keep in touch with friends, John and Big Red in particular. John, who claimed I'd inspired him, had cleaned up his own act and was doing more writing than drinking. Big Red, however, had all but quit playing horn, and that depressed him.

The letters from Kacy began tapering off. In nine months I heard from her four times: a postcard from Guatemala, a long letter from Lima saying they were about to head into the mountains to live with an Indian tribe, then two more from Lima. The first reported that they'd all come down with hepatitis and were thinking of returning to the States, but in the last letter, two months later, they had recovered and decided to go on. Kacy sounded weary but determined. She missed me, she said, and hoped I was keeping myself pure for her return. Though she was only teasing, this struck me as being uncomfortably close to what I was doing, and perhaps it was her distant tweak that provided the first crack in my regimen.

The trouble with disciplined austerity is that it requires deep resolve, and I'm prone to back-sliding at the slightest nudge. I'd hung tough for almost nine months, damn good for a beginner. What got me really rolling downhill was a seventeen-year-old folksinger named Sharon Cross – emerald eyed, red of mane, and a body that made you sit back on your haunches and howl. She was young, innocent, and warmhearted, three attributes that taken separately are charming, but in Sharon combined to produce the one thing I didn't like about her: she was relentlessly, painfully liberal. But she was also lots of fun and sweet company, just what I needed to wean myself from austerity.

I tried to put some heart into the relationship. Sharon did too, of course – there's hardly a woman who doesn't. But we were both aware it wasn't love. I think she was lightly enchanted by my hip working-class cachet while I was enamored of sipping some nectar from the bud. Sharon intuitively understood she had a whole lot of life ahead of her, rich with possibilities, and I was only a place to start. For my part, I felt a lot of my life chasing me, the possibilities dwindling. We were smart enough to keep it easy and not live together.

About the same time I was getting close to Sharon, late June of '64, the Fourth Wiseman appeared in front of City Lights bookstore. He looked old, maybe in his fifties, but was so burned out on speed you couldn't be sure. He might've been a hard thirty. He always wore the same clothes, a brown sport coat with matching slacks, grubby but not tattered, and a white shirt yellowed with speed-sweats, frayed at the cuffs and collar but always neatly tucked in. The Fourth Wiseman stood in front of City Lights from 10:00 A.M. sharp till exactly 5:00 P.M. every day, twirling a green yo-yo and endlessly repeating the one thing that had survived the amphetamine holocaust in his brain, the one ember his breath kept alive. It was a short poem, or mantra, that he mumbled to himself about once a minute: 'The Fourth Wiseman delivered his gift and slipped away.' The whole time pacing restlessly back and forth on the sidewalk, snapping the yo-yo down, letting it hang spinning for a couple of heartbeats, retrieving it with a flick of his wrist – no tricks, no variations, none of that baby-in-the-cradle or walking-the-dog. Just spinning at the end of the string. An austerity of sorts. He ignored any efforts to engage him in conversation or otherwise distract him from his work.

'Delivered his gift and slipped away.' That phrase, and the idea of a phantom Fourth Wiseman, haunted me. Or perhaps, in combination with the spinning yo-yo – a brilliant blue-green, the color of wet algae – I'd been literally hypnotized. I'd drive by almost every day to see how he was doing, and he was always doing the same. Early on I tried to slip him a sawbuck. He was so startled he took it, but when he saw what it was he shook his head as if I'd completely misunderstood and flipped the bill out into the street. A '57 Ford coupe ran over the bill, which fluttered along in its wake, riding the draft. A wino darted out and snagged it about half a block down. The Fourth Wiseman didn't notice any of this, having already returned to his work, yo-yo singing on the waxed twine as he recited his spare testament.

The Fourth Wiseman disturbed Sharon. One of the troubles with the liberal mind is it can't deal with things too far gone to cure with good intentions. She thought he was sad and tragic, a victim, and she wanted to do something about it. She thought a benefit for him – a hootenany – would be wonderful, something for a real suffering human being in the community rather than some abstract cause. I thought it was presumptuous, pretentious, and perhaps a little bit precious to assume he was suffering when, in fact, he seemed satisfied with his mission, or witness, or whatever it was, and that my offer of money had only seemed to confuse and offend him. I told her so. We argued, but that was nothing new.

It was about six months later, Christmas of '64, that things really started falling apart. I remember walking over to Sharon's on Christmas morning and taking a detour past City Lights. There he was, yo-yo blurring in the winter light, reciting his poem with a beatific fervor that brought tears to my eyes. I blurted the question I'd been burning to ask him: 'What was the Fourth Wiseman's gift?'

The yo-yo spun in suspension. When he finally spoke, he said, 'The Fourth Wiseman delivered his gift and slipped away.'

My impulse, hardly Christian on that most Christian of days, was to strangle him, to take him down on the sidewalk and choke the answer out of him, to hiss in his ear, 'Tell me. Tell me *anything*, any truth or lie, that the gift was love or a steaming goat turd or sunlight on our bodies: tell me *anything*: but fucker, you *better tell me something!*'

Maybe he sensed I was about to flip, because when he repeated it again it seemed slightly altered, a shadow change, a glancing inflection: 'The Fourth Wiseman delivered *his* gift and slipped away.'

I walked away, confounded by the slight shift in emphasis, saying to myself, '*His* gift. Delivered *his* gift. *His*.' Confused because I still didn't know what his gift was, or mine, nor, if I even had one, whether I could deliver it or not.

Then came some hard losses. The first was Bottom, the bass player who'd sat beside me on my birthday when Big Red had played 'Mercury Falling,' whose arm had been around my shoulder the moment I first saw Kacy walking naked toward the door. Bottom was a long-time junkie, so his overdose was less a surprise than a raw sadness. They found him in his one-room apartment on New Year's Eve. He'd been dead five days. That we were playing for keepsies was a hard recognition, another rank whiff of the cold mortal facts. Big Red took it particularly hard. When asked to play at the funeral, he simply said, 'I can't.' By then he wasn't playing at all, and after Bottom's death he damn near didn't talk for a month. I sensed that silence, once his element, was beginning to corrode him, and felt helpless to watch.

About a month later, a week or so after my birthday, Sharon and I had a bitter fight about music. About the Beatles, of all people, who were just getting hot. Sharon loved them. I thought it was just bubblegum bullshit, yeah yeah yeah. This was their early stuff we were arguing about, which to my ear was weak. I thought they were a cultural phenomenon, not so much for their music as their long hair and brash cuteness, an exotic British import. As far as I understood it (not very), rock-and-roll had ended in '59. Not just the death of Buddy Holly, Ritchie Valens, and the Big Bopper in that plane crash on my birthday, but also Chuck Berry getting busted on a trumped-up Mann Act violation, and the payola scandals, and good ol' Jerry Lee Lewis marrying his thirteen-year-old cousin. Little Richard had returned to the Church, but because he was wearing lipstick and eye shadow the Church wasn't sure what to do with him. Rock-and-roll had gotten too weird, nasty, and corrupt for the four-square American sensibilities of the early 60's. Besides, the King had abdicated: Elvis came out of the Army and turned his back on rock-and-roll; went in a shit-kicker and came out with schlock. An entertainer. The King made about twenty movies; the first two or three were outright stupid, and after that they rapidly declined. The way I saw it, rock had been taken over by white teen idols, the guys you'd feel safe letting your daughter date — Fabian, Frankie Avalon, Ricky Nelson. But that's marketing, not music. They were the last sanitized gasp of the 50's, and after they vanished into their own vacuity came the Twist and other dance crazes, denatured 'pop,' and then folk music. I figured the Beatles were just a new wrinkle on the old teen-idol number, packaged as a group and imported as an invasion. The odd thing was, due to cultural lag, the Beatles' musical roots were in 50's rock-and-roll.

Anyway, this argument with Sharon was as pointless as most, but that didn't keep it from turning nasty, too bitterly revealing for comfort, and afterwards Sharon and I sort of cooled the relationship. We still saw each other occasionally and even less occasionally slept together, but our fading trust could bear no more permissions.

Sharon left abruptly in the early summer of '65. She came by to tell me she'd decided to take her music to Mississippi and help register Negro voters (they were still Negroes then, though you could tell *that* shit was about to hit the fan). I thought she was doing the right thing for herself and told her I admired her conviction and courage. I didn't tell her I felt a crass glee that her innocence was about to get rolled in some reality, but despite that spot of malice I truly wished her well.

After she left, I drooped around for about a month with a hollow melancholy composed of a self-canceling combination of genuine sadness and deep relief. Women couldn't leave me fast enough, it seemed, sailing off on their spiritual adventures while I stayed behind to move the wreckage around.

Then Big Red left for India. If I hadn't been so wrapped up in my own blues I might've seen he was hurting worse than me. He tried to explain it to John and me our last night together. I mean, Big Red *talked:* a speech, given his usual brevity; a virtual filibuster to forestall his demons. Ironically, he could have said it in four words: the gift was gone. Lost. And for no reason he could understand. It had been given him to hear life's music, to reshape it with his breath, to blow it through our hearts renewed and thereby keep it real. *Keep* it, he insisted, not *make* it. 'You can't create what's already there,' was how he put it, but that, I thought, was picking the artistic fly shit out of the aesthetic pepper, because it didn't change the pain of his loss. From that vision when he was seven, Big Red had understood his gift and had worked hard to sustain it, to deserve it, practiced till his lips were numb and his lungs ached, listened, listened as deeply as he could, listened and connected and listened again, and never dishonored it with frivolity, ego, or greed. And now he couldn't bear the taste of the mouthpiece; it tasted like rancid milk. And all he could hear was noise.

So he was leaving for India. Why India, he wasn't sure, but it felt right. You had to step over corpses on the way to the temples. A beggar's face clotted with flies. Shiva, who created and destroyed. Buddha, who sowed his breath for the harvest of wind. India for no particular reason or belief, except that people he knew who'd been there just shook their heads, and Big Red felt like he needed his head shaken.

John and I drove him to the airport the next morning. I gave Big Red a $1000 severance bonus for years of faithful and felonious service in the auto-dismantling business and John gave him what he called 'a small grant for musical research' as well as a letter-perfect passport, a sheaf of references, and other papers designed to facilitate travel abroad. As we parted at the boarding gate, Red bent to embrace each of us. Direct and simple, that was Big Red's way. No mawkish sentiment about the past, no false and hearty promises to the future. Goodbye and gone.

I'd already decided to take the rest of the day off, so when John suggested we stop by Gino and Carlo's on our way back from the airport, have a drink to honor our departed friend, I was ready. We started drinking around noon and finished a couple of days later when John collapsed in the men's room in some bar. I'd discovered early on in the binge that John had lost his grip on the wagon a week before and was still rolling from the fall. His new work, a long serial poem about the shapes of water and air, was, he claimed, 'an utter piece of shit,' and he'd taken a serene pleasure in composting it along with 'the rest of the offal, refuse, and garbage I seem doomed to produce.' That night, after I'd taken John to the emergency ward, I was lying in bed too exhausted to sleep and no longer drunk enough to pass out when it came to me that the whole problem was with gifts. Big Red had lost his. John couldn't deliver his. And me, I didn't seem to have one at all, no gift to deliver. With that recognition things turned to shit, pure and simple.

After considering this a few days in the grey light of recovered sobriety, I decided I needed a heart-to-heart with the Fourth Wiseman. Since I hadn't been able to crack his mania on the job, I thought I'd follow him home, buttonhole him off-duty as it were, and ask him politely how you could deliver a gift if you didn't have one, or at least didn't know what it was. If he wouldn't talk, I'd cajole, angle, reason, bribe, beg, and, if all else failed, follow my impulse of the previous Christmas and strangle it out of him. But I'd taken too long to gather my resolve into action. July 4, 1965, one year to the tock after he'd first appeared, the Fourth Wiseman vanished – how or where or why, nobody had a clue. I was a day late and a whole lot short.

Scumball's return was another loss in what was quickly becoming a streak, one bad beat after another. He was waiting for me in Cravetti's office. A year and a half in the slammer hadn't changed him much, except the mumble was lower and a little more slurred and his get-out suit hadn't had time to properly scuz. The smile was still an immaculate dazzle and the proposition hadn't substantially changed: 'Georgie, you ready to go for some rides?'

'Scumball,' I sighed. 'You hitting the ground running?'

The mention of his name elicited the full display of teeth. 'Well, Georgie my boy, there's a *lot* of ground to cover, know what I mean? I'm sort of an independent contractor, like you, and like you I'm a stand-up guy. I go down, nobody goes down with me; people like that. I paid my debt to society, now you might say I have a little credit, maybe run up a tab. Did some thinking in slam, and some people I work with like the new wrinkles. For you it's still basically the same number, but the bread, the bread, Georgie, is *lots* better. Say five hundred in front, ditto on delivery. There'll be keys and cover, same as before.'

'Sure,' I said, 'why not?' My incentive wasn't the money, though a grand was a hell of a payday. I suppose it was the promise of action, something to snatch me from the morass, a change that might ring more changes — for the better, I hoped, because if I got much lower I'd be under the bottom.

I didn't notice anything special about the '63 Vette till I cranked it over. The engine had belly, and it was dialed to the dot. This was obviously a street racer, stock to the eye but pure blur under the hood, with a drive-train and suspension beefed to take the load. You just couldn't help yourself. I made another entry in the loss column: I lost my mind.

It was 3:00 A.M. and Army Street was straight and empty as far as the eye could see. However, it couldn't see up the side alleys, and that's where the black-and-white was idling, waiting for an idiot just like me. He must've heard me, because I was going too fast to clock. Whoever had put that Vette together understood in his fingertips the balance between power and stability. The cop's red light started as a pulsing speck in the rearview mirror, but about two seconds after I hit high gear and tromped it on down, the light had disappeared. From the mirror, you understand, not my spine.

I had a lot of things going for me, even if brains wasn't one of them. I had a good jump, haul-ass wheels, an equal or better knowledge of the streets, and a raging desire to keep my sweet self out of jail. What pulled me through, though, was luck — but it was ably assisted, I was pleased to note, by a show of excellent instincts and, believe it or not, enough common sense to understand that while it was indeed exhilarating to be sitting in a machine that could blow the doors off anything the cops had on the street, it couldn't outrun their radios.

To *know* what to do without hesitation carries a bottomless sense of serenity, and I got a nice taste of it as I braked and geared down, gauging beyond conscious thought the variables of speed, distance, angle, force, stress, car-body composition, and the survival possibilities of my own mortal, maimable flesh. I took it sideways in a rubber-shredding, scrotum-cinching arc, hit the concrete streetlight stanchion dead center on the right headlight, simultaneously cramping the wheel to whip the rear end around to crash into the side of the bank on the corner. In one fluid movement I yanked the key and hit the concrete running, first down Mission a block, then sprinting up a side street and then cutting down an alley and then, slowing, a plan taking shape as I got my bearings and breath, over to Dolores. The old oak I'd remembered admiring on one of my walks hadn't moved. I celebrated the steadfastness of trees as I went up it. Some neighborhood kids had lashed a few planks together for a low-rent treehouse high in the boughs. By leaning back against a limb I was able to stretch out. I made myself comfortable while I slowly ate the cover note. It was signed 'Jason Browne,' and while chewing I wondered why Jason Browne would wreck such a beautiful machine. I wondered if he was more desperate than me, then decided it was impossible to know anything like that. I flexed my throbbing left elbow; I must've whacked it in the wreck, but it seemed to work. Everything still functioned, more or less. There was grace in the world. A couple of cop cars cruised by slow, their spotlights stabbing between buildings, but they weren't looking very hard. I waited till dawn collecting such small consolations, then returned to earth.

I called Scumball from a pay phone on 24th and gave him the chrome-on-the-road riff. When he replied, 'Who is this?' he sounded truly indignant, so maybe he'd already heard I'd cut it close. Nothing I could do about that. I used another dime to call in sick at Cravetti's, then caught a bus home to North Beach. After a long, hot bath I opened a bottle of brandy and stretched out on the bed and had a long talk with myself.

You might've wondered where my back-up was. For that matter, why hadn't I pulled over at the first pulse of the cop's light, produced the cover letter, and taken the ticket and ton of horseshit you buy when the heat nabs you clocking double the posted limit and still in second gear? Why indeed, except for the natural aversion to scrutiny in such a vulnerable situation. Was I begging for a fall? Provocative question. Did I want to live? Jeez, I thought so, but my behavior wasn't reassuring. I was beginning to doubt myself, that terrible doubt that's like an obsession without an object. Fact was, though, I'd pulled it off, and I was sure that counted for something; but exactly what, I didn't know. I'd been lucky, I supposed, but despite the gambler's truth that it's always better to be lucky than good, luck is subject to sudden change, and I realized that in my condition I couldn't afford even a drop of bad luck. In retrospect it was a poignantly worthless realization, because I was about to drown in it.

But first, to encourage it, I got roaring drunk. That was a week later, during one of those rare September heat waves when the fog doesn't form on the bay and the city stifles. I must say I was hugely and happily drunk, a welcome change from melancholia-in-the-cups. The happiness was born of some spontaneous eruption without discernible cause, a raw, joyous overflow from the fountain within, a definite sign of life. I decided that rather than swelter in my room I'd sleep out in nature. I considered one of the nearby parks, but there were too many people hanging out on the edges who'd turn you into junk sculpture for your loose change. Then I had a great, happy, drunken idea – that old tree-fort oak over on Dolores, my sanctuary from hot pursuit. I hoofed it on over and climbed into its open arms. It was lovely stretched out on the planks, the stars blurring with heat shimmers as the city cooled.

I slept so well I didn't twitch till the morning traffic began to thicken. I checked for approaching pedestrians through the leaves and shinnied down. As soon as my feet hit the ground, I was dizzy. I leaned against the rough, heavy trunk, waiting a few minutes for my head to clear, and a few more to make sure it would stay that way. When I felt stable and lucid, or as much as my hangover allowed, I headed toward the bus stop over on Mission. I was due at Cravetti's by 8:00.

There is no sanctuary. Down the block I saw a woman starting down her front stairs with a large bag in her arms and a heavy purse swinging from her shoulder. I didn't pay any particular attention till she stopped halfway down and yelled something back toward the house. I couldn't make out the words, but her tone was pissed off. A lovers' quarrel, maybe; back to the world. When she yelled again, her voice strident, I was close enough to make it out: 'The kitchen table, Eddie. *Kitchen* table! Now goddamn it, would you *please* hurry? We're going to be late.' She shook her head angrily.

I was about forty yards from the steps when she shrieked, 'Close the door, Eddie!' A door banged shut and a small brown-haired boy about five years old came bounding down the steps, his arms cradled under a bright yellow lunchpail on top of which were a couple of books and some big sheets of paper; he had his head scrunched down so his chin held the papers in place. He went right through his mother's grasp, giggling, mimicking, 'Come *on*, we're *late*.' His mother, haggard, started after him.

I was about thirty feet away when he tripped near the bottom stair. I thought he was going to fall but somehow he kept his balance. In doing so, however, he lifted his chin from the papers, and an errant breeze lifted off the one on top, which fluttered toward the curb. He almost snagged it, but just as his small hand reached out the paper skirred again, skittered sideways up the block, then, lifting, sailed waist-high toward the street.

I saw it coming and dove for him as he dashed intently between two parked cars and his mother screamed his name. The fingertips of my left hand brushed the leg of his brown corduroy pants. It was that close.

The old guy driving the blue '59 Merc didn't have a chance. The kid was dead before he hit the brakes. When I heard the sound of the car hitting that little boy, a wet smack like a side of beef thrown from the back of a semi onto a loading dock, it was like something reached down into my chest and ripped out my heart. The street was a chaos of brakes and screams. I lay there on the sidewalk, numb except for the burning in my fingertips where they'd grazed his trousers.

When his mother ran into the street, I jumped up to catch her before she could see his body – then realized she *should* go to him, touch him, kneel and hold him, whatever she needed to do.

But she didn't go to his body. She stopped short and pointed a wild, accusing finger at the blood running steadily toward the gutter, floating cigarette butts and a Juicy Fruit wrapper where it pooled against the curb. Her pointed finger shaking, she began a shrill, monotone chant: '*This* . . . is *not* . . . *right*. No. *No*, this is *not right*. *It is not right*. No. *Not right*.' Long after the cops and neighbors had tried to calm her, comfort her, she persisted in the same stunned, determined accusation, until they led her gently back into the house, assuring her everything would be all right.

The cop who took my statement had as much trouble controlling his voice as I did. When I told him about the paper blowing into the street, he unfastened from his clipboard a crayon drawing on cheap tablet paper. A giant sun hovered over a landscape containing a large red flower, three animals that were either horses or deer, and a long green car with shiny black wheels. The sun dominated the upper center of the picture, high noon, solid gold, its light and warmth flooding the scene.

After the cop recorded my story, he rechecked my name and address and told me I was free to go. I'd seen the old man in the Merc being taken downtown in the back of a black-and-white, so I repeated my conviction that it wasn't his fault, that Eddie had bolted blindly between two parked cars and there was nothing in God's green world the man could've done to stop in time. 'Gotcha,' he said. 'They just took him down to get a statement. Routine under the circumstances. The guy was shook, and it doesn't hurt to get him away from the scene.'

An ambulance had taken the body away, and the crowd had thinned to a few gawkers. A couple of cops were measuring skidmarks. A guy with a backpump was flushing away the blood.

'I didn't want to see it,' I told the cop. 'Didn't want to, didn't need to.'

'Me neither, pal.'

'How's the mother?'

'Torn up, like you'd expect, but she'll be all right. Or as all right as you can get after something like this.'

'You know, I just *barely* missed him.' I held up my left hand for the cop to see. 'I touched his pants, that's how fucking close it was. One second closer out of all the time in the world, *one* second, *one* goddamn *heartbeat*, and that guy wouldn't be hosing down the street.'

'You did what you could,' the cop grunted, 'that's what matters.'

The grunt annoyed me. 'Are you *sure?* Are you *really, truly, deep-down positive* about that?' I started yelling. 'Fucking utterly *convinced*, are you?'

'Hey pal,' he bristled, 'don't lay it on me. I gotta see this shit every day, so don't get on *my* ass. Listen, my third month on the street, green-ass rookie, we get a guy out on a ledge fifteen floors up and he's hot to jump. I'm leaning out the window telling him "Don't." I'm telling him every reason in the world to live, and I'm telling him straight from my heart, straight as it comes, how it's *worth* it, *life is worth it*, life is *sweet*, come back inside, give it another shot. And I see he's pressing himself back against the wall, I can see the fingernails on his left hand turn *white* he's digging so hard for a grip, and he's inching his way over to me and starting to cry. And when he's almost where I can reach him, he says in a real soft voice, "You don't know what you're talking about," and he pushes off. Fifteen stories, straight down. Strawberry jam. But even before he hit the ground I knew it wasn't my fault. I'd done my best, and I figure that's all you can ask, all you can ask of anybody, all you can ask of yourself.' His eyes challenged me. 'Unless you want to ask more than that.'

'No,' I said, slumping, 'that sounds like plenty.'

'Okay. You grabbed, you missed, you'll never know if it could've been any different. Don't get down on yourself. Go home, take a long hot bath, crack a couple of cold ones, watch the tube, forget it. Life goes on.'

And that's what I did, all except forgetting. I was weak enough going in, and seeing a happy bouncing kid struck suddenly dead shattered me, just ate me up. Since I didn't know Eddie, you'd think it wouldn't have been so bad, but in a way it was worse, a reminder of the random daily slaughter beyond the tiny circle of my life. Besides, I knew Eddie. I'd touched him.

I took the five weeks of vacation I had coming, bought about three cases of canned stuff – hash, peaches, chili, stew – and about twelve cases of beer, and locked myself in my apartment. I didn't want to see anybody or anything. I took three or four hot baths a day, slept as much as my nightmares allowed, and the rest of the time drank beer and stared at the walls. I didn't know if I was going over the edge or if the edge was going over me. After a week I started pacing back and forth in my small apartment, looking at the floor, every once in a while bursting into tears. I couldn't find anything to hang onto until I remembered the sound of Big Red playing 'Mercury Falling,' and felt the necessity for music. Since I was afraid to leave the apartment, I switched on the radio.

I couldn't find much jazz on the box and what there was seemed too cool and complex. That's when I discovered rock-and-roll. It was the right time. If it was moribund six years earlier, in '65 the stone was rolled away, and that summer there was a revival, if not a resurrection. The Rolling Stones came out with 'Satisfaction,' as in can't get no, sounding as if they might get nasty if some didn't show up soon. Same month, Dylan went electric, bringing the power of the troubadour tradition to the power of electrical amplification, the music driving the meaning like a hammer driving a nail, and he sure wasn't singing about holding hands down at the Dairy Queen:

> How does it *feeeeeel*
> To be all *alloooone*
> Like a complete *unknooowwwwnn*
> Like a *rooooooollllling STONE!*

With the Stones and Dylan, the airwaves suddenly seemed a long way from pretty-boy idols and teenybop dance fads. The mean gutter blues the Stones drew from, Dylan's electric barbed-wire Madonnas, the raw surrealism of the San Francisco bands that were beginning to break out of garages and lofts – all at once there was a mean and restless bite to the music, a hunger and defiance. Yet around the same time, the Loving Spoonful released 'Do You Believe in Magic' and the Beatles' film *Help!*

came out in all its grand and whacky foolishness. That sense of lightheartedness cracked the paralyzing fear of being thought uncool, different, weird – and that dread of appearing foolish is one of the biggest locks on the human cage. So all at once, along with a roots-first resurgence of black music into the mainstream, there was a new eruption of possibilities and permissions, a musical profusion of amazing range and open horizons, from the harshest doubts and indictments and a blatant sexual nitty-gritty unthinkable the year before to a sweetly playful and strangely fearless faith. The stone was rolling, and you couldn't mistake the excitement.

It would be silly to say the music saved or healed me, but in my daily routine of hot baths, of opening cans of beer and food, what I held onto was the music. Not for salvation – nothing can do that for you – but for the consolation of its promise, its spark of life, its wild, powerful synaptic arc across spirit, mind, and meat.

By the end of my five-week vacation I was functional, if barely, and aware that life, even by dragging itself wounded down the path, did go on. When I returned to work, however, I felt like I was coated about two inches thick with cold oatmeal. With the help of time and music I'd hauled myself up from a feeling of gutted doom to one of impenetrable depression. My flesh was bloated, my blood gone rancid, my spirit sour. Partly this was physical – I'd gone to hell from sitting on my ass drinking beer and eating out of cans. I could think of only one thing that might sharpen my reflexes, cheer me up, help me shed some flab – those little white pills with crosses on them.

I'd vowed with every fiber of purpose that I wouldn't do it again, fought temptation like a rabid bear, hung on through the shit-mush and doldrums, and I was so determined to scourge that weakness I decided I'd only buy fifty hits for a last hurrah. In the twisted psychology of collapsed resolve, I figured this lapse was allowable on two unassailable points: first, amphetamines depress the appetite, leading to weight loss, so it was justifiable on medical grounds; and secondly, I was celebrating coming through slaughter, and what's a celebration without treats?

Perked me right up, too, and I needed some enthusiasm to fight back the gloom. Once I got riding that fifty-hit party I knew that what I really needed was to leave, move, split, follow Kacy or Red or any of the others who'd gotten out from under themselves. That I had nowhere to go except somewhere else made me tremendously sad.

I finished the fifty in about a week. Got my nervous system tuned up and my blubber trimmed back, but best of all I didn't try to score more when I ran out. The come-down wasn't that bad – the usual frazzle and funk – or else I was used to misery. My display of pluck was an inspiration. It isn't hard to make the right choices, but sometimes it's hell to stick to them.

In that hopeful mood I met with Scumball on the twentieth of October. He'd left a message for me at Cravetti's to meet him at Bob's Billiards. Scumball hadn't been particularly pleased by the job I'd done on the Corvette. I'd only heard from him once since then, a job in Oakland, but he'd canceled the next day, explaining only that the set-up had fallen through. I figured I'd been scratched from his list of reliable idiots, but then again I'd been out of action for five weeks.

The pool hall was a local hangout where you could shoot more than snooker if you had the inclination and the price. At Scumball's suggestion we went for a walk and were just out the door when he gave me a fraternal pat on the back and said something innocuous like, 'How's my man been?' For some reason, and for the first time, I resented his assumption that we were partners, brothers, buddies, pals. Scumball played the small-time edges, mealy-cheap and tight; there was no hunger or grandeur to his imagination. I almost wheeled around to slap his hand off my back when it struck me what really was eating my ass. We *were* alike, literally partners-in-crime, and for all the soaring grandeur of my majestic and altogether superior imagination, I didn't seem to be doing much. Petty as he was, Scumball did have a certain gift for scamming, and in fact I worked *for* him. I held my tongue and listened.

It was an interesting earful. Scumball was playing a variation on his new theme, and this time a story went with it. The car he had in mind was a mint '59 Cadillac. According to Scumball, it had been purchased by a whacked-out sixty-year-old spinster named Harriet Gildner as a present to some hotshot rock star. The old lady was 'covered up with money,' to quote Scumball, an heiress to a fortune in steel and rubber. The Caddy was all crated to ship when the rock star died in a plane wreck. Since she didn't need the money or the car, and could afford to indulge her sentimentality, she'd stored it in one of her warehouses on the docks. She had a nephew, guy named Cory Bingham, who wanted the Caddy so bad he was wading in his own drool, but the old lady wouldn't let go. She was a major loony, Scumball claimed, and her psychic adviser, one Madam Bella, told her to hang on to it, its time would come.

But Harriet Gildner's time had come first: she fell down the stairs of her Nob Hill mansion and broke her neck, evidently so loaded that the autopsy report indicated traces of blood in the drugs. There was some quiet conjecture that Madam Bella or maybe Cory had given her a helpful nudge to get her rolling, but it was ruled an accidental death. That was in early '62, but her will, while legit, was an homage to surrealism that every relative down to seventh-cousin twice-removed had contested. The legal dust had finally cleared a few months back. The nephew received the Cadillac he'd coveted, but that was all. Scumball didn't remember exactly, but the stipulation in her will, to give you an idea, went something like 'Cory gets the car he panted for, provided he's become a knight worthy of the steed, but he gets nothing else, never ever, and if he ever sells the car he has to pay the estate double the sale price, and if his worthiness is in question the Book of Lamentations should be consulted if the ghosts see fit to reveal it.'

So Cory got the Caddy, others got odd bits and pieces, Madam Bella (her psychic adviser and, Scumball claimed, drug connection) was well provided for, and the rest of the estate was divided equally between the Brompton Society for the Promotion of Painless Death and the Kinsey Institute. I laughed when Scumball told me that, but he shot me a scornful look. 'Fucking dame. Makes me *puke* how it's always her kind that wind up with the big loot and never lifted a finger to earn it, never had to scuffle for one fucking penny.'

Cory didn't care much about the car when he finally got it, an attitude evidently influenced by the fact he fancied himself a poker player, an expensive fancy that had placed him in pressing debt and serious disfavor with collection agencies not listed in the Yellow Pages. Although he didn't say so directly, it was easy to guess that Scumball was affiliated with the people who wanted to be paid. Since the Caddy was the only asset, I gathered Scumball had advised Cory that a mint Cadillac – even one only six years old – was a precious collector's item that should be insured to the hilt, and if anything unfortunate should happen to it – well, the insurance money might cover his IOUs and thereby guarantee him the continued use of his arms, legs, and sexual organs. Cory, quick to recognize wisdom when it threatened to club him, had agreed. The Caddy had been uncrated at a storage garage Cory had rented on 7th Street. A mechanic had checked it out, replacing seals and rubber as needed, and fired it up. It was all set: gassed, registered, ready to roll. Fully insured, of course.

But there was an irritating problem. I'd have to break into the garage to steal it. This wasn't a major difficulty, since Scumball had a duplicate key for the garage lock, but I'd have to make it *look* like B&E to keep the heat off Cory, who was nervous about being implicated, though evidently even more worried about being maimed. I told Scumball that Cory was liable to get looked at hard, considering the recent insurance purchase, and that I wasn't particularly interested in the job since he was liable to crumble like a soggy cookie. Scumball assured me that Cory's alibi would be airtight, that a lawyer specializing in such claims would represent him in all transactions with the insurance people, that he knew for a fact that the agent who'd sold Cory the policy was sympathetic, and that Cory himself completely understood that if he so much as squeaked his body was shark bait.

'Forget it,' I told Scumball. 'The whole thing's got too much wobble.'

Scumball was deeply understanding. He appreciated that Breaking & Entering, even if faked, was a companion felony to Grand Theft Auto, and that working without cover substantially increased the risks. That's why I would get two grand in front and another deuce on delivery.

I'd like to think it wasn't the money that swayed me, but rather some profoundly instinctive understanding that the door was opening on a journey I couldn't deny. I've thought about it since, of course, without concluding much except that somewhere in the welter of possibilities I might've felt a way out. The money, for instance, would support a long vacation to check out other places, new ideas; maybe something would click. I was still miserable, though a notch up from the gutted numbness of the month before.

Scumball smiled with pearly pleasure when I agreed to the deal. He gave me another fraternal pat on the shoulder as he slipped me an envelope with a hundred $20 bills inside. I resented the pat, welcomed the money, and wasn't sure how I felt about the rest.

The job was set for late on the twenty-fourth, giving me a couple of days to prepare. The storage garage on 7th was within walking distance of my place, so I hoofed over that evening to check it out. The lock was a heavy-duty Schlage and the door was steel. Getting in, of course, was no problem – I had the duplicate key – but I had to fake my break-in.

What I did was fairly simple. I bought another Schlage lock, same model as the one on the door, and late that night I went over and switched the new one for the original. I took the original to Cravetti's with me the next morning and used a portable oxy-acetylene torch to cut through the shackle just enough that it would slide out of the staple. I saved the metal drippings, putting them in a film cannister when they'd cooled. I fried the duplicate key beyond recognition and tossed it into the scrap bucket. I worked with a concentration and precision I hadn't felt in a couple of months, and let me tell you it felt good. Felt *alive*, like I was finally rolling with the river.

Then I hit a snag. I couldn't find a back-up driver. All my old outlaw cronies were gone except John Seasons, and he wasn't remotely interested. Neal Cassady was supposed to be around, but I couldn't locate him; he was already turning into a rumor. There was an old friend named Laura Dolteca, but her mother was in town for the week in a last-ditch effort to change her daughter's delightfully wild ways. I couldn't think of anyone else I trusted. Three people, when five years before there had been thirty. It was time to move on. Big Sur. Santa Fe. Maybe across town to the Haight – I'd heard rumblings of some high craziness over there. With the four grand from the Caddy job and another two at home in a sock, I could afford to roam around and see what connected, what pieces fit.

But first the business at hand. When I came off-shift at 5:00 I went straight to my apartment, soaked for an hour in a hot bath, and cooked myself a steak dinner. I ate with gusto for the first time in a couple of months, then did the dishes. At 9:00 I checked and packed my tools: the torched original lock and metal drippings, key to the new lock on the garage, flashlight, gloves, and a few odds and ends like sidecutters and jumper wires. Once everything was all set I stretched out on the bed and dialed up some rock on the box and, riding the anticipation, methodically considered the pile of possibilities and contingencies.

The only three crucial problems I hadn't resolved were where and how to wreck the Caddy and how to get away. I say I hadn't decided, but I had – subject to tough review. I applied all the hard-headed logic I could muster, weighing, balancing, trying to enforce an intelligent objectivity, but I finally approved my original inclinations, which were based on pure sentimentality and an aesthetic disposition for the symmetrical: I'd put it over the same cliff out on the Pacific where Big Red and I had dumped that first car, the Mercury falling into silence. Of course this would leave me on foot about a hundred miles from home, but I saw a pleasing way around that. I'd hide out in one of the rugged coastal ravines for a day devoted to contemplating what to do with my life, then hitch back the next evening. That left a minor hang-up, which I solved immediately with a phone call to Cravetti's, telling them that a buddy of mine had been badly hurt in a logging accident near Gualala and I was on my way up to see him for a couple of days.

I lay there listening to the music till almost 1:30 in the morning, then gathered my crime kit and headed for the door. My hand was on the knob before I realized I'd left the radio on, and just as I reached to snap it off the deejay dropped the needle on James Brown's 'Pappa's Got a Brand New Bag.' I could never figure out whether the new bag was smack, a recharged scrotum, or a new direction in life, but you could sure as shit dance to it. And that's just what I did, bopping around my apartment, little shimmy and slide, touch of Afro-Cuban shuffle here, four beats of off-the-wall flamenco gypsy twist there, a bit of straight-on ass shaking to smooth it out, and ending with a flourished twirl that Mr Brown himself, King of Flash Cool, would've applauded. Yea, if the heart's beating the blood's gotta move. Flushed with dancing, nearly giddy, I clicked off the tunes and lights and hit the street.

The bars were just beginning to empty as I headed up Columbus toward Kearny. Lots of sailor boys fresh from the tit shows and a handful of new fuzz-beard beatniks who looked like they were wondering where they might score a lid of the good stuff. A black-and-white cruised by and I kept on walking as cool as you can get until it turned the corner, then, irrepressible me, I broke into a full-tilt boogie step and took it right over the top into my newly discovered James Brown whoop-da-twirl, a double this time.

The double whoop-da-twirl was actually a one-and-a-half, and I landed facing a young couple that I hadn't noticed behind me on the sidewalk, scaring the holy bejeesus out of them. 'Love each other or die!' I commanded, a line John Seasons was fond of screaming unexpectedly when he was at the peak of a binge. And I'll be go to hell if they both didn't simultaneously blurt, '*Yes, sir!*' They were scared, and that certainly wasn't what I'd intended, nor what I wanted. I could see them flagging down the next cop car with a babbling raw-panic story about some guy who'd spun around and threatened to kill them, so I said, 'Hey, relax. I was just quoting a line from a poem. You know, poetry? And that wild old twirl was straight from unbearable exuberance. Sorry if I startled you, but I didn't hear you coming up behind me.' I bowed to the woman and offered my hand to the young man as I introduced myself: 'My name's Jack Kerouac.'

'I thought you were taller,' the woman said. I could've kissed her.

'You wrote *On the Road*,' the guy announced. 'I dug it.'

We chatted a few minutes as I basked in their reverence, and then I told them I had to go find Snyder because we were taking off in the morning to climb Mount Shasta. Once we reached the peak we'd each say one word to the wind and then give up speech for a year. Bless their hearts, they wanted to go along.

I was turning to go when the woman stopped me with a touch on the shoulder. She reached in her pocket and handed me a small foil-wrapped package. 'LSD,' she murmured. 'Only take one at a time.'

'Thank you,' I said politely. I'd been hearing about LSD but hadn't been interested enough to score. I had enough trouble with peyote. I realized it wasn't exceptionally bright to add drug possession to a list of imminent felonies, but there was no way to gracefully refuse.

'Take it in a beautiful place,' she advised. 'It'll really open things up.'

Well, after all, I *was* interested in opening things up, so why not? Keep the spirit of adventure alive. 'Wish I had something I could offer in return,' I said – *except lies*, my conscience reminded me.

'There's something I'd like to know,' she said shyly.

I braced myself. 'Name it and I'll try.'

'I'd like to know what word you're going to say on top of Mount Shasta.'

'I can't tell you because I don't know,' I said, relaxing. 'I'm just going to say whatever comes to me, whatever I feel. Spontaneous bop of the moment's revelation, you understand. Sorry I can't tell you or I sure would.'

'Just a minute,' she said, rummaging in her buckskin purse till she found a card and a pen. She talked as she scribbled under the streetlight. 'It's a stamped postcard. I'll address it to myself. My name's Natalie. After you come down from the mountain, write what word you said and mail it to me – but *only* if you *feel* like it. No obligation. And I promise not to tell anybody.'

'That's fair. Assuming I make the top and have something to say.' I pocketed the card.

'Can she tell me?' her boyfriend asked.

'Sure, if you still love each other and haven't died.'

They both giggled.

'*Don't* die,' I admonished them, and then I was gone up Columbus to Kearny, strolling up the mountain toward the wild wind and the mighty clouds of joy, letting fly with a bit of the double-shuffle be-bop buck-and-wing as the spirit moved me. From the instrument room of my psyche, a voice as dry as my conscience's but with a more sardonic edge announced, *You're asking for it.* And I answered under my breath, 'That's right, I'm asking for it. Hell, I'm begging for it.' And I bopped on down the street.

I was more subdued by the time I reached the garage on 7th, but still full of juice. I felt alert, confident, inevitable, and I hadn't felt any of that in a long time. I walked up to the garage door like I owned the place, used the key, and swung the double doors open. I stepped inside, shutting the doors behind me, slipped the flashlight out of my crime kit, and stood still in the darkness, senses straining. The air seemed warmer inside. There was a musky odor of gear oil, sharp tang of solvent. I switched on the flashlight.

The garage was full of Cadillac. The car looked about seventy feet long. Where it wasn't chrome, it was pure white, including the sidewalls on the tires. Six years is a long time for rubber not to roll, and though Scumball had assured me there were new tires all around, I wanted to be sure. There were. I checked the plates: current. Despite my attention to safety items as I made my inspection, it was impossible to miss the extravagance of the styling: swept fins that seemed as high as the roofline, each sporting twin bullet taillights; a front grille divided by a thick horizontal chrome bar and studded with small chrome bullets, a pattern repeated on the rear dummy grille that ran across the lower back panel above the bumper; fenderskirts on the rear wells; tinted wrap-around windows front and back; chrome gleaming everywhere. It was an Eldorado, and if memory serves that meant 390 cubes, 345 horses, fed by three two-barrel carbs. You'd need that kind of thrust to move such a chunk of metal.

I opened the door to check the key and registration and was hit by the odor of new leather upholstery and, over that, a fragrance I knew in my loins and reeled to remember: Shalimar. Kacy's favorite perfume. I inhaled deeply, and again, but still wasn't really sure I still smelled it. The uncertainty spooked me. I kept sniffing, starting to tremble, then willed myself back to the job at hand before I snapped my concentration. Forcing myself to relax and slow down, I slipped the registration from the visor and went over it carefully. Clean as a whistle.

The key was under the front seat where it was supposed to be, and slipped smoothly into the ignition. The engine caught on the first stroke and settled into a purr. I gave the gauges a glance; everything looked good. The tank was full. That just left the tricky part, the point of maximum vulnerability. I had to open the garage doors, drive out, stop, close the garage door, reattach the duplicate lock, scatter some metal drippings under the hasp, toss the cut lock out where it wouldn't be obvious but where it could be found without a struggle, then get back into the Eldorado and cruise away. I figured five minutes at the outside if nothing screwed up; two if it all jammed together smooth. What I didn't need was a cop cruising by or some good neighbor with insomnia who collected the Dick Tracy Crimestopper Notes out of the Sunday funnies.

ABCDEFG. Plans. Pure delusions. How can you ever accommodate the imponderables, the variables, the voluptuous teeming of possibilities, the random assertions of chance, the inflexible dictates of fate? You jump out of a tree and walk down the street and a little boy is slaughtered in front of your eyes. The music ends and a woman stands up and takes off her clothes and you fall in love. I was turning the key when I heard a car swing around the corner and come down the street. Then another right behind it, radio blasting rock-and-roll. Both passed without slowing. Then another cruised by from up the block. Far too much traffic for 2:30 in the morning. Maybe there was a party in the neighborhood, a card game, whorehouse, drug deal, who knows. I figured I'd give it a few minutes to settle out.

I decided there were a couple of useful things I could do while waiting, like get the lock and metal drippings out and ready, and then stash the rest of my kit in the glovebox. When I leaned over and opened the glovebox, the powerful scent of Shalimar carried me back into Kacy's arms.

I came back to reality fast, greatly aided by another memory — that I was in the middle of multiple felonies — and by the fact that Kacy wasn't likely to be curled up in the glovebox awaiting my amorous designs. Shalimar is hardly a rare perfume. Maybe Cory Bingham had a girlfriend who used it, or maybe he liked to splash a little on himself and prance around. I shined the flashlight in the glovebox, expecting to find a leaky perfume bottle or a scented scarf, but the only thing in the glovebox was a crumpled piece of paper which on closer inspection turned out to be an envelope. I lifted it to my nose: absolutely Shalimar, not overwhelming but distinct. Of course, logical, always an explanation — a perfumed letter, addressed in a fine, precise script to Mr Big Bopper. That was all, just the name. No stamps or postmark. I turned it over in the flashlight's beam and saw the jagged tear where it had been ripped open. The letter inside was typewritten, single-spaced. I took it out and smoothed it on the steering wheel.

I read the letter seven times straight through right then, another seven later that night, and maybe seven hundred times altogether, but after the first time through I knew without doubt or hesitation what I was going to do.

I can recite the letter by heart. The letterhead was embossed in a rich burgundy ink: Miss Harriet Annalee Gildner. Under her name, exactly centered, the date was typed, February 1, 1959.

Dear Mr Bopper,
  I am a 57-year-old virgin. I've never had sex with a
man because none has ever moved me. Don't mistake me,
please. I'm neither vain in my virtue, nor ashamed. Life
is rich with passions and pleasures, and sex is undoubtedly
one. I haven't denied myself; I simply haven't found the
man and the moment, and see no reason to fake it.

I hope you won't mistake me as a hopeless kook, but one of my deepest interests is the invisible world. Over the years I've employed some of the most sensitive psychics, shamans, and mediums to provide access to that realm of being which defies the rational circuits of knowledge our culture enforces as reality. I've sought those realms out of a desire to know, not a need to believe. I'll spare you the techniques and metaphysics; since they are much closer to music than 'thought,' I assume you'll understand.

To the point then: About a week ago, while I was in my office perusing my broker's report and enjoying a pipe of opium, I was visited by formless spirits bearing a large book. It was bound in the horn of a white rhinoceros with the title stamped in gold: THE BOOK OF LAMENTATIONS.

I asked the spirits to open the book.

'One page, one page,' voices chanted together in reply, then held the book out to me.

It opened at my touch. The page revealed was in a language I'd never encountered before, but somehow I understood clearly as I read that it was a lament of virgins, both men and women, who, by whatever cause or reason, had never known (I quote the text) 'the sweet obliterations of sexual love.' The text continued, a chronicle of regrets, but the page faded as I read. In foolish desperation I tried to grab the book. It vanished with the spirits. But immediately a single spirit (they are invisible, but overwhelmingly present) returned. I could feel it waiting.

'Why was I allowed this visit?' I asked.

There was a giggle, a 17-year-old's nervous glee, and a young woman's voice replied, 'Trust yourself, not us.'

'How will I know?' I asked her.

She giggled again. 'You just *do*. And you'll probably be wrong.'

'Are *you* a virgin?' I asked.

'Are you kidding?' She vanished into her laughter, leaving me confused and, I must admit, distraught.

I didn't fall asleep until late that night, but I slept deeply. When I woke the next morning, shrouded in the membranes of dreams I couldn't remember, I reached over to my nightstand to turn on the radio to a classical station I frequently listen to. Or such was my attempt. I somehow turned the tuning dial rather than the on-off switch. I realized my mistake and turned the right knob, forgetting the station would be at random.

And there you were: 'Helllooo bay-beeee, this is the Big Bopper.' And I was moved. Men that have made sexual advances toward me in the past have always made it seem such an awkward, harrowing pursuit. When I heard the playfulness in your voice, the happy, loose lechery, I knew. And maybe – *probably* – I'm wrong, but that doesn't alter the conviction.

I want you to understand this car is a gift, yours without strings or conditions. It is a gift to acknowledge your music, the desire that spins the planets, and the power it portends. So it is very much a gift to the possibilities of friendship, communion, and love. You owe me nothing. I can afford it because I'm ridiculously wealthy.

If you're ever in San Francisco, please give me a call or drop by my house. I would like very much to meet you.

Sincerely yours,

Harriet Gildner

I sat there in the Shalimar-scented darkness, a man without a gift inside a gift undelivered, a heartfelt crazy gift meant to celebrate music and the possibilities of human love. I would deliver it, all right.

Then a couple of pieces fell together. Scumball had said it was a present to some rock star who'd up and died, but the Big Bopper's name hung on the threshold of memory for a moment before it arced across. 'That's a lot of music to lose,' Kacy had said. Buddy Holly, Ritchie Valens, and the Big Bopper. And now this Cory jerkoff expected *me* to wreck the Bopper's Cadillac, his aunt's gift, to pay off his stupidity at the poker table? Nope. No way was it going to happen. The car didn't belong to him. It belonged to the ghosts of Harriet and the Big Bopper, to love and music. I, too, was probably wrong, but fuck it. You move as you're moved, and what I felt moved to do was drive it to the Big Bopper's grave, stand on the hood and read Harriet's letter, and then set it all ablaze, a monument of fire. I was going to climb the mountain and say my word; deliver my gift and slip away.

I knew this was going to be more difficult than it sounded. Besides a whole pile of luck, I needed a couple of other things I could think of offhand: solid cover and a little information. I figured the cover shouldn't be too difficult. John Seasons and his many official seals could probably handle it as long as I didn't come under hard scrutiny. The only information that seemed crucial was the location of the Big Bopper's grave, and I figured I could find that out on the way.

I carefully refolded the letter and returned it to the envelope, pissed that someone – most likely that asshole Cory – had ripped it open and then crumpled it. The letter was a noble document, a little strange maybe, but that's no reason to treat it like a used Kleenex.

The occasional car still passed on the street, but I felt charmed in my elated conviction of doing right – or at least doing *something*

– and if you're going to throw your ass up for grabs, that's a good time.

I didn't hurry. I cranked the Caddy over again and let it idle while I opened the garage doors. I pulled out into the driveway, put it in neutral, and set the brake. That damn Caddy was so long half of it was in the street. I closed the doors, snapped on the duplicate lock, sprinkled the container of melted drippings around, side-armed the torch-cut original into the space between the garage and the building next door, climbed back in the Caddy, snugged up my gloves, took off the brake, and my ass was gone.

John Seasons answered the door with a distant grin. It was 3:30 in the morning and he'd just finished a poem he thought was worthy. He understood before I spoke that something was up, and fixed me with a cocked gaze. 'My, you're looking *awfully* lively this morning.'

I ran it down for him as quickly and as clearly as I could. 'I bow to the romance of the gesture,' he said, and actually gave me a formal little bow. That he liked the idea made it seem even better.

I explained my need for cover. I told him the Caddy was legally registered to Cory Bingham, so what I needed was either new registration or a damn good reason for being in the car.

John had an innate understanding of such things. 'Do you have any leverage on Bingham?'

'Since I'm off and running, and know the scam, he should be reasonable. I wouldn't say I had him by the nuts, but I could sure yank on some short hairs.'

'It would probably be best for all concerned if the guy took a vacation where he couldn't be reached for a few days. Then he wouldn't have to lie.'

'I was thinking along the same lines,' I said. 'No need to pull on a wet noodle.'

John said, 'All I need from you is a photograph for a new

driver's license, and the rest is easy. And I will need the current registration and that letter from the woman . . . Harriet Gildner, was it? Think I met her once at the Magic Workshop. Definitely out there.'

I had the registration and letter with me. John was impressed. 'Why, George, you're becoming lucidly thorough in your foolishness.'

'I'll take that as a compliment.'

John shrugged. 'Well, at least it's *grand* foolishness.'

'I hate to hurry an artist at work,' I said, 'but do you think you could have the paperwork finished in four or five hours?'

'By dawn's early light.'

'Well, shit, if you have time to kill, how about putting some of your legendary scholarship to work and see what you can find out about the Big Bopper for me? Especially where he's buried.'

'Really, George, that's not my field. Prosody, history, the graphic arts, baseball – those I might be able to help you with. But I lack the proper references for the burial sites of rock-and-roll musicians. However, I recently met a darling young boy who happens to be a janitor at the library. He should be there now, and maybe he can help us out.'

'I just want to get rolling in the right direction.'

'I understand,' John said. 'What's a pilgrimage without a destination?'

My immediate destination was my apartment. I parked around back and climbed the stairs. I stood in the center of the room and thought about what I'd need, and decided to go as light as possible. I threw together a duffle of clothes and my shaving kit, then withdrew my life savings from the First Bank of the Innersprings. I counted it on the kitchen table – $4170, including the $2000 Scumball had fronted me.

That reminded me I had to call. I dialed the new number he'd given me. As always, he answered on the third ring.

'Complications,' I said.

There was short silence, then a displeased question: 'Yes?'

'Of the heart.'

The pause was longer, but I waited him out. 'Well?' he said, not happy.

'Don't worry. The job'll get done. It's just going to take some time.'

'I hope we're talking minutes.'

'Maybe three or four days. Could be a week.'

'*No.*'

'Fuck you,' I said.

'I don't know what your problem is,' Scumball hissed, 'but if you got a dumb urge to play games or mention names I got something for *you* to remember, wise-ass. There's over two hundred bones in the body, and I have friends who'd enjoy breaking them for you, one by one, slowly. When they got done, you'd be a fucking *puddle*, savvy?'

'Fuck your friends, too, and the Sheriff, and the whole posse. If you want your ass covered, tell your shithead friend to be gone for a week. Might do his slimy soul some good to take a long hike in the Sierras. I'll take care of my end. I don't need any premature mention about missing machinery. That might make it tough on everybody concerned. You can keep what I have coming, make up for your inconvenience, but this one gets played my way. I'm going to deliver it where it rightfully belongs.'

'You're gonna eat shit, is what you're gonna do. Save some money for doctor bills. This is gonna make a *lot* of people unhappy.'

'Not for long. And they'll get over it. But you know what? It's going to make *me* very happy. Ecstatic, I hope. I'm going to send it roaring upward in the flames. What do you think of that?'

'I think it'd be nice you went with it.'

'Listen, it's *not* a rip-off, you understand? It's going to go down, like all the rest. A few days' extra time ought to be worth the balance due. Goes in *your* grubby pocket. I'm not jerking you around. It's just something that I need to do, and you can't do shit about it, so why not squeeze a little grace out of that fucking mustard seed you call a heart?'

'Die,' he snarled, and hung up, depriving me of the chance to urge him to improve his imagination.

Given Scumball's nasty mood I figured it wouldn't be wise to hang around my apartment too long – nor the city, for that matter – so I locked up and loaded my stuff in the Caddy's trunk, then cruised over to the all-night Doggie Diner for two large coffees and a double burger, which I ate on my way over to John's.

My traveling papers were ready. At John's insistence, we sat down at the kitchen table to go over them. He flipped through and explained each one. A new California driver's license in the name of George Teo Gass (John's sense of humor), a Social Security card, draft card, and other ID featuring my new name. In addition, a very official looking DMV Certificate of Interstate Transport, a document I didn't even know existed, and I'm not sure John did either. There was a notarized letter from Cory Bingham attesting to the fact that Mr Gass was authorized to transport the vehicle for display at a memorial tribute to the Big Bopper. Cory's letter was accompanied by a sheaf of papers on letterhead from the law offices of Dewey, Scrum, and Howe, which covered the terms and liabilities of the car's display at the memorial. John said that if I got stopped, I should be sure to explain I'd been hired through an agent for the lawyers and had never personally met Mr Bingham or the lawyers, though the agent had told me there was a kind of legal hassle going on between Cory Bingham and the Big Bopper's estate. He even had a card from the agent, one Odysseus Jones.

Poetry or forgery, John Seasons knew what to do with paper and ink. He wouldn't take a penny for it, either. I told him I had a wad of money to cover travel expenses and that proper documentation was foremost in the budget, but John, with the exaggerated professorial tone he used to mock himself, said, 'Ah, but my dear young man, the object of price is to measure value, and the highest value is blessings. One easily infers from the works of Lao-Tze, Dogen, and other Masters of the Path that blessed most deeply is he who helps a pilgrim on the way.'

I was about to insist on a token $50 to at least cover wear and tear on the seals when there was a loud pounding on the door. I spun around, the ruby neon flight-light pulsing in my brain stem, certain one of Scumball's goons had spotted the Caddy down the block. John grabbed my arm. 'Easy,' he said softly. 'Too late for fear.' He went to the door and asked, 'May I inquire who has come to call at this ungodly hour?'

Myron and Messerschmidt, as it happened, both wired to the tits, just hitting town after a forty-hour nonstop run to Mexico and back. They came in babbling, each bearing a large, rattling shopping bag full of drugs available only by prescription in this country, while in Mexico, with its less formal notions of restriction, they were available in bulk over-the-counter, especially at the more enlightened border *farmacias*. The first item out of Myron's bag was a 1000-tablet bottle of benzedrine, factory sealed. They wanted $150, and got it on the spot. John clucked his tongue but I ignored him. I was already tired, and it might be a long drive. Besides, I was bold, imaginative, and decisive; such virtues wither without reward.

While Myron and Messerschmidt rummaged through the portable pharmacy for John's order of Percodan – I clucked at *him* – he accompanied me to the door. 'Any info on the Big Bopper,' I asked.

'Ah, yes. I called my young friend at the library and he went through the newspaper files. The Big Bopper's real name was Jiles Perry Richardson, born and raised in Sabine Pass, Texas. If my spotty geography serves, that's right on the Louisiana border, near the mouth of the Red River. He was working as a disc jockey in Beaumont when he "hit the charts," as they say. My friend said there was no information on his burial site in the papers, but I would assume he was interred in Sabine Pass, or possibly Beaumont. If I were you, I'd head out yonder to East Texas – Beaumont's not far from Sabine Pass – but it would be smart indeed to do a little library research along the way. Shouldn't be difficult to find out where he's buried. But I'd find out before you get too far, because you're going to feel like a dumb shit if you're parked in Sabine Pass and find out his bones found their rest in LA.'

I blessed him for his help and gave him a big hug, putting some feeling into it. He returned it, then held me at arms' length and looked in my eyes. 'So,' he said approvingly, 'the Pilgrim Ghost.'

'Hey, I'm no ghost yet,' I objected, slightly unnerved. But I'd misunderstood.

'No, no,' John laughed. 'Goest. *Go-est*. Like, "The pilgrim goest forth, the journey his prayer."'

'More like it,' I said, relieved.

'Well, give my best to the dragons and wizards, and pledge my honor to the maidens fair. And the pages, if you see any cute ones. And George, seriously: fare well.'

The stars were fading in the dawnlight as I left, forged papers under one arm and a 1000-hit bottle of bennies tucked inside my jacket. The Caddy was waiting where I'd left it, pure white and heavily chromed, blast-off styling and power everything, a cross between a rocketship and Leviathan, an excessive manifestation of garish excellence, a twisted notion of the American dreamboat.

I slipped inside and turned it over. While it warmed up I put the papers in the glovebox and clipped the registration back on the visor. I lined up three bennies on my tongue like miniature communion wafers, swallowed, and stashed the bottle under the seat. I sat there tapping the gas, wondering if I was forgetting anything. But I'd reached that point where anything I was forgetting was forgotten. The clutch plate kissed the power and I came down on the juice. By the time I hit the end of the block I was long gone.

MESOLOGUE

'Blessed are those whose necessities find their art.'

—Schiller

JUST AS GEORGE was taking off on his pilgrimage in '65, we arrived in the present, the tow truck bucking as he geared down for the Monte Rio stop sign.

'Monte Rio,' I announced. Given my nearly comatose condition resulting from the tangled combination of the doom flu, many milligrams of codeine, the paralysis of speed-induced terror, and the hypnotic lull of George's voice, I was as impressed by my perspicacity as my ability to articulate it. 'Monte Rio,' I repeated, enthralled by its existential certainty.

'Yes indeed,' George confirmed. 'Five miles to Guerneville now; got it by the dick on a downhill pull and tomorrow will be a different world.' He hung a left on 12 and took it up through the gears. 'How you feeling? Hanging in there? Ears bleeding?'

I thought about it but I couldn't find the words. I'd shot my wad on 'Monte Rio.'

'Better?' George prompted. 'Same? Worse?'

I nodded.

'All of the above?'

I nodded.

He nodded back. I couldn't tell if he was sympathetically acknowledging my inability to construct and utter words or simply confirming some inner judgment of his own – about what, I didn't know and didn't care. I sank into that luxurious indifference like a high-plains cowboy sliding down into his first bath after five weeks of merciless heat and horse sweat on the trail. The words to 'Red River Valley' were floating through the remnants of my brain. '. . . hasten to bid me adieu . . .' *Adieu?* What sort of horseshit was 'adieu.' Cowboys didn't go around talking French.

George was giving me a look of pure appraisal, friendly but frank. 'Might be smart to stop by the Redwood Health Clinic for a quick check-up. I think you're fine, but opinions ain't diplomas.'

'*Bed!*' I sobbed, distantly astonished that I'd spoken. It was the voice of my involuntary nervous system seizing control from a cowboy-consciousness now bidding adieu to the home of buffalo roaming. Bed. A bed. A physical demand, the need of it pure, unsullied by lengthy evaluation, careful consideration, or thoughtful judgment. Rest, sleep, surcease. The last round-up.

George was passing a log truck like it was frozen in time. Deft, decisive – no question the man could drive. As the log truck faded in the side mirror, he said, 'You're the boss. The first order of business, then, is to get you to bed. When you're squared away I'll haul your rig over to Itchman's.'

My head nodded itself.

'If you got no place particular in mind,' George said, 'how about the Rio del Rio? Bill and Dorie Caprenter run it. Good folks. Towed in their '54 Hudson when they snapped an axle up near Skagg Springs. They'd been out bird watching. The Rio del Rio isn't fancy-ass, but what it lacks in glitz it more than makes up for in comfort. Very quiet. Always clean.'

'Faster,' I said.

George, laughing at my regrettably invincible wit, gladly obliged. Though all the windows were cranked up tight, I could feel the wind roaring against my face. It felt good. It felt even better to be a mile out of Guerneville and closing fast.

The Rio del Rio was on the west side of town, set back in a grove of second-growth redwood on a plateau above the Russian River flood-plain. There were nine cabins, counting the office, all painted dark green with white trim, the green the same shade as the moss tufted between the cracks of the redwood-shake roofs.

George flicked the floorshift into neutral and set the brake. I hadn't realized we'd stopped. 'I'll check in with Bill and Dorie and see what's what,' he said. 'Hang tight. Back in a flash.'

The rain had relented into a swirling mist. Through the wet wind-shield, George seemed to blur as he approached the office. I heard a loud knock, followed in a few seconds by a delighted female whoop, immediately sharpening into a mock scold: 'You crazy ol' ghost, we see you about as often as we do a pileated woodpecker.' My brain refused the comparison as impossibly complex.

I glanced down at my hands folded rather primly on my lap. They seemed far away and unconcerned. I wondered if they could open the glovebox for more codeine. The index finger of my right hand twitched. Where there's communication, there's hope. I was sure George wouldn't mind; there seemed to be plenty, and I might need some later in case I hemorrhaged or something. Might save my life, a life, it was not lost on me, that seemed remarkably free of moral or ethical restraint. Why did generosity seem to inspire my rapacity?

I was still pondering this when I heard the slish-slap of someone running toward the truck. The driver's door flew open and George dumped an armful of paper and kindling on the front seat and swung himself in as he cheerfully announced, 'Okay, pardner, you're all set.' He held up a key, dangling it like bait. 'Lucky seven. You have it as long as you need it, pay when you can. Dorie says there's a special winter basket-case rate of three-fifty a day. *Told* you these were people with soul. Allow me to chauffeur you to your quarters.'

In the middle of a time warp, this was way too much information for me to process. Ten seconds to the cabin. Hours to climb down out of the truck and get inside while George jabbered encouragement, comments, commands. 'Easy does it now. . . .'

Watch those flagstones – slick as snot on a doorknob. . . . Now take a dead bead on the bed there, and I'll put some flames in the fireplace. Little warmth and a couple of days' sleep appeal to you any? You make a conked-out zombie look like a fucking speedfreak, but hey, lookee here, you made it to the land of your dreams! Just peel off those duds and crawl right in. Yes! Curl up like a baby and let it all go so far away your toes will have to shoot off flares to get your mind's attention. That's right. Now I'll go prove I deserved my Fire-Building Merit Badge while you snuggle down solid and sing for the Sandman. Nothing like wood heat to get the warmth to the bones . . .' His voice trailed off as he disappeared through the door.

It was complicated, especially the buttons on the shirt, but I got undressed, slipped shivering between the cold sheets, and pulled the quilt up to my ears. George was back with the paper and wood, saying something I couldn't hear over the crackle of the kindling catching in the riverstone fireplace. He came over and grinned down at me in bed and said something about my wet clothes and picking them up at the office and I could leave his there or keep them if I needed a more diverse wardrobe with a working-class cut to properly woo the Guerneville women, but I was already gliding away, his words lost in the sound of fire and the rainy redwoods dripping on the roof.

'Dreamers awake,' a voice murmured. 'Soup's on.' George held a steaming cup in his hand. 'Hate to wake you, but even if you had a sword stuck through your heart I wouldn't let you miss this soup. This is Dorie's justly famous Cosmic Cure-All Root Broth. Over thirty different roots simmered down slow. And by slow, I'm talking a couple of weeks, you understand? Sloooow. Extracting essences. It'll put some lead in your pencil or I've never been out of first gear.'

I feebly accepted the cup. The broth was almost translucent, with a faint greenish-brown tint. Every swallow had a different taste: carrot, hickory, ginseng, licorice; now ginger, burdock, parsnip, garlic. It felt wonderful in my gut, a calm radiance soaking outward from the center. 'More,' I asked hopefully.

'Whole thermos on the nightstand here,' George said, reaching to pour me another cup. 'Comes compliments of the house with best wishes for a speedy recovery. But it's all there is, they ain't no more – this was the last container from the freezer. You can only make it once a year. Best fresh, Dorie claims, but it doesn't lose a hell of a lot in aging if you ask me. Incredible stuff. Cures flu and the bad blues, gout, malaria, shingles, impotence, schizophrenia, serum and viral hepatitis, terminal morbidity, most moral quandaries, senility, bad karma, and even that dreaded Hawaiian killer, lackanookie.'

I drank greedily while my reviving brain analyzed corporeal input. My joints ached like decayed teeth, the fever (or perhaps the codeine) had turned my skull rubbery, but the piercing headache seemed blunted and the gastrointestinal maelstrom had definitely abated.

'You getting on top of it,' George asked solicitously.

'Leg up,' I mumbled. It was still a long way from my brain to my mouth.

'Thought so. You got some shine back in your eyes.'

'This soup's good. Thank Dorie.'

'I'll do it for sure.' George smiled and turned toward the door.

It took a great effort but I managed: 'And thank *you*, George. Most of all. Your kindness is enough to make me—'

George turned around, a gleam in his eye, the grin following. 'Wasn't leaving just yet. You're not getting off *that* easy. Just wanted to grab myself a chair here so I could make myself comfortable while I finished my story. You should know how it turned out.'

I was confused for an instant, then embarrassed. The story. Oh, shit. I felt like I'd insulted him, and tried to recover. 'George, you're living proof it turned out good.'

'Hard to know for sure.' He shrugged, sliding the chair over next to the bed.

'I want to hear it, George, but I'm afraid I may nod out on you. Full of flu and codeine. Piss-poor audience.' The effort of sustained thought and speech left me weak and breathless.

'Whatever.' George waved a hand in dismissal. 'I need to hear it more than you, anyway.' The hand abruptly reached toward me, as if to touch my face. I flinched slightly, and unnecessarily, for he was just reaching over to snap off the nightstand lamp.

The only light in the room came from the windows, seeping through the redwoods and rolling mist outside. Unless I'd completely lost track of time it was around noon, but the quality of light belonged to dusk. The fire was burning down to a glow across the room, an occasional flare at a pocket of pitch, but its light seemed to reach us only as a change in the density of shadows. I could barely make out George's face.

I stretched out, clenched my muscles, then relaxed and closed my eyes, waiting for him to begin. A minute passed, then another. I could hear him breathing beside me in the dark. After another minute my pathological antipathy for dramatics crawled up my throat like bile. I tried to make it sound light and friendly, but I could feel the sarcasm in my voice: 'George, what happened? You lose the key?'

'Naw,' he said amiably, 'I was trying to remember a feeling. It's important that the feeling is right. You'd think the feeling would be unforgettable – and it *is* – but you never can recall it with the clarity of the original, never whole and present like it was.'

'What feeling?' I said.

'Free,' he said. That got him started, and he didn't stop till the end.

Part Two

DOO-WOP TO THE BOPPER'S GRAVE

*'You need a busload of faith to
get by.'*

—Lou Reed

AT THE MOMENT I took off in that stolen Eldorado I wasn't contemplating the exquisitely bottomless metaphysical definitions of freedom, you understand, I was *feeling* the wild, crazy joy of actually cutting loose and *doing* it. Blinking in the dawnlight shaping the bridge, the bay, the hills beyond, I felt like I'd just kicked down a wall and stepped through clean. Not a hint of what lay ahead or how it would end, but free to find out.

As I crossed the Bay Bridge and took a right toward Oakland and the 580 connector, I was riding on romance, the grand gesture of delivering the gift not because it was essential or necessary to existence – how much really is? – but in fact because it *wasn't;* there was no reason to risk the hazards except those reasons which were my own.

Sweet Leaping Jesus and Beaming Buddha, I felt *good.* Full of powerful purpose and amazing grace. Solid on the path. I gave a little whoop when I cleared the toll plaza and tromped on the gas, the three deuces sucking the juice down, the pistons compressing it into a dense volatility, the spark unleashing the power, driving the wheels. The Caddy handled like a sick whale, but with all the mass riding on air suspension and eleven feet of wheelbase you could eat road in heavy comfort, truly *cruise*, your mind free to roam through itself, rest, or wail on down the line. She wasn't made to race, she was built to roll, and I was holding at a steady 100 without a sound or shiver.

In my defense I'll say that while lost in the flush of freedom and a bit swept away in the righteousness of my journey, I wasn't completely inattentive. I saw the highway patrol car in my rearview mirror about a quarter of a mile back. Just by the way he was coming on, I knew my ass was wearing the bullseye; I was pulling over before he even hit his party lights.

Heart knocking, I scanned the floors and seats for my usual collection of felonies – open containers, for example, or bennies spilling from under the seat – and was relieved to note that nothing was in plain view. Watching in my side mirror as the trooper's door swung open behind me, I told myself to be cool and take the consequences as they came. If nothing else, I'd learn at the git-go if Scumball or Bingham had squealed, and if the paper held up. Then I prayed to any god who'd listen that the cop wasn't some Nazi jerk who'd just had a shit-screamer fight with his old lady before leaving the house.

Praise the power of heartfelt, blood-sweating prayer, he wasn't.

'Good morning,' he greeted me – quite cordially, I thought, considering the circumstances.

'Good morning, officer,' I replied, letting the sunshine beam through.

'I've stopped you for exceeding the posted speed limit of sixty-five miles-per-hour. I clocked you at one-oh-two.' Very precise, a little ice in his tone. Maybe he appreciated accuracy.

'That's correct, sir,' I said.

'Could I see your driver's license and registration please?'

'Of course,' I replied, and the dance began.

No trouble with my license – solid as the law itself. He examined the registration long enough that I anticipated his concern and pulled the folder of papers from the glovebox, the lovely odor of Shalimar now worrisomely mixed with that of fresh ink. Following my old friend Mott Stoker's advice that the only two things to do with your mouth in a tight situation are to keep it closed or get it moving, I got it moving, explaining how I was delivering the car to Texas for some sort of memorial tribute ... didn't really know much about it ... was hired by an agent for the estate and the lawyers had fixed me up with this wad of papers, you see, affidavits and certificates and such. I dumped the whole folder on him. He opened it and began shuffling.

'I haven't read all the legal stuff myself,' I told him. 'There was evidently a hassle between the two estates or some damn thing. Only thing I've checked double-solid is the insurance. I won't transport an uninsured car.'

He grunted. 'Don't blame you, speed you drive.'

'Officer,' I said, edging in a hint of wounded sincerity, 'I've been driving *professionally* for *twelve* years – semis, stock cars, tow trucks, cabs, buses, damn near everything with wheels that turn – and I haven't had a ticket since '53 and never even came *close* to a wreck. Agent who hired me said this car's been in storage for six years while the estate was being settled. Check it out' – I pointed at the odometer – 'seventy miles. *You* know cars: store one six years and seals can dry up on you, gaskets crack, oil gets gumballed in the crankcase. I wanted to know early on whether it's running tight or not, 'cause it's a whole bunch easier to fix it here than in the Mojave Desert two o'clock this afternoon.' I nodded for emphasis, then pointed vaguely down the road. 'And this – light traffic, triple-lane freeway – seemed the safest time and place to check it out. I know I broke the law, no argument there. *But* I didn't do it thoughtlessly or maliciously. Nor recklessly, or not to my mind, since driving's my profession.'

He wasn't impressed. 'The car is registered to Mr Cory Bingham, is that correct?'

'Yup, you got it. Though it may be getting transferred to the Richardson estate – he was the Big Bopper, remember him? This car was supposed to be a gift to him. Except both parties died – this was back in '59 – and the estate was just settled about six months ago. Or that's what they tell me.'

'Just a minute, please.' He took the registration with him back to the patrol car. I watched in the rearview mirror as he slipped inside the cruiser and reached for the radio. Flat electric crackle; muffled numbers. I looked down the road in front of me and hoped I'd be able to use it.

Five minutes later – obviously protected by the righteousness of my journey – I was indeed happily on my way, a ticket in the glovebox, a curt lecture on the-law-is-the-law fresh in my ears if not in my heart, and the bottle of bennies clamped between my thighs. I cracked the lid and ate three to celebrate.

Keeping it down to a sane 75 mph, I cruised south past San Leandro and took 580 toward the valley. I figured I'd take 99 down to Bakersfield, avoid the LA snarl by grabbing 58 to Barstow, then 247 down to Yucca Valley, a short blast on 62 to the junction with Interstate 10, and then hang a big left for Texas. Might've been quicker through LA, but I'd rather run than crawl.

Again it struck me that although I knew I was going to the Big Bopper's grave, I didn't know where it was. One of my major problems with amphetamines is they give me a rage for order, a craving for the voluptuous convolutions of routes, schedules, and plans; and at the same time they wire me to the white lines so tight I don't even want to stop for fuel. John had suggested hitting a library to research the Bopper, sensible advice for someone who felt like taking the time to stop, but I figured I could stop in Texas and look it up there. But maybe he wasn't buried in Texas. Or buried at all, come to think of it – he might've been cremated. After fifty miles I was already obsessively enmeshed in the complexity of possibilities, and needed another fifty to decide I should know what was what and where it exactly was. Otherwise I was likely to go on going till the speed ran out, and with 1000 hits at my disposal that might take awhile. This was essentially an aesthetic question. I wanted to make the trip clean and clear, with elegance, dispatch, and grace. I didn't want to end up pinballing blindly from coast to coast babbling to myself. I wanted to deliver the gift and slip away, not get caught in the slop.

Bolstered by this direct, no-bullshit appraisal of my true desires,

I decided that knowledge and self-control were critical. I'd stop at the next town, go to the library, run down the info I needed, figure out what I was going to do, and do it.

The other imperative was to dump the speed, feed it to the asphalt. Or perhaps dump all but fifty and ration them with my iron willpower; use *them*, not let them use me. If the drugs got on top I wouldn't feel that *I'd* done it, and I sensed that might prove a sadness to last the rest of my life.

I pulled over a couple of a miles past Modesto and dug the bottle out from under the seat. I hit the button for the power window and, while it hummed down, unscrewed the cap, sighed, shut my eyes, then poured the contents out the window. Shook the bottle upside-down to be sure.

Then I got out and picked them all up. Fast. Lots of traffic was ripping by, and some of the bennies were blowing around in the draft. All I needed was for some Highway Patrolman to get wind of a frantic motorist gathering white pills off the blacktop out on 99 and have him stop by to give me a hand.

The thing was, as I was shaking the last bean from the bottle I realized – in one of those magnetic reversals of rationality – this was cheating. To dump the speed wasn't resolve; or if so, the weakest sort. This was actually an act of cowardice – instead of facing temptation, merely removing it. Virtue is empty without temptation. I'd never had any trouble resisting drugs when I didn't have any; only when they were in my hand did the trouble start. I finished picking up the bennies – maybe a hundred short – and screwed the lid down tight. I stashed them back under the seat and promised myself I wouldn't touch them till the delivery was made. Save 'em for the celebration, as it were.

The next stop on my itinerary was a library. I figured a city was a better shot than a small town for the info I wanted, so I waited till I hit Fresno. I stopped at a Union station for fuel and got directions to the library from the young kid working the pumps. 'Gonna do a little reading, huh?' He smirked.

'Actually,' I smiled back, 'I heard Fresno has the only illustrated copy of *Tantric Sexual Secrets*. Stuff on proper breathing and arcane positions that'll keep it up for *weeks*. That's no problem for you young guys, but you get to be my age, all wore down, you need all the help you can get.'

When I pulled out, he was still repeating the title to himself. I felt good about my contribution to scholarly pursuits as I followed his directions into town.

The library was quiet and cool inside. I checked the subject catalogue under *B* for both Big and Bopper, then *R* for Richardson, J.P. Nothing. Since I had the *R*'s open, I looked under Rock-and-Roll. Paydirt. I jotted down the call numbers of everything that sounded useful, then hit the stacks. Nothing. Zero. Not one. Probably a popular subject, but it seemed odd they'd all be out. I checked at the Reference Desk. According to the tall, sharp-boned librarian, they *were* out all right – for good. 'The kids steal them faster than we can put them on the shelves,' she explained.

'*Steal* them? *Why?*'

She lowered her voice to provide me with a model of appropriate volume: 'For the pictures, I suppose.'

'*What* pictures?' I hissed, an attempted whisper.

'Of the stars, I guess. We had a policy meeting yesterday and decided that all the rock books from now on will be in the closed stacks.'

I felt baffled, deflected, so I plunged on to my purpose: 'Do you know where the Big Bopper's buried?'

'I'm sorry?' she said, tilting her head as if she hadn't heard me, a nervous flutter of eyelids.

'The Big Bopper. I need to know where he's buried.'

'I'm sorry,' she repeated, 'but who is – or *was* – the Big Bopper?'

'A rock star. He died in a plane crash in 1959. February third.'

She spent half an hour searching for information, but found nothing I didn't already have. Real name Jiles Perry Richardson. Died at age twenty-seven. Born in Sabine Pass and worked as a disc jockey. Hit single with 'Chantilly Lace.' Nothing in any of the papers regarding the funeral arrangements.

I thanked the librarian for her help and walked out into the bright autumn sunlight. The swept-fin Caddy spacemobile was stretched along the curb like an abandoned prop from a Flash Gordon movie. I wondered about Harriet's taste in automotive styling for a moment, then shook my head. Who's to say what sort of wheels a Texas rocker might tumble to? And maybe Harriet had a sense of humor.

Fresno to Bakerfield was straight double-lane freeway. I kept the needle steady on 90, smiling with the knowledge that every time the wheels turned I was farther away from Scumball's clutches and closer to my destination, as vague as that was. Even though I'd come up empty, the library stop had fulfilled my scholarly obligation. I could enjoy the road, roaring along with the speed coming on solid in my brain, and I figured my itinerary would sort itself out along the way. When you're feeling good, there's no hurry – and what's a pilgrim without faith?

The Caddy needed gas again, so I stopped at a station in Bakersfield, a Texaco on the corner of a shopping mall. While the rocket guzzled Super Chief I hit the men's room and washed my face with cold water. Already I felt road-wired and gritty, and the usual amphetamine dry-mouth had left me parched, so when the Caddy was gassed I drove to the supermarket in the center of the mall and bought an ice chest, a couple of bags of cubes, and a cold case of Bud. I downed two fast, cracked a third for immediate use, and iced a dozen in the cooler, which I stashed in the trunk. The front seat would've been my first choice, but good sense prevailed. The trunk meant I'd have to stop every time my thirst caught up, but it was a lot less likely I'd find myself performing silly exercises for law enforcement officials.

Between Bakersfield and Barstow it was hot and windy. For one of those reasons of odd association, I remembered telling Natalie and her boyfriend that I was Jack Kerouac and on my way to climb Mount Shasta to whisper a word to the wind, and started to feel rotten about the lies. Granted, I'd been covering myself, but other evasions, less sleazy, leapt to mind. Squirm as I might, the truth was that even in my exuberance I'd resented their awed innocence, their eagerness to believe. The cold fact was that I'd wronged them, cheap and cruel. The postcard Natalie had given me was still in my pocket, and I decided to send her a much deserved apology. All the way to Barstow my speed-soaked brain entertained itself by composing and revising appropriate expressions of regret.

It was after dark when I pulled into the Barstow Gas-N-Go and topped off the Caddy for $8, which back then was a hefty cut for fuel. The attendant, a chubby red-haired kid who had to count on his fingers to make change, was absolutely slack-jaw *awed* by the Caddy – washed all the windows and polished the chrome just to stay near it, touching. Handing me my change, he smiled bashfully and said, 'My daddy says a man that can afford a Cadillac sure ain't gonna worry 'bout paying its gas. Guess that's close to right, huh?'

'I wouldn't know,' I told him. 'I can't afford one. I'm just delivering it to the Big Bopper.'

'What's that?'

'An old rock-and-roller. A singer.'

'Here in Barstow?' He looked dubious.

'Nope. Texas is where I'm headed.'

'He's *paying* you to drive this car? Goddamn, I'd love a job like that.'

'No money involved. I'm doing it sort of as a favor.'

'Yeah, hell,' he said, 'I would too. Damn *right*.'

I had an impulse to invite him along but thought better of it. He was too enthralled by the machinery. But when he shuffled along after me as I headed back to the car, his eyes caressing the Eldorado's lines, I invited him to take a slow cruise around town.

'Mister, *goddamn* you don't know how much I'd like that, but I can't. I'm the only one here till Bobby comes on at midnight, and Mr Hoffer – he's the owner – he'd fire me sure as anything if I took off. Almost fired me last week 'cause these two guys from LA came in and did this trick on me about makin' change and the cash box come up thirty-seven bucks short. Mr Hoffer said when I messed up next I was gone. I was already fired from two jobs this summer and Daddy said just once more and he'd kick my ass so hard I'd have to take my hat off to shit. I can't do 'er, much as I'd like to.'

'Well,' I offered, 'how about a spin around the block?'

He shook his head doggedly. 'Nope, better not.'

'Okay, how's this: I'll watch the station – I've pumped lots of gas in my time – and *you* take it for a short ride.' I was *determined*. 'Lock up the cash box if you want. I'll make change out of my own pocket.'

As he considered this, I could feel how much he wanted to do it, but finally he said, 'Naw, I just can't risk it – getting fired by Mr Hoffer, beat on by Daddy. But much obliged for offering. Honest.'

'Tell you what,' I persisted, now maniacal. 'Why don't you drive me around to the men's room. I've never been chauffeured to the pisser before, and at least you'll get a taste of this fine piece of automotion.'

'Yeah,' he grinned, 'I could do that. Sure. Great!'

He was so happy I felt like giving him the damn thing and taking the Greyhound back home. I've never seen anyone more delighted by a fifty-foot drive in my life. I took my time pissing, and when I came out he was sitting behind the wheel running the power windows up and down. I almost had to use a tire-iron to pry him out.

I wasn't hungry – they don't call bennies diet pills for nothing – but I knew from my days of high-balling speed that if you run your gut on empty too long it'll start eating itself, so I stopped at a drive-in joint down the road and dutifully choked down a 30¢ Deluxe Burger and an order of fries that tasted like greased cardboard.

The whole time I was eating I thought about the bottle of benzedrine under the seat. When I drove long-haul it was my habit to reward myself for eating food by eating a handful of speed for dessert, and the old pleasure center never forgets a pattern. I wanted some and told myself no. Instead I cracked another beer and congratulated myself on steadfastness in the face of temptation while I rinsed down the grease and thought some more about the young woman in North Beach.

When I reached in my jacket pocket for her self-addressed postcard, my fingertips brushed the crinkled ball of tinfoil I'd forgotten about – her tender gift, the LSD. Inside were three sugar cubes, their edges crumbled. I remembered her advice about taking one at a time in a beautiful place. Bradley's Burger Pit in Barstow didn't seem like a beautiful place, and I still owed Natalie Hurley of 322 Bryant Street a deserved apology. Using the dash for a desk, I printed in small, firm letters:

Dear Natalie,

I lied to you and your friend. I'm not Jack Kerouac.
My motives for such deceit were complex – joy, fear,
meanness, and self-protection. I regret my thoughtlessness
and disrespect to both of you and hope you'll accept my
sincere apologies.

Sincerely,

The Big Bopper

I shook my head at this perversity and diligently inked the

Bopper's name into a thick black rectangle. Underneath I managed to cramp in 'Love, George.'

It was a clear night, moonless, the temperature warm but cooling fast. Mirage shimmers of rising heat off the desert made the horizon appear to be under water. The highway was as straight as the shortest distance between two points and flat as a grade-setter's vision of heaven. I powered down all the windows, locked the needle on 100, and took it south.

An hour or so later I hit the junction of 62 around Yucca Valley and ripped on down to Interstate 10, stopping in Indio for gas. From Barstow on, my brain had been cruising entranced, but the Indio pit stop had broken the spell. Back on the road, the twitters, skreeks, and jangles of speed-comedown rapidly became unbearable. A brackish exhaustion now stained my attention, my eyes felt like dried pudding, and I grew increasingly distracted, restless, and bored bored bored. I'd been up for a couple of days, one of them chemically aided, and it was catching up hard.

To resist temptation once you've already eliminated it is always easy, but to resist it when it's within easy reach under the front seat is difficult – especially when you've passed the soft flirtations of desire and are down to raw need and can hear those little go-fast pills squealing 'Eat me, eat me.' Difficult, yes, but not impossible, not if you're strong. I resisted the magnetic siren song of benzedrine by fumbling the tinfoil package from my pocket and letting a sugar cube dissolve on my tongue – a sweet, cloying trickle sliding down my throat.

Nothing happened. I should've known better. You can't expect the young to provide reliable drugs. But I was careful. I didn't know anything about LSD except what I'd heard, and most of what I'd heard had come from people like Allen Pound, a kid who drove graveyard at Cravetti's. He'd taken some with a psychiatrist in Berkeley, he said, and it turned him every way but loose. A bookcase became a brickwall. When he rested his forehead against a window, half his head went through without disturbing the glass; he'd felt the cold air outside stinging his eyes while, back in the room, his ears were burning. Always curious, I'd sidled into the conversation and asked him if LSD was like peyote. He smiled one of those cool, knowing smiles that afflict the terminally hip and replied, 'Is a Harley like a Cushman?'

So, even though I suspected Allen Pound of self-inflating bullshit, I was careful. I waited almost seventy miles worth of crumbling nerves before I ate the second cube. Either this had something in it or the stars, like tiny volcanoes, began erupting on their own, spewing molten tendrils of color until the night sky was an entangling net of jewels.

Nothing is more tedious than someone else's acid trip, so I'll spare you the cosmic insights – except for the real obvious stuff, like *it's all one* (more or less), composed wholly of holy parts, the sum of which is no greater or less than the individual gifts of possibility, all wrapped up pretty in the bright ribbon of past and future, the ribbon of moonlit highway, the spiral ribbons of amino acids twining into the quick and the dead, the ribbon of sound unwinding its endless music through breath and horn, the silver dancer with ribbons in her hair. Oh man, I was out there marching to Peoria, aeons out, all fucked up.

I made two intelligent moves, both making up in smarts what they so obviously lacked in grace. First I got off the road. Simply cranked the wheel hard right and drove into the desert, slewing between cactus plants till the exploding Godzilla eyes of on-coming traffic disappeared. Then, once the Caddy stopped, I tumbled out the door and jammed a finger down my throat. Maybe it wasn't too late to puke up the second hit. Of course, maybe I *hadn't* double-dosed, maybe the first was just a blank. But then again, maybe the shit came on slow. I didn't care; I just wanted to get as much of it as possible out of my system before my brain became a bowl of onion dip at a Rotarian no-host cocktail party. I managed to gag up the sour remains of the gristle burger and cardboard fries in a slurry of beer. My mind was vomit on the alkaline sand, as indifferently illuminated by the starlight as anything else of matter made.

I rolled onto my back and watched the stars pulse till I could get my breath. Watched them erupt, swirl, and dissolve like so many specks of sugar in the belly of the universe, only to re-precipitate, glittering. I felt what I always feel when I really look at the stars and remember they are enormous furnaces of light, when I look past them and imagine how many billions more exist beyond vision because their light hasn't yet reached us or they're obscured behind the curve of space, only now I felt this with an unbearable clarity, the impossible magnitude of it all, my own self barely a twitch of existence, a speck of sugar dissolving in the gut, fuel for the furnace, food for us fools. I forced myself to quit looking (otherwise I'd *die*) and curled up, trembling, on the hot desert sand. Eyes clamped shut, I sat on the bank and watched the river burn. Felt my empty body lifted on a wave, lifted on the wind, hurled into the darkness to be lifted again.

I have no idea how many eternities I required to regather myself and re-open my eyes. The stars were stars again, but possibly they wouldn't stay that way if I kept looking, so I cautiously peered sideways across the cactus-studded plain. I don't know what kind of cactus these were, but they vaguely resembled stick figures, legs together in a single line, arms curving up from each side in an ambiguous gesture of either jubilation or surrender. They looked like sentries – not so much guardians, though, as passive observers, witnesses for some unfathomable conscience. Nonetheless I was trying to fathom it when one of the arms moved. I started crawling pronto for the white shimmer of the Eldorado. I reached up to seize the door handle and put my hand right through the starlight mirage of metal. In a panicked glance over my shoulder I saw more cactus limbs move, but, daring a longer look, saw they were staying put, not advancing, and my fear began fading into a very careful curiosity. It took me a few baffled moments to comprehend that the cactuses were dancing to a music I could neither hear nor imagine. I knew that if I wanted to know their music, I would have to join their dance and feel it in the movement of my mortal meat, within time and space, outside in.

I know I danced, but remember neither the movements nor the music. Or anything else until I came to in the front seat of the Cadillac with sweat in my eyes. The sun was up with a passion. I checked the dash clock – 9:30. I felt like scorched jelly. *Need sleep*, my brain was flashing; I hadn't begun to scrape myself from the floor of exhaustion. But the Caddy threw the thickest shade around, and even with all the windows down it was an oven. I *had* to move. I sat up and turned the key, so wasted that for the pain to reach my brain took about ten seconds. I yelped, hands recoiling to my chest. I examined them dully. They were pin-cushioned with cactus spines. Sweat-blinded and on the verge of screaming, I yanked the spines with my teeth and spit them out the window, thinking distantly to myself that if someone were watching they'd probably say, 'Now, *he's* fucked-up: got enough money to afford a fancy car, then parks in the desert and eats his hands for breakfast.'

Even with the spines removed, my hands were almost unbearably tender. I examined them carefully to make sure I'd removed all the needles, then gingerly reached under the front seat for the bottle of bennies. I wasn't tempted. Can you say a drowning man is *tempted* by a life-preserver? Temptation was crushed by necessity. Besides, it's all one, ceaselessly changing to sustain the dynamic equilibrium that maintains itself through change. And that dynamic equilibrium requires human effort. We each have to do what we can. I did seven.

Tuned me right up, too – had those acid-warped synapses firing at top dead center in no time. For example, I remembered the beer in the trunk. The ice was all melted but the water was still cool. I drank two quickly, tasted the next two, and savored another as I lumbered the Caddy back onto the highway.

The next sixty miles were devoted to severe self-questioning of the round-and-round variety. In retrospect I'd been foolish, first of all, to take the LSD, and then to take more. On the other hand, as that old saying has it, when you're up to your ass in alligators it's hard to remember you only wanted to drain the swamp. And what's an adventure without risk, danger, daring? Excitement was the whole point, in a way. Or was I secretly afraid of accepting the responsibility of delivering the gift, that deep down I knew it was an insignificant gesture, a spasm of fake affirmation in an indifferent universe? I didn't have a fucking clue.

And from this speed-lashed tautological self-analysis, only vaguely slowed by beer, out of a puddle of confusion I created a whirlpool of doubt; despite the energetic rush of amphetamine confidence, I felt myself sucked down toward depression. There's no drug stronger than reality, John Seasons once told me, because reality, despite our arrogant, terrified, hopeful insistence, doesn't require our perceptions, merely our helpless presence. I debated the truth of this all the way to the Arizona border. Finally I pulled over and banged my head against the steering wheel to make myself stop thinking.

I started with a light, rhythmic tapping, but that only seemed to increase the babble in my brain and I did it harder, hard enough to hurt. Then I slumped back in the seat, gasping, eyes tightly closed, and immediately had a vision: a tiny orange man, maybe three inches tall, naked, was carrying what appeared to be a piece of glossy black plywood as big as he was across a thin black line suspended in space. He was walking anxiously back and forth on the line, intently peering down. The plywood was cut roughly in the shape of an artist's palette, but lacked a thumbhole. The shape strongly reminded me of something personal, but was obscured in a shroud of associations. Finally it came to me: chicken pox, seven years old, an image of Hopalong Cassidy astride his horse. That was it, a jigsaw puzzle, a piece of Hoppy's black shirt.

The tiny man, the color of a neon tangerine, was still aimlessly walking back and forth along the line, his eyes shifting between the line and the plywood. It wasn't until he turned and walked away from me for a moment that I realized the black line was the edge of a surface, and looking more closely I saw it was a thin slab of crystal suspended in the air; it was exactly at eye level, and without the black line on its upper margin, I might've missed it completely. I tried to stretch myself up to see over its edge, get a better view of the surface the little orange man was stalking, but I couldn't break the angle of sight.

I watched, fascinated, as he roamed back and forth, looking all around, occasionally setting the piece of plywood down and sliding it around with his toe, then picking it up to continue what was evidently a search. I strained again to see the surface, but my gaze was locked dead level with the crystal edge and the parallel black line above it, a shadow laminated to translucence. At last I grasped the obvious: the little orange man *was* working on some crazy fucking jigsaw puzzle.

By the way he moved, lugging the puzzle piece as big as he was, it was plain he had no idea where it fit and, judging from his tight jaw, was becoming increasingly frustrated. I desperately wanted to scan the puzzle, to see what was done so far and what the emerging image might suggest, but despite one last effort of fierce concentration I couldn't see beyond the edge. I wanted to offer the little orange man my help, add my vision to his, but there wasn't much I could do. I decided, though, that I could at least encourage him, and had just opened my mouth to speak when all hell broke loose.

I guess I should say all *heaven* broke loose, because the sky opened and poured rain, rivers and tidal waves of it, a deluge. The little man lifted the piece of puzzle above his head for what meager shelter it offered. I was sure he'd be washed away. But as abruptly as it'd started, the rain stopped, and he immediately returned to his work, even more intently, as if the torrential downpour had washed the image clean. Then the hail began, chunks of ice the size of tennis balls. Again the orange man took cover by lifting the puzzle piece above his head, staggering under the hammerstroke force of the blows, grimacing at the deafening roar, his tiny penis flopping against his thigh as he struggled to stay upright. The moment the ice-storm abated, the wind came up in huge gusts that sent him reeling almost to the edge before he was able to hunker down behind his piece of the puzzle, the power of the wind bending it over him like a shell. No sooner had the wind eased than lightning fractured the sky, fat blue-white bolts sizzling toward his head. He lifted the puzzle piece to deflect the stunning power of the bolts, spun by the brain-wrenching blasts of thunder that instantly followed, and I was already laughing by the time the tomatoes started splatting down, followed by a literal shit-storm of raw sewage, then writhing clumps of maggots, large gobs of spit, and decayed fruit. Once the fusillade of cream pies ended, I was tear blind and gasping for breath, doubled up on the front seat of the Caddy. I swear by all that's holy that I was laughing *with* him, not *at* him; laughing in true sympathy for all of us caught, tiny and naked and nearly helpless, in the maelstrom of forces we can't control. This was the laughter of honest commiseration, of true celebration for the splendid and foolish tenacity that keeps us hanging on despite the blows.

When I finally managed to look again, the little orange man was still standing there, resolutely holding the battered piece of the puzzle above his head even though the sky was clear. He was looking directly at me, glaring. His lips moved, but there was no sound – he looked like a goldfish pressed against the aquarium's glass, working water through his gills. It took a couple of heartbeats for his voice to reach the interior of the Caddy, to break with a deafening boom that rocked the car on its springs and flattened my lungs. He vanished with the sonic blast, but when my hearing returned a few moments later his words were waiting for me, not shrill or angry or bitter or even very loud, but absolutely corrosive with disdain: 'That's right, you idiot – *laugh*.'

'Fuck you!' I screamed back, enraged by the injustice of his flagrant misunderstanding. 'You don't know *shit!*' There was no reply.

Seething, I fired up the Eldorado and aimed it down the road, yelling, 'How could you *say* that? I was laughing *with* you. *Completely* with you.' But even righteously wronged, I heard the false note in 'completely.' I *was* laughing with him, at least 80 percent, and another 10 percent from relief that it wasn't me, and another 10 percent just because it was funny. So even if my claim wasn't *completely* true, it was true enough, and I didn't deserve his contempt. 'You mean little orange shithead!' I railed. 'Jerk! Who are you to judge my laughter? You know I would've helped you if I could. That black piece shaped like a palette – it's part of Hopalong Cassidy's shirt. I put that one together when I was *seven*, you asshole.'

By then I was tapering off to mutters, the dull throb in my skull reminding me I'd been beating my head against the steering wheel, and I twisted the rearview mirror around to check for damage. Fear hit me like a hell-bound freight. It wasn't the small lump or little smear of blood that jolted me. It was my eyes. They were crazy.

I pulled over immediately. At the rate I was going, I'd be lucky to make Texas by Christmas – if I made it at all. I was insane. Out of my mind. Why kid myself? I'd been beating my head on the steering wheel, watching a naked little orange man running around working on jigsaw puzzles. Worse, I'd talked to him. The night before I'd died in a whirl of starlight and danced with a cactus to music I couldn't remember. The night before that I'd stolen a car and crossed a man who was at that very moment probably rounding up a posse of well-paid goons who would be grossly pleased to turn me into a shopping bag full of charred meat and bone chips. By any objective standard of sanity, I wasn't. Not even within hailing distance, not if facts were faced and no bullshit allowed. But even granting that I was totally flipped out, maybe this was only a temporary condition, the result of drugs, exhaustion, stress, dislocation, and a weak psychic constitution going in. Maybe I didn't even know what crazy was, in its deeply twisted forms and dark forces. Maybe I *wanted* to be crazy so I wouldn't have to go through the normal rationalizations and self-justifications of unfettered indulgence. And thus my speed-racing mind babbled on until I finally gave up and pulled back onto the road. If it really got bad, I could always pound my head on the wheel and try another vision. That I'd seen the little orange man secretly cheered me; vision belonged to pilgrimage, and despite all my romantic notions, I'm a classicist at heart. I was disappointed, however, in the *quality* of the vision – neither heavenly nor beatific, more on the order of grotesque slapstick. Maybe I should've pounded my brain with something heavier. I wondered what sort of vision a solid whack from a ballpeen hammer might produce, or what undreamable cosmic insight might accompany the blow from a wrecking ball. I wondered how much it cost to rent a crane for thirty seconds. I wondered if the orange man had been a real pilgrim's vision, or just a leftover from last night's acid feast, the deluded projection of spiritual hunger. I wondered what spirit was. I wondered what I actually wanted out of all this. I wanted to get there, wherever *there* was. I wanted to deliver the gift. I wanted to lie naked against Kacy and have her turn sleepily and snuggle as I ran my hand along her fine warm flank. I wondered where she was and what she was thinking, then I wondered why I was delivering Harriet's gift to the Big Bopper when both were dead, gone, and done with. Was it because I couldn't deliver my own gift to the living? Babble babble babble on into Arizona. When I looked in the rearview mirror again my eyes didn't look so crazy, just tired and confused. I needed a break.

I got it on a long stretch of empty highway about five miles out of Quartzsite, Arizona, when I saw a figure walking east on the shoulder of the road, back turned toward me. True, I was tired of listening to myself and felt a sudden desire for company, but there was something in the walk, in the slope of the shoulders, the sense of weight, the trudge, the isolation against the landscape, something indefinite but definitely wrong that made me come off the gas. When I was fifty yards away, down to a roll, I saw it was a woman. She wasn't hitching. She didn't even glance up as I passed.

It's always tricky when it's a woman alone in a lonely place and you're a man; no matter how noble your intentions, you have to be considered a threat – there's just too much ugly proof you are. I pulled off about seventy yards past her and got out. She walked closer and then stopped. She was short, chubby, in her early thirties by my guess, with messed auburn hair cut short, wearing faded jeans and a wrinkled grey blouse clinging where sweat had soaked through. At that distance I couldn't see her eyes, but her face looked dull and puffy. It wasn't something wrong that I'd noticed, but that something was missing: no purse. Five miles from the nearest town, no broken-down cars on the shoulder, and no purse. I felt a sickening conviction that she'd been raped or mugged. I couldn't think of anything to say, so I waved, smiled, and leaned against the Caddy's left-rear fin, waiting for her to offer some sign, but she stopped and stood still, watching me. I didn't feel fear from her, no wariness at all; just fatigue.

'You all right?' I tried to put into my voice the truth of my concern, but it sounded clumsy even to me.

Her chin lifted half an inch. 'I don't know,' she said. It sounded like the truth.

So I told her the truth, too. 'Well, I was asking myself the same question about forty miles back down the road, and I didn't know if I'm all right either. But I *am* headed for Texas, and I'd be glad to give you a ride anywhere between here and Sabine Pass, with no come-on, no hassle. If you'd prefer, I'd be glad to call you a cab in the next town to pick you up – even pay the fare if you're short – or call a friend to come pick you up. But if you'd rather just walk on along, say the word and I'm gone. Or if there's some other way I can help, I'll see what I can do.' This had turned out to be a speech, but I was having trouble keeping the truth simple.

She walked five steps toward me. 'I'd appreciate a ride into town. Thank you.' She said this with a sad formality, as if manners were all that remained of her dignity.

I went around to the passenger's side. 'Do you want to sit up front with the idiots or would you rather sit in the back and be chauffeured like a princess on her way to the casino for an afternoon of baccarat and dashing young men?'

She smiled thinly to show she appreciated my attempt. She had lovely eyes, the dark, lustrous brown of raw chocolate. I wasn't an expert, but I was sure she'd been crying. 'The front will be fine,' she said, 'with the idiots.'

I ushered her into the front seat and said, 'I know where you're going, but where are you coming from?'

'Same place. Quartzsite. That's where I live.'

'Well then,' I asked, irrepressible, 'where've you been?'

'Changing my mind,' she answered, her voice husky.

'Yes indeed, I know what you mean. When I'm not changing mine, it's changing me. We'll have to discuss the importance of change in sustaining equilibrium as well as its relation to timing, knowledge, spirit, and the meaning of life. And what love and music have to do with the purpose of being. When we get those figured out, we can tackle the tough ones.'

She looked at me sharply, a flash of irritation, a hint of contempt. 'I have two young kids. Boys. Allard's seven; Danny's almost six.'

Her name was Donna Walsh. Besides the two boys, she had a husband, Warren, who'd lost his job in the Oklahoma oil fields and finally joined the Air Force in desperation. He was learning aircraft mechanics so he'd have a trade when he got out. He was overseas, Germany, and she and the boys were staying in his uncle's trailer in Quartzsite.

She'd fallen in love with Warren her last year of high school and slept with him the night after the senior prom because she was tired of making him stop when she didn't want him to. She got pregnant, and in Oklahoma if you got pregnant, you got married.

Warren had left for Germany six months ago, in April. This was only a year's assignment, then he'd have another year of service in the States, and after his discharge he'd get a job with one of the big airlines as a jet mechanic. Warren could do just about anything with machines, she claimed, especially engines. She wished he was home to fix the '55 Ford pick-up, which had leaked so much oil the engine burned out. Repairs would run $200 to fix it, but Johnny Palmer at the Texaco said it wasn't worth fixing. Not that it mattered, really, since Warren could only send $150 a month, and that had to cover everything. Tech Sergeants didn't make much, but like Warren said, learning jet mechanics was an investment in the future.

Warren was basically a good person, Donna said, but it was a lot of responsibility and pressure to get married so young, with two babies right away. And when he got laid off in the oil fields, he'd started drinking too much, and he only hit her when he was drunk. Not that he beat on her much – she didn't want to give that impression. It had only been three or four times tops, and once she'd asked for it by nagging him about finding a job, and he really had been trying.

Another time it was just one of those things: she was cooking dinner and little Danny was three and he wouldn't quit crying and it was hot that evening, over a 100° easy, and Danny just wouldn't stop and Warren had drunk way too much beer and started screaming at him to shut up, which only made Allard start in crying too; and Warren had slapped Danny so hard it sent him flying against the dinette, and when he did that Donna didn't even think, just swung on him with what she happened to have in her hand, a frozen package of Bel-Air corn, and it opened Warren's left eyebrow along its whole length – he still had the scar – but he didn't make a peep, even with the blood running all over his face, he just stood up real slow, pushed her against the fridge and started hitting her in the body with his fists, hitting her hard in the stomach and ribs and breasts until she passed out.

He didn't come back for a week after that, a week in which it sometimes hurt her so bad to breathe she'd hold her breath till she got dizzy, a week when it was all she could do to make peanut butter and jelly sandwiches for the boys. She'd called around to Warren's family and friends, but nobody had seen him. When he came back he was pale and both his eyes were black-and-blue; he'd needed nine stitches to close the cut. He was sober when he came back, and he was sorry. It was the only time she'd ever seen him cry. She made him promise never to hit the boys like that again.

That was the last time he'd beat on her till just before he'd finally given up job-hunting and enlisted. She was asleep when she heard him stagger against the table, then lurch toward the pull-out sofa bed they shared in the front room. He loomed over her. She was lying on her back looking up at him, but there was enough glare from the porch light shining through the uncurtained window behind him that his face was hidden in shadows. She could smell the whiskey.

'It's all your fault,' he said quietly.

Donna saw the blow coming but couldn't move. He hit her in the belly, doubling her up. She couldn't breathe or scream or kick. Paralyzed, terrified, she watched his fist ball up again tighter and tighter till she thought the knuckles were going to pop out of the skin. She thought she was going to die. She heard what a scream sounds like when you don't have the breath to scream. But he didn't hit her again. He hit himself square in the stomach, right where he'd hit her, and began to methodically beat on his own face. Gasping, she inched across the bed until she could throw out an arm and reach him. He stopped at her touch. His fist opened and he reached down and touched her hair, lightly, and then down to the base of her neck, gently massaging as she choked for air. Still rubbing her neck, he pulled the sheet back slowly and lay down beside her and took her in his arms. She was naked; he was fully clothed. They held each other tightly, silently, for a long time. Donna said it was the most intimate she'd ever felt with him, and was aroused even as she cried. She pressed her thighs along his legs and wiggled in closer, but he had fallen asleep or passed out.

Warren always sent the money every month with the same short letter. 'Hi. How are you? I'm working on B-52s. Keeps me busy. You boys mind your momma.' He'd called on the Fourth of July. Mostly he'd talked to the boys, who were so thrilled they just jabbered away about everything. When she got the phone back, she couldn't think of anything to say, so she just said they all missed him. She wanted to tell him how much she missed him, and how, but the boys were yammering and tugging at her and he was too far away. She'd written him every week till that phone call. Now it was about every two weeks. It was so hard to say what you felt when you couldn't look at each other.

She told me all this as we sat beside the road and, after a while, drove the five miles to town. She spoke in a husky monotone, staring down the highway as if she were trying to describe a picture she'd seen as a child. She needed to talk. If you can't believe she'd open up to a total stranger – a man at that – well, it stunned me, too. Stunned me. I sat there with speed racing in my blood and didn't say a word; just listened. Sometimes it's easier to be honest with a stranger, someone you know you'll never see again. Safer. No obligation but the blind trust opening the moment.

As we pulled into Quartzsite I told her I was starved and offered to buy her a late lunch if she wasn't in a hurry. She said she had to be at the trailer by 4:30, when the boys got home from school. Usually they were home by 3:00, but today the lower grades were putting up Halloween decorations.

We stopped at Joe's Burger Palace and ate in the car. We picked at our burgers in silence for a few minutes, a comfortable silence, then made small talk about life in Quartzsite. But small talk seemed to diminish whatever had passed between us, and after a few meaningless exchanges she shifted around on the seat to face me and told me, without introduction, what had happened that morning. As she spoke, her voice gathered force, but it barely escaped the undertow of weariness in her tone.

'I got up at six like always, then woke up the boys and got them dressed. Danny couldn't find his blue socks. They're his favorites. He couldn't remember where he'd left them. I told him it wasn't going to hurt him to wear his brown ones for a day, and he started crying. Kids can get *so* strange about clothes, like they're little pieces of their lives. So I hunted for his socks and finally found them under his pillow. *Under* his pillow, can you believe that? They were so filthy I think I found them by smell. It reminded me everything was dirty, and I *had* to do the laundry.

'I got Danny's socks on him and then made their oatmeal and poured their milk. Allard was telling Danny all about skeletons and ghosts and how ghosts can just *wooooosshh* at you out of nowhere, and when he was *wooooosshhhing* his hand to show what he meant he knocked over his milk. I wiped off the table and was about to get what had dripped on the floor when I smelled something burning: I'd put the oatmeal pan back on the burner but hadn't turned it off like I thought. The oatmeal was charred to the pan. I filled the pan with water and some baking soda to soak, but the smell of burnt oatmeal had filled up the trailer. By then the boys were going to be late for school, so I got them all gathered up and figured I'd take care of the mess when I got back.

'I walked the boys to school, which is about eight blocks, but when I got back to the trailer I couldn't open the door. I don't mean it was stuck or I'd forgotten the key – I just *could not open it* and go back inside to the smell of burnt oatmeal and spilled milk and dirty laundry. *Physically* couldn't. So I turned around and started walking.

'At first I thought I'd go to Curry's market a couple of streets down, but I walked right past it – just as well, 'cause my purse was in the trailer. Then I thought I'd go by the old Baptist church, but when I saw it, with all the stained glass and heavy doors, I didn't want to go in. I walked on past the church and just kept *going*, know what I mean? Not thinking about anything in particular except how good it felt to be moving in the clear air. Just walking. When I reached the highway and saw the broken white lines going on so far in the distance that they seemed to turn solid, I felt happy. I kept walking. Two or three cars stopped but I shook my head. I wanted to keep going.

'I know I'm a little overweight but as I walked along I started feeling lighter and lighter and lighter, like the wind could pick me up and fly me away, the way I felt it could when I was a little girl. Then it all collapsed in me and I started crying.'

Donna blinked rapidly as she remembered that moment, jaw quivering, but there were no tears. She shook her head. 'But you know how it ended. Here I am. But I walked a long way down the highway thinking how every promise gets broken one way or another, how every hope you have is hoped for so hard and so long it's almost like praying, praying so you can believe in *something*, but it never turns out that way. I'll tell you what really got me blubbering, was that I *knew* I was going to turn around, cross that damn road, and come back. *Knew* I couldn't leave. I'm ashamed to admit it, but there's been a few nights when I felt like the best thing to do was get the butcher knife out of the kitchen and go stab the boys in their sleep, kill them before they found out what happens to dreams. Is that *sick?* But you can't do that any more than you could let them come home to an empty house with Daddy in Germany and Momma run away crazy. They're too real to hurt like that, too real to escape. So I'm coming back because I don't *really* have a choice. I didn't understand it, but I made a choice with Allard and Danny. I'm going back and opening that goddamn door of that trailer and walk into the smoked-in smell of scorched oatmeal and curdled milk and filthy socks. Now that's *grim*.'

'I admire your courage,' I told her.

Donna shook her head. 'If I could walk away and be happy, I'd still be going. But something *that* wrong gnawing on my heart, I could never be happy. Not that I'm happy now, with no break from the boys and the walls pressing in and a husband I don't know about, but this way there's a *chance* things'll work out. Maybe not, but I have to do what I think's right and hope it is, I guess.'

'I hope so, too,' I said, 'and I think it is. But if Warren ever hits you again, I'd get out from under. No maybes. Just leave.'

'Yeah,' she said, 'I told myself that.'

'Promise yourself.'

'What about you?' Donna asked. 'You coming or going?' She was deflecting the pressure of the question, not begging it, and she'd had enough pressure for the day. So, still sitting in the Caddy, our half-eaten burgers long cold, I told Donna what I was up to, my own mess and now this journey. I didn't mention Eddie getting run over – it wasn't necessary – nor that the car was stolen. I did tell her about dancing with a cactus and the little orange man and the upwelling babble in my brain. In the course of explaining, I was taken with a strong intuition that she'd appreciate Harriet's letter, so I asked. She thought about it a moment and said she would. I dug it out of the glovebox and handed it over.

Donna sniffed the envelope. 'Ooo-laa-laa.' She giggled. 'Miss Harriet was serious.'

She read the letter slowly, nodding, shaking her head, smiling.

When she finished she folded it neatly, returned it to the envelope, and began to weep. *So much for my deep intuitions*, I said to myself, but then she reached for me across the front seat and we held each other.

As it turned out, however, my intuition was better than it seemed at first. It wasn't the letter that got to her, she said, as it was remembering that Ritchie Valens had died in the same plane crash. Ritchie Valens, it turned out, was one of the reasons she'd slept with Warren that first night, the night she got pregnant with Allard. Not Ritchie Valens personally, but a song of his called 'Donna,' Donna the heartbreaker, a lament for his lost love. The school she went to in Oklahoma was too small to afford a band for the senior prom, so they'd used records. And when Ritchie Valens sang her name that night in the dimly lit gym – Donna in her gown with her hair done up and an orchid on her wrist, her stockinged feet sliding on the waxed floor as she danced slow and close with Warren – she wanted to grow up into the woman she felt in herself.

When I admitted I didn't recall the song, Donna looked at me with deep suspicion, like a border guard confronted with dubious credentials, but then she shook her head, smiling, and said, 'Well, it doesn't make much sense without the song.' And in a high, clear voice with just a touch of a whiskey edge and a power and clarity that left me breathless, she sang:

> *I had a girl*
> *Dooonnaa was her name*
> *And though I loved her*
> *She left me just the same*
> *Oohhhhh Donnnaaa*
> *Ooohhhhh Doonnnaaaaa . . .*

And I was thinking she'd break my heart when she abruptly stopped and said, 'That's why I'm crying about the letter. And because it's sad that they never had the chance to meet. And because it's really a sweet thing you're doing – a little crazy, but sweet.'

'Then allow me to deliver this gift in your name, too – as a tribute to Ritchie Valens, music, and the possibilities of friendship, communion, and love.'

She cocked her head and gave me a smile that was in odd but happy contrast to the tears on her cheeks. 'That would be nice,' she said.

'Well I'm a nice, sweet guy and it's a very romantic journey – some might even call it foolish, or pointless. You wouldn't happen to know where the Big Bopper's buried, would you?'

'No,' she said, 'but I just thought of a good gift for you.' She sounded excited. 'It's in a big box under the bed, lugged all the way from Oklahoma: a battery-powered record player and a young girl's collection of forty-fives to play on it.'

'You're kidding. Old forty-fives? Are they mainly from the Fifties?'

'I was seventeen in '59. Your record player was all there was in Braxton, Oklahoma.'

'Mainly rock-and-roll?'

'What else was there?'

'Well, listen, that's what I'm supposed to do on my way *back* from delivering the Caddy – look around for Fifties record collections. I've got this friend in 'Frisco named Scumball Johnson, a used car salesman, and he collects Fifties rock the way some people collect baseball cards. Kind of a hobby, but he's real passionate about it. When he heard I was making this trip, he gave me a thousand bucks to buy with, and out of that I can cover my travel expenses home. I told him I didn't know diddley about the music but he said that was no big problem – if in doubt, buy everything. He buys 'em, sells 'em, trades 'em, reads these obscure little collectors' magazines with circulations of half a dozen – you know, just a nut. So, since you've got the records and I've got the money and we're both in the same place, I could buy some now.'

'No, I want it to be a gift,' Donna said firmly.

I was ready for this. 'If you insist, I'd be honored to accept the record player as a gift. Scumball doesn't collect record players. The records, those I have to pay for. That's business. Of course they've got to be in good shape. Not scratched or warped, labels intact, things like that.'

She eyed me with open doubt, and I wasn't sure whether she was considering the offer's intrinsic value or its clumsiness. Frankly, I thought I was pretty slick. Finally she said, 'Okay, but the record player's a gift – as long as that's understood.'

'Understood and gratefully accepted.' I bowed as much as I could in the front seat. 'I'd like to take a look at the records, but I'm not sure what your situation is. I'd be glad to drive you to your trailer if you think your neighbors wouldn't take it wrong. And I wouldn't mind at all if you'd rather have me call you a cab and meet you somewhere else with the records – *and* the record player. What do you think?'

She fixed me with those lustrous brown eyes and a smile. 'I think you're a very thoughtful man. And for all your supposed craziness, very, very careful. We can go to the trailer. None of the neighbors thinks anything about me as far as I know. About the only person I ever talk to is Warren's uncle when he comes around the first of the month to collect the rent and try to feel my ass.' Her nose wrinkled with disgust. 'The kids'll be home in a couple of hours. I can move the mess around while you check out the records.'

The trailer, closed all day in the heat, reeked of burned oatmeal, curdled milk, and dirty socks, just as Donna had said. She stopped in the doorway, took a deep breath, and let it out slowly in a murmuring sigh. 'Ah, home sweet home. You're welcome to it. See if you can find a place to sit down.' She left the outside door open and went into a tiny room at the back of the trailer. She didn't have far to go: the trailer seemed about seven feet long. I hadn't spent that much time around kids, but even if they sat stone-still that place would've been cramped.

Donna was back in a couple of minutes with two large plastic cases, each half again as big as a portable typewriter case. One was turquoise with yellow flecks, the other light green. The latter contained the record player. It was a bit dusty and the batteries were long dead, but the turntable spun smoothly and the needle looked sharp. Sounding upset, Donna said it worked fine the last time she'd played it. I assured her of my utter confidence that new batteries would do the trick and, if not, that I was an ace mechanic, but she insisted on searching for the four-cell flashlight so we could use its batteries to test the machine. She couldn't find the flashlight and grew increasingly distracted. 'The boys were using it last night to play flashlight tag. How can they lose *everything* they touch? I mean,' she spread her arms, 'how can you lose *anything* in a place this size? Damn flashlight's bigger than the table.'

She was still looking for the flashlight when I opened a small compartment on the side of the case and found a cord for a 12-volt connection; you could plug it right into the cigarette lighter. I held it up. 'Forget the flashlight. Lookee here at the miracles of modern technology – I can run it straight off the car's system.'

The turquoise case was full of records. There were three tightly slotted rows, all but a dozen in paper slip jackets. Most looked like they might've been pressed the day before. 'You sure kept your record collection immaculate. Hardly a speck of dust. No reason you shouldn't get top dollar.'

'You'd never know to look at this place that I used to be a tidy young lady, would you?'

'I bet two rambunctious young boys really sharpen your personal sense of order.'

'Ain't that a fact,' she said ruefully. 'Listen, I'm going to attack the dishes. Take your time going through the records. And take anything you want; they're all for sale.'

I went through the records quickly. A fairly comprehensive collection, to my limited knowledge. I found the Big Bopper's 'Chantilly Lace' right off, a bunch of Elvis, Jerry Lee Lewis, Fats Domino, Bill Haley & the Comets, Chuck Berry, Buddy Holly galore, five or six of Little Richard's wailings, the Everly Brothers, some folk and calypso, and a whole bunch of groups and people I'd never heard of. Ritchie Valens's 'La Bamba' and 'Donna' were near the end of the last row. I set 'Donna' aside.

She was behind me at the sink, scrubbing dishes. I told her I'd set 'Donna' aside and asked if she had any other favorites.

She damn near wheeled on me. 'Take "Donna,"' she said flatly, 'that's the one I really want gone.'

'No sentimental favorites?'

'Not anymore.' She turned back to the sink.

I counted the records and then my money. I was short out-of-pocket and had to go out to the Caddy for the roll in the duffle bag. When I came back in, I counted out the cash on top of the turquoise case. 'Okay,' I said, 'let's get down to business. I get two hundred and seven records at two bucks a pop, makes it four-fourteen, so I'll call it an even four-fifteen if you'll throw in the carrying case.'

Donna was shocked. 'You're buying *all* the records for two dollars *each?*'

'I know that seems low, but Scumball says it's standard price for good-to-excellent condition. I don't know what the market's like here, but even in 'Frisco he can't get more than three dollars a pop. And I *am* buying them all, remember, not high-grading it for the good stuff.'

Donna pointed at the turquoise case. 'You're gonna give me over four *hundred* dollars for those records, is that what you're telling me?'

'Four-fifteen,' I corrected her. 'I'm sorry, but I really can't go higher.' I tried to look sorry.

Donna was shaking her head. 'You know those records aren't worth nothing much. You're just looking for a way to give me charity. I appreciate it, George, but that ain't right.'

The truth was, I didn't have the vaguest idea what used records were going for, but two dollars seemed fair to me and that allowed me to put some honest righteousness in my bluff. 'Donna, I'll write down Scumball's number. Call him at work and he'll tell you whether I'm bullshitting or not.'

She decided to believe me. 'No, there's no need for that. God, I guess not. You'll have to excuse me, but I was figuring a dime at the most, and you're telling me two dollars. Four *hundred!* Hell, if I knew I was sitting on a gold mine, I'd of sold 'em a long time ago.'

'Glad you didn't.' I grinned. 'And I *know* Scumball will be.'

Donna insisted on coming out to the Caddy to say goodbye – plus she wanted to make sure the record player worked. I plugged the adapter into the cigarette lighter and hit the switch; the turntable began revolving. I was tempted to play 'Donna' and ask the real one to dance a slow one right there in her scuffed yard in front of God and the neighbors, holding her close before I aimed it back down the Interstate. But seeing as how she didn't need the pain, I picked a Buddy Holly at random. It dropped smoothly onto the turntable and the tone arm lifted over and laid the needle in the groove:

> *I'm gonna tell you how it's gonna be:*
> *You're gonna give-a your love to me.*
> *I wanna love you night and day,*
> *You know my love not fade away.*
>
> *Doo-wop: doo-wop: doo-wop-bop.*

My love is bigger than a Cadillac,
I try to show it and you drive me back.
Your love for me has got to be real
For you to know just how I feel.
A love for real not fade away!

I hit the freeway full-bore and feeling good, a farewell kiss from Donna still warm on my cheek. Since I had the record player all set up, I figured I might as well listen to 'Chantilly Lace,' seeing as how I was riding its ripple of consequence into my present madness. I dropped it on the box. There was the sound of a phone jingling, then a low lecherous purr:

Hellooooo, bay-bee.
Yeah, this is the Big Bopper speaking.
[a prurient laugh]
Oh, you sweet thang!
Do I what?
Will I what?
Oh bay-beeee, you know *what I* like:

And *then* he starts singing.

Chantilly lace and a pretty face
and a ponytail hangin' down,
a wiggle in her walk
and a giggle in her talk
Lawd, makes the world go 'round 'round 'round . . .

Listening, I agreed with the Bopper that we all need a little human connection, some critter warmth. It was sad, but in the music was an invincible joy that proved sadness could be balanced, if not beat, and for a while there, rocking toward Phoenix with

Donna's record player turned up full blast, so exhausted I could barely blink, I was serene. Mostly it was the music, the captivating power of the beat; I didn't have to think. No wonder the young loved it. Adolescence is excruciating enough without thinking about it; better to fill your head with cleansing energy. I kept filling mine, hoping this feeling of serenity could last forever, but when I started to nod at the wheel it clearly was time for either speed or sleep. Acting upon the sanity serenity inspires, I pulled into the Fat Cactus Motel on the outskirts of Phoenix, signed in semiconscious, and raced the Sandman to Room 17. It was a dead heat.

I woke around noon the next day, reborn. I showered for about forty-five minutes, washing off the road grit and speed grease, then put on clean clothes. I felt fresh, fit, and ready to take on Texas. After filling the Caddy with high-test, I stopped down the street and stretched my shrunken gut with a tall stack at the House of Pancakes.

I said I felt good, and that's a fact, but you can always feel *better*. My nervous system, after the cleansing flush of sleep, was beginning to twitter for its amphetamine, asserting a need that was undoubtedly sharpened by the knowledge that the means of satisfaction was near at hand. I invoked my recently refreshed sense of purpose and limited myself to three. A man buffeted by general weakness and a tendency toward utter indulgence needs to bolster his resolve with such acts of self-control. Of course, it's not a tremendous consolation to tell yourself you only took three when you could have taken thirty, but Fortune favors those who at least *try*.

Eight miles out of Phoenix, Fortune, quick to pay off, rewarded me with Joshua Springfield, make of him what I might. At first it was difficult to make anything of him, just the shadow of a shape in a blaze of light, but as the angle of vision changed with my approach I saw what was what – apparently, anyway – and pulled over in response to his upraised thumb.

This man is proof of the impossibility of description. He was large and round, easily over two hundred pounds, with short legs, large torso, and a massive head, yet altogether there was a sense of spare grace in the proportions. He was moon faced, so smooth as to seem featureless, or maybe the features were blurred by the power of his dark blue eyes, a color at odds with the short, tightly curled reddish hair that covered his crown like a fungus attacking a pink balloon. He was wearing a lime-green gabardine suit apparently made by a tailor suffering severe impairment of his sensory and motor faculties. The color of his suit clashed with his red shirt, though it matched the body feathers of the parrots printed on it. Joshua was standing on a large rectangular silver box the size of a footlocker, and it was the dazzle of sunlight off the silver box that made him appear, despite his considerable substance, apparitional.

'Good afternoon,' he greeted me in a mellow bass. 'It is kind of you to stop. I hope you won't mind being burdened with this heavy and rather unwieldy box.'

He wasn't lying about that: we both were panting by the time we got it secured on the back seat. Back on the road, still mopping sweat, I said, 'Must be the family gold in there to haul it around hitching.'

'Ah, if it was gold I assure you I wouldn't be hitching. I would rent a helicopter. But since it isn't gold, and since I've never learned to drive an automobile, I must accept the luck of the road and the kindness of fellow travelers like yourself.'

'My pleasure. Do you mind my asking what *is* in the box? I'm always curious about what I've been wrestling.'

'Not at all. It's not very spectacular, I assure you. Merely equipment I use in my work – amplifiers, speakers, that sort of thing.'

'You an electrician?'

'I dabble. By vocation I'm a chemist, so I suppose it's accurate to say that the electrical is within my field.'

'A chemist,' I repeated. Visions of sugarplums danced in my head. 'What exactly do you do?'

'Oh, the usual. Dissolve and coagulate; join and sunder; generally stir the elemental soup.'

'Well, yes . . . but what sort of substances do you make?'

'For the last twenty years I've primarily been interested in medicines, but I've made all sorts of things – metal polish, soap, plastics, paper, cosmetics, dyes, and the rest.'

'Have you ever heard of lysergic acid? LSD?'

I listened carefully for a note of caution in his tone, a trace of reserve, but he was direct: 'Yes. I ran across it in Hoffman's work on grain molds.'

'Have you ever made any?'

'No.'

'Taken any?'

'No.'

'You weren't curious?'

'I'm curious both by nature and aesthetic disposition, but I've found that psychotropic drugs are like funhouse mirrors – they reveal by distortion.'

'And you want a funhouse with honest mirrors?'

Joshua thought for a moment. 'Actually, I guess I'm more interested in a funhouse *without* mirrors.'

'You think it would still be fun?' I'll admit to a snotty note of the disingenuous in my tone.

'Why else would it interest me?' he replied sharply, lifting his arms in exasperation. One sleeve came to midforearm, the other to his knuckles. When I didn't reply he continued in a softer, but still testy, tone, 'There's no need to poke at me like a crab in a hole. If you have a point, come to it; if you have a question, ask.'

I lacked a point but had far too many questions, and the three hits of speed were kicking into high, so instead I told him my tale much like I'm telling you, the road and story rolling together,

Phoenix to Tucson and on down the hard-rock highway. Joshua listened with complete attention and without comment, which unnerved me at first and made me hurry for fear of boring him. But when I realized he was absorbed, not bored, I relaxed, and that inspired my honesty. I told him the car was stolen, that I'd been taking drugs and might be crazy. This information didn't seem to alarm him; his hands were folded on his lap and he briefly turned them palms up, as if to indicate it was an insignificant matter of fact.

I didn't finish bending his ear until we were passing the Dos Cabezas range. Joshua turned his attention from me to the mountains, then stuck his head out the window and craned his neck to look at the sky. When he sat back and settled himself again in the seat, he said, 'There are many possible responses to being lost in the wilds. You can stay put and wait for help. You can build fires and flash mirrors and construct huge SOS signals by piling stones or dead branches. You can pray. You can hurl yourself off a cliff. You can try to find your way out by backtracking, or you can plunge on ahead. Or sideways. Or in circles. Or randomly, willy-nilly. I don't think it probably makes much difference what method you adopt, though it *is* a reflection of character, and certainly an expression of style. The romantic is a dangerous impulse, easily confused with the most pathetic sentimentality, yet so wonderfully capable of a magnificence borne and illuminated not by mere endurance, but by a joy so elemental it will gladly risk the spectacular foolishness of its likely failure.'

'So you approve?'

'My approval isn't required. I will confess I'm prey to such gestures myself, though they generally offend me with their excesses. A splash where a stroke would serve. The jelly of adjectives instead of the bread of a noun. Ah, but if the connection is made, the arc completed: what powerful grace! An eruption so marvelous a million spirits are joined!'

'What you're saying basically, if I understand it, is that my ass is up for grabs.'

'You're strafing a mouse, but yes, essentially.'

'What about your ass, Joshua?' I said. 'Is it up for grabs, too?'

He gave me a huge moonbeam smile, the kind we draw as children on the round faces of our imagination, U-shaped, the corners of the mouth nearly touching the eyes. 'Of course my ass is up for grabs. It is a perpetual condition of asses.'

'You don't seem unduly concerned,' I noted.

'I'm not. I don't *care* if it gets grabbed. I might not like it, of course, but I don't care.' He gave me a wonderful wink, convivial and conspiratorial, and at that moment, though I wouldn't realize it till later, our journeys were joined. I'm sure Joshua had already recognized this and was acknowledging it with the wink – but then he was a chemist, and finally it was a matter of chemistry, of congruence and charge.

As we started up Apache Pass, Joshua explained he was on something of a journey himself. As he talked, it became clear that Joshua was one of those eminently functional people who are remarkably crazy, a psychic equilibrium that few can sustain, and which may well constitute a profound form of sanity. Or may not.

'I'm on an experimental field trip,' he explained. 'As a chemist it is one of my duties to stir the soup. Not to season it necessarily, but to keep it from sticking to the bottom and, not incidentally, to see what precipitates or dissolves. Perhaps I flatter myself in thinking I'm an agent of the possible, but we all suffer our vanities. Like your little orange man protecting himself with a piece of the puzzle. Classically it's the catalytic burden, but why snivel or shrivel at the load when the trees can bear the wind with such grace, and the mountains bear the sky? "Don't matter if the mule's blind, just keep loading the wagon." In that silver box burdening the back seat is a self-contained amplification system, from turntable to two powerful speakers. There is also a microphone hook-up. Primitive, really: twelve-volt DC, nickel-cadmium battery. Electrical amplification is a new force in the world and it needs to be assessed. Can clarity be made clearer by amplification? Is sound meant to be carried beyond the natural range of its source? Or are we about to start worshipping another overpowering technological distortion as some degraded puritanical form of magic?

'My experiment is crude, but not without certain possibilities of elegant resonance. I intend to go to San Picante, a small village of perhaps ten thousand souls; it's in New Mexico, out of Lordsburg and up through Silver City, in the Mimbres mountains. No trains have ever passed within ninety-four miles of San Picante. At approximately four o'clock tonight – or, more precisely, tomorrow morning – I will set up my amplification equipment and put on a recording of an approaching train – at full volume. I've tested it, of course, and the effect is *quite* impressive. I'm planning to do this in a residential area, and if a crowd gathers, I may hook up the microphone and make a few remarks.'

'If I was you,' I told him, 'I'd make tracks. Some folks might be a little upset about getting the ever-loving shit scared out of them just so they can lose two or three hours' sleep before they have to go to work.'

Joshua inclined his massive head an eighth of an inch in acknowledgment. 'I concur; that's highly probable. But without that probability, how can we court the marvelous exception? Speaking as a *true* scientist – as opposed to those who line up to lick the tight ass of Logos, if you'll forgive my justified vulgarity – I maintain a *reluctant* objectivity that I'm willing to abandon at any hint of the marvelous. In my first science class in college, we each looked at a drop of our own blood under the microscope. I saw a million women naked, singing as they ascended the mountain in the rain. Who's to say what can happen when literally *anything* can happen? These people tonight may hear the train and walk radiantly from their houses, jolted into the reality of their being. But if their reactions confirm your grim predictions, you are a capable driver. Even excellent.'

I noted my inclusion in his 'experiment' and took it as a shy invitation rather than an arrogant presumption. I was about to respond when Joshua pointed down the highway. 'Look at that lovely live-oak. This is an outstanding tree. You look at it and immediately know it couldn't be anywhere else. This tree could *not* be on television. That's a good sign, don't you think?'

I didn't know what to think, so I smiled and said, 'Joshua, you're crazier than I am.'

He leaned his head back on the seat and shut his eyes as if preparing for sleep, but immediately leaned forward and looked at me. 'George, my friend, when I was seven years old, living with my family in Wyoming, one day I was sitting in a mountain meadow examining the patterns the wind was making in the grass when a raven flew over my head and asked in one hoarse syllable, "*Ark?*" Having been a Sunday School regular, I was convinced this was the very raven Noah had sent out centuries before to seek out land – the raven that preceded the dove, remember, never to return? – and now, after what an unimaginably mysterious and exhausting journey, had found land but lost the Ark. I could feel its joyous message dying in its throat. So I set to work building an Ark in our backyard, using scrap lumber from a nearby construction site. It wasn't much of an Ark, more of a pointed raft, but I worked on it with singleminded concentration and completed it within a week. Then I climbed aboard and waited for the raven to return. After three weeks of my absolute intransigence, my parents had me committed.

'The doctors told me I had misunderstood. They said all ravens uttered a harsh croaking sound that could be easily mistaken for the word *Ark*. That, I thought, was fairly obvious. But they hadn't been in the meadow with me; they hadn't *heard* it. I understood their doubt, but not their adamant refusal to admit even the slightest possibility that they might be wrong. Nor could they offer textual evidence from the Bible of the raven's fate, though it was impossible, they said, that this bird could've flown since Noah's time, that it would have died of old age, and so forth. Despite this they claimed to believe in God. And yet they could not see, or refused to see, that if God could create the earth, and sky, and water, and stars, He could surely keep a poor lost raven aloft. Theirs was a disgusting violation of logic and an insult to intelligent inquiry. That's why it's a relief and a pleasure to meet people like you, people who understand—'

'Joshua,' I interrupted, not wanting him to think I was dense, 'I notice you seem to have included me in your plans for tonight as the getaway driver, and I just want to keep things clear and plain. That's sort of one of my rules for the trip: no bullshit.'

'That's rather bold,' he said, blinking. 'But I meant as a cohort and friend, not just as a chauffeur.'

'I accept the honor of being your accomplice.'

He broke into a smile I'll never forget, that still shines on me sometimes with unexpected blessing. That smile was what I was agreeing to.

'And,' I added, 'I hope you'll accept *my* offer to continue on with me and make this delivery to the Big Bopper's grave. I would welcome your company.'

Joshua sighed. 'There are lessons not even the wisest counsel can prevent us from learning. Nor should it. Each raindrop is different unto the river and equally waters the trees. After two years of pale green walls and apostate doctors I knew the raven wouldn't come to me, so I went looking for it. I found it in the trees, in the sky, in the water, the flames, and in myself. I have built many arks for many ravens, burned many empty nests. I have some experience in these matters, George, believe me. I am no more a teacher than you are a student. But it's best for both of us if I don't accompany you. Yours is the journey of a young man.

I'm nearly fifty. What help I might offer would merely obstruct you; my company would prove a distraction. Trust me when I say that you are much more essential to me than I am to you.' He reached across the front seat and patted my shoulder. 'You do understand?'

'Of course not,' I said, stung at his refusal. 'I don't understand anything these days. I guess I do understand that you can't drive and I can – which, if I understand it right, is what makes me necessary.'

Calmly, patiently, Joshua said, 'That's a beginning.' Then added, with a pointedness his patience couldn't restrain, 'It was an *invitation*, George, and can be declined.'

I wasn't sure if he meant his or mine, and decided it didn't matter. 'I thought I made it clear I'd be glad to help.'

Joshua leaned closer. 'Well then,' he whispered, 'let's conspire.'

It wasn't much of a conspiracy. We'd pull into San Picante well after dark, find an appropriate neighborhood, Joshua would set up his equipment, we'd send a train screaming through the residents' peaceful slumbers, Joshua would deliver his remarks, and then we'd split – and be prepared to do so triple-lickety in case of enraged pursuit. I had a few quibbles, questions, and doubts. About my fear that the Caddy was far too conspicuous for the job, Joshua argued that, on the contrary, it possessed 'the perverse invisibility of insane proportion.' As for its being stolen, he claimed this would make it harder to trace to us and, moreover, that the legal status of automobiles was an unnecessary burden on minds about to undertake an important scientific experiment. He did agree that I should smear mud on the license plates to 'confound identification,' though he personally felt we had nothing to hide and shouldn't behave as if we did.

I wasn't particularly hungry myself but, playing the thoughtful host, asked Joshua if he was. He said he wouldn't mind a milkshake, so we stopped at a Dairy-Freeze in Lordsburg and grabbed four shakes to go – vanilla for me; raspberry, butterscotch, and chocolate-chip for Joshua. I washed down four hits of speed with mine, seeing as how I'd be up late doing some tight work. Joshua declined my offer of the open speed bottle, claiming the milkshakes were sufficient. He drank alternately from the three cups, consuming them at an equal rate and with obvious pleasure.

I pulled in at the local U-Save for ice, potato chips, and Dolley Madison donuts, then gassed the Caddy to the gunwales. As we headed into the mountains, I asked Joshua what he planned to say, assuming there was time for a speech. He said he had nothing in particular in mind; perhaps just a few general comments on the nature of reality and the meaning of life – nothing beyond what the moment might offer. Sounded an awful lot like me lying to Natalie and her friend about the word I'd whisper on the peak of Mount Shasta.

On roads that narrowed as they climbed through the night, we talked about moments and what they might offer. We were an hour early in San Picante – a result, according to Joshua, of my driving faster than his calculations – but the town was already long asleep. Even Dottie's All-Nite Diner was closed, a fact that for some reason irritated me and amused Joshua immensely. We cruised the small residential areas off the the main drag until Joshua found exactly what he wanted, 'a pure-product middle-class tract subdivision, sumptuous with stunted dreams, ripe for the river.' He said he could feel it, and I, more nervous by the minute, hoped he knew what he was doing.

I parked in the shadow-deepened darkness of a large tree. Joshua took about fifteen heart-thudding minutes, nine hundred long moments, to get the sound system hooked up in the back seat. The battery, turntable, and amplifier stayed in the silver box; the speakers, which had some sort of adjustable metal tabs, were fitted into the open rear windows. Joshua hummed the sprightly 'Wabash Cannonball' as he worked. For my part,

I worried, studying the county map I'd bought in Silver City while gassing up, and by the time Joshua had his instruments set up I'd memorized every possible escape route, from major roads to obscure hiking trails. I was looking for feasible cross-country routes when Joshua slung the microphone over into the front seat and then crawled over himself. 'Are you ready for a ride in the patently unreal,' he asked cheerfully.

'I guess,' I said.

Joshua looked out the window. 'I'm afraid this tree may cause some distortion in the sonic configuration from the right speaker. Can you back up about fifty feet?'

In the interest of clarity, I kissed our cover goodbye and backed up as requested. As soon as I cut the engine, Joshua reached over into the back seat and hit the start switch on the turntable. I heard the record drop, then a whisper of static as the needle touched down.

Joshua touched my arm in the darkness and whispered, 'Isn't this an amazing moment? Not the vaguest idea what will happen.' Beside me, I could feel him swelling with happiness.

You could hear the train coming far down the tracks, wailing on fast and hard and louder than I ever imagined it would be, mounting to a crescendo that was everywhere and right on top of you at once, its air horn blasting you out through the roof of your skull. I'm telling you, the fucking street *shook*. The Caddy started flopping like a gaffed fish, bucking so bad I instinctively jumped on the brakes. I *knew* that train was a fake, an utter hoax, and it *still* scared me shitless. I cringed to imagine the havoc inside those sleepy houses, houses never rattled by the roar and rumble of the railroad. I glanced over at Joshua. His eyes were mild, lips parted, but as the silence gathered mass in the wake of the ghost train's shattering passage, before the muffled screams and curses issued from the houses and lights flicked on randomly down the street, a tiny smile lifted toward his cheekbones as he bent his head to the microphone like a man about to pray.

Directly across the street I saw a grimacing face flash behind a parted curtain, then heard more shouts and shrieks. Imagined many trembling fingers dialing numbers that are found in the front of phone-books under *In Case of Emergency*. I hoped Joshua wouldn't *literally* wait for a crowd to gather. A front door two houses down flew open and a huge man in rumpled pajamas lurched out onto the front lawn brandishing a baseball bat. He didn't seem radiantly transformed to me; on the contrary, he appeared monstrously pissed. I was reaching for the ignition when Joshua's voice, amplified to a deafening roar, stunned the night: 'REALITY IS FINAL!' He paused, then added softly, 'But it is not complete.

'How *could* it be complete without a Mystery Train hurtling through our dreams? How could it possibly be complete without imagining that together we have all dreamt it up, to *make* it real, so that at this moment, right *now*, our entire lives could come to this? A rather provocative state of affairs, don't you think?

'The train we dreamt of was the *Celestial Express*. I don't know about you, but my arms are tired from trying to flag down the *Celestial Express*. The train we dreamt of was an old freight hauling grain, refrigerators, newsprint, tractor parts, munitions, salt. The train we dreamt of was the *Dawn Death Zephyr*, burning human breath and broken dreams for fuel. The train we dreamt up was the raw possibility of any real train we want to ride.

'All aboard! All aboard that train!

'But of course we're already all aboard. That is the practicality of the joke. A joke, I promise you, that wasn't intended to demean you as fools or scare you witless, but rather to illuminate your own face in the rain and hear the thousand songs in your blood. To perhaps touch your mother's breast the way you did, a week old in a magical world – her clean mammal warmth most magical of all. To refresh the magic. The real magic of holding each other in our real arms.

'We hurt each other. We help each other. We kill each

other and love each other and generally seem to suffer the slaughter of bored failure in between. We treat others – people, plants, animals, earth – with contempt, deceit, unbound venality, slobbering greed. What faith we muster is often blind with self-righteousness or merely a garbage can lid to keep the flies from making maggots, the dogs from scattering our trash on the front lawn, our dirty little secrets and decaying shame displayed for all to see. And then a small child cuts a crooked cherry limb for a sword, lifts the garbage can lid for a shield, and sallies forth to vanquish the real dragons guarding the real grails, the empty grails depicting in precious stone the marriage of the sun and moon.'

Joshua paused a long moment, the echo of his last words rolling down the valley, then continued with a boom: 'I'm not talking about *religion*. I'm not trying to sell you a ticket on the train. I'm neither owner nor conductor; I'm a passenger just like you. Maybe some seats on the train are better than others, but all religions are basically the same. After that, the churches and temples fill with accountants, warriors, and delusion – and, quite frankly, I would have them fill with rivers, with ravens, with real wishes.

'Reality is final, but not complete. We will fade into the rain, the river, the restless and infinitely suggestive wishes that spawn our faces. A raven will appear or not. All we have is what is real. What we can comprehend, replenish, sustain, create. And if the possibilities are beyond our comprehension, they are not beyond our choice or, by that same choice, our faith. The *is* is the real-right-now it all gets down to, and I assure you I know how really and truly hearts are mangled, how the weight of our loneliness collapses on us, the way doubt and ignorance leach our salts. We don't know if we're solid, gas, or liquid; light or space; deranged angels or the devil's fools; all or none or some of the time; or who, what, where, how, or why-oh-why the is *is* – except as we make it so, affirm it so, and live it as our own witness.

'But here we are. Here we are tonight, alive. We live by life.

And we are bound by being, by being life, to make and accept our choices as the truths of ourselves and not excuses wrenched from the impossibility of choosing. All I truly want to say is that I know the choices aren't easy, that there's a wilderness between intention and consequence, that if you've never been lost you have no way to understand how lucky you are. I address you out of commiseration, not instruction, hoping to remind you that we can hurt each other or help each other, fester or flower, freeze or leap.

'Leap.'

He'd barely uttered the word when I caught the muzzle flash in the corner of my eye, and in the same instant the left-rear speaker was wrenched from the window and Joshua sagged against the door, hand to his head, blood seeping between his fingers. I leapt across the front seat and pulled his hand away. Expecting the worst, I was elated to see a shallow scratch instead of the brain-dripping hole I feared. I decided it must've been a fragment from the speaker or the bullet. I also decided that an explanation for the oddity of the wound could wait, which is about the same instant I was deciding we should get the fuck out of there. I made another leap – back behind the wheel – and was twisting the key when a hand seized mine. Joshua's.

'No.' He meant it.

'They're shooting at us,' I said reasonably.

He shrugged. 'It wasn't a very inspired speech.' He idly wiped at the trickle of blood tangling in his left eyebrow. 'One has to accept criticism.'

'You're bleeding,' I told him.

'It's nothing. A wood fragment from the speaker, I think.' He picked up the microphone and handed it to me. 'You try.'

By now people in bathrobes or half-dressed were pouring outside, the name Henry being screamed. I sat with the microphone in my hand, my mind – so recently and incessantly possessed of babble – a blank. I waited about fifteen seconds for the next bullet; then, unable to bear the suspense, I jerked the mike to my mouth and bellowed, 'You've got three minutes to kill us! That's all my nerves can stand!' My voice sounded weird to me, fractured, hollow. 'If you haven't killed us in three minutes, I'm going to respond to my friend's statement. I'll be brief. Then we'll leave.' *Why three minutes?* I thought to myself. Why indeed? Why not?

Joshua was climbing into the backseat. 'Forsaking me in my time of need, huh?' I said.

'On the contrary, George,' he grunted as he squeezed on over, 'I'm checking on the damage to the speaker. There's tremendous distortion somewhere. You sound like a frog chewing ping-pong balls.'

'It's the fear and madness,' I explained.

'Nonsense. They've shot a speaker. You *do* understand they were shooting at the speaker, not us?'

'Whew,' I said, letting the sarcasm drip, 'that's a relief.' I glanced at my watch, suffering a moment's panic when I realized I hadn't marked the beginning of three minutes. At least a minute had gone by, it seemed to me, so I called it two, wondering if anybody was actually keeping track.

Outside, a woman yelled, 'Eddie, get back in here.'

From up the block, a man shouted, 'Goddamn it, Henry, that's enough shooting. You're crazier than they are. There's no reason to kill them.' I hoped that sentiment was sweeping the neighborhood.

'Ah-ha,' Joshua said behind me. 'The bullet hit the edge of the speaker; a wire pulled loose when it fell. Just what I thought.' He started humming 'Zippity-doo-dah' as he commenced the repairs. He had remarkable grace under pressure, or a serious mental defect.

In clock time, every second is of equal duration, but our experience proves this simply isn't true. The duration between tick and tock stretches, compresses, and, to judge from this occasion, sometimes stops. I stared at the second hand until I was sure it was moving again, figuring I'd lost half a minute minimum during my watch's malfunction. That would make it three minutes, maybe more. I switched on the microphone.

'Time's up,' I announced. 'Thank you, folks. We meant you no harm at all and hoped you'd feel the same way.' Evidently Joshua had reconnected the wire because my voice was loud and clear. Which was a waste of a good sound system and speedy repairs, since I had nothing more to say; and even if I did, my mouth was suddenly too dry to speak. I flipped off the mike and dropped it on the front seat. Then, with a desperation disguised as bravado, I opened the door and slowly got out of the car, careful to keep my open hands in plain view. I walked around to the front of the car, then climbed up on the warm hood, and then onto the roof. There I stood in the clear-night mountain air, looking at every face I could see, people standing in protective clusters, faces at windows, families jamming doorways or half-hidden on darkened porches, and then I began to applaud, steadily, sincerely, and painfully, for my hands were still tender from the cactus waltz.

'Get your worthless asses outa here!' a voice snarled from the shadows.

'Yeah, before you get 'em kicked,' the guy with the baseball bat added.

I continued my applause.

'You people're crazy and shouldn't be loose.' It was an old woman's voice, sharp with a judgment born of experience, cranky with the fuss caused by fools.

I clapped madly.

The shouts stopped and I could hear my applause echoing down the street. I don't know the sound of one hand clapping, but I can tell you for sure what two sound like. My hands hurt, but I continued my ovation.

And finally a person I couldn't see – just a shadow on a porch at the end of the block, not a clue if it was man, woman, or child – joined my applause. *Only* one, true, but that was enough. Besides, nobody booed. I stopped clapping.

'Thank you for your patience,' I said, and jumped to the pavement, opened the door to Joshua's honoring nod, cranked the Caddy over, and we made away in the night – a departure, in my view, not without a certain touch of panache.

Within two miles the graceful dignity of our exit was fouled by a flashing red light, and what had been a cool slipaway became a for-real, rootin'-tootin', flat-out, ass-haulin' and bawlin'-for-momma getaway.

As the red light hammered on behind us, I turned to Joshua for instructions. He was holding the microphone by its cord, swinging it like a pendulum to the pulse of the red light, his other hand pressing a chartreuse handkerchief to his forehead. He was lost in either thought or shock.

I prodded him: 'I believe some sort of law enforcement official is signaling us to pull over.'

'Ignore him.'

'He won't go away.'

'That's sheer conjecture on your part, George,' he replied, still swinging the microphone. He stopped abruptly when the sheriff hit his siren. 'That siren is certainly obnoxious, isn't it?'

'Unless you're deaf,' I agreed.

'Ignore it if you can,' Joshua advised.

I kept it just above the speed limit, the sheriff on our tail like glue. About a mile on, as we entered a long straightaway, he swung out and pulled even with the left-rear window. I decided I'd treat him like any other motorist, hitting my highbeams to indicate it was clear to pass.

The sheriff killed the siren and pulled up even with the Caddy. He used the roof-mounted bullhorn to issue a crisp, professional request: 'Pull over, cocksuckers!'

'Must we also endure slurs on our sexuality,' I asked Joshua, who was reaching over into the backseat.

'Yes,' he grunted.

'Sticks and stones, huh?'

'Within reason.'

'PULL OVER AND STOP OR I'LL SHOOT!' the sheriff commanded.

'What about bullets?' I asked Joshua.

'We should display compassion for his crabbed and envious mind,' he replied mildly, turning back around in the seat and gazing thoughtfully down the road as he fiddled with the microphone in his hand.

'*NOW*, MOTHERFUCKERS!' the bullhorn boomed.

The next thing I heard was Joshua's voice, still mild, but at a decibel level far beyond the capabilities of the sheriff's puny bullhorn: 'Sir, we don't recognize your authority to detain scientists at work or pilgrims on their appointed way.'

I glanced over to see how the officer was responding to this modest objection just in time to see him lift an ugly sawed-off .12-gauge from the floor rack. There was a burst of static or sputtering over the bullhorn, followed by a rage-gored bellow: 'RIGHT *NOW*, FUCKERS!'

'*EAT SHIT!*' Joshua screamed.

I don't know who was more shocked, me or the sheriff. As if blown apart by the sonic blast from Joshua's souped-up system, the Caddy and his Dodge swerved away from each other. I recovered and he didn't. However, he did manage to slow it down enough that when he twirled off the shoulder and took out thirty yards of barbed-wire fence he didn't roll it.

'Stop,' Joshua recommended.

I pulled over and we looked back. The red light was still flashing, but erratically. The interior light came on and we could see the sheriff jump out and immediately go down screaming, tangled in barbed wire.

'He's fine,' Joshua said, 'merely rendered inept by his rage and our magic. Let's leave him here, preferably with haste.' He clicked the mike switch on and murmured cheerfully, 'Good night, officer.'

I pulled back onto the road and put my foot in it, romping it up into triple digits within fifteen seconds.

After a minute Joshua asked, 'How fast are we traveling?'

'About a hundred and ten.'

'Is that necessary?'

I thought about it for a moment. 'Not really. But you said "with haste" and, given the likelihood of pursuit, I find speed comforting.'

'Then by all means enjoy it. And should it contribute to our safety, all the better.'

'Speaking of escape, Joshua, it might not be a bad idea to get rid of the silver box and its contents – that's the sort of evidence that could really nail our sacks to a wall. Unless you don't want to dump it. Sentimental attachment, investment, whatever.'

Joshua smiled. 'I'd already decided to give it to you in appreciation for your help. A gift to the giver, as it were. It's yours to dispose of as you will.'

'Joshua, did anyone ever tell you you're a sneaky ol' fart?'

'I always thought generosity the simplest of virtues.'

'Thanks,' I said, nodding my acknowledgment.

Joshua nodded in return. 'Good. Enjoy it. I've spent months refining it.'

'Will it handle a forty-five RPM?'

'Yes. The train recording is a forty-five.'

'Would you mind if I played some records from a friend's collection on my new machine? As loud as possible?'

'Rock-and-roll, I assume?' He didn't sound enthusiastic.

'That's right,' I said.

'Am I being punished, or is this an attempt at persuasion?'

'Neither,' I said. 'In celebration.'

'George,' Joshua muttered, 'it isn't sporting to flog a man with his own rhetoric; our mouths too often prove larger than our hearts.'

'Tough,' I said.

We started with Chuck Berry's 'Maybelline,' followed by Jerry Lee Lewis's 'Shake, Rattle, and Roll,' which we were doing, and that followed by four hits of speed for me and one for Joshua, bless his heart, who decided he at least owed it to the music to hear it in its proper context. I even saw him tap his foot a few times as he stared straight down the road, lost in what marvelous eruptions of mind I couldn't imagine.

At Joshua's suggestion, we drove around at random till well after dawn. His theory held that we could confuse any pursuit by confusing ourselves; to lose them by getting lost. Getting lost, however, turned out to be difficult. Usually we hit a dead end and had to turn around, so more than once we had the vague feeling of having been there before. Joshua would say, 'Let's take the next right and then drive for nine minutes and take the next seven lefts.' Almost always we wound up at a gate or dead end. Besides, there were frequent road signs telling you where you were and how far it was to the next place. But it worked. We saw a few cops, but none who seemed to notice us.

Joshua and I parted company in Truth or Consequences, New Mexico, a town he selected from a highway mileage sign as appropriate to our farewell. I let him off just inside the city limits, within easy milkshake distance of a Dairy Queen that was about to open for the morning. He thanked me for the ride and a memorable night. I thanked him for the silver music box and for making me feel possible. I was sad to see him go.

I took 25 South toward Las Cruces and the intersection with 10. I looked for some company but there wasn't a thumb on the road. I missed Joshua's bent but somehow reassuring presence, and that, along with feeling bone weary and emotionally drained from the night's adrenalin hits, left me blue. It's common cultural knowledge that the best cure for the blues is music, so I turned Little Richard up full volume and listened to him rave about a woman named Lucille.

No doubt about it, the music helped keep the blues at bay, but what helped even more was a quiet afternoon spent on the banks of the Rio Grande, watching the wide dirty water roll by. I'd stopped to take a quick piss, but by the time my bladder was empty I was caught in the soothing pull of the river. I decided to rest for half an hour and ended up sitting there damn near till dark. Drowsing off on occasion, I watched the water move, calmed by its broad, sullied, inevitable force. When I finally fired up the Caddy, I felt like I'd had a good night's sleep. Nothing was left of the blues except the shadow that's almost always there.

I stopped in El Paso to gas up for the West Texas run. I fueled myself with two tacos from Juan's Taco Take-Out Shack, of which I ate one and two bites of the second, followed by benzedrine, of which I ate five. Thus fortified and clear of mind, I put the Diamonds' 'Little Darlin'' on the box and began the slow curve east into the hill country.

I even had myself something of a plan. I'd haul down to Houston, grab a motel, sleep till I woke up, chow down, then hit the library or do whatever else was required to find out *exactly* where the Bopper's bones had found their repose. I felt sure he was buried in his hometown, or else in Beaumont, but it was time to know for sure. Past time. I'd been sloppy, a truth I calmly acknowledged and calmly vowed to change. Yup, no doubt about it: time to gather everything tight and true. I felt a surge of purpose and knew I was going to pull it off. I was closing on the end, about to deliver.

Clint, Torillo, Finlay, up the Quitman Range as the moon rose, past Sierra Blanca and down to Eagle Flat and on through Allamore, Van Horne, Plateau, I took West Texas at full gallop, whipping it down the highway behind the cut-loose combo of drugs and rock-and-roll. 'Pow! Pow! Shoot 'em up now ... ah-hoooo, my baby loves 'em Western Movies.' Blues dusted, even the shadow blown away. I didn't need Joshua or Kacy or sleep. I remember saying over and over for miles, lyrics to my own music, 'Myself, this moment, this journey.' Seriously.

I pitted for gas at the 10–20 Junction Texaco Truck Stop. A scrawny young guy buttonholed me outside the men's room and asked for a ride to Dallas. His eyes alone constituted probable cause, and his breath was so cheap-wine sour it would've straightened out a sidewinder. I told him I was taking the other fork, to Houston, and that I didn't feel like company anyway, that for the first time in too long I was enjoying being alone.

I pulled back on 10 with Little Richard wailing 'Tutti Frutti' up my spine. With a quickness and accuracy that would shame your average computer, I plotted time and distance, assessed my neural system for evidence of fatigue, considered a snarl of intangible intrinsic needs, and determined seven bennies was the optimum dose. I washed them down with a cold beer. The run to Houston was going to be long and empty – exactly what I wanted. I leaned back in the Caddy's plush seat, powered down a window for fresh air, flexed my fingers on the wheel, and screwed the juice to it till the stars blurred. I was a white rocket in a wall of sound; pure, powerful, ready to tighten down and deliver the gift, kiss the Caddy's grille against the Bopper's stone, soak down the backseat with gasoline, then set Harriet's letter ablaze and toss it in, a little torch to spark off a magnificent fireball, love's monument and proof. Yes, mama, yes. Wild into the wilderness. Wop-bop-a-lu-bop. Flower and root.

And there, right there, precisely at the diamond point of affirmed purpose, riding that bridge-burning music and wholly committed to my unknown end, I caught the shadowy semblance of Double-Gone Johnson in the headlights' halo and got myself turned around. Not *completely* around, or not immediately, but a definite hard left, 90°, due north.

Later I wondered why, given my mood, I even thought to stop, but the fact is I was stopping *before* I thought. Neural impulse, social reflex, whatever: I snapped to him. Whether this was wise or stupid, lucky or fucked, are judgments I leave to you. But before leaping to a conclusion, let me describe the man as I saw him – the raw impressions in the headlights as I slowed, the finer details as he eased himself in – and ask you to consider what you would've done in similar mood and circumstance, in that same span of three skipping heartbeats I had to decide.

The color of his stingy-brim hat might've stopped me by itself: a screaming flamingo pink, about three decibels short of glowing in the dark, and hardly muted by a satin band of neon lavender. The hat might not stop you, but not because you didn't see it.

He was tall, six-one or -two.

Not hitching, or no sign of an upraised thumb or flagging arm. Standing tall and straight.

Holding a squarish, shiny, mottled-white object, which on closer examination was a King James Bible bound in the hide of some South American lizard.

Slender, but without any sense of being skinny.

Black. That alone would've stopped me for sure, a black man hitching on a Texas freeway at 2 A.M. in 1965, because he was either fearless, magical, desperate, or seriously dumb – and which, or what braid of those strands, is the kind of question I find intriguing.

I suspected it was fearlessness, the sort that springs from a deep personal sense of heavenly protection, for he was dressed as a clergyman, and though Double-Gone Johnson was indeed a minister of the faith, he was also, as his vestments revealed, a man of the cloth in the sartorial as well as the ecclesiastical sense. A frockcoat of black velvet, its severe cut gracefully tailored into sleekness. Black velvet pants, modestly pegged and impeccably fit. Black alpaca sweater. A clerical collar, but with a color variation: instead of a starched white square at the throat, a patch of glowing lavender satin cut from the same electric bolt as his hatband. To the ecclesiastical basics he added a black velvet opera cape lined in a silk the dyer's hand had tortured into the same shade as his hat. A pair of snakeskin cowboy boots completed his wardrobe.

I rolled to a stop and reached across to open the passenger door. 'Houston bound or anywhere in between.'

Double-Gone stooped to look me over with his dark brown eyes – not wary or nervous, but languidly alert. He had wide, fleshy lips and, when he smiled, an expanse of stong white teeth. He reached in and gently placed his lizard-bound Bible on the front seat, but he didn't get in himself. 'One moment please,' he requested in a caramel baritone, holding up a long finger.

I thought he was gathering luggage I hadn't seen or was going to take a leak, but instead he circled the Eldorado, touching the hood and front grille, running his hands along the chrome and the roof line, over the twin-bullet taillights, nodding rapidly, crooning to himself as he made the circuit, 'Yes. *Solid*. My, my. You long and sweet. Oooh baby, *yes*. Fo' real and fo' sure. Much, much, much, far and away truly *too much*.' All the way around and back to the open passenger's door. He slid himself in, picked up his Bible, gently shut the door, and bestowed onto me a full-force smile. 'The Holy Spirit must love yo' act to lay it on sooo *thick*.'

'Actually,' I confessed, 'I stole it.'

'Well all right, yes,' he blinked, 'sometimes yo' forced to gather the Heavenly Bounty with yo' own two hands, I dig that, but it makes fo' a *bad* situation, catch my riff? Means the Law be looking fo' it. Means they find it, they gonna find *me in it*, and that's a hard five in the slammer if yo' black and in Texas, both of which I am, and those are conditions that don't allow for much innocence and *no* justice. And since I *do* truthfully enjoy fresh air and wide open spaces and woman's sweet flesh and *all* the Holy Manifestations of the Almighty Light, I do not have the time fo' the time, you dig it? So bless ya fo' offerin' a pilgrim soul a boost along the way, but man, y'all best be getting on without me, sad to say.'

'Good enough,' I said, and waited for him to get out.

Instead, he sank back in the seat, rolled his eyes heavenward for guidance, then closed them as he sighed to himself, 'Double-Gone, you be *long gone* if honky Law comes down on yo' ass; jus the nigger to make their night. White man and a black man in a stolen cherry Cadillac with California plates, *who* they gonna believe stole it? Man, even if this righteous white cat next to you confesses all the way to the fucking Supreme Court, yo' ass is down fo' five. Count on it.'

'*Stolen*,' I interrupted his reverie, 'may be too harsh. Legally, I have a pile of illegal documents that explain I'm merely transporting this car to a memorial service. I've been stopped once already, just out of Frisco, and the paper stood up. And—.'

'Yes,' Double-Gone swung in eagerly, 'talk that talk.'

'And morally, I'm actually delivering it as a gift of love from a spinster woman who was awakened by the music.'

'Oooeeeee! More!' Double-Gone clapped his hands. 'Pile it on!'

'But it's only straight to tell you that early this morning a sheriff, in hot pursuit of a car *real close* to matching the description of this one, ran off the road, though he might feel he was forced off.'

'Thas *ugly* news. Kind of thing might be misunderstood as attempted murder or some such bad shit.'

'However,' I went on, 'that was in the mountains of New Mexico, and like I say it was early this morning, and time *is* distance.'

Double-Gone nodded, but without conviction.

'And you'll notice in the backseat a box of about two hundred rock-and-roll records and a funny-looking sound system so powerful it'll cave in your skull.'

Double-Gone brightened. 'Thas better, yes, now we're back in the groove; thas the kinda music I *like* to hear.'

'*And*—'

'Do it to me!' Double-Gone urged.

I did. '*And* in the glovebox is a bottle of maybe nine hundred amphetamine tablets, factory fresh.'

'Great Lawd God o' Mercy!' Double-Gone shouted, palms raised heavenward in jubilant surrender. 'We best eat 'em up 'fo the Law seizes 'em as evidence.'

This struck me as enlightened strategy. Houston was still somewhere over the horizon, and I could feel exhaustion creeping in. Besides, as Double-Gone had astutely noted, there's no call to leave incriminating evidence lying around. We both took a small handful, though Double-Gone had big hands.

I lifted the box of records off the backseat and handed them over. 'You're the deejay.'

'Awright! I dig it! And now get ready fo' KRZY brain-blasting radio, the Reverend Double-Gone Johnson keeping the beat and whipping some o' that sweet gospel on yo' ears.'

'Well, Reverend Double-Gone,' I said, swinging the Caddy back onto the road, 'you're riding with Irreverent George: glad to have you aboard.'

'Five,' he laughed, extending his hand.

I took it. 'Now maybe between cuts you might explain your religious affiliations and the exact nature of your ministry, because I've never in my life seen such downtown vestments, nor a clergyman who gobbled bennies for communion. It's always been my understanding, and certainly my experience, that amphetamines are the Devil's work.'

Double-Gone snorted. 'Lord made the Devil to play with. *Made* it all, every thing and every being; *is* it *all*; and *will be* long past that blast on the clarion horn that lifts us up into the

Unending Light. What you gotta dig from the jump is there ain't no salvation lackin' some sin to salvage yo' ass from. Otherwise, we all be bored shitless and I'm outa work.'

'I'm ripe for conversion. What's the name of your church?'

Double-Gone groaned – at the forlorn hopelessness of my spiritual state, I thought at first. 'Man,' he sighed heavily, 'my whole life been a trouble with names.'

He elaborated as we ripped down the road, his baritone beating back whatever song was blaring from the speakers as I jammed the white lines together, thinning them into a shimmering string, still happily unaware that it led into the labyrinth, not out.

Double-Gone was going home to Houston after nine years of scuffling in LA. He'd taken off at fifteen, when his parents split up; Momma could no longer abide Daddy's drinking, and Daddy couldn't stand his nighttime janitor's job at the Texaco building without some lush. Double-Gone was the youngest child by six years; three older sisters were married and gone by the time his folks called it quits. 'No reason to hang anybody up,' he explained, 'Momma, Daddy, or me.'

Double-Gone wasn't his given name. '"Clement Avrial" is what they hung on me – after my granddaddy – but with all due respect fo' tradition, *Clem* jus don't make it. Sounds like yo' 'bout half a jump ahead of a dirt clod, with an IQ 'round room temperature. So when I cut for the coast I changed my name to Onyx . . . and dig, man, I was fifteen, wanted a little *flash* in my life. No sooner make LA than I latch up with this white hooker chick grabs her own kicks from tender young black boys like me. Right after we make it – and this is my first piece we talking about; my *cherry*, right? – and I'm still collapsed there on top, fuck-stunned and gaspin', she start up giggling like girls do and her giggling jus keeps growing till it's some *crazy* laughing. Ask her what it is, she laughs so hard it takes her a minute to strangle it out. "Onyx," she howls, and that *really* cracks her up. So there I am, can't figure my toes from my nose, my dick from a popsicle stick, but I do got one thing covered fo' sure, and that's that I don't want *no* name that's a joke I don't get. So I slid on out, got dressed, and found my way to the door. She's *still* laughing. Ah, women is a wonderful grief. Learned early on jus to love 'em and not worry on figuring 'em out. Different species. But how it is, you see, is the Lord don't make mistakes, just mysteries – and man, he made one fo' sure when he made women.

'Anyway, what I done was have *no* name. Hacked it back to plain Johnson. Decided if I couldn't dazzle 'em with bullshit, I'd hit 'em with mystery. Worked, too – snagged a bunch – 'course it mighta had more to do with my natural good looks and smooth moves. Tried to put a coupla girls to work, but LA is tight turf and mean streets, you understand? I stepped on some big toes inside hundred-dollar shoes and got my sixteen-year-old ass thumped good . . . or good enough to spend a few weeks in LA General eating through a straw. No *fun*, but it sorta opened my eyes by swelling 'em shut, you might say.

'When I limp outa General, I decide I be doin' it the American way. Got on at Denny's washing dishes graveyard. Rented me a room was so small you couldn't spring a decent boner without getting pressed up against a wall. Bagged enough plate scraping to keep my guts from greasing my backbone. Start at the bottom and work my way up – that's the plan, man. Read them Help Wanteds like a map to the City of Gold, and I took me a smile an' shoeshine to every interview, but they don't call it nigger work because there's a bunch o' white folks lining up to do it, I know yo' hep to that. I worked my way *sideways*, one shit job after another, till I looked in my wallet on my twentieth birthday and didn't have the jack for a free blowjob and a bottle o' Ripple both. Life's a groove, and thas the truth; but man, the bullshit can break ya down.

'So I start workin' the street again, *real careful* this time, penny-ante hustling. You know the gig: weed by the matchbox, numbers and nowhere cons, fencing stuff so hot it's third-degree burns jus lookin' at it. And when yo' margin's ten percent of alley discount, yo' lucky to get high fo' a night on what you clear on a diamond ring. I was being *bad*. Small-time bad. *Loser* bad. I was goin' down like one of them dinosaurs in the tar pit. Started lushing and joy-popping and sleeping where I fell. Couldn't get my soul up off the ground.

'But the evening of January seventh, jus last year, 'bout as down drunk as a man can be, I get lost going 'round the corner to the liquor store and end up right in front of this concrete building with a bitty purple neon cross 'bove this slab-oak door with a sign says BESSIE HARMON'S CHURCH OF ENDLESS JOY. I turn right around to make me a fast getaway from *that* shit but my lush feet get all tangled up and I go lurching 'gainst the door. And man, that door's *pulsating*. I press my ear on it and what do I hear but a hundred human voices rocking high up in the gospel. Push open the door into a room musky with rapture and full of shiny black faces all lifted heavenward in song, eyes closed, singing fo' all they worth, and right now, *wham!* the singing stops and Bessie Harmon grab the pulpit and cries out in that raw crystal trumpet voice, "Do you want to *feeeeellllllll* the *mighty, endless joy?*"

'A hundred hearts shout *yeah* with a single voice – a hundred *and one*, 'cause I figured it wouldn't hurt me none to feel a little myself, seeing as how I'd been short some lately.

'Bessie let the silence work a second, then say soft, matter o' fact, "Well, it's easy." Then she leans out over the pulpit, her sweet face shinning like a black moon, and whispers, 'All ya gotta do is *open* your *heart*.'

'I do like she said, opened up my ol' raggedy-ass heart, and the Light came *pouring* in, flooding me so full I overflowed on the spot. When the singing started again I was right up there with 'em, and I was dancin' in the aisle like a man who'd never be empty again.

'I went home with Miss Bessie herself that evening fo' some of her *personal* ministry, and she laid it on me as I laid her down:

"I seen 'em gone on the light and gone on the music, but yo' *double-gone*, Johnson, and I can't wait to get next to ya." I didn't hang her up, ya dig? And when she moaned out "O Lawd, Lawd, Lawd!" in that deep springwater voice, you *knew* He heard our human prayers, loud and clear.

'Bessie brought me into the Church and kept me at her place to continue her personal ministry. She started me reading the Bible and learning the hymns and jumpin' her bones when the spirit moved her – and she was a woman *full* of spirit, my-oh-fucking-my. You ever get a chance to hear that Bessie woman sing "Amazing Grace" lying naked on silk sheets, yo' liable to have yo'self a religious experience that whups the shit outa talking to angels.

'Bessie got me going on the preaching gig. Jus seemed to come to me on the natch, like it was waiting there all my life, lying low in the weeds. Bessie taught me high and godly preaching's one-part Bible, one-part style, and ninety-eight-parts heart and soul. I hear what she laying down. In five months she made me Assistant Minister of True Witness and cut me ten percent of the plate.

'End of the year we're packing 'em to the rafters. My job was warm-up . . . get the hellfire lickin' at their heels. I'd bring that powerful need down like a hammer, smash the lid open on all their sin and sickness, get 'em squirming with guilt and failure, and then Mama Bessie'd come on and vault they po' souls into heavenly bliss. But man, even though we *raking* in the bucks, I can't stand making 'em *sweat* like that, playing the heavy. *I* wanted to lift 'em up, but Bessie wasn't hearin' none of it. *I* wanted to add some electric guitar, a little bass, a taste of drums to the hymn singing. Bessie say no way and never happen. Plus she being a restless woman, she laying the hot-eye on this pretty-boy mulatto. I come home the other night, she says why don' I make myself *triple* gone fo' the evening, she had some emergency salvation work to do on Sammy – this mulatto cat, dig? – who was having some spiritual crisis in his pants. Now I'm a man who knows that when it's got to the point where yo' just standing in the way, it's time fo' *somebody* to make a move, so I hit the petty cash box on my way to the door.

'So here I am in downtown LA, old threads on my frame, nothing but this Bible Bessie gave me on my twenty-first birthday and three hundred and change to get me clear, standing on some nowhere corner at midnight with the bad blues in my heart and no clue what to do, when the Lord tells me plain as I'm telling you, "Go *home*, Double-Gone; go *home* and flourish." Now when the Lord speaketh, you *heedeth* – and pronto, my man. I'm choosing between a used car and some new threads, and I figured I couldn't get much of a short for three bills but I could boss up my wardrobe good, so I go for the clothes – Lord likes his evangels to be lookin' sharp, not like some low-rent Yankee philosopher or some such shit.

'So now *here* I am, almost *there*. What I got in mind fo' my old hometown of Houston is the world's first rock-and-roll church. Bring the Light down strong on the young so they *know* their bodies and souls are one, and joy ain't no sin, or not in *my* gospel. Should rack me some healthy in-come once we get rollin'. Maybe branch out with a couple of rib joints. Lord put me on it, so you know it's got to be good. Got that can't-miss feeling. I mean, there's three things *at least* that black folks do better than you whiteys ever dreamed of, and that'd be sing the blues, do ribs up right, and go to church.

'Which brings me smack-back to my troubles with names. "Double-Gone" got my personal handle covered, but now I need a name fo' my church. Something says *what it is* – you dig it? – and hooks 'em solid. Something wild, but cool too. Been twirling some around in my skull between rides. Let me whip out a couple, see what ya think. Dig this one: The Holy Writ Church of Awesome Joy. *Too* much, huh? Then let me lay down something else: The First Church of the Monster Rapture

Hits. "Monster" too *down*, ya think? Scare the kiddies? Well, here's something more quiet and smooth: The Full Soul Church of Pure Joy. How 'bout Soulful Church of Rocking Joy? The Rocking Joy Church of Atomic Gospel? You know, something *modern*.'

I stepped in with a suggestion. 'Why not keep it simple? Something like The Church of Faith?'

Double-Gone was offended. 'Thas too tight-ass white. No *pop* to it, man. You Unitarian or something?'

'All right, how about The Rock Faith Church of the Wild Shaking Light and Wall-Blowing Glory?'

'Now yo' at least *breathin*.'

That encouraged me. 'Okay now, hang on: The Whirlpool Church of Undreamable Felicity.'

'Hey now! Whoa up, mule! What's this "Felicity"? That the same chick I knew in Watts with them tight pink shorts spray-painted on an ass guaranteed to make yo' heart stand still?'

'Just another word for happiness,' I explained.

''Deed she was, but I don't want no congregation where you gotta put a motherfuckin' dictionary in the hymnal.'

'Well,' I said, 'you should look for a name in what *you* actually feel. It's your church, right? Something like The Open-Heart Church of the Flooding Light.'

'Thought of that,' Double-Gone said, 'but "open-heart"? "Floodlight?" Sounds like serious surgery. But I dig yo' drift. Now check this out: The Gospel Wallop Church of Eternal Bliss.'

We went on and on, riffing back and forth, a playful speed-rave ring-shout, trading solos over whatever tune he'd dropped on the box. Nothing stuck, but we had fun.

The sun was trying to come up when we stopped for fuel and donuts at a Gas Mart outside Austin. Frost sparkled on the oil-stained cement of the pump bays. The donuts were stale the week before, so we ate some more speed to cut the grease. I was beginning to feel gone and gritty. The pale dawnlight scratched my raw eyes, and my neck and shoulder muscles felt torqued down tighter than the nut on the Caddy's flywheel. I needed a long hot bath and a good day's sleep. I was looking forward to Houston.

Double-Gone was shuffling records as we fishtailed off the frost-slick on-ramp back onto the highway and I took it up to cruising speed, the needle locked solid between the nine and the zero.

'This indeed be the Lord's bounty,' Double-Gone chuckled, tipping a record to read the label in the strengthening light. 'Yes, oh yes! Head full o' volts and some good boogie fo' the box and a short so boss it could be the Lord's chariot driving to the Pearly Gates. I catch what yo' doing besides some widow's memorial gift or some such?'

'The memorial is the paper cover. And she was a spinster, not a widow. I'm delivering it to the man who moved her. You're holding him in your hands there someplace: the Big Bopper.'

'The Bopper?' Double-Gone looked dubious. 'Thought the Bopper went down with Holly and that Valens cat.'

'Exactly. He died just before she was going to ship this Caddy here off to him. Had it all crated up and ready to go. Put it in a warehouse when she got the sad news.'

'Man, that is *sad*.' Double-Gone patted the dash consolingly. 'Machine like you all caged up in some dark corner.'

'Then when *she* died,' I continued, 'her jerk-off nephew scored it from the estate.'

'Yo' breaking my heart.'

'The nephew's up to his nuts in gambling debts. He and this low-life by the name of Scumball – he's the brains – insured it at top value as a mint collector's item or cultural artifact or some damn thing, and I was supposed to make it look like Grand Theft Auto before I totaled it.'

'You *wreck*, they *co*-lect – that the gig?'

'That *was* the gig. I stole it and kept going. And here we are.'

'I'm digging it.' Double-Gone nodded. 'And speaking as a humble servant of the Lord, my heart tells me it's righteous in His eyes.'

'Glad you and the Lord agree.'

''Course I don't feature the Law's gonna pump yo' paw and give you a good-ol'-boy slap on the back and cut you loose, 'cause there be good reasons that lady holding the scales got a blindfold over her eyes. And those two cats back home prob'ly ain't over*whelmed* with joy . . . 'fact, maybe they dialing the number gets answered by the kinda people like to hear bones snap.'

'Yup, that's the kind of noise they made when I told them how it was, but I got the goods to take 'em down with me, and I made *real sure* they understood how it was.'

'That is: *if* yo' alive. But say these goons wreck you *and* this lovely chunk of automotion? *They* collect and *yo'* be wrecked.'

'First they have to find me, then they have to catch me.'

'And they don't know where yo' going to, right?'

Oh, fuck! Harriet's letter. Cory Bingham had read it, and I told Scumball I was taking the Caddy where it belonged. How specific had I been? But the sudden dark lash of dread-squeezed adrenalin had locked the memory vault.

'Yo' looking ill,' Double-Gone pointed out.

'Well, they *might* figure it out, but I'd call it long odds on short money.'

'These cats connected?'

'Connected to what?'

'I mean,' Double-Gone said patiently, 'do they have friends, family, or business associates here in the Lone Star state that Ma Bell could put 'em onto faster than even you can drive?'

'I don't know. One of them, maybe. But hey, they're looking to take in forty or fifty grand at the outside, and that's an expensive effort you're talking about.'

Double-Gone was shaking his head. 'I know some cats whose souls so twisted they'd snuff you for a six-pack and the giggle. Cats like that everywhere. Then you got those jus out to make a name or impress the Man. It ain't *always* the money; the Man's got to save face an' set good examples fo' the boys.'

'Reverend, you're not lifting my spirits.'

'First yo' spirit gotta understand *what is*. We ain't jus talking 'bout yo' ass, dig? What about the Bopper's people? You give 'em this fine automobile, you might be givin' 'em the gift o' grief.'

'Wait a second,' I said, sensing the misunderstanding, 'I'm taking it to the Bopper himself.'

Double-Gone blinked. 'Say what?'

'The Big Bopper. I'm delivering this car to *him*, with love from Harriet, ashes to ashes and dust to dust.'

'The Bopper *dead*, man, crashed and burned.'

'I'm hip.'

Maybe my tone was a little sharp, because Double-Gone's response was icy on the edges. 'Well now, you *hip* that the dead *can't drive?*'

I laughed with relief. 'Listen, I forgot you don't have the whole picture, and damn near forgot I do. See, what I'm up to is this: I deliver the Eldorado here to the Bopper's *grave*, soak it down with a gallon of high-test, stand on the hood while I read Harriet's letter – kind of a eulogy – and then it's up in flames.'

Double-Gone pinned me with a bulge-eyed stare: 'Yo' *sick*, man.'

'Ah,' I replied, 'but wait: I not only deliver this lost gift of love, and honor the power of music to move us and complete another connection in the Holy Circuit, but my two scuzzy friends also collect their insurance money.'

'I'm hearing you, but *they* don't know that. Far as they know, you got it parked on Sunset and Vine with a FOR SALE sign taped up in the window.'

'Wrong,' I said. 'They *do* know it. I told them I'd wreck it, but it was going to take a little longer than usual.'

'Why sure,' Double-Gone took on a look of feigned innocence, 'they ain't saying to themselves, "Well here's a speed-cranking daddy with a two-monkey habit running loose with our fifty-G pay-off machine, our income fo' sure on the line and, should the Law come down, maybe our asses, but George say *be cool, don't worry*, and you know ol' George wouldn't think of anything like a paint-and-plate job or a side-street discount or even keeping it stashed somewhere fo' a steady blackmail income. Naw, shit man: we trust ol' George. Sure, we'll do like he say and hang here cool and make no whatsoever effort to bust his fucking chops."'

'Double-Gone, I got the perfect name for your church: The Come-Down Tabernacle of the Grim View.'

'Lord give us eyes so we could dig it *all*, not jus what we *want* to see. Besides, man, it breaks my po' heart to picture this fine, high-styled piece of fast machinery wasted in flames. And it would be double-sadder, a true burden o' sorrow, if you happened to be sacked up in the trunk.'

'Wasn't that long ago you said what I'm doing is righteous in the eyes of the Lord.'

'No doubt about it, but being righteous ain't no excuse fo' bein' dumb.'

'You think I'm being dumb?'

Double-Gone nodded once solemnly. ''Fraid I'd have to cop to that.'

'Well, man, looking at it through the Lord's eyes, tell me a smarter way.'

Double-Gone grinned. 'Now George, you *know* I never claimed to that. Only total fools think they looking through the Lord's eyes. Ain't you never dug the Book of Job?' He slapped the Bible on the seat between us. I felt the sermon coming.

'Now ol' Job was a truly righteous cat with all this wide-flung real estate and livestock and a loving wife, not to mention seven boss sons and three daughters so good lookin' make yo' teeth chatter.

'But Satan hanging around the scene, strutting to and fro in the earth and bopping up and down. Lord spots him and says, "Hey Satan, dig my servant Job. He loves me like he should and does no evil."

'Satan says, "Well sure, no shit and no wonder: you got him *covered up* with goodies. Take *them* away and Job'll spit in yo' eye."

'Lord knows that's jive, so he tells Satan, "Do what you want to convince yo'self – just don't touch his flesh."

'No sooner said than Satan lays it on Job hard: sends these goons to rustle the mules; drops a gob of fireballs on the servants and sheep; blows a horrible wind outa the mountains that flattens the eldest son's house where the sons and daughters partying and they *all* wasted. Now what do you think Job says to all this ruination and heavy grief? He say, "The Lord *gave*, and the Lord *taketh* away. *Blessed* be the name o' the Lord."

'The Lord's loving it. He tells Satan, "Hey, I told you my man was cool."

'But Satan comes back with the big scoff: "Well fuck, why not? Didn't hurt *him* none. You put some pain on Job's own frame, he'll curse yo' name as a ratprick bastard; can count on it."

'The Lord tells Satan, "Go ahead; his ass is yours – jus spare his life is all."

'Now Satan's got it tight when it comes to putting the serious torment on folks, and he smotes Job with horrible pus-bubbling boils from wig to toes. It's an agony so hard makes piss dribble down yo' leg. Job's wife flips out when she digs the pain he's in. She tells him, "Job, curse the Lord and die. This ain't making it."

'But Job don't budge. Tells her to hush her fool mouth. Tells her, "Shall we receive good at the hand o' God, and shall we not receive evil?"

'Then a bunch of Job's buddies shows up to comfort him. Job's all naked and pus-runny and covered with ashes, and when they clock how monstrous his hurt be, none of 'em can speak fo' seven *days*. But Job's boils eatin' him up something fierce, and he commences to snivel and bad mouth ever being born, and generally lays it down that he's a righteous cat that never crossed the Lord and can't believe he's done *anything* to deserve such bad action. But dig this close: he don't ask the Lord to *end* the suffering. *No*. All he prays for is the *strength* to endure it. *That's* righteous.

'But his buddies be getting in his shit, saying stuff like, "Job, my man, you *musta* sinned else the Lord wouldn't be on yo' case. 'Or like, "You getting worked over for thinkin' Job mo' righteous than the Lord."

'Job calls 'em what you been calling me: "miserable comforters." But he won't cop to being a sinner 'cause it ain't the truthful fact. His buddies all whipping on him hard, telling him to repent and trust the Lord and Job's jawing right back at Elihu and Eliphaz and Bildad and them other cats to bug off, he ain't got nothin' to repent for, always trusted and obeyed the Lord, and near as he can dig he's getting fucked over fo' no reason.

'Then all of a sudden – *bam!* – the Lord's voice comes roaring out the whirlwind, and He gets *down*. What he lays on Job and his buddies runs like this: "Maybe yo' getting fucked over – but hey, yo' mine to fuck. *I am the Lord!* You get whatever it is you get and what you get is yours, high times or bad blues, good luck or tough shit. I gotta maintain a harmony so far beyond yo' experience that it's fucking *pathetic*."

'But jus to make sure, the Lord lays it down in all His beautiful sweetness and light, puts it right in their faces: "Do *you* know the treasures of the snow? Do *you* make the tender buds open in bloom? Is it *you* that feeds the baby lions? *You* that makes sure the ravens have food or divide the waters so them big ol' hippos have rivers to loll in? Can *you* bind the sweet influences of the

Pleiades, or loose the bands of Orion?" Ooowheeeee, I love that one – he's talking *stars*, man. And the Lord goes wailing on: "Is it *you* that lets the heart understand? Did you give yo'*self* life? Do you *really* think you knowing better than me what's what and what ain't? That you got more than a few pitiful clues what it's all about? What *I am*? Well, get hip: no fuckin' way."

'Now when a man lays it down, liable as not it'll bounce back up in his face. But when the *Lord* lays it down, it *stays* down – and Job, he copped on the spot, saying "I was blind, but now mine eyes doth see. Do what Thou wilt. I can dig it."

'So the Lord healed his boils *like that* and no scars neither, and gave Job back *double* all his camels and she-asses and other livestock, plus ten *more* children – seven boys so tall and strong they coulda whupped ass on the Celtics, and three daughters *so fine* you immediately jump to hard. And if that wasn't fair enough, He let Job live another hundred and forty years so he could play with all his grandchildren and *their* children and on and on like that fo' many sweet and swinging generations till Job cashed out, being old and full o' days.'

I spoke right up: 'How does that make me dumb? You didn't hear me claiming I saw through the Lord's eyes either, did you?'

'See?' Double-Gone sounded exasperated. 'Yo' taking it *personal*. Yo' putting yo'self in the way. Point is, don't even *try* to understand the Lord's will; jus follow.'

'I'm hearing you,' I said – a little testily, I suppose – 'and I'm *all* for it. I guess *I* don't know what His will happens to be.'

'Finest thing that Bessie woman ever preached me was "quit trying and stop denying." *Feel* it. Feel it like you feel music. Like you feel sunlight on yo' skin. Like it feel when you lie down with a sweet-lovin' woman. I swear, you white folks damn near a lost cause.'

'Not much I can do about the color of my soul,' I said, jaws tight.

'You know why the Lord gave black folks so much soul?' Double-Gone asked, his tone suddenly playful.

I wasn't feeling playful. 'No. Why?'

'To make up fo' what he did to our hair.' His dazzling smile, combined with the pink flash of his hat, almost made my raw eyes water. ''Course,' Double-Gone continued, 'it ain't really the color o' the soul that matters, though having some cultural heritage is a mighty help when it comes to feeling the spirit move.'

What I was feeling again was the babble rising in my brain so bad I wanted to scream. But I took a deep breath. 'You still haven't told me how I'm being dumb.'

'George,' Double-Gone said quietly, 'yo' being dumb because you getting in yo' own way. You dumb because you got the man and the music confused. You dumb because you got so high an' mighty on yo' own righteousness that you didn't cover yo' ass – them others be foolish dumb, but that's *dangerous* dumb, getting so sucked up in yo' own wild wonderfulness that you don't take care of business. The Bopper buried in Houston?'

The question, erupting in the litany of my idiocies, caught me by embarrassed surprise. 'Well, you know, actually I'm not sure where he's buried,' I hemmed, then hawed, 'I assume Sabine Pass – that's his hometown – or maybe Beaumont.'

'But you don't know for sure.' This wasn't a question.

'I've been moving fast lately.'

'Not knowing where you going – tell me that ain't dumb. Lazy dumb. You think jus 'cause you on the journey that the Lord gonna do *all* the work?'

'No,' I agreed. 'I was calling it "sloppy dumb" to myself right before I saw you standing beside the road, that hat of yours warming the night.'

'Hope to shout. Be a little awkward turns out the Bopper's sixed in San Jose. But I'd imagine those two cats you cut on know jus where to send them flowers. People like that pay some mind to details; them that don't, they pay the dues.'

'Gotcha, man, loud and clear. But you're telling me what I already know, which maybe isn't much for a dummy like me. Tell me a smarter way. I'm all ears.'

Double-Gone shifted his weight slightly and leaned toward me. 'I was you, *no way* I'd get near the Bopper's grave. I dig *high*, and I groove on *risk*, but when I see 'em together, like in *high risk*, I stop for a close look, and what I be looking fo' is a way around it.'

'Not much glory in that,' I said. This sounded poor, but it usually does when you're defending your ignorance.

'George,' Double-Gone said sadly; 'even money says goons be waiting at the grave to hand you yo' ass on a platter and bring yo' little romance to an ugly end. You go on ahead and you liable to join the Bopper, and on yo' stone they'll chisel, "This man *looked* to suffer."'

I felt the first brush of a hustle. 'And what are *you* looking for?' I asked as pointedly as possible.

'Man,' Double-Gone huffed, 'don't shine the light on me when I'm sneaking up. Breaks my rhythm.'

'Even money says it has something to do with confusing the man and the music.'

'You on the beat, George. You do dig I don't got my heart in it to *push* the point – I don't like bad-mouthing the dead, 'specially if they was so wild alive – but I don't think the Bopper's yo' man. Got my reasons. Number one is like I say: if they gonna hit ya, his grave's the place. Number two, I ain't convinced the Bopper deserves it. That's cold, I know, but there it is. He only made it once, and that was some diddley novelty number with fun and joy, but nothing *deep*. Here, let me drop it on the box and you can hear—'

'No need,' I cut in. 'I heard it already and I'm hearing you. But I'm not delivering it to the Bopper as a reward for musical excellence or a pack-train of hits; I'm delivering it because it was *meant* for him, Harriet to the Bopper, soul to soul, the way love's supposed to be.'

'Now you jus *got* to know that ain't true.' Double-Gone was adamant. 'That spinster woman never laid eyes on the cat. He sneak up and do her doggie-style in the dark, she wouldn't even know it was the Bopper's bop.'

'She was moved by his music. That's good enough for me.'

'Hallelujah brother, I'm hearing *that*. But you got to ask yo'self jus where that music coming from.'

'Says on the label he's singing it and playing it and that he wrote it, so I'd say it's his.'

'You mistaking the flower fo' the root,' Double-Gone gently chided. 'Where you think rock-and-roll come from?'

I was getting annoyed. 'Hey, I never claimed to know jackshit about music.'

'That a fact?' Double-Gone was polite. 'Well, you remember me playing Elvis doing "Don't Be Cruel," right?'

'Yeah,' I said, wary.

'And Elvis doing "All Shook Up"?'

'Yeah.'

'Jerry Lee working out on "Great Balls of Fire"?'

'Yeah.'

'Any idea who wrote those numbers?'

'No.'

'Black cat name o' Otis Blackwell.'

'Otis does good work.' I was getting the point.

'Remember "Hound Dog," monster hit fo' Elvis? Black woman named Mama Thornton did that song early on, long 'fore Elvis's pouty face and cute wiggle came on TV and got so many teenybop panties damp that America's daddies was scared shitless their daughters was gonna crawl out in the yard and howl at the moon.'

I smiled at the image, but I wasn't talking – mainly because this was obviously a time to listen.

Double-Gone continued, 'You ever heard of T-Bone Walker? Joe Turner? Sonny Boy Williamson? Big Bill Broonzy? Mississippi John Hurt?'

'Can't say I have.'

'They were playing the rock-on blues and paying some nasty dues when Elvis was still a gleam in his daddy's eye.'

'Double-Gone,' I said, growing tired, 'I told you out front I don't know shit about music. I spent my youth turning wheels and chasing truck-stop waitresses. Didn't even have a fucking radio in any of my rigs.'

'But what you don't know *either*,' Double-Gone said with surprising vehemence, 'is when the *need* could arise. Little knowledge maybe give you some angle on the action, help you see yo' way clear of mean trouble, spare yo' heart some grief. That's why I'm hipping you to the straight fact that if you follow rock music back down the tracks, yo' traveling through rhythm an' blues, plain ol' dirt blues, jazz music, back-porch jugband, field-hollers, an' right on to the heart of 'em all, music born in the simple joy and hurt of living, and thas *gospel* music. You travel back to them raw human voices lifted up in praise an' pain, yo' gonna see a *trillion* black faces never been on no TV, never heard no big concert crowd go crazy, never rode in no fine cars, didn't never see fucking *penny one* fo' pouring their souls empty, and never broke faith when their music was stole.'

'Double-Gone,' I said, 'that's a righteous claim, delivered with honest passion and high eloquence, but you're not getting this Cadillac.'

'But man' – he smiled hugely – 'I'd look so *gooood* cruising the street – that'd be after I arranged for some changes in paint and I.D. numbers, new plates and paper.'

'You did it to yourself. If you hadn't got me so paranoid about Scumball running me down, I wouldn't feel so responsible.' That much was true, but the unspoken reason was even simpler, and one I'm sure he both understood and appreciated: it was mine to deliver, not his.

Double-Gone was all sympathy. 'Responsibility is a heavy burden, brother. Let me take this load off yo' hands.'

'It isn't gonna happen,' I told him. 'You know that.'

'George, you jus jumpin' on my little joke there about copping it fo' my *personal* use. Not so. Far too hot fo' a new cat in town. I was gonna pass it on to Chuck Berry or Otis Blackwell or Mama Thornton or somebody nobody ever heard of singing his heart out in the choir.'

'Nope. That'd just transfer the grief you're so certain is coming my way. Hate to see Chuck Berry or any of them busted up over this sweet Eldorado.'

'I wasn't jivin' on that, George. I think they'll be looking fo' *you*, and if they do some *finding*, you liable to get messed around.'

'And I know you weren't jiving about the music,' I said in an attempt at graciousness. 'The music belongs to its makers.'

'Yeah, thas true, but the thing is I didn't take it far enough. See now, gospel music don't *belong* to black folks. We just hear it best. Gospel music, rock music, Beethoven music, country music, *all* that music rightfully belong to the Holy Ghost. That Harriet woman, she feel her love *through* the music. Jus happened to be the Bopper's, may his high soul rock on fo'ever, but when you get down to the nitty-gritty, it belong to the Holy Ghost. You want some burnt offering, light a candle fo' love on the stone altar, thas fine. But if it's crowded at the Bopper's grave – you hearing me? – you can always deliver it right to the Holy Ghost. He'll see the Bopper gets it.'

I started to reply when Double-Gone suddenly held up a palm for silence. His hand was trembling. '*Got it!*' he rejoiced. 'The Lord – bless Him! – just spoke it aloud smack-dab in the center of my brain. Now get a good grip on the wheel there, George, 'cause here it is: THE ROCK SOLID GOSPEL LIGHT CHURCH OF THE HOLY RELEASE!'

'I love it,' I said, glad to share his joy, and no sooner had I spoken than a voice – though it sounded like my own – spoke in my addled brain, saying, *If not to his grave, to the place he died*, and a whole new possibility opened: the enlargement of the gesture to include Ritchie Valens for Donna and Buddy Holly for the millions who loved him and, yes, for the Holy Ghost, too. Considering Double-Gone's warning that Scumball might have some rotten friends waiting for me at the Bopper's grave, it made better sense to deliver the Caddy to the site of the plane crash itself, let the gift honor them all and at the same time cut the risk.

I told Double-Gone. '*Yes!*' he shouted. 'Thas fox-solid smart. Didn't I tell yo' disbelieving ass the Lord got us covered? *Didn't I jus finish preaching the Book o' Job to open yo' ears to His whirlwind voice?* O mercy, mercy, and hallelujah to the Holy Ghost, you jus got the Lord's Word plain as fucking day, jammed up and jelly-tight, jus like He spoke the name of my church in my ear.'

'Hold on,' I cautioned. 'I don't mean to doubt, but I'd have to say I didn't hear the voice real clear. Might've been me babbling to myself.'

'George,' Double-Gone warned, 'take His blessings as they flow.'

'I'm just not sure it *was* the Lord.'

'*Had to be*. I know, 'cause he jus got done talkin' to me, whippin' that fine name on my brain. Figured long as He was on the scene, help you out too – Lord don't waste a move, dig, and the way we haulin' ass He didn't want to run us down twice.' I must've looked as dubious as I felt, because Double-Gone kept on. 'You making a mistake here, George my man. Don't mess yo'self around heaping doubt on what comes down. You hear what I'm saying? Do you?'

'Count your blessings.' It seemed clear enough.

'Not count 'em like nickels, no. Take 'em in *deep*. *Dig* 'em. *Use* 'em. *Ride* 'em over the mountain. And most of all, the *very most* of all, give something *back*. Keep that juice movin' down the wire. Keep that voice raised in prayer and praise. Reflect the Holy Spirit's bounteous generosity, make His abundance yo' own. Reach down in yo' soul's bankroll and peel off what you think's *right*.'

'When I heard that sweet name of your church, Reverend, I knew nothing was going to make me happier than offering a small donation toward making it real . . . call it an investment in the faith.'

'Now what's *this?* I didn't see no collection plate passing by.'

'Only because you can't afford one yet. You'll need a collection plate and rough-hewn wood for a cross and maybe a month's rent on a storefront where you can gather your flock.'

'You don't mind me prying,' Double-Gone asked, 'what was yo' piece of this car wreck action?'

'Four grand, half up front, which is the only half I'll ever see.'

'If my math'matics ain't failing me, thas two thousand.'

'Minus expenses,' I reminded him. 'The paper was free from a friend, but bennies, gas, food, and motel rooms add up, plus I bought this record collection from a woman in Arizona for four hundred.'

Double-Gone jackknifed like he'd been kicked in the guts. 'Ooooo, it *hurts* to hear that sum went down fo' this pile o' vinyl. Got its moments fo' sure, but I damn near come to gagging seen it all cluttered up with this Pat Boone and Fabian and Frankie Avalon.' He chuckled. 'That woman musta done you right . . . right up one side and down the other.'

'She needed it. Tap City, with two kids.'

'Uh-huh. So you down to twelve bills or thereabouts?'

'Thereabouts.'

'Well, half would seem about right. Spirit ain't cheap, you dig that, I know.'

'Is it tax deductible?'

'Now what's this shit? Spirit don't charge no taxes, man — just dues.'

I had an impulse. 'Way I understand it, standard tithe is ten percent, but since you're double-full of the spirit, I'll double it up. So let's say two and a half. *But*, you got to throw in your hat.'

'Man,' Double-Gone grimaced, 'you *hard*. From six bills to two-fifty, plus my lid. And what you want it fo'? Just pale you out worse than you already are.'

'I like it,' I said.

'Me *too*, man — thas why I *bought* it.'

'Two hundred, then. I'll use the fifty bucks to buy my own. Should be able to get one *easy* for fifty.'

'George my man, why you want to do me like this? I put my best preachin' on ya. Practical *salvation*. You be headed right to Goon City if I hadn't put you straight. And do you *deep down* think the Lord be talkin' to you if he wasn't already on His way down to lay The Rock Solid Gospel Light Church of Holy Release on his faithful servant here?'

'That's why it's two-fifty *and* the hat.'

Double-Gone glared down the road, muttering, making a show of it — then, with a big double groan, took off his hat and handed it over. I put it on. He watched me, shaking his head as I admired it in the rearview mirror. 'Don't make it, George. Not an inch.'

'What I *really* dig is the color,' I said. 'Looks like a flamingo getting hit with a million volts.'

'Ruint my color coordination,' Double-Gone grumbled. 'Feel *de*frocked. I jus' don't think I can abide this, George; takes away from the man I *am*, dig? Man's got to feel good about himself. Now it might make me feel better — fact, I *know* it would — if you throw in some of them go-fast pills.'

'Leave me a hundred. And Double-Gone? No more sniveling.'

'You right. You did me. It's down, done, gone, and forgotten.' He gave a forlorn little wave in the direction of my head. 'Bye, you boss top. Wear him well. And now, 'bout that charitable contribution . . .'

We jammed on down the line as Double-Gone counted out 100 hits of speed for me and the rest for him, which he stashed with the money in a secret pocket in his cape. Then he leaned back, smiling. 'You a strange cat, George; good, but strange. Just can't figure where the fuck you at.'

'Twenty miles out of Houston, closing fast.'

'You know that ol' truth, you can run but you can't hide? I'd pay some mind to that.'

'Get thee behind me, Satan.' I smiled when I said it.

'George,' Double-Gone said tenderly, 'I'm behind you all the way. Thas why I'd like to see you make it.'

'Faith, Reverend.'

'There it is.' Double-Gone grinned.

We parted company a half-hour later at the steps of the Houston Public Library where, taking Double-Gone's advice to heart, I intended to do my research. In farewell I told him, 'You preach that solid rock gospel light, Reverend Double-Gone. I hope you and your flock flourish till you're all so fat with blessings you curl up and die of happiness, old and full of days.'

Double-Gone graced me with a stylish benediction, though it was difficult to tell if it was the sign of the cross or a Z hacked in the air by some bebop, speed-gobbling Zorro. 'George, I want you to get it done, my man. Now you get *on* the beat and *stay* on it, hear?'

I waved and started up the steps when his baritone, calling my name, turned me around. He pointed his right index finger straight at my head. 'And George: hang onto yo' hat.'

I wasn't sure whether to take his words as a stern injunction to guard his recent and rightful property or as a graceful acknowledgment that he was letting it go. Either way, I decided, was fine. Later I realized both readings were wrong. The Good Reverend was neither admonishing nor releasing; it was pure, rock-solid gospel-light prophecy.

A heavy-tongued church bell began to toll, its resonance muffled in the rev and honk of downtown morning traffic. I hit the library right on the beat – a short, lean black man in work khakis was just unlocking the door. He held it open for me as I entered, his sharp brown eyes flicking upward to check out my stingy-brim.

I stopped and turned around. 'Good morning, sir,' I said. 'I'm a wondering scholar just wandering through and have found myself with an urgent need for some reliable information about a plane crash that sadly claimed the lives of some notable musicians on the third day of February, 1959.'

'Reference Desk be to yo' right, sir.' He pointed mechanically.

I leaned in close and lowered my voice: 'What do you think?'

'Beg yo' pardon, sir?' he asked nervously.

'I noticed you checking out my new hat.' I tugged the brim down a notch. 'What do you think?'

He shrugged his bony shoulders, his eyes looking steadily past me. 'Don't think nothin' in particular. Brightly colorful, fo' sure. But that's jus looking, not thinking.'

'Do you think it possesses that elusive quality known as *soul*?'

'None that jumps right on me ... but then that's rightfully something fo' you to be thinking on.'

'That's interesting,' I said. 'I bought it because it was *beyond* thought. And also for the practical reason that I need something to reinforce my skull in case my brain blows.'

He looked in my eyes and said in a forceful whisper, 'You either messed up on drugs or natch'ly crazy – not sure which, don't care – but you fo' sure looking trashed and sour, so you might think about wandering *on*, 'cause you don't be *cool*, you gonna *lose*. This library don't tol'rate no misbehaving. You be covered with *po*lice yo' first wrong move. Got that?'

'Got it. I want information, not trouble,' I assured him, disconcerted that my playfulness had obviously hit him wrong.

He slipped the key from the door lock and, as he turned to face me, snapped it back on his belt. ''Nother thing: *fuck* yo' hat.'

'Hold on. I apologize for crowding you. I only meant to be friendly, but I guess I'm just a little too giddy and excited and exhausted. Been a wild ride.'

'I jus bet it has. Now if you'll 'scuse me, I got work to do.'

'That's why I'm here, too.' I smiled. 'So let's get on with it.'

'Mind yo'self,' he called over his shoulder.

I did, being absolutely sweet and professional with the reference librarian, a middle-aged brunette who went out of her way to be helpful. I went through everything she dug up, mostly news-paper clips with the same wire-service stories, plus a couple of record industry journals and a few paragraphs in music histories. Subtracting the duplications, there wasn't much, but the one thing I *had* to know – the location of the crash – I found right away. However, I stayed with it like a serious pilgrim, and my diligence was rewarded: the Big Bopper was buried in Beaumont. I'd been on the track all the way.

When I left the library two hours later, I was a bunch less dumb but also twice as depressed, sorely pissed, more determined, strangely fearful, and – still in seeming accord with the Lord's will – completely confused, especially about what my next move should be. I slid behind the Caddy's wheel and turned the key. Then I decided *Nope, no more wasted motion*, and shut it down. I leaned back in the seat and shut my eyes, took seven deep breaths, slid my stingy-brim down to cover my face, and considered the general mess.

For openers, I was better informed, and that was to my favor. I knew within a few square miles where I was going – certainly an improvement – and I had a fairly solid idea of the events surrounding the crash.

The chartered plane had left the Mason City airport at 1:00 A.M. headed for Fargo, North Dakota. It was snowing and cold, but nowhere near a blizzard. The plane evidently crashed shortly after take-off, for when the flight was overdue in Fargo the owner of the charter service took another plane up to search and spotted the wreckage northwest of the Mason City airport in a snow-crusted field of corn stubble. Around 11:30 that morning the coroner arrived to confirm what the extent of the wreckage made obvious, that the four people aboard were dead: Buddy Holly, 22; Ritchie Valens, 17; J. P. Richardson (aka the Big Bopper), 27; and the pilot, Roger Petersen, 21. According to the wire service reporter, the plane was no longer recognizable as such, and the victims' identities were impossible to determine without extensive lab work.

I was depressed as much by my morbid imagination as by the bare sadness of their deaths. Sitting there in the bright, warm library, everything neatly organized, I'd felt for a horrible moment the gut-wrenching fear as the plane plunged, heard the begging, blurted prayers as the earth whirled up to meet them, all possible future of their music lost in the instant of impact, from life to death in the span of a heartbeat, just like Eddie.

They shouldn't have been flying to Fargo, in a plane they'd chartered themselves, but they didn't have much choice. For six days they'd been living on piece-of-shit buses without adequate heaters during a mean Midwestern winter. The tour, in fact, was billed as the Winter Dance Party. Six days on a cold, slow bus. Six days, six gigs, and drive away whipped. Trying to sleep sitting up half-frozen in the seats; kidneys punished by shocks that had turned to jello 30,000 miles before; sick from exhaust leaks; wearing clothes that hadn't been laundered since who could remember when. The Big Bopper, nursing a bad cold, broke down and bought a sleeping bag to keep warm. Finally

Buddy Holly decided to charter a plane along with two of his band members, Waylon Jennings and Tommy Allsup, and fly ahead to Fargo, get everyone's stage clothes laundered, and log a night of true sleep in a hotel room with the heater turned up high. The Big Bopper, whose frame matched his name, found the cramped seats particularly unbearable and persauded his buddy Waylon to give up his seat on the flight. At the last moment, Ritchie Valens wanted to go, and pestered Tommy Allsup into flipping a coin to decide who would get the last seat. Allsup reluctantly agreed, but only if he got to use the Bopper's sleeping bag if he lost. Ritchie called heads, and heads it was.

The promoters of the Winter Dance Party, Super Enterprises and General Artists Corporation, evidently believed good business is best defined – as it so often is in this country – by fat black ink on the bottom line. You want to fatten the take, you cut frills like heaters in the tour bus, laundry, or an occasional open date for rest somewhere among those all-night bus rides between Milwaukee, Kenosha, Eau Claire, Duluth, Green Bay, and all the other exhausting points along the way. Fair profit from able dealing is one thing; exploitive greed, that gluttony of heart and ego, starves everything near it as it buries its face in the trough. When you wrong the people who make the music, you wrong the music; and if Double-Gone had it right, if the music does belong to the Holy Spirit, you wrong the Holy Spirit, too. You fuck-over the Spirit, you deserve what you finally get.

My cold, vengeful anger and the freshened sadness at their deaths inspired me to honor their lives and music, and I was glad Buddy Holly and Ritchie Valens were now included. Mine was a tooth-sunk, jawlocked, bulldog determination, the kind that makes you die trying. But I feared that determination, not only because I was afraid of dying, trying or otherwise, but also because I didn't really understand my deepened resolve. I wanted to deliver the gift and slip away. There was no need for the further entanglement of these interior motives. Just as we can disguise greed as ambition, we can dress obsession as necessity. I was afraid of not knowing which was which, afraid of losing the thread of my purpose. I was afraid I would be equally destroyed by certainty and doubt.

I sat there with my hat over my face, trying in vain to think my way through this new confusion. At last I decided motion was best, that I'd take three beans and I-35 up through Dallas and on past Oklahoma City to Posthole Joe's Truck Stop Cafe, where I'd see if Joe still made the best chicken-fried steak on the twenty-four thousand miles of Interstate that used to be my home. I'd be hungry by then if I laid off the speed, and I intended to do just that. I was already out on the fried, jittery edge, just asking for it, and I didn't want to waste myself on what amounted to crazed recreation. I had to get tougher.

A plan took shape. After Posthole's chicken-fried steak with biscuits and gravy, I'd maybe take four more – but *no* more – hits of speed for dessert, and then ride on up to Kansas City, Kansas City here I come. From KC to Des Moines was only about a 2½ hour run, and I could do that with my eyes closed if I had to. But I didn't have to, I reminded myself. I'd sleep if I got tired. But it was mighty tempting to think that if I kept at it I could be soaking in a hot bath by midnight. After that, a solid eight hours of shut-eye, a good breakfast, then an hour's drive up to Mason City and the crash site, rested and sharp for the ceremony.

I cranked up the Eldorado and got rolling, my eyes literally peeled for that elusive sign that would read 35 NORTH: DALLAS, POSTHOLE JOE'S, K.C., DES MOINES, MASON CITY, CRASH SITE, DELIVERY, AND MAMA ON DOWN THE LINE, a sign made even more elusive by the design of downtown Houston, yet another city where the traffic engineers evidently take their professional inspiration from barbecue sauce dribbled across a local map. To find a fast lane pointing north took me ten minutes, so I put my foot in it to make up for lost time.

The day was clear and bright, but the temperature seemed to plummet as the sun climbed. From Dallas to Oklahoma City is a flat, straight shot, with nothing much to entertain the eye except the oil rigs looming like huge skeletal birds, each mechanically dipping and rising as if locked in a tug-of-war with a cable-fleshed worm, slowly pulling it out only to have it recoil into the earth, yanking the bird's head down with it.

North of Gainesville I crossed the Red River, the Tex/Okie border in the north, the Tex/Louisiana boundary to the east. I remembered the Big Bopper was born near the mouth of the Red River, and doffed my hat in respectful salute. I also remembered a record I'd seen while going through Donna's collection, 'Red River Rock' by Johnny and the Hurricanes; I dug it out and put it on the box, though by then I was fifteen miles into Oklahoma. Still, it seemed an appropriate gesture. The water bearing my blessing would eventually get there.

My eyes felt like they might start bleeding if there wasn't a total eclipse of the sun within minutes. I tried pulling my hat down for shade, but they're not called stingy-brims for nothing. My mouth was drier than a three-year drought and my stomach had shrunk to the size of a walnut. I'd gassed up just out of Houston and again before leaving Dallas, but twenty miles across the Oklahoma line I stopped again. The place was called Max and Maxine's Maxi-Gas Stop, and the paint-flaked sign promised HOT GAS, COLD BEER, & ALL SORTS OF NOTIONS. I told the young pump jockey to top it with ethyl and walked into the store. To my hollowed senses it seemed I was walking through pudding that hadn't quite set.

I bought a case of Bud, a bag of crushed ice, a bottle of eyedrops, and one of the two pairs of sunglasses left on the rack, preferring the wrap-arounds with the glossy yellow frames over the green up-swept cat-eyes studded with rhinestones. The lenses of both were caked with dust.

I restocked the cooler in the trunk, holding out a couple of bottles for immediate consumption. By the time I had the others properly iced, my fingertips were so numb I could barely pinch a twenty from my wallet to pay the attendant. It was a pleasure to slip back inside the warm Caddy. I drank a beer, then treated my eyes to some drops; they stung like hell at first, but gradually soothed. Still blinking, dabbing at the dribbles of eyewash on my cheeks, I angled back onto the freeway. Once I was up to cruising speed, I looked around for something to wipe the dust from my new pair of Foster Grants and, when I automatically glanced up to check traffic, a sheet of white paper came swirling across the road from the right shoulder and I stood on the brakes, a scream gathering in my guts as I waited for the sickening thud of flesh against metal.

But there was no thud, no Eddie, no child ruined against the blinding chrome; only the shriek of rubber and the brake shoes smoking on the drums as I fought to keep the rear end from whipping around – but when I heard another wheel-locked scream behind me and caught a flash of a pick-up in the rearview mirror bearing down on my ass, I cranked the wheel hard right, whipping the rear end around as the pick-up, bucking against its clamped brakes, cleared me by half a hair. I came to a stop way off on the right-hand shoulder, turned around 180°, looking straight back at where I'd just come from as adrenalin swamped my blood. I could hear myself panting. Hear my heartbeat and the barely audible throb of arteries in my neck. Hear the pounding slap of heavy boots running on pavement, growing louder as they approached: the guy in the pick-up.

He almost tore off my door, an act I considered understandable given *his* adrenalin surge, his rage at my sudden and inexplicable braking, and his size. He looked like he could go bear hunting with a pocketknife and come home with meat for the table. He was wearing grungy Levis, a heavy plaid flannel shirt, a blue down vest with one pocket half ripped off, and a scuffed yellow hard hat with a Gulf Oil logo.

'What the *fuck* do you think you're *fucking* doing, you *fuckhead?*'

This wasn't a particularly civil question – not really a question at all, in fact – but was fair enough, under the strained circumstances, to deserve a prompt and truthful answer. 'A week ago in San Francisco I was walking down the street and a little boy five years old came running down some stairs and one of the drawings he was carrying blew out in the street and Eddie – that was his name, Eddie – went right after it without a thought. I saw it coming and dove out full length to try to stop him but my fingertips just barely grazed his pants as he scooted off the curb between two parked cars and got splattered by a '59 Merc before your heart could skip a beat. I don't know if you saw it, but a piece of paper blew out on the road right in front of me back there and I locked 'em up on gut reflex because I never, ever-again want to see a little five-year-old mangled on the pavement, dead in his own blood.'

'Yeah, okay,' the guy said. He shut the door softly, turned, and walked away.

Sometimes there's nothing more devastating than understanding. I burst into tears. I didn't try to fight it. I slumped over the wheel and wept for Eddie, for the kind understanding that confirms one's pain and changes nothing, for every shocked soul forced to bear helpless witness to random mayhem, and, with a self-pity I couldn't escape, for myself.

When I began to notice cars slowing to check out this Cadillac pointing ass-backwards to the flow of traffic, I snuffled my nose clear and got out and made a cursory, tear-blurred check of the car to see if I'd bent or broken anything in that high-stress 180° onto the shoulder. As I squatted to check out the front end, I saw the piece of paper plastered against the grille. It was a mimeographed note, the ink sun-bleached to a faint violet shadow. My eyes hurt to read it, but I finally made it out:

Dear Parents of Second Graders

The second grade is having a classroom Halloween Party
on the afternoon of October 31. Students are encouraged
to wear their costumes to the party. The Halloween Party
will be held during the last two hours of class time.
Students will be dismissed at the regular time unless Rainy
Day Session applies. Buses will run on normal schedule.

I wish you all a scary (but safe!) Halloween.

Sincerely,

Judy Gollawin
Second Grade Teacher

The note really tore me up. One happily mindless mistake and
the party's over, kid. A single misstep and you break through the
crust. I got back in the car and slumped against the wheel and
let the tears roll. Not sniveling, or not to my sense of it. Crying
because it hurt.

You might be able to grieve forever, but you can't weep that
long, so after a while I wiped away the tears, folded up the note
and put it in the glovebox with Harriet's letter, and got myself
turned around and back on the road, taking it up till the needle
quivered between the double zeros of 100. This might've been
terrifying if I'd stopped to think, the slowest mind in the west
going that fast, hellbent for glory, goddamn it, no matter if I
had to stop and weep at every scrap of paper that blew across
my path, every sweet kid skipping off to school, every splash of
blood on the highway.

Within twenty miles I was overtaken by an undreamable feeling
of peace, no doubt a combination of raw exhaustion and emotional
release, but I didn't try to figure it out. I realized, to my baffled
delight, that I'd blundered into a wobbling balance, a vagrant

equilibrium, a fragile poise between water and moon, and I was riding the resolution of a wave.

It was a short ride, about an hour and a half between the last tear and Posthole Joe's, and it felt so good I slowed down to savor it. As I passed Oklahoma City there was still an hour before sunset, but under a sky grown so leaden through the afternoon that it was almost dark, only a faint pinkish light, the ghost color of my florid hat, was holding at the horizon.

My peace deepened when I pulled into the lot at Posthole Joe's. The long, flat-roofed diner was the same dingy white with tired red trim, the light inside still softened to an inviting glow by the exhaust-grimed glass of the windows. Two Kenworths and a White Freightliner idled in the lot. This was a memory exactly as I remembered it, familiar and sure, a reference solidly retained, and it gladdened me that something had prevailed against change. As I walked toward the door my peaceful happiness began expanding into a sense of elation I could neither understand nor contain, only welcome. When I stepped into the warmth and rich tangle of odors inside and saw Kacy standing just to my left – tall loose blond, lovelier than I could've hoped to remember, wearing the white rayon dress and brown apron that Posthole's waitresses have worn forever, just standing there out of nowhere taking the orders of two drivers in a booth against the wall – my elation vaulted into joy, and I yelled her name and took her in my arms.

The deepest memories are the claims of the flesh, and as soon as my arms brought her close I knew I'd made a mistake. She wasn't Kacy, but that information was caught in the joy-jammed circuits of my brain, arriving just a helpless instant before her knee flattened my testicles.

'Sorry,' I gasped on my way to the floor. 'Honest. Mistake.' I barely managed to wheeze out 'mistake' before I curled up on the scuffed beige linoleum and abandoned apology to agony. I could no longer speak, but for some reason I could hear with an amazing clarity.

'Well, *shit*!' Kacy's double shouted down at me.

'Man oughta look before he lunges,' one of the guys in the booth offered as a judgment or general truth. His buddy snickered.

The waitress knelt and touched my shoulder. 'You all right?'

From my new point of view it was obvious she wasn't Kacy's twin, or even a sister, but the resemblance was close enough to fool the desperate or hopeful. I couldn't answer her question, though.

She gently squeezed my shoulder. 'I'm sorry. You scared the hell out of me, grabbing ahold like that. You want to stretch out in a booth or something?'

I shook my head. 'My . . . fault.'

She snapped at the two men in the booth, 'You boys done hee-hawing, maybe you could give him a hand. Christ, *I* don't know what you're supposed to do for that.'

The philosopher in the booth said, 'Shot you gave him, Ellie, ain't a hand he needs, it's a search party – to go looking for his gonads. Reckon first place I'd check is up around his collarbones.' His buddy thought this was even funnier.

I reached around and patted her hand resting on my left shoulder.

'You gonna make it?' she said tenderly.

I nodded once, patted her hand again to express my thanks, then flopped over on knees and forearms, ass in the air, and started crawling for the door. I'd lost my appetite and my happiness.

'Tommy! Wes!' she barked. 'God*damn* it, help him up!'

They both started to slide from the booth, the witty one whining back, 'Don't go chewing on *our* asses. Wasn't us copping feels. Man deserves what he gets.'

I stopped and rolled over onto a hip, raising a palm to stop them. After a few breaths I'd gathered enough surplus air to form the words into half-gagged croaks. 'What you get . . . belongs to you . . . yours.' I nodded vigorously for the emphasis my voice couldn't supply, then added, 'I'll crawl.'

I negotiated the yard to the door, pulled myself to my knees, then used the doorknob to leverage myself upright. I wasn't standing tall, but I was on my feet. I touched my head to make sure I hadn't lost my hat. The waitress and truckers were watching me, a guy at the counter I hadn't noticed before had turned around to stare, a pair of heads were craning from another booth, and a cook I didn't recognize was peering from the kitchen. 'Sorry,' I told them, 'for disturbance. Good night.' I tipped my flaming flamingo hat politely, thinking its color was about three shades lighter than my nuts felt, then eased out the door. The Caddy was gleaming across the lot, and I headed toward it with a mincing, bow-legged shuffle, slow and easy.

I didn't realize till I opened the Caddy's door and was trying to figure out how to slide in without adding to my pain that the waitress had followed me outside and was standing in front of the diner, her arms wrapped around herself against the cold. She'd wanted to make sure I made it, or so I assumed. I wished fleetingly that her arms were wrapped around *me*, but in my condition that would've been cruel for the both of us, so I simply waved. She waved in return and slipped back inside.

Using the car door and steering wheel for support, I eased myself onto the seat, my groans and whimpers amplified in the Caddy's voluminous interior. To keep my pelvis elevated, I braced my shoulders against the seatback and my feet against the floorboards. But you can't drive all stretched out like that, so I held my breath and assumed the standard position; the pain wasn't any worse, and at least I could drive. I pulled back onto the highway, running it up through the gears as fast as I could so I wouldn't have to think about moving my legs again.

I couldn't help thinking about Kacy, though. The mistaken moment in the waitress's arms was a cruel reminder of how much I missed her, how much I wanted to hold her real and right now.

The feeling triggered a rush of memories, each sweet particular sad with loss. If I had a shred of sense, I thought, I'd hang a U for South America, and go get her. If the gift is love, why wasn't I delivering my own, face to face, belly to belly, heart to beating heart? But that good sense met the stronger conviction that Kacy couldn't be hounded into love. She might appreciate the gesture, but not the pressure. To chase her was to lose her. I could dangle my throbbing balls in the ice chest to numb that ache, or pull in to the closest emergency room, or knock over a pharmacy for every narcotic in the locker, but there was nothing I could do about the pain of wanting Kacy, nothing except forget her, and her memory was all I had.

There's a shock-trance that mercifully accompanies trauma, shutting the brain down to dumb function and removing you far enough to withstand the pain. Even more fortunately, it renders you incapable of convoluted metaphysical thought and prolonged self-analysis, truly subtracting insult from injury and properly placing the anguish of inquiry far beyond the immediate agony of the flesh. When the dam breaks there's no need to examine it for cracks or to discuss the intricacies of hydraulic engineering; you best head for higher ground. The body knows what *it*'s doing.

As the shock gradually faded, my balls settled into a tender, throbbing ache and my mind added primitive consideration to mere perception: I was exhausted. Given that exhaustion – so sorely compounded by my recent testicular trauma – I wondered whether I should stop in Wichita for food and a good night's rest, or just pop the four bennies I had coming for dessert and bore on for K.C. and Des Moines. I wondered briefly if the problem was with *my* plans or plans in general, and why I seemed to keep falling into traps I didn't know I'd set, but I caught myself short of that metaphysical deadfall and stepped instead into the snare of compromise: I ate the four bennies on the spot and an hour later, when I stopped in Wichita for gas, after examining myself for damage in the men's room stall and finding them both tender but without obvious need of medical attention, I walked gingerly across the street to Grissom's Liquors and Deli, where I got a fatty ham sandwich on Wonder Bread and a half-pint carton of limp slaw.

I ate in the car, distracting my palate with a perfunctory reconsideration of whether to grab a room for the night right there or make a run at Des Moines, four hundred miles upstream. It was 7:13 P.M. by the station's Hire's Root Beer clock: I could make Des Moines by midnight easy, which meant I could still soak an hour in a hot bath, get a solid eight hours of snooze, dally over breakfast, and hit Mason City by high noon. This sounded so much like a plan that I summarily abandoned it. I'd play it on the move – it always seemed to come to that anyway. In the unlikely event that none of the billions of unforeseen complications occurred, I could always fall back on the plan.

I headed 'em out for Kansas City feeling refreshingly realistic – getting nailed in the nuts will do that to you – and also, to my surprise, feeling playful enough to slap Jerry Lee Lewis on the box, keeping time with my fingers on the steering wheel because it proved too painful to tap my foot:

> *You broke my will,*
> *What a thrill!*
> *Goodness, gracious,*
> *Great Balls o' Fire!*

I made the selection as an arrogantly humble acknowledgment that I could take a joke, accompanied by a silent prayer that the gods had a sense of humor.

Sailing along the Interstate somewhere between Wichita and Kansas City, I suddenly found myself deep in the drunken memory of a North Beach midnight where somebody was yelling to me through time, 'You show me *one place* in the Bible where

God the Father or Jesus Christ His Son *laughs*, and I'll convert to Christianity. Otherwise, fuck it.' Whose voice was it? One of the Buddhist poets, it sounded like, maybe Welch or Snyder, but whoever said it was two tables away in the wine-blurred babble and clatter of Vesuvio's, where I was enthralled by the sight of a voluptuous redhead named Irene throwing back a shot of Jack Daniels at the end of the bar. That was its own joke, being an adolescent American male, because if it didn't get me high, have a pussy, or hit 65 in second gear, it wasn't of compelling concern. Who cares about the place of humor in the cosmic order when you're nineteen years old and never had a blowjob? When there's drugs to take and tracks to make and music that carries you away? I hadn't sinned enough to need salvation, and hadn't lost enough to truly laugh.

> *But what a thrill!*
> *Goooodd*-ness, *Graaaa*-shuuus;
> *Greaaaaaaaaat Balls o' Fire!!!*

Indeed. And if neither the Father or that lucky ol' son had the required sense of humor, perhaps it resided in the Holy Spirit, in speed and music and fucking your brains out, in roaming the mountains and roaring through the night, the bare wire, the straight shot. That might be funny.

It was altogether too fitting that my little reverie on the possibilities of divine humor was obliterated by the pulsing flash of a red light in my rearview mirror. Since I was going close to 100, it wasn't gaining much, which gave me time to die a thousand deaths before I instinctively punched it and instantly changed my mind. I came off the gas and pulled slowly into the right-hand lane, hoping with all my heart that it wasn't a cop, and if it was, that he had someone other than me in mind.

It was a fire engine, a big red fire engine. I pulled over to hug the shoulder as it wailed by. I was just about to put my foot back down on the pedal when another red light came streaking up, and then another: a state trooper followed by an ambulance. Wreck ahead, probably a bad one. I told myself that if I saw another mangled five-year-old kid I'd *drink* that bottle of speed, bash the Bopper's Cadillac through the Heavenly Gates, and grab God by the throat and demand a justification, an explanation, and some satisfaction. A dead kid isn't funny.

It was two miles up the road, and I was the fourth or fifth car on the scene. The cops had blocked both northbound lanes about two hundred yards from the wreck. I couldn't see much in the distracting light of flares and whirling red flashers, but it didn't look like the fire crew was necessary – they were standing around jawing as the flames died down. The charred hulk of an upside-down car was lying diagonally in the right lane, nose just touching the shoulder, rear end jutting out on the road. The air reeked of burnt rubber and scorched grease. It looked bad, so bad I didn't want to look again; in ten years of driving and towing I hadn't seen many much worse.

I powered down my window and yelled to a nearby trooper, asking if they needed any help.

'Nope, no thanks,' he called back. 'It's not as bad as it looks. Tow truck lost it – clevis snapped. Nobody inside. We'll have a lane open in about ten minutes.'

Wonderful news all around. I had to strain to see the tow truck another hundred yards down, its flashers barely visible in the oily haze. Probably take a squadron of troopers to write up the citations on the driver. Never lost one myself, but there's lots of good drivers that have. The trooper didn't mention the safety chain, but I fraternally hoped it had failed and hadn't been forgotten.

They opened the left lane about fifteen minutes later. By then traffic was backed up a quarter-mile, but I was right in front. I was so gleefully anticipating some open road to run on while half the night shift of Oklahoma law enforcement was otherwise engaged that I was almost past the smoldering hulk before I recognized it was a '59 Cadillac – impossible to tell the model, but even crashed, burned, and upside-down you couldn't mistake the space-shot styling.

I didn't know if this wreck in my path was supposed to be funny or not. I didn't laugh, but I smiled – grimly, I admit – because if I took it as something beyond indifferent coincidence or random connection, then I had to think of it as a sign or omen, and to decide whether it augured well or ill: well if it foreshadowed accomplishment, the gift aflame, delivered, nobody inside, nobody hurt; ill if it portended some pitiful failure, a weak connection snapping, an opportunity squandered to ignorance, negligence, delusion – merely lost instead of released. I wasn't sure what it meant – nothing new there – but I didn't like it.

However, I liked the open road a lot and put everything else behind me in no time flat, including endless speculation about unclear omens. This seemed an ideal time to put KRZY back on the air, and since 110 mph requires most of your attention, I just grabbed a handful and stacked them on the spindle, announcing to the night, 'This is KRZY coming on to darkness, Floorboard George flopping the sides and babbling in your ear. What you hear is what you get, and it sounds like what we got is Jerry Lee and "A Whole Lot of Shaking Going On." Won't be doing much shaking myself, you understand, having received a bad blow to the go-daddies earlier this evening, but you guys go right ahead and strut yo' stuff.'

Less than halfway through the stack, the program was interrupted by the greatest traveling salesman in the world. Clad only in dark pants and a white undershirt, bouncing up and down barefoot alongside the road in 35° weather, I might've guessed he was the craziest fucker within a thousand miles, or the best Human Pogo Stick act west of the Mississippi, but it never even crossed my mind that he might be the greatest traveling salesman in the world until he was in the Caddy and shaking my hand, introducing

himself as Phillip Lewis Kerr, 'please call me Lew,' and handing
me a silver card with deeply embossed blue print that read:

PHILLIP LEWIS KERR

Greatest Traveling Salesman in the
World

(212) 698–7000

He was an old guy, easily in his early sixties, belly slumping over
his waistband, but not at all sloppy – in fact, his general bearing,
the close-cropped grey beard and neatly trimmed mustache, the
small blue eyes forcefully alert and mildly amused, the directness
of his manner and speech, all combined to imbue him with the
calm dignity of a man who knows what he's about, even if he's
hitchhiking half-naked on a freezing night.

I introduced myself as he stowed a battered leather attaché case
under the front seat. His feet were broad, gnarly toed, and blue
with cold; I don't know whether I shivered in sympathy or at
the icy blast pouring in through the open door. Suddenly I was
freezing.

'Hey, Lew,' I hissed, jaw clamped to keep from chattering.
'Unless you got more gear to load, how 'bout putting some door
in that hole.'

He looked at me, startled. 'Oh! I *am* sorry.' He swung the
door shut, killing the domelight. In the darkness his voice was
disembodied. 'That was thoughtless of me, George, inexcusably
thoughtless. The warmth was so welcome I didn't imagine you
could be cold. And it *is* cold outside, I assure you.' I felt the seat
tremble as he shivered beside me.

I put the Caddy back on the asphalt and eased it up through
the gears, still very much aware of the tenderness in my loins.
Reminded by my own discomfort, I asked Lew if he'd like the
heat turned up.

'Oh no, not at all. It's better to thaw slowly. At my age the cell walls can't tolerate rapid changes; they rupture.'

'Never considered that,' I said truthfully. Everything he was saying seemed forthright and direct as it entered my ear, but seemed to make oblique jumps in my brain. We weren't connecting. I was willing to grant that the problem was in the receiver. However, I didn't want him to get going on his cell walls the way old folks sometimes do, elaborating their ills with lurid physiological details of how the flesh fails – I had a couple of aching examples of my own – so I changed the subject by asking him if he was going to Kansas City.

'I'll be going there, yes. Yourself?'

'Des Moines – and I'm running late. I may just drop you off at the closest warm place to an off-ramp.'

'Well,' he began, pausing so long I thought he was through, 'you must have left *awfully* late, because at this speed you would *have* to be early.' He smiled tentatively.

I smiled in kind. 'Lew, you mind if I ask if you always dress like this for freezing weather?'

'My goodness, no,' he said. 'I sold my coat, shirt, tie, socks, and shoes to a young fellow that works in the oil fields. He had a date with a young lady this evening, but he'd stopped with his friends after work for a few drinks and didn't have time to drop by a haberdashery.'

Again, this didn't sound right to me. 'Didn't he want the pants, too? He'd look strange wearing crusty old Levis with a coat and tie.'

'Oh, he inquired about the trousers, but I couldn't risk the possibility of being incarcerated for indecent exposure.'

'Rather die of regular exposure,' I asked lightly.

'I figured someone would come along shortly. And besides, the trousers were too small.'

'I'm glad you explained things, because I'd have to wonder why the world's greatest salesman couldn't afford to put some fabric between his flesh and a nasty night. That your usual line, men's clothes?'

'I sell anything and everything. I've found that in the long run diversity is stability.'

'Looks like you're about sold out.'

'Indeed I am. It's been an interesting trip.'

I figured out what was bothering me. 'You know, Lew, I've wanted to ask you a question ever since you handed me your business card here, but I can't see a way to ask it without sounding offensive, like I was challenging your credentials, and that's not what I mean to do.'

'George,' he said, 'I'm a salesman. I started with a lemonade stand in Sweetwater, Indiana, when I was five years old. I learned very early that it was expensive to take offense. It deflects you from your purpose.'

I wanted to ask what his purpose was – profit? the transaction itself? the necessary appeasement of demons and dreams? – but didn't want to lose my original question. 'All right, since you won't take offense, I was wondering about what it says on your card, that you're the greatest salesman in the world.'

He interrupted softly, 'Actually, the greatest *traveling* salesman.'

'Right. But it was "greatest" that grabbed me. I mean, how do you *know* you're the greatest in the world, traveling or standing still? Is there some measure, an objective standard, a committee of judges, a general consensus, or do you just step out and claim the title?'

'George, you're a remarkable man, the one out of a thousand whose first reaction doesn't concern farmers' daughters.' Evidently sensing my puzzlement, he added helpfully, 'You know, the traveling salesman and the farmer's daughter – there's a tradition of jokes. I'm sure you've heard some.'

'Yeh, sure, but I can't remember any offhand.' In fact I was trying hard to remember one – an act, considering my mental state, akin to fishing in a parking lot – when I realized that he'd evaded my question with a little flourish of distracting flattery. But I was too tired and too wired to play whatever game I sensed was going on, so I rammed straight ahead – not *heedlessly*, for I did understand *something* was going on, but with a wariness recklessly short of giving a rat's ass. 'Lew, I asked the question because I wanted your answer.'

'Mr Gastin,' he said, his voice soft as a cotton swab, 'I thought I'd lost you there for a minute. Perhaps you should disregard your tardiness and rest in Kansas City. And though obviously less capable, I would be glad to drive.'

The abuse of amphetamine is notorious for producing bad paranoia, and I got a sudden, deep stab: old Lew was a hit man hired by Scumball to murder me and wreck the car. I had to be cool, keep a sense of craziness in the air, keep my control – I doubted if he'd make his move while I had the wheel in my hands, especially at 110. 'Appreciate your concern, Lew.' I giggled. 'I admit that my mental health is not all it should be. Not at all. Lately I've been having these recurring losses of thought, and frankly I'm alarmed by their increasing frequency. Only thing that seems to stop them temporarily is a hard knee in the balls. But again I think you've squirmed the question. It's a fair question. Why don't you answer it?'

'If you insist,' he said evenly, 'though it's pointless.'

'Not to me.'

'But George, you would have absolutely no way of knowing whether I was lying or not.'

'That's exactly my point,' I said and, not having the slightest idea what my point was, jumped: 'You see, it doesn't matter if I can know the truth of what you tell me; the point is, I trust you to tell the truth, exactly as you trust my belief. And if the truth is boring or embarrassing, then tell me an illuminating lie. We've got to have faith in each other. I get a little incoherent when I'm this far gone, especially considering I'm pretty fucked-up to start with, so let me put it as bluntly as I can: Answer or get out.'

He said it quietly, as if to himself, 'No.' I then understood that he wasn't a hit man, but I'd already committed myself. I was lifting my foot from the gas and angling for the shoulder when he said, only slightly louder, 'No, Mr Gastin, I will not converse under duress. And certainly if trust is your point, duress betrays it. If you'll withdraw your ill-considered threat, I'll answer the question gladly, as I intended. After all, I did invite it. And it *is* a fair question.'

That coercion denies trust is obvious. I was properly chastened, both for my glaring lack of logic and my paranoid delusion. 'You're welcome to the ride,' I said, 'whether you answer or not.'

'Thank you.' There wasn't a trace of triumph or mockery in his voice.

I was about to burst into tears again, felt my throat tighten and my eyes begin to burn. I turned and screamed. '*Fuck this song and dance!* You wandering half-naked and coming on so calm and coy, who the fuck knows what *your* game is? Who knows whose ... whose ...' but I'd lost it, and in frustrated rage slammed my open palm against the dash, the slap sharp as a gunshot.

Lewis Kerr flinched badly, recoiling toward the door. But he spoke in the same tone of imperturbable sympathy. 'George, if you'll permit a candid observation, you're in bad shape.'

'*No shit!*' I howled in agreement. 'Would you sell your soul?' I hurled it at him, more demand than question, and without immediate reference except my bad shape.

He looked confused for a moment, then said, 'Don't be silly.'

'Do you *have* a soul to sell?'

'Yes, I make that assumption.'

I wanted to nail his slippery ass down. 'Why,' I asked him, my throat tight, 'are you being so fucking *careful?*'

'Because you're *not*,' he shot back, some heat in his voice for the first time.

'Why should I be?'

'Because you're terrified, and terror inspires disastrous stupidity, and stupidity is slavery. Because, George, you're not a slave.'

If you've ever been inside a slaughterhouse and seen a big, prime steer crumple and splay at the stun-hammer's blow, that's close to what I felt like – both steer and observer. I was floating out of myself. I couldn't think in words. I couldn't tell if I was breathing or not, if my tongue was still in my mouth, if it was the car or the road moving, or the night moving through us both. My normally narrow field of awareness was suddenly constricted to a single sensation of terror. Not the profound cellular fear of death, or of time's star-jeweled movement and stone gears grinding on, or the gangrenous dread that I was among those randomly picked to be randomly destroyed, any time now, without warning. No, it was an embarrassing terror, like you were lost in your own house.

Though it had been a long silence, Lew continued as if he'd only paused. 'Or I *assume* you're not a slave, much in the way I assume a soul.'

I didn't say anything. A person driving 110 mph down a road whose existence he questions should neither be required to think nor allowed to.

'But,' Lew continued, 'enough of my assumptions; you'll accuse me of evading the question while I was merely framing a reply.'

He paused as he shifted his weight on the seat, then continued, 'I'm a proud man. It's a pride based on accomplishment, not on arrogant assumption – or so I like to think. Pride is a powerful strength, and therefore a dangerous weakness. I try to temper it with honest humility. I don't brag. I don't gloat. I don't flaunt my achievements. I sell. In the fifty-nine years since I sold that first glass of lemonade on the muggy streets of Sweetwater, I have devoted myself to the mastery of selling. I've sold seven *billion* dollars worth of products. I've made millions in profit and commissions. When I was nineteen years old I sold a hundred and sixty-eight used cars off one lot in Akron, Ohio, during a twenty-four-hour period – that's seven cars an hour, one every eight and a half minutes – though of course I wasn't handling the paperwork. I sold out a semi-truck full of vacuum cleaners in Santa Rosa, California, in two days. Before I was thirty years old I went to Labrador and sold refrigerators to Eskimos. They had no electricity and lots of ice, but I had the ability to see possible applications for the product where others saw only the superficial absurdity of the venture: refrigerators, being insulated, are much like a thermos – they can keep, say, fish from freezing in a frozen climate, as long as they're not plugged in. Further, if properly drilled and vented, a refrigerator also makes an excellent smokehouse, thereby preserving with heat in a structure designed to preserve with cold. I sold the motors separately to the Air Force and used the money to buy electric heaters, which I sold to Indians in the Amazon Basin. They understood both the intrinsic beauty of the coils and their decorative possibilities. The electrical cords were similarly used for adornment, and for binding. The dismantled sheet metal frames proved to have a thousand applications, including arrow points.

'Through my thirties and forties I traveled the world selling every commodity you can imagine, including cinnamon in Ceylon and tea in China, the whole time refining my abilities and distilling the principles of the craft. The principles, I discovered, were surprisingly simple: listen well and tell the truth.'

Abruptly he leaned down and picked up his attaché case. He set it on the seat between us and snapped it open for my inspection. It was crammed with neatly stacked piles of money, twenties being the smallest visible denomination. 'That's a lot of money,'

I said, no doubt hoping to impress him with my firm grasp of the obvious.

'I don't even count it anymore. My accountant handles all that. I have no wife, no children, no expensive tastes. I've found it's wise to keep one's pleasures simple and that in my case, even the simple pleasures are ruined by indulgence. I enjoy the constant anonymity of motel rooms, the neutrality of passing through. I relish the stimulus of travel and contact. I'm still compelled by the possibilities of my work – each knock on the door, the face revealed as it opens – but beyond my work I need very little and want even less. So to me this money is relatively meaningless, even as a measure. Rather than make the excruciating and impossible decisions about who might best benefit from my surplus, it all goes to buy land to be held undeveloped in various land trusts for perpetuity.'

'You're a very romantic salesman,' I said. While I believed the money in the attaché, I wasn't sure I believed the explanation.

'Romantic?' he repeated. 'Well, I do believe there's a connection between ability and possibility.'

'Maybe you have a romantic heart and a classical mind. I'm just the opposite, I think. It gives me fits. Does it bother you much?'

'I think I mentioned,' he said dryly, 'that my pleasures can't bear indulgence.'

'Mine seem to encourage it.'

Lew shrugged. 'You're young. The price goes up.'

'You know,' I said, 'you probably *are* the greatest traveling salesman in the world. I just have this feeling you are, know what I mean? I believe you.'

'Oh, well, perhaps – but it's certainly not a claim I'd make for myself.'

I didn't get it. 'But it's there on *your* card, right?'

Lew said primly, 'Perhaps it's not a claim I'm making, but a title I'm accepting.'

'So there *is* a body of judges, or a committee, or something like that?'

'Yes, something like that.'

I was pleased, having figured out enough to feel functionally recovered. 'So, who says you're the best in the world?'

'The gods.'

No, I thought to myself, *why the fuck don't you learn?* What I managed to say was, 'Gods? Plural?'

'Yes. Plural.'

'How did they tell you you were the greatest in the world? Divine revelation? A plaque?'

'They called my answering service in New York.'

'Lew, you've *got* to be shitting me. Be careful; my mind's extremely frail these days.'

'So I noticed. That's why I *have* been careful. But it's the truth nonetheless. The gods left a message with my answering service . . . a number, no name. I returned the call. A woman answered – a secretary, I assumed from her manner – and put me on hold for a moment. There was a rapid clicking sound on the line, and then suddenly a very aggressive male voice demanded, "Would you sell a rat's asshole to a blind man and tell him it was a diamond ring?" I didn't have time to think, of course, so I replied from principle. "Only if I charged him at the fair market value for rat rectums and was utterly convinced the blind man had the imagination to appreciate the brilliance of the stone."

'"Excellent, Lew," the voice replied. "We'll get back to you." The connection went dead. I immediately dialed the number again but received a recording that informed me the number was no longer in service.

'Three days later, again through my answering service, I returned a call to a nameless number. This time it was a deep male voice that answered. "Yes?" he said. I gave my name and noted I was returning a call.

'"Kerr? Kerr?" he muttered, and I could hear papers rustling.

"Oh yes, here we have it. Mr Kerr, we're the gods. We consider you the greatest traveling salesman in the world and would like to employ your talents."

'I thought it was a joke, of course, so I said, "Suppose I'm not available?"

'"Then neither are we," he said, and what impressed me wasn't so much the implied threat as the tone in which he said it – an indifferent statement of finality.

'So I asked, "What would I be selling?"

'After a thoughtful pause, he answered, "Well, you wouldn't really be *selling* anything. You would be returning lost goods and collecting the delivery charges."

'"What sort of lost goods?"

'"Ghosts," he said matter-of-factly, as if we were discussing light bulbs or paper towels.

'I was incredulous, naturally, but just as naturally I was intrigued by the inherent possibilities, so I asked, "Will the people know their ghosts have been returned, or even that they were lost in the first place?"

'"No," he said, "or not unless you tell them."

'Now that piece of information made it infinitely intriguing . . . essentially selling an invisible product that a person wouldn't even be sure they'd bought. I had another question: "Suppose these people refuse to pay the delivery charges?'

'"Then you're not a great salesman. But," he added, after just the right length pause to let the challenge stir me, "we wouldn't have solicited your talents if we weren't confident of our choice."'

I couldn't help myself, and interrupted, 'And you fell for it, Lew? Hell, you're not the greatest salesman in the world – *he* is. Or they are. Tell me, where do you send the money?'

'That was exactly my next question to him.'

'Well,' I prodded, '*where* do you send it?'

'That's what truly confounded me. He said, "Keep the money. We can't use money. We're gods."'

'No. You're kidding.'

'Yes. And no, I'm not kidding you. Provocative, isn't it? It's either the gods or the product of a highly unusual human mind. Or minds, perhaps. Can you comprehend the effort and expense required to perpetrate a hoax of that magnitude without any return on the investment except your own amusement?'

He had a point: it was awfully elaborate for a practical joke. But it seemed to me some important points hadn't been covered. 'Where do you pick up these lost ghosts you're supposed to return?'

'I don't,' Lew said benignly, 'they evidently pick me up.'

Holy shit, I hope he doesn't mean me. The thought streaked through my buckling brain; my heart had grown legs and was running up my throat.

Lew must've sensed my fear because he immediately explained, 'I don't mean they pick me up hitchhiking. Ghosts don't drive, or not that I'm aware of. The ghosts find me, I gather, along the way. Invisibly attach themselves. I don't even know they're with me until I hear their names spoken, which is the same name as the person who lost the ghost. That sounds garbled. Let me try to be more exact. I return calls left with my answering service. I usually get a woman's voice, and she gives me a list of names, usually seven to nine. I transcribe the names in my notebook and then go on about my normal travels. Without any search or intention on my part, I invariably end up meeting those people whose names are on the list. Sometimes it takes two or three months to exhaust the list; the shortest was five days for seven names. Do you understand my point now? No one could endure the incredible expense or egomania necessary to sustain that godlike illusion. They would have to place me under constant surveillance, and I've hired the best private investigators available – who assure me there are no tails or bugs or any sort of monitoring devices.

You see, whoever it is would have to employ people to run into me, people whose names are on the list they give me, and that means they would have to know my moves in advance – and I assure you I've made it a point lately to act randomly. My only conclusion, George, is that it *is* the gods, whoever *they* may be. Here, let me show you.' He fumbled around for a moment, and finally produced a small leatherbound notebook slimmer than a wallet. He flipped through it quickly, then stopped and turned back the page. He offered it over for my inspection. I eased off the gas and then took a look. He was pointing to a page with a list of seven names. 'See?' he said. 'Right here. Number four. George Gastin.'

I wished for a long time that I could've thought of something witty to say, something like, 'Lew, perhaps these "gods" of yours are simply deranged angels,' but lately I've come to believe that my response had a certain eloquence. I looked at my name there on the list and said, '*Arrrrgggggghhh.*'

'My sentiments exactly.' Lew nodded, watching me intently. 'But what I'd like to know, George, the question you might trustingly and truthfully answer for me: if *not* the gods, *who* paid you to do this? And why is he, or she, or they, going to such great trouble to drive me crazy?'

Hook, line, sinker, and the rod and reel, too. He was good. I sighed. 'What are the delivery charges?' Why start fighting after you've already landed yourself?

'So you deny any knowledge of what's going on?'

'Lew,' I raised my right hand, 'I swear that the following is the most complete and accurate and honest truth I have ever uttered in my life: I don't have the barest fucking inkling what's going on. Not at all. Not any.'

'Well, George, that makes two of us, a virtual unanimity at this particular juncture of time and space.'

'I don't think so,' I disagreed affably. 'One of us is a great salesman; one of us is kind of a lost soul. The great salesman is not merely great, he's the best in the world, so accomplished that he alone is capable of inventing challenges for himself, because he knows if he quits exploring and extending his talents, polishing his brilliance, he won't have anything to justify his pride. But that's his problem. The lost soul's problem is terminal confusion, and it doesn't help that he's a romantic sucker for truth, beauty, love, hope, trust, honor, faith, justice, and all those big *gleaming* abstractions that his spirit constantly fails – or so he secretly believes. Plus he's suffering from exhaustion, sexual injury, and drug abuse. The salesman, being a keen observer, notes this, but since he has no goods to sell in a situation of outstanding sales potential, he brilliantly contrives to do exactly that: sell nothing. Which he proceeds to do, flawlessly, after a bit of sleight-of-hand jotting in the dark. Both the conception and execution are, in fact, so flawless that the lost soul sees it clearly and *still* has no choice but to buy his ghost – which he can neither see nor feel – because even if he's almost positive it's bullshit, he – being lost, romantic, and generally fucked-up – can't risk the slim chance that it *is* the truth. And if it *is* the truth, if the gods think it important enough to return lost ghosts – though he doesn't remember either having one or losing it – he'd be a fool not to accept delivery and pay the charges. So: Bravo, Mr Kerr. You are indeed the greatest traveling salesman in the world. How much do I owe you?'

'That's the beauty of it, isn't it, George? And that's why I'm beginning to believe it really is the gods: there are so many possibilities for disbelief, so much beyond proof. It's perfect.'

'And the price of this perfection?' I sourly reminded him.

'George,' he sounded pained, 'if *the gods* don't take payment for returning your ghost, how could *I* possibly ask any reward beyond the privilege of delivering it?' He tapped the leather attaché case. 'I certainly don't need the money.'

'You can afford to do it for kicks.'

'You *could* believe me, George, even though I'm not sure I

believe this myself. *Trust*, remember? You keep missing your own point, so it's no wonder you're confused.'

'So what you're saying is there's no charge? I get my wayward ghost back for free?'

'Not exactly for free. The gods have no use for money and I personally take no commission, but there *is* a fee for the transaction, sort of an emblematic tax on the thermal exchange – call it a donation to cover charges on the cosmic freight. It's a dollar ninety-eight. Symbolic, like I said, but the gods insist on it.'

'What happens if I just flat-ass refuse to pay? Do you repossess my ghost?'

'I don't know. Nobody's ever refused.'

'Who gets the money?'

'I've been including it in my land trust purchases. So far I've collected one hundred fifty dollars and forty-eight cents. The gods said they didn't care what I did with it as long as it was collected. This figure is obviously capricious; the gods didn't say so, but I gather it's meant as a symbolic reminder that there are things beyond the normal considerations of price and value.'

'Would they accept *symbolic* payment?'

Lew cocked his head. 'I don't know. It's never come up. But speaking as their ignorant agent, I don't see why not.'

Without slowing down I reached over into the backseat and snagged my secondhand Salvation Army jacket. I tossed it to him. 'A symbolic payment to keep you warm in a universe getting colder all the time. I'm going to let you out here because my brain's near death, and I want it to die in peace.'

'I understand,' said Lew as he put on the jacket. 'It's interesting, you know: invariably when I return a ghost the person suddenly wants to be alone.'

'Or together with his ghost. Sort of a second honeymoon.'

Lew looked at me sternly. 'I'd be particularly wary of irony, George; it mutilates what it's helpless to transform.'

'Now how can I be careful of irony when I didn't even know I'd lost my ghost?'

'That's a point,' Lew said, zipping up the jacket.

'You don't happen to know where I lost my ghost, do you? Or when? Or how? Or why?'

Lew picked up his attaché case. 'No, I don't.'

'What do the gods say about these lost ghosts?'

'Nothing.'

'Did you press them?'

'Of course. I'm a curious man myself.'

I had my neck bowed. 'So, what did they say when you pressed them?'

'They told me not to worry about it. The gods don't seemed disposed to idle chatter. I'm just given a list of names. It's all very crisp and distant.'

'And you're sure it's gods, plural?'

'Positive. I wouldn't make a mistake on something like that.'

'Last guy I gave a ride to was the pastor of the Rock Solid Gospel Light Church of the Holy Release. The Lord speaks to him. One god. *Mono*theism, right? And you're telling me gods. At least more than one. Voices out of the blue and out of whirlwinds and over the phone – evidently the spirits are just babbling away out there. Not that I've personally heard them. They haven't said diddley-shit to me. Well, maybe a whisper once or twice, but nothing I could be sure of.'

'You know what frightens me?' Lew said. 'I'm afraid I'm going to get the gods on the phone one of these days and be sitting there writing down names of lost ghosts to return and my name is going to be on the list.'

'Just drop your buck ninety-eight in the pot like everyone else.'

'I guess so,' he said uneasily, 'but for me I don't think it would be that simple. They say the only mark you can't beat is the mark inside. I'd probably try to sell it back to them.'

'They'd probably buy it.' I slowed to let him off. 'I really am sorry to put you out like this. I don't know what's going on, but I guess I should thank you for your help in keeping it going.'

'My pleasure,' Lew said. 'I know you'll ignore me, but George, you shouldn't go on much farther without some rest. It's not helping.'

'Three more hours and I'm soaking in a hot bath.' I pulled over onto the shoulder and stopped. 'I'm tempted to kidnap you for company and counsel, but I need to be alone for a while to think, to make up my mind.'

'Make up a good one,' the greatest traveling salesman in the world advised me as he offered a little wave in farewell.

As I nosed back onto the blacktop I caught a glimpse of him in the rearview mirror as he sprinted across the freeway to the southbound lanes and stuck his thumb up for a ride back the way he'd come. Something else to think about.

But I don't remember thinking about that or anything else on the drive into Des Moines. I don't remember the drive, either. The only evidence that I actually did it is that I woke up in a Des Moines motel the next morning. Between dropping off Lewis Kerr and waking up is pretty much a hole; there are a few clinging fragments, and if they were the high points I can understand why the rest are forgotten. Perhaps my strongest memory is a feeling of frustrated rage that I'd been cheated out of Paradise. I remember a huge green figure that seemed to beckon to me. I recall giving money to a sallow young man with a prominent Adam's apple who — except for a bright green blazer — looked like an apprentice embalmer. There was one sliver of pleasure, the immense relief I felt as I slid into a steaming bath, but the next memory is of screaming awake in cold, grease-slicked water, terrified I'd drowned my ghost. I remember clawing and sloshing my way out of the tub, the freezing linoleum, and — most vividly — the explosive bitterness in my mouth as I scrabbled on hands and knees to puke in the toilet. I remember passing the wall heater as I crawled toward the bed and stopping to crank it up full blast before I died of exposure. Still dripping wet, I heaved myself up on the bed and wriggled under the covers. The last memory-shard of that night is so faint it may have been a dream: uncontrollable shivers that became convulsions; praying they would stop before my skeleton flew apart; begging the mercy of every god I could remember, from Allah to Zeus. After that, nothing.

Memory did not resume gently. I woke the next morning convulsed by a heart-stopping shock that was like getting hit with a souped-up cattle prod. *Phone!* my brain screeched. *Nightstand. To your right.* I saw it. A green and yellow plastic phone that resembled an ear of corn. 'Please don't!' I blurted just as it rang again. I reached to pick it up and make it quit when an alarm went off in my brain stem — *who knows you're here? who knows you're here?* — and the crank of adrenalin turned my mind over; it was idling rough, but it was running. The phone rang again. *Nobody knows I'm here, wherever it is.* The phone rang again. Maybe it was the gods returning my call. It rang again. Whoever invented the telephone's alleged 'bell' should have his skull drilled with a dull bit until it's a gossamer of bone. I snatched up the receiver, lifted it to my ear, but didn't speak.

'*Good* morning!' a scratchy recording of a pert female voice began brightly, 'this is your wake-up call as requested.' I didn't remember requesting one, but then again I didn't remember much of anything. I relaxed as the voice continued, 'Thank you for staying with us at the Jolly Green Giant Motel. If you're hungry, may we suggest Pancake Paradise, conveniently located next to the motel. And please keep in mind that any prolonged irregularity in your bowel habits or the presence of blood in the stool are both warning signs of rectal cancer and you should see a doctor immediately. It's been our pleasure to serve you. We hope you've enjoyed your stay. If you'll be journeying on today, have a safe and successful trip, and do stop and see us if you get back this way again.'

Rectal cancer? Blood? Stool? My brain denied it. I kept the phone to my ear. '*Good* morning!' she began again, and I listened intently through 'signs of rectal cancer,' then decisively hung up. The room was gorged with rank humidity. I was sweating and shivering. The bed looked like I'd been cavorting with a school of mermaids all night. I was simultaneously numb-dumb and jangled with an unfocused frenzy. Muscles in my body twitched randomly. I wasn't feeling well. In fact, objectively, I was a wretched mess. Subjectively, however, all I needed was a dozen hits of speed. Soon. Otherwise I was going to turn into a big clot of algae.

The speed was in . . . where? The bottle. The bottle of speed. Now I was getting somewhere. Under the seat of the car, right. Car? Where's the car? Parked where? Keys? Pants? To think and crave at the same time is extremely difficult, particularly when you're handicapped by the loss of recent memory.

If you think I bolted bare-ass from the room, keys clutched in a sweaty palm, and careened around the parking lot looking for something large and white with swept fins sporting dual bullet taillights and a bottle of amphetamine under the seat, you've forgotten – as I had until that moment – my purpose in subjecting myself to exhaustion, amnesia, drug withdrawals, the dangers of the road, and rectal cancer in wake-up calls. It was delivery day, arrival, the point of completion, and I'd damn near forgotten. 'You pathetic piece of shit,' I said aloud. 'Must really be important, a deeply serious matter of love, music, spirit. But first get that speed. Don't stand there jerking yourself off with this gift-of-love horse-shit. You can go get the speed or you can get serious.'

I got serious. It wasn't what I felt like doing – what I felt like doing was a tall stack of crank – but when Saint George came galloping in on his ethereal white charger, I submitted to what I wanted to be rather than what I was.

Following Saint George's command, I marched to the bath-room. The undrained water in the tub was slicked with grey congealed oils, but it was an enchanted lake with lily pads compared to the toilet, which I understandably, if unfortunately, hadn't flushed after vomiting. 'Take a good look in the mirror,' Saint George ordered. I obeyed. Not as bad as the toilet bowl, but if the blood in my eyes had been in my stool I would've been fanning the Yellow Pages under *Physicians*.

'This is what you've come to,' Saint George sneered. 'But you don't have to live your life like this. You don't have to die with pee-stains on your underwear in a scabby motel room reeking of disinfectant, holding your broken dreams in your arms like some ghostly lover whose every touch you failed. This bathroom is the image of your soul. Clean it up.'

I cleaned the bathroom till it sparkled, then started on myself. First a hot shower, then a cold one, followed by a shave and a clean change of clothes. That my duffle bag and shaving kit were already in the room was proof I'd at least retained some mental functions the night before. Though I was trying to be playful about it, I was distressed by the black-out. My last coherent memory was of Lew Kerr selling me my ghost, and that was hardly encouraging. I hoped my ghost wasn't as fucked-up as I was. 'You fight with what you have,' Saint George rebuked me, his formidable white charger trembling for action. 'Go eat, and then let's do it.'

When you're bullwhipping yourself with self-loathing, there's a tendency to want to spread the pain. I made a point of returning the key to the office instead of leaving it in the room, hoping that the sallow young man was on duty; a few lashes might get his blood moving. That I was disappointed to find a freckle-faced woman in her mid-twenties in the office was evidence of my mean mood. She was pleasantly chubby, with a cute nose and bright hazel eyes, wearing more make-up than she needed – the milky farmer's daughter of a traveling salesman's wettest dreams. I was disconcerted by her healthy glow, but any inclination to spare the lash vanished at her cheerful chirp of a greeting: '*Good* morning, Dr Gass.' Hers was the same perky voice I'd heard on the wake-up call.

'Wrong.' I slapped the room key on the counter. 'It might've been a bearable morning had it not been besmirched by the malignant anus of your wake-up call.'

The weight of her collapsing smile bowed her head. I felt like I'd run over a puppy. 'I like words,' I told her. 'I read the dictionary with breakfast. I'm secretly vain about my abilities to express myself in all sorts of situations, and in company ranging from scumballs to poets. Perhaps it's because I've been sick with the flu this week, but I find I can't even *begin* to express my disgust at the utter tastelessness of including the warning signs of rectal cancer in a wake-up call.'

She lifted her face, tears trembling in the corners of her eyes. 'Try "putrid." Or "hideous." "A grossly thoughtless insult to human sensibility and the hope of a new day." That's the best one so far. "Sick" and "disgusting" are the most common.' She paused to knuckle the brimming tears. 'I get ten complaints every morning.' She sniffled, sniffled again, then tried to smile.

I wasn't moved. 'If you get complaints every morning,' I said icily, 'why do you persist in including it? Why not remove it?'

'I *want* to,' she pleaded, 'but Mr Hilderbrand won't let me.'

'*Who* is Mr Hilderbrand?' He was going to pay double, for my pain and hers.

'He's the owner.'

'Is he here?'

She shook her head. 'Excuse me a moment, please.' She went into an adjoining room, out of view. I could hear her blowing her nose.

I was waiting like a moray eel when she returned. 'Will Mr Hilderbrand be in soon?'

'Not till this evening.' Her voice was a bit tight and breathless, but steady.

'Do you have his home number? I see no purpose in haranguing you if you're only doing it at his insistence.'

'He's at the hospital most of the day.'

'A mental hospital, I assume.' Spare the rod, spoil the child. Too blind to see.

'Oh no, of course not. His wife is dying of cancer. Rectal cancer. I mean, don't you *see?* That's *why*. Harriet – that's his wife – knew something was wrong but she was too embarrassed to go to the doctor or even tell Mr Hilderbrand until it was too late. It's so *sad.* Embarrassed by a thing like that. They've been married *twenty-nine years.*'

'Do they love each other?' It was a foolish question, but far less foolish than I felt.

She appeared baffled by the question. 'I suppose so. Twenty-nine years is a lot, and he spends all his time with her at the hospital.'

I couldn't think of anything to say, foolish or not, so nodded my head as if I understood.

She continued, 'For a while I told him about the complaints, but he wouldn't budge. He said people have to face what's real. That it needs to be reinforced or they'll ignore it.'

'I agree. But why make *you* say it? Why make you suffer the consequences?'

'Well, to tell the truth' – a flicker of a smile – 'Mr Hilderbrand has a squeaky voice, and it's worse on tape. And every day for the last six weeks he's been at the hospital with his wife – that's suffering enough without the complaints. So I try to handle them and not bother him.'

'What's your name?'

'Carol.'

'Carol, you have a fine heart.'

'That's nice of you to say.' Her eyes glistened with tears. She gave a funny little shrug of her shoulders, swiped at the tears with a tissue crumpled in her hand, then managed an awkward smile.

'Could I borrow a paper and pen? I'd like to leave Mr Hilderbrand a note.'

'Of course.' She was glad to have something to do besides fight back tears in front of a stranger.

I explained. 'I'm going to suggest to Mr Hilderbrand that instead of enforcing reality on the wake-up call he instead have *all* the warning signs of cancer printed on a piece of paper and placed in every room as a bookmark for the Gideon Bibles . . . sort of diagnosis and consolation at the same time. Slip them right in there at the Book of Job.'

Carol hesitantly slid a ballpoint pen and a livid green sheet of paper across the counter. I didn't understand the hesitation till she said, 'But Dr Gass, we don't place Bibles in the rooms. Mr Hilderbrand won't allow it. He says it's presumptuous . . . not everybody is a Christian.'

'But it's *not* presumptuous to wake up guests, whatever their religious preferences, with graphic descriptions of the warning signs of rectal cancer?' I felt sense disintegrating.

'I guess Mr Hilderbrand doesn't think so.' I noted a new, non-committal coolness in her tone. She was tired of dealing with me.

I picked up the pen and briskly began, *Dear Mr Hilderbrand* . . . but then couldn't think of anything to say. The last hour I'd been riding that combination of self-loathing and false power that accompanies the fervor of renewal, the righteousness released by fresh conviction, but it was fading fast. The pen trembled in my hand, and I put it down. 'I don't know what the hell to say,' I confessed to Carol. 'I can't *think* with this damn flu.' I suddenly wanted to bury my face in her bosom and weep.

'Ralph – he's the night manager – he said you didn't look well.'

'I was a zombie.'

'Well, I hope you feel better soon, Dr Gass. And I hope you

won't hold the wake-up call against us.' This was a reasonable facsimile of her perky self, but not the real item. She'd receded.

So had I. 'Thanks. I hope I feel better, too. And now I understand how you knew my name – the night manager told you.'

'Ralph was concerned. He said if you stayed past checkout to look in on you. . . . That sounds bad, like it was the money, but it was to make sure you were all right.'

'What did he say? "Look for a guy I can practice my embalming on?"'

Carol tittered. 'No, he just said you looked sick and tired. And that you were wearing a colorful hat.'

'He liked the hat, did he?' I reached up and gave the narrow brim a tug.

'He said you asked him if he *understood* your hat.'

'Well, I was extremely ill last night. The fever was peaking. I suppose I was babbling. To tell the truth, I don't even remember talking to him.'

'Dr Gass, do you *really* wear that hat so the gods can spot you more easily?'

'Did I say that?'

'That's what Ralph *said* you told him. I don't think Ralph realized how sick you were. *He* thought you might be a little loony-tunes.'

'I can certainly understand why,' I chuckled nervously, 'going around saying things like that. Or it may be that Ralph doesn't *personally* feel the gods are watching. And maybe he's right.'

'Oh,' Carol said. Now we both were nervous. 'Do you mind my asking what sort of doctor you are? Ralph didn't think you were a medical doctor, but I said you could be a professor.'

'Bless you, but you're both wrong – though *you're* closer. I'm a Doctor of Divinity. I'm doing missionary work for the Rock Solid Gospel Light Church of the Holy Release.'

'It's pretty much Methodists around here,' Carol said.

'It's a new church,' I explained, 'greater ecclesiastical emphasis on the role of the Holy Spirit as manifested in love and music. Which reminds me that I must be on my missionary way. It was a pleasure to meet you, Carol. I hope our paths cross again. Good day.' I was out the door, feeling I'd handled the explanations and my exit with dignity and aplomb.

Out in the parking lot, the dignity and aplomb quickly withered: I couldn't find the Eldorado. I felt the keys in my pocket; all I lacked was the car. I went around back. No Caddy. I circled the entire motel, shivering with cold and impending collapse. Nothing. As gone as any memory of where I might've parked it.

Trying to fight down the panic, I returned to the office. Carol seemed startled to see me.

'I can't seem to locate my car,' I told her, my attempted smile more like a twitch.

She put her hand to her mouth. 'Oh, I'm *sorry*. I was supposed to remind you – Ralph asked me to . . . but I got involved talking and . . . oh, I'm *really* sorry. It's parked in front of the restaurant . . . the pancake house next to us.' She pointed helpfully.

'I don't remember parking it there,' I said, excruciatingly aware as soon as the feeble words left my mouth that that was obvious.

'Well, according to Ralph you were very upset.'

'Did he say why?' I wasn't sure I wanted to know.

'Because the neon letters were the same color as your hat,' Carol said.

I shouldn't have asked. 'The fever.' I shook my head sadly. 'I must've been delirious.'

'I don't know if it's true, but Ralph said they almost called the police.'

'Oh?'

'You were threatening to tear the sign down with your bare hands.'

'I was? I *like* the color.'

'But it wasn't Paradise.'

'*What* wasn't?' I demanded. I needed speed just to keep up with the conversation.

Carol shied at my tone. 'I only know what Ralph told me.'

'Yes?' I urged.

'You were upset because the pancake house wasn't Paradise. The sign said it was, but it wasn't. And if it wasn't, you said they shouldn't use an honest color like your hat's for false advertising.'

'Sounds like my sort of logic. Wish I could've been there.'

'It *is* kind of funny.' Carol grinned, glee flashing in her lovely hazel eyes. 'I always thought Pancake Paradise was a really stupid name. Mr Hilderbrand's ex-partner owns it, a Mr Granger. They bought the motel and restaurant together, but they couldn't get along – mainly because Mr Granger is such a jerk – so they split it up. The restaurant isn't doing so good now that Mr Granger has it. He's never there. He's more interested in chasing women. He thinks he's *so* neat. He's always coming over and asking me to go out and have a drink with him, and he's *married*.'

'Do they make good pancakes over there?'

'Urp.' She giggled.

I liked her giggle. 'Well, if it isn't Paradise and they serve urpy food and Mr Granger is an adulterous jerk, why don't you and me go over there and tear the sign down together right now. Strike a blow for truth, justice, beauty, and good eats. Then, soon as I take care of a little business, we can run away to Brazil.'

She wasn't shocked or offended. She just looked at me and shook her head.

'You can say no.'

'Dr Gass, I *have* to say no.'

'No you don't.'

'I *work* here. I *live* here. I don't *know* you.'

I lost heart against that three-gun salvo of logic. 'You're

right. You have to say no, I guess, and I have to wonder if that's the reason I asked you. I mean that respectfully, as a compliment. So maybe in the future, under the influence of different circumstances, different signs.' Graceful exits were becoming my specialty.

'Don't do it,' Carol warned me. 'They'll call the cops for sure this time and put you in jail.'

'The Paradise sign?' I waved my hand in dismissal. 'I'm too weak to do it without your help. But I wasn't really intending to anyway. I'm not *that* dumb. Or that smart, maybe. Besides, I've got plenty of other foolishness to keep me busy today, and though it's proving difficult to release myself from your captivating company, I best get on to it. Call farewell to your rejected suitor as he rides into the desert.'

She shook her head. 'You *are* loony-tunes.'

My first step out the office door I saw the Caddy's bullet taillights jutting between two pick-ups. I decided the best tactic was to stroll over casually, jump in, and make tracks. Everything with an easy quickness. The place could still be simmering with animosity. I was about halfway across to the Caddy when I heard Carol's maiden voice, a bellnote cutting the cold air: 'Fare-thee-well!'

I turned around and cupped my hands: 'I'll never stop loving you!'

That sent her jumping back inside the office door. I'd forgotten for a moment she worked there, lived there, had to say no. So had she.

The Cadillac, praise my autonomic nervous system, was securely locked. I opened the driver's door and slid in, relocking it immediately. It seemed to me there were a lot of faces peering through the windows of Pancake Paradise. I squirmed on the freezing front seat; no wonder Preparation H, Doan's pills, and amphetamines are a trucker's best friends. I shouldn't have thought of amphetamine, but instead of reaching under the front seat, I reached up and turned the key. The engine cranked slowly, not enough juice in the cold, but then it caught – ragged at first, but warming toward a purr.

I was so intent on the engine sounds that it took me a moment to notice, right next to my door, the two huge men dressed identically in blue bib-overalls and white T-shirts. They looked like twins, except the one standing to the rear had a silly, glazed smile on his face and a very distant look in his pale blue eyes, while the one rapping on my window with knuckles the size of unshelled walnuts had a very close look in his eyes and no smile at all. I figured that together they could rip the door off the Caddy faster than I could slam it into reverse and pop the clutch, so I powered the window down a short inch and pleasantly said, 'Good morning, gentlemen.'

The one with the close look and no smile didn't believe in such idle pleasantries. 'Wha'chu out there in the parkin' lot bellerin' about?'

'Love,' I said, nudging the stick into reverse.

He hunkered down and grinned hugely against the glass. 'Yup,' he rumbled, 'ain't love a bitch?'

'Glad to see you're a man of understanding,' I told him, glad indeed. It was nice to see him smiling.

He pointed to his massive chest. 'I'm Harvey.' He pointed at the other young giant. 'That there's Bubba. He's my brother.'

'George, here.' I nodded to Harvey, then raised my voice so his brother could hear me: 'Ho there, Bubba. I'm George. Glad to meet you.'

Bubba rotated his head slightly to look at me, a movement that elicited the uneasy feeling that someone I couldn't see was running him by remote control. His mouth began to work for words, a labor that didn't change his happy, vacant expression.

'What's happening, Bubba?' I encouraged him.

'Bubba like head,' he announced.

'Don't we all. But love's a bitch, Bubba. You listen to your brother Harvey here.'

'We're looking for a whorehouse,' Harvey confided. 'Promised Bubba we'd get us some pussy once the crops was all in. One we been to last year and year before got closed up. You know where one is?'

I looked them over carefully, then lowered my voice. 'Not a whore*house*, but I know where you can get you a couple of *fine* women that'll party you boys till you beg for mercy.'

'Tell me slow so I can remember,' Harvey said.

I pointed at the door to Pancake Paradise. 'Right inside.'

Harvey shook his head. 'Been inside. Didn't see none. Just waitress ladies in there.'

'Whoa down now, Harvey. The *women* aren't in there, but their *pimp* is. Name's Granger. *Granger*. He owns the place. Don't talk to anyone else. Just Mr Granger. He'll pretend he doesn't know what you're talking about and tell you to leave and generally act mad – that's what he did with me at first – so what you have to do is tell him you're going to come out here in the parking lot, you and Bubba, and you're going to tear down his fucking lying Paradise sign with your bare hands unless he sets you up with Mandy and Ramona.'

'Mandy and Ramona,' Harvey repeated.

'They're my recommendation. You boys might want bigger girls to romp with, but I'll tell you, I spent last night with Mandy and Ramona, and look at *me*.'

Harvey leaned close against the glass and gave me a long look. 'Whooooooweeeeee,' he clapped his hands, beaming.

'Now the thing about Mandy and Ramona is they're both about five-foot-ten, and Mandy's got an ass like a valentine and Ramona can suck the knots out of an oak. And let me tell you true, they're both big where it really matters, you know what I mean?'

'Sure *do*.'

'That's right, Harvey, they've got the biggest hearts that ever poured selfless love out on a lucky man. You don't just *come* with these two, you *arrive*.'

Harvey looked puzzled but agreeable.

Bubba joined the conversation. 'Bubba like head.'

'Well then,' Harvey said decisively, grinning at his brother as he stood up, 'let's go get us some from that Mr Grange in there.'

'Wait, wait, wait,' I cautioned. 'Mr Gran*ger* might not be in. If he's not, get his home address. Tell whoever has it that you want to sell Mr Granger some buckwheat flour. Be *really* polite to everybody. None of them knows Mr Granger runs the wildest call-girl operation in the county. And remember: he doesn't like dealing with strangers, which is why you'll probably have to threaten to tear down this Paradise sign here – shit, I actually had to start rocking on it before he called the girls. And be sure to tell him that if he even *thinks* about calling the cops, you'll run his ass through your harvester and chop him up for silage.'

'That'd be *murder!*' Harvey was shocked.

'Well Good Christ, don't do it! Just *threaten*. Now the sign, of course, you *can* tear down. You see, you got to show pimps a little muscle or they'll just ignore you. Personally, I don't hold with hurting people.'

'Me neither,' Harvey said. 'I go to church come Sundays. Bubba don't like church much.'

'Yeah, but he likes head, and that's just as good.'

'Come *on*, Harv,' Bubba whined, tugging at his brother's arm.

'Now another thing,' I said as I slipped the clutch, 'whatever you do, stay away from the motel over there. It's *swarming* with undercover cops. You'll be in jail before your overalls hit your ankles.' The clutch engaged and I started to move. 'You boys have yourself a *good* time. Give Mandy and Ramona my best.'

They waved gratefully as I pulled away.

Siccing Harvey and Bubba on Granger and his false Paradise was mean, dangerous, and stupid, but it was not without wit, and there was the intriguing possibility of justice. Besides, I felt so rotten I wanted it to spread. Benzedrine withdrawal is not conducive to exquisite moral judgments, especially when there's a bottle of relief as close as the floor, a whole bunch of tiny white prisoners bearing the sign of the cross, each pounding on the glass and begging, 'George! Please save me. Swallow me now. Help! Please!'

I couldn't bear their pitiful wails, so I pulled over just before the Clear Lake/Mason City on-ramp, took the bottle out from under the seat, and, holding my breath, leaped out of the car and dashed around back and locked them in the trunk inside the cooler, plucking out two cans of beer to make room. I noticed the ice had hardly melted. Colder days and colder nights. I thought about dumping the ice to lighten my load, but that meant opening the trunk and resisting the temptation of that bottle of go-fast again, and once had been tempting enough. Let the ice melt in the blaze, sizzle through liquidity as it leaped from solid to gas. Let the cooler melt and the beer explode. Fuck yes, let it all roar upward in the cleansing flames. Ready or not, I was on my way, the last run. Even if I was crazy, it didn't matter now.

Part Three

THE PILGRIM
GHOST

'The self-seeker finds nothing.'
> —Goethe

RIGHT FOOT NAILED to the juice, needle jammed in triple digits, running full bore and pointblank, I made Mason City in about forty minutes. Given my punky reflexes, to justify flying like that was difficult, but it was a question of paying attention either to haul-ass driving or the wharf rats chewing on my nerves. I was, however, hanging on – like an old toothless hound with a gum-lock on a grizzly's ass, perhaps, but hanging on nonetheless. Two cold beers helped, the alcohol numbing the rawer edges while the liquid replenished my parched cells. I would've downed two more if I thought I could've opened the cooler without jumping the bottle of speed; yet another obstacle of my own devising, almost enough to make me curl up on the floorboards and weep. But that I was standing fast against the howling neural need for chemical refreshment made me believe I had a chance – slim, for sure, but gaining weight.

I didn't have a plan, though, which was just as well, since I lacked the sustained coherence to carry one out. However, in a typical burst of perversity I recalled all the recent stern injunctions to be careful, attend to details, assess the full range of possibilities, and generally keep in mind that fortune favors preparation – though it seemed to me that both mind and fortune were drunk monkeys in the tiger's eye. Startled by the Mason City city limits sign, I decided to at least lunge at the basics, so I made a jangled survey of the essential steps: eat; fill the Caddy with high-test; buy some white gas; and find out as exactly as possible where the plane had gone down. I did briefly consider how to get myself and my gear back from the crash site after burning my ride, but I figured a phone call to Yellow Cab could cover that. The first thing was to deliver the gift; then I'd worry about slipping away.

My first stop was the Blue Moon Cafe for an order of bacon, eggs, a short stack of buckwheat cakes, and some information. They had everything but the information, but one waitress conferred with the other, the other waitress queried the cook, and then the three together quizzed the other four patrons. The consensus was that Tommy Jorgenson was the person most likely to know exactly where the plane hit ground, and that I could probably find him at the Standard station eight blocks down on the left.

I finished what I could of my breakfast, left a $10 tip, and humped back out to the Caddy through the stinging cold. I'd overheard a ruddy-faced guy in a John Deere cap trying to sucker the Blue Moon's cook into betting that it wouldn't snow before dark, and as I fired up the Caddy I wished the cook had jumped on the wager. Not that I would've – you could feel snow gathering in the air. I just hoped it held off for a couple of hours. I didn't need to get sideways on a snow-slick road and wrap the Caddy around a power pole a few miles short of my destination. I'd come too long and too hard for that kind of cruel irony. Once the Caddy was warmed up, I drove downtown to the Standard station at nary a quiver over the posted 25 mph.

Tommy Jorgenson surprised me. I suppose his name had made me expect a tall, slowly thoughtful Scandinavian instead of what I got, a short wiry guy with spring-coiled black hair and intense brown eyes that never quit moving even when he was looking straight at me – one of those restlessly kinetic people who wash their ceilings every week just to burn off the energy. Until you get to know them, you suspect they're secretly banging speed.

But they don't need it. They run off their own systems, DC; they're just naturally wrapped tight.

I told Tommy to fill 'er up, then got out and followed him around as he put the nozzle in the tank and started on checking the oil and cleaning glass. I introduced myself as a reporter for *Life* magazine and told him I'd been on vacation visiting my sister in Des Moines when I'd gotten this wild idea about doing a major feature on the three musicians who'd been killed in the plane wreck – sort of a retrospective memorial piece – and that I was interested in visiting the crash site.

Tommy shot me a glance as he wiped the dipstick. 'Isn't there no more.' He dropped the dipstick back into the hole.

'What do you mean,' I chattered, 'it's *not* there? It *has* to be there. It's a place, a site, a point in fact – even if it's been paved over for a parking lot, it's still *there*.' The cold was numbing.

Tommy pulled out the dipstick and held it up for my inspection. It was a hair under full. I nodded rapidly, as much to move some blood to my brain as to indicate that the oil level was fine.

Tommy said a bit sharply, 'Of *course* nobody's *moved* the place. I meant there's nothing left to see. They had the wreck cleaned up right away and the field was plowed and planted the next spring.'

'Now we're talking.' I grinned.

'You still want to check it out?' Tommy replaced the dipstick and dropped the hood.

'You bet.'

'Why?'

'Good question.' I stalled, thinking to myself, *Fuck good questions. What I need are good, precise, unequivocal answers.* 'I have lots of reasons, all complicated. I guess the main reason is simply to pay my respects. Another's more practical. I've got this idea for a lead running around in my head. Something like: "On a snow-swirling night in early February, 1959, a small Beechcraft left the Mason City airport and shortly thereafter crashed in an

Iowa cornfield. Along with the pilot, three young musicians were killed: the Big Bopper, Buddy Holly, and Ritchie Valens. As I stand here at the precise point of impact on a late October afternoon six years later, there is no visible evidence of the wreckage. For six springs this field has been plowed and sown; for six autumns the harvest reaped. The earth and the music heal quickly. The heart takes longer."' I paused for whatever effect a pause might have. 'I know, it's rough as hell, but you get the angle. I suppose the best way to put it is that I'm hoping to draw some inspiration from the place.'

'I'll draw you a map,' Tommy said.

Music to my ears, the last piece clicking into place. I was starting to like the little dynamo. Maybe the reason Tommy throbbed with energy was that he didn't waste any. I felt like grabbing a pair of jumper cables and hooking us up, brain to brain – boost some of his juice. The cold was draining mine through the corroded terminals. 'I take it,' I said, 'you've been out to the crash site.'

'Yup.'

'Recently?'

'Nope. Last time was early '62, over three years ago.'

'You see it after it happened?'

'My old man's a deputy sheriff. I heard the call come in on the box at home. I'd been there the night before, at the Surf Ballroom, where they played that night. That was over in Clear Lake. Almost every kid from around these parts was there; we don't draw much top-line entertainment in these parts. It was a good show, but not great. They looked tired and beat. 'Course I was shit-faced on vodka. What we called a Cat Screwdriver – half a pint of Royal Gate, half a pint of Nehi orange soda. So when the call came in, even though I was hung over down to my ankles, I had to go out and see if it was true. Had no idea how true it was. Turned me inside out. Must've puked for an hour.'

My stomach churned in empathy. Breakfast wasn't setting well.

The bellyful of cold beer had congealed the bacon grease into a solid, sinking chunk; if it kept falling, it was sure to come back up. It's hard to grit your teeth when they're chattering, and it was my turn to ask why: 'But you went back in '62, right?'

Tommy's sigh plumed in the air. 'Yeah. Actually, I went out there a couple of times a month for a while. Don't know why. Nothing to see but the corn growing. I had a chopped '51 Ford coupe at the time, metal-flake green, dropped a T-Bird engine in it. All souped-up and nowhere to go. Or nowhere better. One thing, it was real peaceful just sitting there watching the breeze move the cornstalks. So, I'd tool out there fairly often – ain't far, and there's a long straight stretch where you can run flat out, coming and going. But after I blew the transmission, I went out less and less. Last time was February third, '62. The anniversary. Don't know why, though. Never thought about it. Just did.'

Before I could ask my next question, he turned and was moving back along the Caddy. By the time I caught up he was topping off the tank. 'Don't mean to pester a man on the job, but I wonder if you know who owns the land where the plane crashed? Figure I should get permission before I go trespassing around in somebody's corn patch.'

'Corn's in,' Tommy noted, withdrawing the nozzle and shutting down the pump.

'That's just less cover for my ass.'

Tommy smiled. 'Bert Julhal used to own it, but I heard Gladys Nogardam bought it from him a couple of years ago. I'm not sure about that, wouldn't bet on it anyway, but I'm pretty sure ol' Gladys bought it. She must be a hundred years old now and people say she's still sharp as a tack.'

'What's her story?' Information is ammunition, and I had a bad feeling I'd best load up. A woman that old and still lucid would undoubtedly know her own mind, which would make changing it more difficult in case she didn't dig my romantic gesture. I hadn't been around a lot of old women lately, and the few I knew no longer seemed inclined to suffer what they found disagreeable.

Tommy was shaking his head. 'Never met the woman myself, but I've heard a lot about her. She lived over in Clear Lake for about twenty years, married to Duster Nogardam. Duster was this big Swede dentist, but what he was famous for was skeet shooting. He was on the '34 Olympic team, came in fifth or ninth or something like that. Anyway, sometime after that – don't remember exactly – he went out pheasant hunting over on the Lindstrom place and just vanished. Car parked right beside the road. Never seen or heard from since. She finally inherited his estate. She got a little weird, I gather – wandered around at night, stuff like that. She bought the Julhal place because she said she was too old for city life and needed some fresh air. That's what she told Lottie Williams, anyway. I heard it from my mom. You know how small towns are – live in each other's pockets. Old lady Nogardam don't work the place, of course. Leases it to the Potts brothers is what I heard.'

'Wait a minute. Let's take that back. Her husband just *vanished?* Poof? No trace?' For some reason I wasn't liking that at all.

I liked it three times less when Tommy said, 'Same thing happened to her first two husbands, too. That's the *strange* thing.'

'Three husbands and they *all* disappeared?'

'Yup.'

'*Who* says? I mean, are we talking rumor, fact, or what?'

'My old man's a deputy, right? He read the police reports.'

'How'd she *explain* it? They must've grilled the ever-loving shit out of her – three husbands vanishing is damn near impossible. Hell, *two*'s impossible.'

'According to Dad, she said she couldn't explain it. She said explaining it was their job.'

'And they couldn't, right?'

'Like Dad said, "Coincidence isn't evidence."'

'I assume her husbands all had hefty estates. Or some heavy insurance.'

'Nope,' Tommy shook his head, 'that's the kicker. Duster had a few bucks, and the second one – I think he had a ranch in Arizona – was barely making ends meet, but the first one was hocked to his armpits. He was a linoleum distributor in Chicago. They'd only been married a couple of years. She and Duster had been together for twenty or thereabouts; ten with the guy in Arizona, I think.'

'And she had alibis and all that?'

'Airtight, ironclad, not a crack. For all of them, not just Duster. Or that's what my dad said.'

'I don't get it,' I said, flapping my arms for warmth.

'Don't feel like the Lone Ranger.'

'What do *you* think? She hire it out, they just get called to their Maker, take a walk, spaceships come down and spirit them away, what?'

'Spaceships,' Tommy said.

I couldn't tell if he was kidding or not, and suddenly I didn't care. I was freezing, and in a rotten mood to start with. Spaceships, sure – made as much fucking sense as anything. I reached for my wallet. 'How much do I owe you?'

He glanced at the pump. 'Six eighty-five ought to get it.'

'You carry white gas?'

'Gallon cans. Nothing in bulk.'

'Gallon's perfect. I've got a little single-burner Coleman in the trunk to brew up coffee – put a little antifreeze in my system.'

'Might try a jacket along with it,' Tommy observed.

'No shit.' I chuckled, handing him a twenty. 'I gave mine to some poor bastard I picked up hitching last night. All he had on was an undershirt.'

'You meet some nuts, all right,' Tommy said as he took the bill. He headed for the office, calling over his shoulder, 'I'll bring you the map and the white gas with your change. Might be a few minutes with the map.'

'Hey, no problem,' I called after him. 'And you keep the change. Good information's more valuable than gas. And that map: I would really appreciate it if you make it as precise as possible . . . you know, "*X* marks the spot."'

Tommy stopped to protest the tip but I waved him on. 'The magazine pays for it. Legit expense. Hell, I'd give you a hundred if they'd hold still for it.'

I waited in the Caddy, letting it idle with the heater on full blast. I made a mental note to buy a heavy jacket before I left town, chastising myself for giving mine to Lewis Kerr when I remembered the foilwrapped cube of LSD that was still in the pocket. This added another dimension of possibilities to last night's transactions. I hoped the acid somehow managed to get into his bloodstream – not that the world was ready for a hallucinating Lewis Kerr, though the notion pleased me immensely.

I wasn't happy about Granny Nogardam and her missing husbands, so I gave this a few minutes of serious worry, cursing my luck. Why couldn't it *ever* be simple? Why wasn't the landowner some crop-failed farmer who'd be overjoyed to let me do any damn fool thing I wanted for twenty bucks and a six-pack, and throw in a ride back to town? But what the hell, maybe she would, too. No way to know till I asked. And I'd be doing that soon enough. I felt a tiny, voluptuous tremor of anticipation surge through me then, a little premonitory quiver of impending completion, and it thrilled me. I closed my eyes to savor the feeling and saw the Caddy parked in the middle of an ivory desolation, gleaming white-on-white. No sound. No movement. Then a flat, muffled WHUMP! as the white gas ignited and then a blinding roar as the gas tank exploded. Yes, yes, yes. Signed with love; sealed with a kiss. The gift delivered. I was dreaming on the verge of occurrence. I felt its inevitability in my bones. It was *meant* to happen. *Had* to be. No question.

When Tommy came hustling across the slab a few minutes later with the map and white gas, I was ready to make the last move, set the last piece in place. I was wasted but drawing strength from the promise of imminent release, about to lay that burden down.

The map, as I expected, was deft and precise. Tommy went over it with me quickly, and unnecessarily since the route was so simple – maybe ten miles of straight roads with only three turns to remember. In the field in back of the house marked NOGARDAM was a large *X*, carefully circled. I thanked Tommy for his help and insisted he keep the change, my sincerity not the least compromised by the fact I'd solicited his help under false pretenses.

Heading out of town, I remembered I should buy a warm jacket and generally get my shit together . . . have things organized in case Granny Nogardam proved intractable and I was forced to hit and run. I was all set to let it rip, but as Joshua and Double-Gone had cautioned me, that wasn't sufficient justification for the wholesale violation of common sense.

As if in reward for my display of mature judgment, I immediately spotted a JC Penney's and was about to hang a left when to my right I saw a hand-lettered sign propped against a sawhorse next to a Phillips station:

CAR WASH $1

BENEFIT METHODIST CHOIR

I hung the right on impulse, figuring the least I could do was send the Caddy to its sacrifice clean.

The Methodist Choir Car Wash crew seemed to be composed entirely of ruddy-cheeked, blue-eyed, vestal eighteen-year-old girls, all of whom, unfortunately, were bundled against the cold. I wondered who sang bass. They were swabbing away on a '63

Chrysler, with an old Jimmy pick-up next in line. They were singing 'What a Fortress Is My Lord' as they worked. The young lady who bounced over to greet me said it would be fifteen or twenty minutes if I didn't mind waiting. I told her that would be fine as long as they'd keep an eye on the car and hold my place while I trotted across the road.

I was back in fifteen sporting a new red-and-green plaid wool jacket and carrying a bag with insulated longjohns and a pair of pink mohair earmuffs that almost matched my hat. The girls were still rinsing pig shit off the Jimmy, so I used the Phillips men's room to slip into my long-johns. By the time I was properly dressed for the weather, the choir was ready to baptise the Caddy. Before I pulled it up I took my duffle bag from the trunk, using their witness to curb any temptation to hit the cooler for crank.

While they scrubbed off three thousand miles of road grime and sang 'Rock of Ages,' I sat in the Caddy getting my gear together and cleaning up beer cans and donut wrappers off the floor. I divided my possessions into three categories: immediate getaway essentials, basically the clothes on my back and the balance of my funds, which looked considerably depleted; the second category was walkaway, namely my duffle bag and everything I could fit into it; the third category was breezeaway, and included the first two plus everything else I felt like taking, notably Joshua's sound system and the record collection. I figured the cooler was dispensable, but I'd take the speed. I deserved it.

I finished arranging my gear at about the same time that the Methodist Choir was wringing out their chamois. I powered down the window to pay and learned that the price included vacuuming the inside, and for another 50¢ they'd do the interior glass. Sounded like a deal to me, so I got out and wandered over to a phone booth while four of them, Windex squirting and vacuum humming, swarmed inside.

Just for fun I decided to give Scumball a jingle and tell him the deal was about to go down: time to relax. I dialed the last number he'd given me. On the third ring a recording informed me the number was no longer in service.

The girls were still working so, hoping to hear a friendly voice, I tried John Season's number. Nobody home. I hoped he wasn't out drinking, then recalled the remark about a physician first healing himself.

I thought about calling Gladys Nogardam, but decided against it. Let us both be surprised.

The Caddy looked so good I tipped the gospel ladies a five-spot, much to their wowed delight. They wanted to ask me about the car and California and the strange record player in the back seat, but I told them I was running late for a religious duty of my own and departed with a gallant tip of my hat.

Going slow and easy, I rolled out to the crossroads noted on Tommy's map and took the left. Thinking it would be an appropriate touch, I put some music on the box, first the Bopper with 'Chantilly Lace,' then Ritchie Valens's 'Donna.' I took a right on Elbert Road, and two miles later a left. Feeling serious, confident, ceremonially formal, I put on Buddy Holly's 'Not Fade Away,' drumming my fingers on the steering wheel rim as I checked the mailboxes against the map: Altman, Potts, Peligro, and there it was – Nogardam.

A white farmhouse with dark green trim, freshly painted, it was set back from the road and fronted a large fenced field of corn stubble. Next to the house was a garage or some sort of storage building, but no car or other sign of occupancy. I turned down the gravelled drive just as Buddy belted out the last line, 'Love that's love not fade away.' I clicked it off on the last note and shut down the Caddy. *Wop: doo-wop: doo-wop-bop*. On the beat, right on time; there, ready, and arrived. I took a deep breath and stepped out to ask Mrs Nogardam's permission – not that I was going to need it, just that it would make things easier. As I walked toward the enclosed porch I found myself repeating her name to myself like a charm: *Nogardam; No-gard-am; No-guard-em*. I certainly hoped so.

She caught me badly off guard. The porch was damn near dark and I'd already given the heavy screendoor frame two strong, confident raps before I realized the front door was open behind the screen and she was already standing there. 'Oh,' I said in a burst of wit, 'I didn't see you.'

'Obviously.' Her voice was raspy but plenty forceful. In the interior shadows of the darkened house, further obscured by the screen, I could barely make her out. There was enough light to see she was hardly a withered crone – in fact, though indeed stooped with age, she was just a bit shorter than me, which must've put her over six feet in her prime. She was wearing a dark grey dress of some coarse material, her shoulders draped in a black shawl. Her hair, pulled severely back, was the silver color of leached ashes. Her face was deeply wrinkled, and the lines drew inward toward her eyes, eyes the color of dark beer held up to the light, a gold at once clear and obscure, eyes that were watching me unblinking, waiting.

'Mrs Nogardam?' I inquired tentatively, trying to recover my equilibrium.

'Yes.'

I tipped my hat, hoping to make it look boyishly charming.

'That's a ridiculous hat,' she declared, her voice like a file hitting a nail.

'Yes, ma'am,' I said benignly, buying time while frantically considering an angle of approach. That she wasn't going to invite me in for a glass of warm milk and a plate of cookies was plain, nor would she likely yield to stuttering good intentions and scuff-toed boyish charm. Her unflinching gaze made up my mind. I touched my hat brim again, a gesture I hoped looked absently wounded, and said, 'Sure it's ridiculous, but that's altogether appropriate to the rather strange journey that brings me to your door. I call it "strange," but it has also become urgent and compelling, important enough that I would call it "essential," at least to me, and a journey that's impossible to complete without your kind permission, Mrs Nogardam.'

'Whistles and flutes,' she said.

'No ma'am,' I assured her, 'even worse: I'm going to tell you the truth.'

That got her interest. She cocked her head slightly and folded her arms across her bosom. Encouraged by her attention, I laid it on her, the whole truth and nothing but, the condensed version, about ten minutes straight as she listened without comment, shift of weight, change of expression, or any indication of judgment. Told her how I came to have the car; quoted Harriet's letter; explained Eddie, Kacy, Big Red, John, Scumball; the Big Bopper, Buddy Holly, and Ritchie Valens, and their music; mentioned Joshua, Double-Gone, Donna, and the rest. I told her as directly and forcefully as I could and, considering the duress of necessity, did an amazing job, damn near eloquent. I finished by telling her exactly what I wanted to do – to let it all roar upwards in an offering to the ghosts, the living spirits, the enduring possibilities of friendship, communion, and love. I concluded with a flourish: 'It is all grandly romantic, yes; ridiculous, of course; surely melodramatic; indubitably flawed; rightfully suspect – but it is as real to me as hunger and thirst, as crucial as food and water. I've told you my truth, such as it is. I've done everything I have the wit and spirit to do. This is the end of my journey. Now it's up to you, Mrs Nogardam. Please permit me to complete it.'

She uncrossed her arms. 'You're a fool,' she said flatly.

'Yes ma'am, I believe I've conceded that point.'

'I'm ninety-seven years old.'

I didn't see the relevance of that, but murmured politely, 'People in town said you were over a hundred.'

'People in town talk too much for people who have little to say. In that they're like you, Mr Gastin.'

'Be that as it may, Mrs Nogardam,' I said, trying to keep a nasty edge from my tone, 'what do *you* say?'

'I already said it: you're a fool. And one of the few blessings of my age is that I don't have to suffer fools – either gladly or at all.'

I felt like tearing down the screendoor and strangling the old witch, but instead took a deep, shuddering lungful of air. 'Then don't. Just tell me yes or no.'

'That's why you're a fool,' she snapped. 'You want to be told. You think you've earned the right simply because you have an idea that you've allowed to bloat into a need. Because you're paralyzed with confusion. Because you've driven a few thousand miles on drugs and good intentions and a fool's hope. Phooeey. Does believing you're in love make you capable of love? Are you a priest simply because you're willing to perform the sacrifice? What rights have you *earned* in these matters? Mr Gastin, there's no permission I can give you; only folly I can prevent. If you want to make this grand offering of yours, this homage you've concocted as some secret proof of your worthiness, this testament to a faith you so obviously suspect, don't saddle *me* with the responsibility of judgment. It isn't a question of my yes or no.'

'You mean it's up to me?' I didn't follow at all. She was full of judgments, it seemed to me.

'Of course it's up to you, since you won't accept anything other than certainty. Very well, then: if you can go out in that field and find exactly where that plane crashed, you'll have earned the right to deliver your gift, as you call it; and you'll not only have my permission to set it ablaze or any other fool thing you choose, but I'll gladly come out and dance around the fire with you, and pay to have the remains hauled away. But if you *can't* discover the precise point of impact, you must give me your word that you'll go on your way without bothering me further.'

'With due respect, Mrs Nogardam, I've come a long way, I'm

very tired, and I'm not in the mood for proofs of my worthiness, or yours.'

'Then leave.'

'The fact that it's your property by purchase doesn't grant you the privileges of the heart. People own a lot of things that don't belong to them.'

In the dim light I saw her bony fingers flutter at her throat. 'Well, dear me. I must say, Mr Gastin, that that's pretty high-falutin' from someone whose property is literally theft, whose gift is stolen. But you *are* right, and I do agree. In fact, I have walked out in that field and felt exactly where those young men died. *Felt it*, do you understand? I am able or allowed to do so. And *that*, not ownership, is my claim to privilege. If you can do the same, you'll have as much right in the matter as I do. But any shenanigans or tomfoolery, and I'll stop you.'

'You will?' I wasn't challenging her, merely curious about the means.

'I'll certainly try. And if *I* can't, there's neighbors or the sheriff.'

I softened my tone and played the ace she'd dealt me: 'I told you the truth because I want to do this without deception on my part or objection on yours. I didn't have to tell you the car was stolen; I could've said it was mine, or a friend's, or thousands of other lies. But I want this to be *right*. That's why it's a point of honor with me to tell you I *already* know where the plane crashed.' I took Tommy's map from my jacket pocket and unfolded it, spreading it flat against the screen for her to look at. 'There it is.'

Her attention locked on the map. After a minute of hard scrutiny, she stabbed with a crooked finger and asked, 'Here? The *X*?'

'Yes, ma'am. The man who drew that map for me saw the wreckage before it was cleared, and came back many times afterwards.'

'The map's wrong.'

I hadn't even considered that possibility and was momentarily confounded. 'Well, now,' I began with feigned reluctance, '*you* say it's wrong. *He* claims it's right. He was *here* and you *weren't*. You say you *felt* it. He *saw* it. It seems awfully relative to—'

'If you want to discuss philosophy,' she bluntly interrupted, 'I suggest you try the university – they've made an institution out of mistaking the map for the journey.'

'I'm not trying to be offensive, Mrs Nogardam. All I'm saying is you *could* be wrong. That's all. That it *is* possible you're mistaken.'

'Then go look for yourself. You have till dark. No tricks.' She shut the door.

The door was white, and shutting it had the bizarre effect of making the porch seem brighter. I stared at it, all at once pissed off, crushed, set to explode, dejected, gutted, wrecked, enraged, and lost. I headed back to the Caddy in a dazed stomp, mumbling aloud, 'Why, why, why, why, why, why did it have to be some batshit old lady culled from the geriatric ward, some vestal guardian of corn stubble? *Fuck her*, goddamn it anyway . . . just get in the Caddy and crank it up till the head glows and turn it loose right through the motherfucking fence out into the field and grab your shit and touch it off and run like hell . . .' mumble grumble till I was standing next to the Caddy. The air seemed to have thickened. I gazed out into the field toward the general area of the *X* on Tommy's map. '"Go look for yourself." What the holy shit does she *think* I've been doing?' I opened the Caddy's door, slid in, and slammed it behind me.

The sound of the slamming door carried across the harvested field. As if precipitated by the sonic disturbance, big fat flakes of snow began to fall. Just what I needed. Was it meant to cover the clues I was supposed to seek, or was it supposed to cloak my getaway? Or was it a shroud to conveniently cover that old witch's body should I follow my deepest impulse and beat her to death with a ball peen hammer? Did it in fact signify anything other than what it was? Snow.

I was getting all wound up for another bout of metaphysical babble. The snow was swirling thick, silent, peaceful. I leaned forward, my chin resting on my hands on the wheel, and gradually relaxed as I watched snow swaddle the field; mound on the fenceposts; settle then melt on the Caddy's hood, still warm from engine heat; stick to the windshield for a heartbeat, the intricate crystals dissolving into slow rivulets sliding down. Within fifteen minutes, about the time the snowflakes began sticking on the cooled windshield to obliterate my view, a weary calm came over me. I decided to try it her way first; maybe I'd learn something. I zipped my jacket all the way up and slapped on my new earmuffs.

I must've spent a couple of hours in that field searching for physical evidence that was perhaps being obliterated as I sought it, and for some sort of metaphysical evidence that I wasn't sure I'd recognize even if I were capable of sensing it. Wild, dense, relentless, the snow fell, cutting visibility to the length of a stride. I tried to approach the task methodically, crossing back and forth between the east-west fences, trying to maintain roughly parallel lines, but when the tracks of your last pass are buried before you can start back, when you can't see the fences till you twang into them, when you're essentially following your frozen face, that method is doomed. I had no idea whether I was constructing a crisp, evenly proportioned grid or merely lurching back and forth in the same groove. But I *did know* that I was rapidly losing feeling in my extremities in absolute direct proportion to the feeling of immense futility swelling in my heart. By the time I floundered back to the Caddy I couldn't even feel the cold anymore, just a powerful desire to lie down on the front seat and sleep. Maybe even die. It was all the same.

But first I had to get into the car, and to get the door open took a good jerk, and then another to free my bare hand from the frozen handle. It was almost as cold inside the Caddy as in that forsaken field. After considerable crude fumbling with the key, the Caddy turned over torpidly, then caught. I used my elbow to turn the heater up to cook and spread my hands in front of the vent.

My fingers resembled some mad confectioner's display of blueberry popsicles. As they thawed toward tingling, I thought about energy and its wondrous, manifold, interpenetrating forms: thermal, kinetic, moral, hydraulic, metabolic, all of it. The energy required to warm you, maintain you, move you. Ergs – that basic grunt unit – in waves, calorie, current: x ergs required for each step on the journey, each turn of the wheels, each prayer uttered, answered, acted upon. The energy captured, transformed, released. The energy just to drive the welter of transactions. This was a melancholy contemplation, because while the world plainly vibrated with energy, personally I was just about out, the flesh sorely overdrawn and the soul about to be foreclosed. What remained to me as possible energy, the power I would need to act on the intractable Mrs Nogardam and answer her psychic pop quiz, was energy that I, with sad realism, understood was *false*: money, amphetamines, and madness. But I'd said I'd give it everything I had.

Once my fingers were again semifunctional, the tips alive with a burning ache, I dug out my bankroll and counted out $2000 in a hundred $20 bills. I folded and wadded them in my jacket pocket, flexed my fingers a few times, and headed back to Mrs Nogardam's lair to talk business. I left the Caddy running in case the negotiations dragged on; I didn't want to come home to a cold house. Besides, I had plenty of gas and nowhere left to go.

She'd seen me coming and had the door open, her gold eyes boring into me through the screen, only this time I saw her, too, and didn't knock. Instead, the hand I raised contained $2000. Fanning the bills like a deck of cards, I pressed them against the screen for her authentication. 'What you see, ma'am, is what you get. That's two grand, a considerable dent in my cash assets – leaves me enough for a half-dozen grilled cheese sandwiches and a Greyhound ticket home. And it's all yours, right now, *if* you let me honor the dead.' I tapped the money lightly against the screen. 'So what do you say we cut the horseshit here and both make ourselves happy?'

'You can't buy it,' she said, her voice flat as Iowa. The door closed.

I kicked the aluminum-framed bottom of the screendoor, screaming in frustration, 'Be reasonable, you old cunt!'

The door flew back open. 'You mind your foul mouth, Mr Gastin, or your time will be up right now. Do you understand?'

The fire in her eyes had the paradoxical effect of forming ice in my scrotum. I flapped the money weakly, then tucked my hand into my jacket pocket as I nodded my meek understanding.

She continued, 'I made the conditions clear. It is almost three o'clock. By five it's dark.'

'But ma'am,' I pleaded, 'it's a snow storm out there.'

Her eyes didn't leave me. 'So it is.' The door closed.

I trudged back to the Caddy through snow up to midcalf, though it seemed to have slackened a bit. Before getting back in my snow-bound landrocket I scraped the crust off the windshield with my coat sleeve. Softened by the heat from inside, it wiped right off.

I leaned back behind the wheel, a clear view through the windshield now, and watched the snow fall like cold confetti on my stalled parade. I felt utterly, dismally deflated. To try and buy it had been stupid. I closed my eyes and tried to concentrate on the options, but either my concentration was shot or there weren't many options. I could leave, try to find Tommy, and bring him back with me, though he'd probably come on-shift at 6:00 and was gone for the day. Besides, I'd have to convince him to drive out and tangle assholes with Granny, and there was no guarantee the old hag would acknowledge Tommy's memory of the crash.

Nope, I decided, it was pretty much down to satisfying her or running her over, and I didn't have the energy for either job.

Well, not *on* me. The trunk, however, wasn't that far away. After all, it had taken me this far, and I sure didn't seem to be getting anywhere without the help. I would take three – no more – to freshen up. I promised myself that if I took them, I'd try her way one more time before resorting to mine. I reached down and turned off the engine and was withdrawing the key when I noticed that in the course of my brief reverie it had stopped snowing. The sky was still leaden, but the scene to my eye was silent, pristine, clear. Looked like a sign.

When I opened the cooler in the trunk and seized the bottle of crank like an osprey nailing a fish, I perceived a small problem. Instead of a bottle of small, neatly cross-hatched white tablets, I had a bottle about a quarter full of a pale white liquid: I hadn't screwed the lid down tight and water from the cooler had trickled in, dissolving the tablets into a thin slurry. Well, as long as only the form and not the substance had been altered, I'd merely have to make a careful guess at the proper dosage. Recalling from high-school chemistry that alcohol lowered the freezing point, I fished a six-pack out of the cooler while I was at it, and then closed the trunk.

I ended up having a wonderful wake in the front seat: three sips of speed, four beers, and a solid hour of Golden Oldies turned up so loud they blew the snow off the Caddy and loosened the siding on Granny Nogardam's house. I listened to everything I had of the Bopper, Buddy, and Ritchie, hoping the sound of their music would stir their lingering spirits to help me.

A love for real not fade away!!!

'Not!' I screamed. 'Not! *Not!*' I hoped Granny was listening.

I stumbled from the Caddy and headed out to the field in the long-shadowed dusk. I hadn't left myself much time. As I went over the fence I yelled, 'Bopper, my man! Buddy Holly! Ritchie! Talk to me. Tell me where to deliver this load of a gift. Got love and prayers for you. Got 'em from Harriet. Got 'em from Donna, Ritchie – she's sending her best. She's sort of fucked-up in Arizona right now, but she's trying, man. Everybody's trying, you guys hear me? Double-Gone, Joshua, Kacy, John – they all send their love. The real kind that doesn't fade away. So even if it doesn't matter to you guys now, don't mean shit to your gone spirits, it matters to me, to us. So talk to me. Guide me. Tell me where you want this monument to love and music burned, where you want the dark lit up.'

The snow started falling again, lightly, a few drifting flakes. No voices answered, inside or out, but I felt a faint tug of direction and began walking, starting around the fence-line and then spiraling inward, closing as the snow fell faster, thicker, until I could hardly see my own feet, till I felt like I was vanishing, and then my left foot came down on something solid. I knelt and searched with both hands in the snow until I touched it, slick and cold, and lifted it close to my face for a look. I bit back a scream when I realized it was a bone; then laughed with crazy relief when I recognized it as an antler, a deer's shed horn, a thick main beam forked into two long tines, weathered a faint moss-green, nicked here and there with sharp, double-incised grooves where rodents had chewed it for minerals. I couldn't stop laughing. 'Great. Just what I needed. A fucking deer horn. Don't you guys understand I already got enough pieces for the puzzle? Probably got more fucking pieces than there *is* puzzle. Come on, now: help me out, don't mess me around.' I brandished the horn to emphasize my point. It slipped out of my numb hand, burying itself base down in the snow, tines spread upright like the forks of a river joining to plunge straight down into the earth. And there it was, by sheer accident, right in front of my face: a divining rod, a witcher's forked stick, a wand to dowse the spot where their ghosts broke free of their broken bodies. The key, or at least a tool to pick the lock.

With snow mounding on my flamingo hat, piling across the plaid shoulders of my jacket, my hands, feet, and face frozen beyond feeling, I worked the field with the bone wand held steadily poised in front of me, my whole being condensed to the receptive tip, waiting for its plunge. I spiraled slowly out from the center of the field, wired to the slightest stirring, faintest sense, a pulse, a trembling, anything. And I didn't feel the slightest quiver of response – nothing; zilch; zero. It was solid dark when I gave up.

The porchlight was the only sign of life at the house. I expected her to be waiting behind the screen, but the door was closed. I knocked. Coming back defeated across the field, I'd tried to compose a new plea, but it no longer seemed to matter. When she opened the door I didn't even look up.

'Well?' she demanded, friendly as ever.

I felt the tears coming and, afraid my voice would crack, shook my head without speaking.

'You'd better go now,' she said, and for the first time, I sensed a hint of sympathy in her voice.

Not much, but it encouraged me to give it a try. 'I'd guess somewhere near the center of the field. It's the only place I felt anything. I found a deer horn there, close to where the X is on the map. But you already said that was wrong.'

'It is.'

'You couldn't be mistaken?'

'It's unlikely.'

'Would you tell me where the spot is?'

'No. You agreed to the conditions. You didn't fulfill them. Now kindly leave.'

'I want to come back tomorrow and try again.'

She didn't answer or give any indication she'd heard.

I'd tried everything except begging, so I figured I'd give that a shot: 'Please, Mrs Nogardam. *Please?*'

'I told you *no*, Mr Gastin. Now I want you to leave.'

I slammed my fist against the screendoor frame, jolting it open for an instant before the spring whipped it shut again. '*Damn* your cold ass,' I wept. 'How can you possibly judge what I'm all about, what this means to me, how much . . .' but I stopped because she hadn't even flinched, not a blink, a start, a step back, nothing. Just watching me with those dark gold eyes.

I wiped at the tears with my sleeve, some clinging snow from my stingy-brim plopping to the porch floor. 'Why can't I make you see how much this matters? And not just to me, either. Donna, Joshua, Double-Gone, my friends in San Francisco – what do I tell *them?*

'Tell them you failed. Tell them pity is a polite form of loathing. Tell them I didn't pity you.'

'What fucking *right*—' I started to rage but she suddenly lifted an arm and pointed past me into the darkness. I stopped cold.

'Mr Gastin, if you want to work off your anger and confusion there's a snow shovel leaning against the back of the porch. You'll need it to clear a path to get out. Good night.' She shut the door.

I picked up the shovel on my way back to the Eldorado. I started the car to let it warm up, took a little gulp of speed to lubricate my muscles, then started shoveling. There was about 200 feet of driveway out to the main road and I dug right in, not a thought in my raving mind except moving snow, and without thought there was no confusion, just the scrape of shovel against the gravel roadway, the grunt of breath as I lifted, pitched, and took another bite. In about twenty minutes I finished, walked back down the cleared drive, and replaced the shovel, figuring that I was, if nothing else, a success as a human snowplow.

Back across the drifted yard, I used my forearm to wipe snow from the corners of the windshield, then wiped the same forearm across my sweaty face. I was so warm, in fact, that when I slipped behind the wheel, I had to turn down the heater. I took another gritty swig of speed to replace lost fluids, turned on the wipers to clear the slush from the windshield, clicked the lights to highbeams, dropped it into reverse, and came off the clutch. The drive wheels spun for a second, then gripped. Aiming between the bullet taillights, staying light and steady on the gas, I backed out to the road.

When I felt the rear wheels on the pavement I stopped, slammed it into low, and screaming 'Oh *baaay-beeee*, you *know* what I *like!*' I stood on the gas. There was a shuddering second before the rubber fastened the power to the road and then I was smoking back down the driveway like a silver bullet, a dead bead on the fence, hoping I'd have enough speed to crash through into the field.

I never found out. Just as I nailed it into second and felt the Caddy leap forward in a spray of gravel and snow, a blast of flame exploded from near the porch and the Caddy's right front end collapsed, the momentum snapping the rear end around so hard I felt it wanting to flip, but I squared it away as best I could and whipped around through a full 360°, showering snow. Then, I cut the lights and engine and bailed out, still uncertain what had happened.

Mrs Nogardam was standing in front of me in a white parka, hood drawn tight about her face, the shotgun in her hands pointed at my throat. 'I asked you to leave,' she said with a mean, even patience.

'Ma'am, that's what I was doing.' I couldn't keep the pounding of my heart out of my voice.

'No, you were just being foolish.'

'I stand corrected,' I said, beginning to relax – she wasn't going to shoot. 'And it looks like I might be standing here corrected for a while longer, because I think you just shot my way out. Where were you aiming?'

'Where I hit: the right-front tire.' She lowered the gun slightly. 'If you've got a spare, change it. If not, it looks like you'll have to use some of that money on a tow truck.'

The possibility of that irony made me reckless.

'Ma'am,' I asked mildly, 'is that by any chance a Remington twenty-gauge pump?'

'It is.'

'I had one just like it when I was a kid growing up in Florida. Used it on quail. You use yours on your husbands?'

Reckless, but it got to her: her eyes flashed and the gun barrel came back up to lock on my throat. Her voice was tight. 'I find it difficult to believe you grew up, Mr Gastin. I find about as much evidence for your maturity as the police found for my involvement in my husbands' disappearances. None. Because there was none.'

'You realize, of course,' I said softly, 'you'll have to kill me. I'm not giving up. This is something I *have* to do.'

'No you don't,' she said. 'But you probably will. That does not mean you're going to do it here. I was calling the sheriff about the time you were putting the shovel back. I told him I thought there was a prowler. I doubt if he'll hurry – I'm not popular with local law enforcement – but he should make it in twenty minutes or so, and then you can discuss rights and wrongs with him. Or you can hurry and change your tire. Or you can try to take this gun away. I won't kill you – believe me or not, I've never killed anything in my life. But you might live the rest of yours without a knee, or the ability to reproduce.'

'I was wrong,' I told her. 'You didn't shoot your husbands – you froze 'em to death. Or froze 'em out so bad they were glad to vanish.'

Though she didn't reply, her shoulders seemed to slump. I think I could've gotten to her in half an hour, but I didn't have the time. If she was bluffing about the sheriff, she was bluffing with the best hand. 'I have a spare in the trunk,' I told her, hoping a new tire was all I'd need.

She held the shotgun on me as I fumbled the spare tire and tools from the trunk, and kept it on me till I was down on my belly digging out a place for the jack. While I can usually change a tire in five minutes on dry ground, I didn't know how long it would take in the snow, so I ignored her to concentrate on my work. There was no reason to slow things down with more nasty exchanges. We were done talking. I'd be back. She had to sleep sometime.

I set the jack solid under the axle and then crawled out to spin off the lug nuts. I glanced in her direction to see how close I was covered, and for a strange, splintering instant I thought she'd disappeared. But she was there, all right, sitting cross-legged in the snow, gun cradled across her left arm, her head bowed against the snowfall – a few flakes blowing from the storm's edge, a handful of stars glittering where the sky had cleared – and she looked for all the world like an old buffalo hunter hunkered down to wait out the weather.

I went back to work. The tire was shredded. There were pellet dents in the hubcap and a few concave dings in the fender, bare steel glinting through the chipped white paint and primer. I slipped the lug wrench over the first nut and twisted, leaning into it. The nut broke loose with a tiny shriek. I spun it off and dropped it clattering into the hubcap.

The sound had barely faded before she began to speak. I was stunned by the change in her voice, that hard edge turned to a delicate keening. 'I loved them all, you know. Kenneth was the first. We were young, two years married. He had a lot of debts, a lot of doubts about himself, and we had some troubles – but when it was there for us, it was really there. I thought he'd just walked away from it. Snapped one moment and just kept going. Men can do that. I never tried to look for him. I was six months pregnant and somehow believed the baby would bring him back. The baby was stillborn. The minister and I were the only ones at the funeral, and the minister was there because he got paid. I used to visit the grave every day, hoping I'd find Kenneth waiting. I never did.

'Joe, my second husband, disappeared out rounding up strays on the Arizona-Mexico border. The sheriff thought he might have been killed by drug smugglers. Stumbled on them by mistake and tried to stop them. Joe would have: he was big and rough, not a drop of sentiment in him, but he was so decent he was almost fragile. I *knew* he hadn't just kept riding.

'I remember pacing in the ranch house as it got later and later. Praying on the flagstone floor that he was all right. Beating on it with my fists.

'I looked for Joe. Months after the posse had given up I was still out there every day. People said I was crazy, hysterical, a ghost-chaser. I looked in every baranca, arroyo, draw, and canyon, behind every tree and boulder for thirty miles. I never found a trace. But after a while out there alone in the mountains, looking so hard, so devoutly, I got so I could ride up a gully and *feel* the presence of death – tendrils, subtle odors, a particular stillness – and after three years of looking I could feel death where only a hair remained, or a fleck of dried blood, and soon I could feel it when there was nothing at all. You called me a hard woman; well, it's a hard knowledge.'

'Ma'am—' I started to defend myself, but she sliced right through it, the old flint in her voice, 'You listen while you change that tire. If you want to talk, talk to the sheriff.'

That shut me up. I spun off another lug nut as she continued. 'I might still be riding that border if Duster hadn't come along. His wife had died of cancer six months before and he was traveling around hunting and fishing, trying to let go. He stopped by the ranch house asking for permission to hunt doves down by the pond. We talked a bit, and the next day he came to hunt again and asked me out to dinner. I warned him about my husbands disappearing but he took it the same way he took my heart, with a kind of crazy, carefree seriousness. Duster was a rare man. He knew who he was, so he loved you for who *you* were, not something he wanted you to be.

'Twenty-one years Duster and I were together, most of them around here. And one day he went out pheasant hunting over at the Lindstroms' place and disappeared. I can't tell you how hard that was. The police kept after me for months. I couldn't blame them. But what could I tell them? I didn't know what to tell myself. But I made up my mind I'd find Duster, and when the hullabaloo died down I started looking. I looked every night for seven years. Every single night.

'You see, Mr Gastin, that's how I learned to sense the dead, to feel the earth reveal the spirits it's claimed, to sense the presence, read the signs. I learned it by looking for those dearly lost to me.'

I had the spare on the axle and was finishing the lug nuts. 'Did you find him,' I asked.

'Mr Gastin, I'm sorry I have to be so stern with you. You *are* foolish, yet I admire your spunk.'

'Then give me another chance at it when it's not snowing. You had years of practice.'

'No,' she said, 'not here.'

'Then where?' I asked, cinching down the last lug nut.

'I don't know. You can always try to get back to the beginning, but I'm sure you understand how difficult that is, and dangerous. Take it where you find it – that's my advice.'

'I'm not sure I understand,' I told her politely, 'but that's hardly a new state of affairs.' I worked the jack out and stood up. She stood up with me, the gun barrel pointed down at the snow, but she watched closely as I put the blasted tire and the tools back in the trunk, then back around and into the car. As I closed the door she stepped around to the driver's side. When the gears meshed, as simple and smooth as that I understood what she was guarding in the field. I powered down the window. 'Maybe I haven't earned the right to deliver the gift,' I said, 'but I do think I've earned the right to ask you what you're protecting here. I just can't believe it's the ghosts of three rock musicians.'

'I'm protecting my ignorance,' she said.

That wasn't what I'd expected. 'I thought ignorance was my affliction.'

'You're hardly alone.'

'What is it you don't understand?'

Her head turned slightly to gaze out across the field. 'I told you I looked for the spot where Duster vanished, looked for seven years, and this is where I found him. I was sure of it. In the center, near where you found the antler. Of course, the antler wasn't there then. This place is about nine miles from the Lindstroms', in the opposite direction from where we lived at the time, but the feeling was powerful and clear. I thought maybe he'd been murdered and his body buried here.' She closed her eyes, then immediately opened them. 'The truth is, I *hoped* he'd been murdered . . . I wanted a *reason*, you see—'

'I see,' I said. 'I *thought* it was your husband you were protecting. Now it makes sense.'

'Don't be so sure,' she said sadly. 'When I dug down that night, yes, there it was, a human skull. But it was the skull on an *infant*, Mr Gastin, a baby less than a year old, and it had been there long before my husband or your musicians died. There were no other bones. Just the skull. You could almost hold it in the palm of your hand. So you understand why I couldn't let you drive this car out there and set it on fire? There are forces here beyond my understanding, so I had to insist that you prove yours.'

I felt my skull shining in the moonlight. I finally managed to say, 'I'm not sure I wanted to know that.'

Mrs Nogardam leaned her hooded head to the open window and gave me a quick, dry smile. 'Neither did I. It only added to the confusion. But if we don't want to know, why do we seek?' She smiled again, almost girlishly, then stepped back from the car, the shotgun swinging up level with the grille to remind me to act intelligently.

I backed out to the paved road, swung to the left, and got on it as fast as the snow allowed. For someone with nowhere to go I sure found myself in a hurry to get there, although on reflection there was a place I wanted with an overwhelming desire to reach, and that was *far away* from all the madness, the ghost salesman and ghost guardian and the moonlit skulls of children and a gift that didn't seem to want delivery — but most of all I wanted away from my continual inability to make sense out of any of it, and my tumorous fear that there was no sense to make.

When I met a sheriff's car at the first crossroads — had she actually called, or was this a routine patrol? — I came very close to turning myself in. I stifled a powerful impulse to put a broadslide block on his cruiser and jump out jabbering, 'Officer, this Caddy's so hot the paint's runny and that bottle of white stuff on the front seat is pure Hong Kong heroin I sell to schoolchildren and the papers in the glovebox still have wet ink and the baby's corpse in the trunk is missing its head and my goodness is that an open container in my hand, you child-molesting Nazi cock-sucker. Oh, pretty please: lock me up! Yes! I *need* custody.'

But I didn't. We eased past each other on the snow-slick road. I watched his taillights in the rearview mirror as they disappeared into where I'd been, the point from which I was unraveling. Where next, and why? *Drive*, I said to myself, *for Christsake find out where you're going*. Yet even that pure injunction was stymied: because of the snow, the roads were so treacherous I had to doodle when I wanted to jam. I couldn't even get it up past the posted till I hit 135, freshly plowed and sanded. I took it south, back toward Des Moines, mainly because there were more stars in that direction.

I don't want to give the impression I was flying apart. In fact, I was fairly stable, paralyzed as I was by the triangulated suck of stark confusion, dread, and depression. It was just as Gladys Nogardam had so coldly put it: I'd failed. If I was smart, I told myself, I'd simply shoulder my duffle bag and walk away from the whole fucked-up mess. Quit while I was only behind. I'd entered that state of mind where flight is spurred by the vulnerable belief and poignant hope that what's chasing you is worse than what's waiting ahead. But if I wasn't smart enough to cut my losses, at least I was bright enough to stop and catch my breath.

After knowing Joshua Springfield, how could I possibly have resisted the Raven's Haven Motel on the north edge of Des Moines? The office reeked of the liver-and-onions frying in the manager's adjacent apartment. On a small table opposite the business counter was a stuffed, ratty-feathered raven mounted on a jack-o-lantern. The manager kept eyeing me nervously as I signed in, then examined the registration card closely as I dug in my pocket for money.

'Ah, under occupation here, Dr Gass . . . what sort of pharmaceutical testing do you do?'

'Freelance,' I explained. 'But right now I'm working for the Feds. Some of them damn beatniks are putting ground-up marijuana in Saint Joseph's Baby Aspirin. Found a batch up in Fargo this morning. Company says it was a split shipment, Fargo and Des Moines, so I'm down here to check it out. I'll try to run it down in the morning. Haven't slept in two days, that's why I'd appreciate it if I wasn't disturbed. I get disturbed easily. And whatever you do, don't tell anybody – no need to start a panic. They might not even be on the shelves yet. But just between you and me, don't give your kids Saint Joseph's.'

'I thought marijuana was green. That should make them easy to spot.'

'It *is* green, pal, in its natural state – and I'm glad to see an alert citizen – but they're bleaching it with mescaline tritripinate.'

'Somebody ought to shoot the lousy bastards,' he said with disgust.

'Tell you what: we break the case, I'll give you the names of the jerks as soon as I get them. Maybe try to work something out with the Feds to take their time, know what I mean? You can close the case before the shithooks even have a *chance* to call their fancy New York lawyers. You got a card with a number where I can reach you on short notice? You should be ready to move on it in a hurry.'

He gave me his card along with the room key, though he didn't seem particularly eager to give me either.

'Citizen involvement,' I told him as I headed for the door, 'that's what separates the sheep from the goats.' I turned around at the door. 'Another thing: you on city water?'

'Yes,' he said uncertainly.

'A word to the wise: get bottled. A retarded baboon could dump a vial of chemicals in the water supply any time he took the notion. Lysergic acid, hashish extract, opium crystals – a pound of any of that shit in the water supply could take out Des Moines for a week. You have a cup of coffee one morning and ten minutes later you're up on the roof here trying to plug your dick into the neon sign. Don't think I'm kidding.'

'Bottled water,' he repeated.

'You got it. In this day and age, you can't be too sure. Hard to be sure at all, in fact.'

I fetched my duffle, a six-pack, and the bottle of crank from the trunk and then started looking for #14. I wondered about my perverse delight in jacking around the Harveys and Bubbas and Walter Mittys of the world. To beat up on the defenseless didn't show much character, nor much heart. No wonder I failed or fucked-up at every opportunity.

But the self-flagellation, meant to raise the welts of self-pity, stopped the moment I stepped into my room – not that it was breathtakingly spacious or tastefully appointed. Standard issue down to the smoke-yellowed floral wallpaper, a linty-green Sear's close-out carpet, Magnavox fifteen-inch black-and-white TV bolted to the desk, and a lumpy double bed that had probably known more sexual joy and despair in a month than I had in twenty years – but # 14 offered the welcome sanctuary of transient neutrality, space without claims.

I locked and bolted the door, set my bag on the luggage rack, opened a beer, and moseyed into the bathroom hoping to find a spacious tub. The tub wasn't luxurious, but it was adequate. I wiggled the bead-chained plug in tight and opened the hot water all the way. As the steam curled, I stripped off my grungy clothes and pawed through my duffle looking for something I hadn't worn recently. Making a mental note to do laundry in the morning, I grinned at my display of confidence. But indeed, this was the trick – to carry on as if everything was normal. I needed rest, especially rest from thinking, but had to make some decisions about what to do now that I'd failed the delivery and lost my way.

In the time it took me to shut off the hot water, I decided I believed Gladys Nogardam or else was scared shitless of her, either of which was sufficient reason not to attempt a midnight run on the crash site, a notion I hadn't realized I was still seriously considering. Nope, I was in over my head with Mrs Nogardam. But the point she'd made about returning to the beginning made more and more sense. In the spiritual inflation of enlarging the gesture – abetted by the baseless paranoia inspired by Double-Gone that Scumball's goons might be awaiting me – I'd lost my original purpose and therefore my way, the simple, uncomplicated point of delivering it to the Bopper's grave and then quietly slipping away.

According to the information I'd found at the Houston Public Library, the Bopper, as I'd assumed, was buried in Beaumont. The obvious move was to drive down and make delivery, and that's what I decided I'd do after a good night's sleep. While this amounted to a two thousand-mile detour, I could chalk it up as a learning experience. That was the ticket: get up early and back on track, rested, refreshed, and wiser. And no picking up any hitchhikers along the way or talking to anyone who might possibly deflect me from that simple task. I was too suggestible, too vulnerable to my own doubts. And another decision: if I didn't pull it off this time, I'd just forget it and walk away. Abandon the journey as a fair try that failed, a victim of my own fuck-ups and fate. Sad, but no cause for shame.

I went in to check the bathwater and jerked my hand right back out – I wanted to soak myself, not cook lobsters. I was reaching for the cold water handle when it crossed my mind that I didn't know which Beaumont cemetery had won the Bopper's bones. It was about 8:00 and I was fairly sure Texas and Iowa were in the same time zone. With any luck the Beaumont Library was still open.

If the bathwater had been 20° cooler, I wouldn't have phoned the library before it closed and my story might've ended up in a different place altogether. The temperature of water – such a simple thing. Everything intimately and ultimately involved, millions of convoluted contingencies, none of them meaningless, any one potentially critical, and potential itself subject to the infinite dimensional intersections of time, space, and luck. Obviously a mind is not enough.

I sat my bare ass down on the desk chair, put the beer within easy reach, then dialed information through the motel office. The number in Beaumont was busy, so I asked the operator to try Houston. The call went through smoothly, answered by a woman on the second ring: 'Houston Public Library, may I help you?'

'Could I have the Reference Desk, please?'

'This is the Reference Desk.'

I put some honey in my tone. 'Well now, ma'am. I have an unusual request, but so far in my research I've found that the world would get pig-ignorant mighty quick if it wasn't for the patience and dedication of you librarians, so I'll just blunder ahead here and trust you to sort it out. What I'm doing is some research on early rock-and-roll musicians and I'm having trouble with some background on a Beaumont musician known as the Big Bopper. That was his stage name; his given name was Richardson, J P, Jiles Perry. Now the thing—'

'I bet y'all want to know where he's buried.'

That snapped me to attention. 'Now, *how* did *you* know *that?* You librarians telepathic?'

'No sir, y'all just the *third* person today wanted to know where this Bopper's buried, and a man in yesterday wanted the same information. That Bopper's sure been popular around here the last few days.'

'Myself, I'm doing an article for *Life* magazine. I don't know if these other folks are reporters, scholars, or just interested citizens.'

'I don't know either. They didn't say. But I can tell without going to the clippings that Mr Richardson died in a plane crash on February the third, 1959, up around Mason City – that's in Iowa – and he's buried over in Beaumont at Forest Lawn. Is that what y'all wanted?'

As I inched forward on the chair, my bare ass squeaked on the vinyl. I shared the sentiment. 'The burial place, yes ma'am, that's what I wanted. I'm not interested in the crash site. Is that what the other researchers are covering, the crash site?'

'Truth be told,' she lowered her voice confidentially, 'the two men that were here today seemed more interested in the man that was in yesterday than they did in Mr Richardson. They didn't come right out and say so, but I gather this other fellow, he'd taken some research notes from them? They asked Helen – she works the early shift – what he looked like, what sort of car he was driving, what he wanted, that sort of thing. They talked to Peebles, too – he's the morning custodian.'

'Sounds like the usual research rivalry to me. You wouldn't believe how some of these scholars carry on.'

'Lee – that's the janitor, Leland Peebles – he didn't think so.'

'No?'

'No sir. He said he talked to the young one with the crazy hat yesterday when he first came in – he was wearing this bright pink hat, but I didn't see him. I don't come on until noon. Anyway,

Peebles said the young one was either crazy or on drugs, and he thinks the other two are after him for stealing their car or some money.'

'I don't see what that has to do with the Big Bopper.'

'I don't either, but it must have *something* to do with it – this Mr Richardson's the one they all asked after.'

'Well, I want to thank you for your help with this. It's appreciated, believe me. And you sure got my curiosity going about those other three guys; hope we're not all covering the same ground.'

'Glad to help y'all. 'Night, now.'

No, I said to myself as I frantically redialed Houston Information for a number for Leland Peebles. *Just help me. I'm the good guy.*

Mr Peebles recognized my voice before I got seven words into my awkward ploy. 'Mister, there's no way I wanna be even *re-mote-ly* involved in this shit. *None* fo' me, thanks jus the same. I don't know you an' I don't know them, but I tell ya what I *do* know, and that's that them men lookin' fo' you is *exactly the sort you don' want to be findin'*. Big and nasty sort, you understand? I got my own burden of griefs, don't need yours *or* theirs. Hullo an' goodbye.' He hung up.

'Hold on!' I shouted. When there was only that empty hum in response, I fell apart. Paranoia started playing my brain like a pinball machine, racking up seventeen free games by the time I got the phone back in the cradle. Lights and rollovers were flashing and popping, flares exploding in the darkness, livid yellows and lurid reds. I saw the two goons in the motel office, *right that minute*, showing my picture to our helpful manager. 'Yeah, sure, the guy in fourteen, that's him. The one works for the Feds.' I saw myself tied to the chair I was sitting on, a guy about twice Bubba's size gagging me with a ping-pong ball and a swatch of wide adhesive tape while the smaller one fished his tools from a black doctor's satchel.

One shoe in my hand, an arm up a pantleg, I was scrambling around for clothes, knocking over the beer on the desk as I thrashed around on hands and knees groping for my other shoe as the cold beer dribbled off the edge of the desk onto the small of my back and down the crack of my ass, my brain screaming *HEMORRHAGE!* when a dry voice spoke to me with neither disgust nor loathing, just calm amusement. 'George, not only is the mind not enough, it is evidently too much.'

And that voice snapped my panic, pulled the plug. It was me, of course, unless I'd locked someone in the room with me, but the voice seemed to come from outside that elusive entity I generally considered my self. I reached back and gingerly touched the wetness along my ass, then examined my fingers. Beer. I cringed with humiliation: I'd blown apart under pressure like a cheap transmission scattering down the stretch. I wondered abjectly what sort of quivering puddle of shit I'd turn into if Scumball's specialists ever caught up.

I mustered a sort of fatal dignity and went into the bathroom, glad the mirror was so fogged with steam I couldn't see my face. With a towel from the rack I sopped up the beer, then gathered the cleanest clothes I could find and laid them out neatly on the bed. So the bad guys were hot on my trail. Would Zorro fall apart? Shit no. Hopalong Cassidy? Are you kidding? Davy Crockett, John Dillinger, Zapata, Errol Flynn – would those guys be scrabbling around on a motel room floor too panicked by the mere *idea* of the crunch coming to pick up their fucking shoes? Surely you jest. I went back in the bathroom and wrung out the towel in the washbowl, then, facing myself, swabbed at the mirror. No dashing Zorro there, no cool-eyed Dillinger; neither swash nor buckle. Just crank-eyed, lip-quivering, day's growth, sweat-gritty, wrinkle-dicked me. I walked over to the tub, lifted myself in, and sank.

I tried not to think, but it was like trying not to breathe. My first thought, oddly enough, was that I should call Gladys Nogardam and warn her she might expect some bad company. On second thought, I figured I should call the Houston Library and leave a warning for the goons, should they consider heading *her* way. That gave me heart. If a ninety-seven-year-old woman could stand her ground, then so could I. If Joshua Springfield could ride his *Celestial Express* into a sleeping town and challenge the prevailing dreamless version of reality and not even flinch when the shooting started, surely I could dream on. After all, Gladys admired my spunk, or so she said, and they'd shot at me as well as Joshua. And Donna trying to wash the stink of sour milk out of that sweltering trailer and feed the kids – if she could go on, what was stopping me? Besides fear, doubt, and no direction known.

What to do, where to go; the same old boring shit. Go to sleep. Go roaring back to Beaumont right into their teeth and touch it off on the Bopper's grave. Or go to the phone, call a taxi for the airport, book a seat on the next flight to Mexico. Fuck the gift and fly away.

Thinking, thinking, stopping only long enough to add more hot water or crack another beer. By two in the morning I was out of beer, my face was raw from the steam, and my body was beginning to pucker and prune pretty seriously, so I stood up, dripping and shriveled, and watched the water spiral down the drain, a circle sucked through itself, disappearing to wherever it went – pipes, sewer, sewer pond, evaporating back to the air, falling again as rain for the roots – and remembered again Gladys Nogardam saying, 'You can always try to get back to the beginning.'

I spent the next hour pacing the bedroom naked, trying to figure out some sort of beginning to return to, thinking I had to be desperately lost if I was trying to find a beginning just to begin again, assuming I was capable of distinguishing beginnings from endings, assuming they weren't just illusions.

That's how it was in room 14 of the Raven's Haven Motel in Des Moines, Iowa, at 3:00 in the morning, full of failure, dread, doubt, beer, and speed. Pacing, pacing, pacing. I think it was the monotonous rhythm of walking rather than the monotony of thinking that conjured the echo of the beginning I sought. Big Red Loco taking the bandstand to play 'Mercury Falling,' shaping his breath into the silence we'd heard together as the stolen car flopped over the edge and fell, fell, fell, vanishing then bursting within the roar of waves breaking on the rocks. The same night the small Beechcraft fireballed into an Iowa cornfield. The first night I held Kacy naked in my arms. That was the beginning I wanted returned. Not to recapture the past but to open the present. Not a *re*birth, you understand, but *this* birth. This life. My bewildered love, my fucked-up music, my shaky faith. But even so, it was a love with hope, a music I could still dance to, and a faith suddenly steadied by the feeling I'd finally got it right, that I knew where I was going: full circle, back to that turn-out above Jenner. A familiar plan to me, maybe even the original one, and it made me laugh. My laugh sounded a little unnerved, oddly wild.

I dressed, packed my gear, left $10 on the dresser for the phone calls that probably saved my ass, and went out and started the Caddy. While it patiently idled, gathering warmth against the predawn freeze, I stowed my duffle and celebrated the new beginning of the end with a sip of speed chased with beer, the first of the last six-pack left in the cooler. Either I'd been lost in concentration or he hadn't yet appeared, but it wasn't till I popped the emergency brake that I noticed my ghost. He was sitting on the passenger's side of the front seat, watching. Our eyes met. 'You're crazy, you know,' he said.

'I know.'

'Well, suit yourself.'

'Leave me alone unless you're going to help,' I said, but he had already vanished.

I swung the white rocket around in the parking lot, eased out onto the empty street, and eight blocks later found the on-ramp I wanted. The freeway was a little slick, and snow from yesterday's storm was plowed up along the shoulders. I took it easy, getting the feel of the road. When I hit the I-80 junction I stopped for gas. I sat staring at the dinosaur on the Sinclair logo while the yawning attendant topped off the tank. I took I-80 West, headed for the California coast. A big Kenworth rumbled past me as I pulled onto the freeway, and I honked and waved. He tooted back. The road was slushy in spots, but generally good. A green mileage sign read OMAHA 130. I put Bill Haley and the Comets on the box, 'Rock Around the Clock,' and then put some leather to the pedal, some sole on the go. If anybody was chasing me, they were going to be further behind. I was still eighteen hundred miles out, but I was closing fast.

I made Omaha before 6:00 Central, light just beginning to pale the sky. There was a strong cross-wind from the north, but the road was clear. It looked like straight sailing to the coast. I hoped to reach Jenner before the next dawn and figured that if I gained two hours in time changes and averaged around 80 mph, I could make a few stops and still have time on my side. Things were looking good.

A couple of things, however, were nagging at me. One was the gut-shot spare in the trunk. Or non-spare, since it was worthless. The rubber on the right-front was new, but I've never liked running without some extra on board; I can't stand how dumb you feel when you have a flat. And although I have no statistical proof, personal experience has convinced me you're fifty times more likely to have a flat when you don't have a spare.

Then there was my ghost. Not that he'd returned to ride shotgun or anything alarming, but that he'd made an appearance in the first place. I figured he was a hallucination born of psychic distress and physical exhaustion, and I was certainly no stranger to hallucination. It seemed like only yesterday I'd been waltzing with a cactus under the melting desert stars, and it *was* yesterday that I'd seen Kacy in an Oklahoma waitress and got my gonads tenderized. I knew a hallucination when I saw one, and I'd driven truck long enough to know what tired, wired eyes could do with a heat mirage, tricks of light and shadow, semblances suggested by blurred or distant shapes, ghost-images dancing down the optic nerves when an oncoming driver neglected to dim his highbeams and left you half-blind and batting your eyes in his wake, all kinds of wild shit out there in the dark. But I'd never seen my ghost before.

Granted, there's a first time for everything, but it nagged me, like I said, particularly since Lewis Kerr had only the night before supposedly returned my errant ghost. I didn't want to consider the possibility it *was* my ghost, for as nearly as I understood it, ghosts were disembodied spirits of the dead, and I wasn't dead, of that I was certain – although, like a clutch plate with an oil leak, that certainty was beginning to experience some slippage. If ghosts were spirits of the dead and I wasn't dead, maybe it was a preview of coming attractions, a warning to watch myself. Or perhaps – and this struck me as so ludicrous I immediately accepted its possibility – I was being haunted by my own ghost.

It *was* mine. I was convinced of that, although recalling its visit I had to admit I hadn't so much seen it as *felt* it, or maybe I'd seen it *because* I'd felt it so clearly. But ghost, hallucination, mirage, psycho-projection, whatever it was, it was *of me*.

And yet I wasn't alarmed. For one thing, I didn't think it was real, at least not *real* in the sense that little Eddie's blood was real, or Red's music, or Kacy's coiled warmth. And real or not, my ghost hadn't seemed threatening. If anything, it apparently wanted to help – it had pointed out I was crazy more as a reminder than a judgment or warning. Maybe I now was crazy enough to have split in two, which was all right with me; I could use a spare mind.

In Lincoln I stopped at another Sinclair station for a fill-up. I was beginning to think of that green dinosaur as a personal good luck charm. I wanted his pressed oils to power my run to the coast. I told the pump jockey to stock it to the top with gravity's wine. When he looked baffled, I pointed to the dinosaur revolving above us atop the stanchion and explained, 'Some of that prime, high-test dinosaur juice from the Mesozoic crush. Gas.' He seemed glad to tear himself away from our conversation and get pumping. As I opened the trunk to get out the mangled tire, I cautioned myself that Lincoln, Nebraska, at 6:30 A.M. was not a good place to succumb to an attack of the mad jabbers.

The tire was the shredded mess I remembered, but the rim looked fine. I held it up for the attendant's inspection: 'You carry my size?'

'Think so, mister,' he said, staring at the blasted casing. 'Jesus Christ, what did you *do* to it?'

'Misjudged an old woman's determination.'

He shook his head. 'Boy, I *guess* so.'

Although he did have one in stock, he couldn't – or didn't want to – mount it until the number-two man came on at 8:00 to cover the pumps. He looked alarmed when I volunteered to mount it myself, or to watch the pumps while he did it, and mumbled something about insurance problems. Fuck him, I decided. The right-front looked plenty good to get me to Grand Island; in fact the rubber was good enough all the way around to get me to Alaska if I wanted to risk it.

Nebraska is a flat state – the roads so straight they have to put rumble-strips on them to keep you from going into highway trance – but it's great terrain for making time, and I kept it up in the high 90's as I blew down the pike. The traffic was light, and the hard cross-wind let up not far out of Lincoln.

It was beginning to look like a classic autumn day, crisp and full of color, when I hit Grand Island one hundred fifty miles and ninety minutes later. I'd barely entered the city limits when I saw a sign that read AL HAYLOCK'S TIRE N' TUNE, and damned if the sign didn't feature a picture of a rubber tree. Yes sir, that's the kind of advertising to attract a man looking for the beginning, the raw material, the unrefined source. When the mechanic said he'd need about ten minutes to mount the tire, I told him to change the oil and filter while he was at it, and to give it a quick tune as well. I used his restroom to drain some beer, then went off in search of a donut to throw my growling stomach.

There was a greasy spoon two blocks west, the mechanic said, so I headed in that direction. A long stretch in the fresh morning sunlight felt good after sitting behind a wheel for hours. I was checking for traffic as I crossed a side street when my glance was seized by a huge chartreuse sign on the roof of a building about the size of a large cable car: ELMER'S HOUSE OF A THOUSAND LAUGHS. All the Os in the sign were tilted like heads thrown back in laughter, and in fact had faces painted on them, closed eyes and big open mouths out of which emerged, in pale flamingo script, assorted hee-haws, yuks, chortles, snorts, whoops, hyugha-hyughas, and other expressions of amusement and delight.

I was attracted by the oddity of the place, but admonished myself not to court distraction when things were clicking along just fine. Besides, the place looked closed. And just as I made up my mind, someone started waving a white flag in the store window as if signaling my attention or his surrender, or perhaps a meeting under the sign of safe conduct.

As I approached, I saw the waving flag was none of the above, but instead a floppy, butcher-paper sign a woman was taping inside a front window. HALLOWEEN SPECIAL, GET YOUR TRICKS HERE. Who could resist? Especially when I noticed that the woman behind the glass had the dourest face I'd ever seen. She looked like her breakfast had been a bowl of alum and a cup of humorless disgust.

On the door, in small, neat script, was another sign: 'A practical joke is one that makes you laugh.' Above it was one of those plastic squares with two clock faces commonly used to indicate store hours, but the hands had been removed. On one clock face the sun-leached letters read: 'Time flies like an arrow.' On the other: 'Fruit flies like bananas.'

I was having serious second thoughts, but pushed the door open anyway, freezing immediately when I heard a hoarse male voice whisper urgently, 'Edna, did you hear that? *Oh Christ*, I think it's your husband.'

'It's just one of Elmer's jokes,' a weary female voice informed me. 'A recording. Breaking the circuit in the door activates it. I tell Elmer it's bad for business but he don't listen to me.' The speaker was the dour-faced woman I'd seen in the window. She didn't look any happier in the dingy glow of the two forty-watts lighting the store. She was in her fifties, a few inches over five feet but showing all the signs of shrinking fast. She was dressed entirely in dull black except for a large, round pin on her bosom, a grinning, bright orange pumpkin with the legend KEEP FUN SAFE FOR KIDS. As I looked at her narrow, tight-lipped face, the legend seemed less a plea for the safety of innocence than a personal admission of its loss – her matte-brown eyes had given up on fun long ago.

'No problem.' I smiled to show her I could take a joke. My instinct was to cheer her up.

'There's not much stock left,' she said, 'but go ahead and look around. You need any help I'll be behind the counter.'

It was a joke shop: joy buzzers, whoopee cushions that emitted long flatulent squeals when you sat on them, fountain pens designed to leak all over the unsuspecting user, plastic lapel flowers with hidden water-filled squeeze-bulbs to flush the sinuses of sniffers, kaleidoscopes that left the viewer with a black eye – that sort of thing, and more bare shelf than merchandise.

A section of plastics caught my eye. A pile of dogshit that looked so real you could smell it. Below that a display of severed extremities – fingertips to put in somebody's beer, whole fingers to wedge in doors, the entire hand for under the pillow or the lip of the toilet bowl. Not to mention plastic snakes, spiders, bats, scorpions, flies, and hideously bloated sewer rats that I instantly envisioned floating belly-up in suburban swimming pools. Next to the animals were plastic puddles of vomit with realistic chunks of potatoes and half-digested meat. None of them made me laugh, but I'll admit to a smile.

In the next aisle were books of matches that wouldn't light, rolling papers saturated with invisible chemicals guaranteed to gag the smoker, exploding loads for cigarettes and cigars, and boxes of birthday candles that appeared normal but could not be blown out. The last struck me as cruel. If you couldn't blow out your birthday candles, your wish wouldn't come true; not that it did anyway, which was a different sort of cruelty. But if the candles couldn't be blown out, was the birthday eternal, the wish kept alive without a future to grant it, deny it, betray it? The candles didn't make me laugh, but since they provoked me with possibilities I decided to buy a box.

The next aisle was devoted to humor of a chemical nature. A handsomely packaged soap that promised to turn the user's skin a gangrenous green a half hour after application. Something called Uro-Stim, invisible when dissolved in liquid and guaranteed to create in any drinker the frantic need to piss. I immediately thought of a couple of long-winded North Beach poets who could use a few hits in their pre-reading wine. There was also Rainbow P, a little packet of six colorless capsules that would turn your urine a choice of colors. I thought Uro-Stim and Rainbow P might make a devastating combination – send the victim hopping pigeon-toed and grimacing to the pisser only to deliver a stream of bright maroon urine . . . looking down, stunned, and thinking, *It can't be me! Jesus, who was I fucking last night?* I started laughing, clearly getting in the mood.

I skipped a section of playing cards – some shaved or marked for tricks, others obviously for viewing ('52 Different Beauties – No Pose the Same') – and browsed a miscellaneous aisle of Chinese handcuffs, balloons called Lung Busters because you couldn't blow them up with anything lighter than an air compressor, and a cheap-looking fry pan ostensibly coated with a revolutionary stick-proof compound, although the accompanying literature guaranteed this miracle coating would melt into industrial-strength epoxy within two minutes of heating, locking your eggs to the pan.

What sort of mind thinks of such things? I wondered as I shuffled on past the mustache wax that caramelized fifteen minutes after you put it on, a dusty box of Chocolate Creme Surprises (the surprise was either a licorice-tapioca filling or a hidden capsule of raw jalapeno extract), a display of rubber kitchen utensils, and, all alone at the end of a bare shelf, a big magenta tube with a screw top that looked like a tinker-toy package except for the gold lettering that identified it as 'S.D. Rollo's Divinity Confections, The Finest Sweets This Side of Heaven.' No telling what those were. I unscrewed the lid to take a peek and *great fucking Jesus!* a giant spring-coiled snake shot halfway across the store, its flannel skin a blinding yellow with glaring polka-dots of baby blue and a flamingo pink only slightly more muted than my hat, its black button eyes glossy as sin and its tongue of red stiffened velvet ready to lie for pleasure. The shock of the vaulting snake made me drop the box of Uro-Stim, then step on it as I moved to retrieve the snake from over by the whoopee cushions. Blushing brighter than the serpent's scarlet tongue and trying to babble an apology to the sour-puss clerk, who hadn't even *looked up* from what she was doing, I was stumbling in total disarray when a familiar voice called, 'Hey, George,' and I wheeled around to see my ghost pointing to a stack of small white boxes. 'Get me a couple of these, would you?'

'What are they,' I asked, but then he was gone.

'I beg your pardon?' called the woman behind the counter.

In my attempt to turn around, I tripped on the damn snake and fell against the shelf of whoopee cushions, instinctively grabbing one to break my fall. Which it did, to the long accompaniment of what we young boys in Jacksonville used to call a 'tight-ass screamer,' only this one ended more like a siren sinking in bubbling mud.

'My goodness! Are you all right?' She was peering down at me, sounding even wearier than before.

'Fine, no problem,' I mumbled, flailing my way up off the floor with the whoopee cushion under one arm and a hand around the snake's throat.

'I tell Elmer he should put a warning on that darn snake, but he thinks there's already too many jokes that are explained. He thinks people can't develop a sense of humor unless they *experience* the joke themselves. Here, let me help you get that snake back in the can.'

'No, that's okay; I got him.' I was enjoying jamming him back in his container. 'And don't worry about that package I stepped on; I was going to buy it anyway.' I screwed the lid down on S.D. Rollo's Heavenly Confections with mad delight. 'How much is this obnoxious snake anyway?'

'Nineteen ninety-five,' she said, sounding dismayed.

'That's a lot.' I'd figured it'd be around two bucks.

'The company that made it, Fallaho Novelties, went out of business a couple of years ago. They don't make them with flannel bodies anymore – make them overseas cheaper with plastic now, but the plastic don't hold up. Three or four leaps and the plastic cracks. And the spring's some new alloy, not steel. Elmer wanted to keep it as a collector's item, but he already had eight or nine of them so I insisted it go on the shelf. Elmer just marked the price way up there where he said somebody would have to be crazy to buy it.'

'You and Elmer are partners in the store, is that it?' Suddenly I was interested in old Elmer.

'I'm his wife.'

'Ma'am, if you tell me Elmer has cancer or has mysteriously

disappeared, I'm going to jump through your front window and *sprint* for the Pacific Ocean.'

Her lips parted in surprise. 'Why would you do that?'

'Because I'm crazy enough to buy this damn snake,' I said, smacking the can down on the counter, 'plus the whoopee cushion here, and the Uro-Stim and some Rainbow P, and these birthday candles you can't blow out, and a couple of boxes of that stuff over there, whatever it is – my ghost wants some. What is it anyway?'

'Rabi-Tabs. They're little tablets you put under your tongue that work up into a froth. Supposed to make you look like you're foaming at the mouth. Like you have rabies.'

'I'll take two.' I went over and plucked them off the shelf. 'Anything else you want, Ghost?' I said loudly. He didn't reply. I picked up the squashed box of Uro-Stim on my way back to the counter.

'Is that who you're talking to? A ghost?' Dismay and weariness joined forces in her voice.

'Yup. I think so.'

'Elmer'd like you.'

'Ma'am,' I asked gently, knowing better, 'where *is* Elmer? What's he up to?'

'He's in the hospital. In Omaha.' She said it as if surprised I didn't know.

I felt guilty for having forced the painful information. 'I'm sorry to hear that. I hope it's nothing serious.'

She looked up at me and said in a flat voice, 'I thought everyone knew. It was ten months ago, last Christmas Eve. He went to midnight mass and slipped this new dental dye in the communion wine. Turned everybody's teeth bright purple. People were furious. It was *Christmas*. They knew who did it, of course, and they turned on him. He went running from the church – laughing like crazy, they said – and his feet went out from under him on the icy steps and he cracked his head. He's been in a coma ever since, in the VA down there. The doctors say they don't know what's keeping him alive.

'I go over there every weekend. He doesn't recognize me, though. He has this huge, happy smile on his face. It never changes, or not that any of us has ever seen. I tried once to pull the corners of his mouth down – so he'd look more dignified, you know? – but they went right back up. But he never opens his eyes, never looks at me, never says a word. I don't know if he's happy or paralyzed or near dead. I'm selling off all the stuff in the store. I guess I'm just waiting for him to die, and I don't even know why I'm waiting for that.'

'I think he's happy,' I said. 'And I think this weekend he's going to open his eyes and look in yours and say, "Honey, let's run away to Brazil and start all over." But if he doesn't, if he dies, I hope you can find it within yourself to sit on his headstone and laugh, really *laugh*, from way down in your guts, for him and for you.'

'It's not funny,' she said.

'*Some* of it surely is. Why lose that, too?'

'Because you just do,' she said sourly, and started ringing up my purchases.

'You should smother your husband,' my ghost said, appearing briefly over her shoulder before he faded.

'Did you hear that?' I asked her, though she'd given no indication she had.

'No,' she glanced up, 'what?'

'My ghost said, "Mother him."'

'You're just like Elmer. He loved Halloween.'

'My ghost's like Elmer. I'm really like you. Except I'm not waiting. You know why? Because time flies like an arrow.'

'I know, I know,' she waved a hand, 'and fruit flies like rotten fruit.' She handed me my bag of purchases. 'You and your ghost have a nice Halloween.' I wish she could've smiled when she said it.

I went straight back to the tire shop. The Caddy was ready and waiting, chrome flashing with sunlight. I put the bag of tricks on the passenger-side floor, except for the whoopee cushion, which I carefully placed on the passenger seat. If my ghost showed up again, still along for the ride, I wanted to find out if he'd set it off. This might well have been the first fart trap ever designed to detect the physical presence of a ghost. Never too crazy for empirical experiments in reality.

I paid for the tire and tune-up, then wheeled the car around the block a few times to make sure it was running tight. Couldn't have been better. I headed back out for I-80, stopping along the way for dinosaur power at a Sinclair, and then at the Allied Superette for a couple of six-packs of Bud to restock the cooler. By the dash clock it was 9:20. I took a little sip from the crank mix to keep me on track, and a few minutes later I was ripping down the Interstate, California-bound.

Using my benny-quickened brain, I calculated that the Caddy would be introduced to the Pacific in about twenty hours, some twelve hundred minutes. I had roughly two hundred records in the back seat, two sides each, say three minutes a side, six per disc – well how about that? Talk about your celestial clickety-click, that was about twelve hundred minutes of music if I listened to it all, and that was exactly my intention. I could feel myself starting to hit the nerve snap-point of too much speed and not enough sleep, and music soothes the beast. I set aside everything by the Bopper, Buddy Holly, and Ritchie Valens; it seemed only fitting to save them for the last wild-heart run at the sea.

Between watching the road and shuffling records it took me about ten minutes to get set up. The spindle on Joshua's turntable would take a stack of ten, which meant all I had to do was flip them every half-hour and change the stack on the hour. The first tune, Elvis' 'Now Or Never,' sounded about right to me. I leaned back and cruised as I listened to him croon.

From Grand Island through North Platte and on to the state

line, Nebraska – if you can believe it – gets flatter. You don't really have to drive; just put it in boogie and hold it between the lines. It's boring, and I suppose it was boredom that inspired the idea of sailing the records out the window once the whole stack had played. By the time this occurred to me I already had a stockpile of twenty records, so by restricting myself to one toss for every two cuts, I had some physical activity every six minutes. The interim was well occupied with drinking beer, listening to the music blast at cone-wrenching volume, choosing suitable targets, and, best of all, matching titles to their fates. For Brenda Lee's 'I'm Sorry,' for instance, I just plopped into the slow lane to get run over. The Everly Brothers' 'Bird Dog' I sailed out into a cornfield to hunt pheasants. 'Teen Angel' I saved till the highway cut in to parallel some railroad tracks, but I undershot it badly into a weedy ditch. Since I had some slack, I saved a few titles for more appropriate places – 'Mr Custer' definitely belonged to Wyoming, while the Drifters' 'Save the Last Dance for Me' was obviously meant for a late-night fling.

Those whose titles didn't suggest targets became general ammunition in my war on control, and were gleefully winged at billboards and road signs, and especially at speed limit signs. To sail a record out of a car moving 95 mph and hit anything except the ground is a real trick, and about 98 percent of the time I probably missed. But I tell you, it's a *magnificent* feeling when you connect. Damn near blew my shoes off with joy when I sent 'The Duke of Earl' tearing through a Bank of America billboard. And as to the musical question 'Who Put the Bomp in the Bomp-Da-Bomp?' I'm not sure, but I know the record itself put one hell of a bomp on a 65 mph sign – folded the fucker almost in half, much to my delight. I celebrated this rare bull's-eye with a toot on the horn and a solid squeeze of the whoopee cushion, happy as a seven-year-old with a slingshot in a glass factory. Shit, even the misses were fun – sailing gracefully out over the fields to drop like miniature spacecraft from Pluto.

I was having so much fun my ghost couldn't resist. I'd just barely missed a Burger Hut billboard with 'Theme from a Summer Place' when he appeared in the passenger seat.

'Ah ha!' I pounced, 'you're not real: the whoopee cushion didn't go off.'

He ignored me in his excitement. 'Salvoes,' he urged, 'fusillades, machine guns, cluster bombs. Shotgun the fuckers! To hell with this johnny-one-note stuff.' And he was gone.

I was reluctant but had a few spares, so I picked up five together, waited for a large green road sign announcing 'CHEYENNE 37,' came within a hundred yards and, allowing for some lead, snapped them backhanded out the passenger window. But something wasn't right – the weight, the throw, the aerodynamics – because one nosed down and the other four fluttered and died way short of the target. I wrote it off as bad advice and told my ghost to forget it. I didn't hear any argument.

If throwing music away like that seems sacrilegious . . . well, maybe it was. But I'd already decided to send the records and sound system down with the ship; they belonged with the Caddy as part of the gift, but rather than do it all at once I was delivering pieces along the way. The Bopper's records, Buddy's, Ritchie's – I still intended to send them over the edge with the blazing Caddy, maybe even stacked on the spindle as a crowning touch. The rest I felt free to fling like seeds across the landscape, scatter like ashes. If they happened to collide with bill-boards, road signs, and other emblems of oppressive enterprise and gratuitous control, all the better – that seemed altogether congruent with the spirit of the music, doubly fitting considering it was also a lot of fun.

I gassed at a Sinclair station in Cheyenne, tipping my flamingo hat to the dinosaur, then hauled on for Laramie. I was starting up the east slope of the Rockies, where driving required a bit more attention, but there were still plenty of opportunities to cast the music far and wide.

'What's that, Mr Charles? "Hit the road, Jack"? No sweat.' I reached out the window and fired it straight down; hard to miss when you're right on top of it. No need to tell me not to come back no more, no more, no more, no more.

When Frankie Avalon asked the musical question 'Why?' I told him it was just to see how far he could sail into the sagebrush, that's why. And I flung him out there as far as I could.

'And Tom Dooley,' I said aloud to myself and my ghost if he was listening, 'sweet Jesus, man, you've been hanging your head since the Civil War, poor boy. Let me cut you some slack.' And with a sharp backhanded toss I set him free.

Just out of Rawlins, about to crest the Continental Divide, I tired of the game and decided to use the thin air to go for distance – but was going so fast I couldn't keep the longer shots in sight. When I hit the crest I pulled over, scooped up my pile of reserves and, after pissing beer into both watersheds, alternately sailed records east and west, watching them hang majestically and curve away, a few disappearing before I could see where they hit, and I'd bet some of them carried for miles.

I returned to the Caddy refreshed, though my break from rapid motion made me realize I was probably a bit overamped on speed; I made a mental note to lay off for a while or I'd be chewing on the steering wheel by midnight. Generally, however, I felt wonderful. I was on the Pacific side of the country, halfway to the edge with a downhill run, looking good and having fun.

It didn't last long. 'Hound Dog' had just finished playing, and either the bennies had sped up my hearing or Elvis was singing slower – something was out of time. The next platter down was the Kingsmen's 'Louie, Louie.' If you want to hear music for the end of the world try a 45 of 'Louie, Louie' played at 33 and progressively fading to about 13:

Looouuuuiiiiieeeeee, Looouuuuiiiiieeeeeeeeeeee,
Oooooooohhhhhhh yeeeaaaaaaaaaaaahhhhhhhhhhhhhhhhh
Weeeeeeeeeeeeeeeeeeeeeee

Goooooooooooooooootttttttaaaaaaahhhhhhhhhhhhhh
Goooooooooooooooooooooo
Nnnnnnooooooooooooooowwwwwwwwwwwwwwwwwwwwwwww

The battery was dying in Joshua's magic box. 'Aaawwwwwwww fuuuuuuuccccccckkkkk,' I said, trying to maintain my sense of humor as I reached back and snapped it off.

'*Music!*' my ghost demanded, suddenly beside me in the passenger's seat. 'Sounds! Give me the *beat!*'

'If you don't like it, leave,' I told him, slowing to pull over.

He whined like a five-year-old. 'But it's *boring* without music.' He disappeared.

'Just take it easy.' I wondered if he could still hear me. 'Your man's on the job.'

I stopped and got out. I could've switched batteries, but Joshua's sounded so low I probably would've had to roll start the car, and I hate running on low power. To dig out Donna's machine and plug it into the lighter socket seemed smarter; this would do till I got to Rock Springs, where I could buy new juice for Joshua's system. In theory this sounded good, but when I lifted Donna's record player from the trunk I noticed the tone arm was jammed down on the turntable, and the needle was broken. Somewhere along the line – probably in Gladys Nogardam's driveway – the cooler must've slid into it. Or maybe I'd thrown the shot-up tire on it. Didn't make any fucking difference *how* at that point – it was useless. I considered trying a needle swap but figured by the time I discovered they weren't interchangeable I could be leaving Rock Springs with a new battery. Till then we'd just have to do without music.

Two silent minutes down the freeway, my ghost reappeared beside me, commenting in that nasal snottiness five-year-olds find so withering, 'Well, *my man;* where's the *music?*'

I ignored him. No reason to pamper hallucinations.

'I *need* the beat!' he demanded. 'The sound of fucking music!'

'I'll sing for you,' I offered sarcastically.

'Why don't you just turn on the radio there?' He pointed. 'They're amazing inventions. Magic. You click on the switch and sometimes music jumps right out.' He disappeared.

It was embarrassing. Like I said, I don't normally have a radio in a working vehicle. Music is fine, but all the deejay chit-chat and commercials poison your attention. But the fact was I hadn't even thought of the radio.

I was glad my ghost had, though. We picked up KROM out of Boulder, almost solid music and a lot of it what I'd been listening to a couple months earlier holed up in my apartment trying to stay sane. After a steady diet of Donna's collection, it was a nice leap forward to hear what was blooming from those roots. My ghost must've enjoyed it, too; not a peep out of him for fifty miles.

When he reappeared again it wasn't to complain about the music, but to offer an observation. 'Jeez, George, maybe *I'm* the paranoid one, but at the speed we're traveling it seems hard to believe that black car behind us is catching up – well, not actually catching up, but sort of *settled* in, if you know what I mean.'

Two big mothers in an Olds 88. I use the mirrors on reflex and was sure I'd checked in the last half-minute, so unless I'd missed them or was slipping badly they hadn't been there long. Considering their adverse impact on my pulse rate, I saw no reason for them to be there any longer than necessary. I was doing a smooth 90 at the time, coming off a long downhill stretch, and I had lots of pedal left. I was just stomping on it when I saw another car coming fast down the hill and, unless the dusk light was playing tricks, this one had a bubblegum machine bolted to its roof and generally conveyed the feeling of a state trooper. So rather than punch it, I let the accelerator spring push my foot back up to a more sensible 65 mph.

By coming off the gas suddenly like that, the Olds, if it wanted to stay on my tail, would've had to hit its brakes, thus making its intentions obvious, or at least provide some rational basis for the

paranoia playing my heart like a kettle drum. If the Olds passed –
the exact move I was hoping to force – I'd at least get a good look
at them, and with any luck the trooper would nail their ass. I'd get
two birds with one stone. Just call me Slick. Unfortunately the
Olds must've spotted the trooper too, and didn't gain an inch.

The Caddy, Olds, and trooper's Dodge settled into a stately
procession, an extremely nervous one from my vantage, marked
by a great deal of wishing, hoping, and nonchalant concealment
of visible felonies, and not untainted by a certain mean irony as
Bob Dylan asked through the magic of KROM radio,

> *How does it feeeeelll*
> To be on your *ooooownnn*

'Tell you the truth, Bob, not too fucking good right now,
sort of caught between goons and the heat out here on the
alkali Wyoming sage flats with a bad case of dread and my
ghost hiding under the front seat, but I guess that's what makes
existence the wonderful adventure it is.'

We kept moving in strict formation, me in front, my worries
right behind at hundred-yard intervals. Dylan finished his biting
lament and the KROM deejay was announcing a license plate
number for some promotional contest – if it was yours and you
called within ten minutes you won two tickets to hear Moon
Cap and the Car Thieves at the first annual KROM Goblin
Rock-and-Roll Horror Romp at Vet's Hall. I'd rather have been
there than where I was and, worse yet, with a decision to make:
should I take the upcoming Rock Springs turn-off or not? Not,
I decided; I didn't know the turf, a severe disadvantage if I had
to run for it.

The black Olds, however, did take the exit, making me wonder
for a minute whether they were simply a couple of big guys
out for a drive. That left just me and the trooper, me wildly
radiating innocence and the trooper, I hoped to Christ, receiving.

Unfortunately, a discreet glance in the rearview revealed he actually seemed to be sending, since he was holding the radio mike to his mouth. Maybe a little spot-check on a five-niner Cadillac Eldorado, California license plate number B as in busted, O as in Oh-shit, and P as in prison, 3 as in the square root of nine, 3 as in trinity, 3 like the wise men. Such moments have led me to the firm conviction that driving our nation's highways would be a hell of a lot more fun without license plates.

I held my speed at an even 65 for the next few minutes, then held my breath as I saw him coming up quickly behind. But he went on around, giving me a long look as he passed.

He saw a smile. Far better for a paranoid to have them in front instead of behind. Unless they're playing games, as he apparently was, because in less than a mile he began to slow down. *Now what?* I silently shrieked, but ahhh, blink-blink, he was taking the Green River exit.

I continued driving as if he was right behind me, but after a few more miles and no sign of him, I romped on it. On the radio, the Rolling Stones were laying claim to their cloud, a position I shared, though by then it was dark enough that no clouds were visible.

No more than three minutes later, just as I made a mental note to gas at the next available station and pick up a battery, another trooper passed me in the eastbound lane, his brake lights casting an apocalyptic glow in my rearview mirror as he slowed to cross the divider strip. I momentarily lost sight of him as the road, approaching the Green River bridge, swung abruptly.

I snapped off my lights and started looking for somewhere else to go – there's almost always a frontage road along rivers, and I hoped I could make one out in the fast-fading light. And there it was, just on the other side of the bridge; no need to signal or slow down much. Then I started looking for cover, a campground or spur road or anything. I came off the gas, though, going too fast to see, and to slow down seemed smarter than turning on the headlights. I finally spotted an abrupt right that dropped down to the floodplain; it looked like gravel trucks had used this through the summer. Banging bottom and rattling my teeth, I took it at full speed. I whipped the Caddy around so I was facing back up the road, backed in close to some willows, then shut the engine down and started gathering the beer cans and other incriminating evidence. I needed something to carry the empties so I dumped my joke house purchases on the front seat and used the bag. The first thing I heard when I opened the door was the river. It *sounded* green. I wondered if that was the reason for its name, but doubted anything so seductive. Probably it was named for the color of its water, though all I could make out in the heavy dusk was a broad shimmer of light.

I hid the beer cans and benzedrine behind a clump of willows, then strolled down to the river, keeping a sharp eye out for traffic on the road to my right. Far downstream I could see the headlights of cars crossing the I-80 bridge.

At the river's edge, it was cold. As I stood there watching the light fade, three dark shapes winged over, one crying, '*Argk! Argk! Argk!*'

Ravens. '*Argggk*,' I called back weakly, but they disappeared downstream.

My ghost appeared in front of me, standing on a rock about ten feet out in the river. 'You're crazy,' he announced. 'Barking at the sky.'

'They were ravens.' I defended myself. 'Looking for the ark. Noah's Ark, remember? All the animals two by two. You know, I've always wondered how it was that ravens were able to reproduce if Noah sent one off that never came back. That only left one, right? So how—'

'Please.' My ghost stopped me. 'Let's listen to the babble of running water; it's so much more soothing than the ravings of your poor mind.'

'Hey, you're *my* ghost – you've got to be crazy, too.'

'I don't have to be anything,' he said, vanishing.

I bent over and scooped up some water and splashed it over my face, trembling as it ran down my neck. It was cold. When I opened my eyes, blinking water from the lashes, I thought I saw a flicker of light upstream. I wiped my eyes and looked again. Still there. I couldn't tell if the light itself was flickering or if something was crossing in front of it. I walked upstream till I could see more clearly. As nearly as I could tell, it was behind a screen of willows. A campfire, I decided. Maybe Smokey was having a wiener roast for his forest friends. I splashed another sobering shot of water on my face to sharpen my focus. Yup, I was sure I saw Bambi's shadow, and then Thumper's. But whose shadow was that, the tall naked woman unfurling her wings? I headed back to the car.

'Where are you going now?' my ghost demanded. I couldn't see him but his voice was clear. 'Don't you think it might be wise to wait a few minutes before resuming this fool's errand? I like it here by the river.'

'I'm going swimming,' I told him.

'The river's this way.'

'I'm going to the car first. For a present.'

'George,' my ghost said with strained patience, 'hasn't it ever struck you that you're one of those warriors who, every time he girds up his loins for another reckless leap into the unknown, gets his little pee-pee caught in the buckle?'

'There's always a first time,' I said without breaking stride.

'And a last,' he reminded me.

On the way back from the car with the can of S.D. Rollo's Divinity Confections in my hand, I cautioned myself over and over *Don't expect it to be Kacy; don't even think of it*. A far-fetched notion, I realized even at the time. I picked the slowest water I could find, a long bellying pool downstream from the flickering firelight. I caught a faint scent of wood-smoke.

I stripped to my shorts and, holding the Divinity Confections aloft, waded in to mid-thigh, then launched myself gently into the current. The water was so cold that all bodily sensation gasped to a numb stop, and if I hadn't been so full of crank I doubt they'd ever have started again. After two stunned minutes of mechanical exertion I was across, crawling out on the opposite shore like some blue-fleshed proof of unnatural selection.

I flopped around on the sandy beach to reheat my body, then still shivering badly, picked up the can of Divinity Confections and lurched upstream toward the fire. While the road-side of the river had a wide floodplain, the other side rose into steep rockface bluffs with only a narrow, willow-choked flat between river and rock. I crashed my way through the willows, muttering and grunting to myself until I realized I probably sounded like a rabid bear. I felt the crosshairs centering on my heart. No need to frighten anybody into such unthinking defensive behavior as shooting me, so I stopped and hollered, 'Hello there! Company coming with gifts and good cheer!'

'*Please*, go away,' a young woman's voice answered close by, genuine appeal in her tone.

'Nothing to fear,' I called back, moving forward a few steps and stumbling into a small clearing. The fire was built against the base of the bluff, set back under a ledge that high water had cut through the centuries. The woman was standing in front of the fire shaking her head vehemently. She wasn't tall, she didn't have wings, and, of course, she wasn't Kacy. She was a couple of inches over five feet, and what I'd taken for wings from across the river was a poncho made of an olive-drab Army blanket.

'Please listen a minute before you send me away,' I asked. 'I'm probably stone crazy and a fool to boot, but my intentions are wholesome and altogether honorable. I was attracted by the light, and I just swam that icicle of a river because I wanted to bring you a present – whoever you are.' I held up the can of Divinity Confections as if it were irrefutable truth.

'That's nice of you,' she said evenly, lowering her head

'but I don't want company. I'm not in the mood to entertain.'

'Don't worry,' I assured her – as if there was assurance to be found in a wild-eyed, sand-blotched fool wearing nothing but his soaked jockey shorts and waving what looked like a large tinker-toy can. '*I'll* entertain *you*. Please? I just want to talk to another human being.'

'All right,' she said reluctantly.

Her name was Mira Whitman, twenty years old, and she listened to my tale of low adventure and high stupidity as she sat on a log in front of the fire, her shoulders hunched and head down, staring at her fingers entwined on her lap. She had a small, squarish head, brown hair cut short, with a thin, sharp nose at odds with her broad cheekbones. Her face was deeply tanned.

When I finished my narration, bringing her right up to date on my mission and the imminent delivery at the continental edge, she said, still staring at her hands, 'I guess you are kind of crazy. But, you know, at least it's a *real* craziness; at least it has a point. And I hope you make it, if that's what you want to do. Wreck that car, I mean.'

'That's what I want to do. But I didn't tell you I'm starting to see my ghost lately. He just shows up. He looks just like me only he's not flesh and blood. I talk to him. Do you think that's cause for alarm, or does it matter?'

'I have no idea. You're talking to the wrong person. I mean, I don't really even understand what you've been telling me. Don't you see that? I have *no* understanding. It's all I can do right now to wake up in the morning and see the river. Or a leaf. Or an ant.'

'Why's that,' I asked gently, quickly adding, 'But don't tell me if it has anything to do with a man – one who loves you or doesn't, beats you, adores you, who's died or's dying. I don't want to know. Seems like every woman I've talked to in the last year has man troubles.'

She glanced at me, then looked down at her hands. 'I thought you were *doing* it for love and music?' But fortunately, before I had to defend the untenable, she went on, 'But no, it's not a man. That just hurts. Or infuriates. No, it's *me*. Or not me.' She bit her lip and glanced up again. 'I got lost.' This time she didn't look back down. 'Does that make any sense?'

I sighed. 'Sounds painfully familiar.'

'No.' She was adamant. 'With you it's meaning. Making it *mean* something.'

'And with you?'

She looked past me into the fire, then back to my face. 'You're nice, George. And I like what you're trying to do. But it's pointless for me to talk about it. For you the words help carry it, give you something to hold on to, but for me they tear it out of my hands, or turn it mushy.' She started to add something, then changed her mind, her gaze moving back to the fire. 'I've enjoyed talking to you, George, but the best thing you could do is leave.'

'No,' I told her, 'I won't.' That surprised her. Me, too. 'I want to know what happened and what you're going to do about it, or what you're trying to do. You sit here and tell me you're lost and imply you have no sense of being real, and I see the real light from this real fire dancing in your real pretty brown eyes, and I *know* you're wrong, me who doesn't know very much at all. Maybe what you lost is a feeling, maybe a feeling I've lost, too, or that we're both trying to create, or fake, or somehow just patch enough together to make it through another day.'

'You're so *hungry*,' she said, looking straight at me.

I looked straight back. 'Maybe you're not hungry enough?'

'I'm not *like* you,' she pleaded, 'can't you see that? You with your lost lover and stolen car and wild adventures all over the country. For you – oh, Jesus, this doesn't make any sense – for you it's like you can't blow up a balloon big enough to hold it all, can't find a balloon *large* enough . . . and me, it's like a little balloon I was blowing up every day, and every day the air leaked out until I was emptying faster than I could fill it. Ever since I was twelve, right around junior high, I've just *dwindled*. I'll spare you adolescence in a small town in Colorado. I wasn't pretty. I wasn't popular. I wasn't particularly smart. I didn't have any friends that were the way I thought friends should be, men *or* women. But it was manageable. As soon as I graduated from high school I left and moved to Boulder. The Big City! I had a tiny apartment and I cleaned motel rooms in the morning and worked at Burger Hut in the evening. I liked being on my own, doing what I felt like when I didn't have to work, but I was still shrinking. I could feel it every morning, like I was running away from myself over the hills. Then I got a break: this woman who came into Burger Hut all the time mentioned a job was opening at a radio station down the block, KROM, not as a deejay or anything, just a receptionist, record librarian, general assistant . . . and I got it. The pay was two dollars an hour, but I loved the job. The people were nutty and it was always chaos and it was fun being involved with the music. Music touches people, you know that, and I was part of it, and it had been a long time since I felt like a part of anything.

'Then about three months ago they started this big bumper-sticker promotion. You know: you put a KROM bumper-sticker on your car, and if your license number's announced and you call in, you win some kind of prize – albums, merchandise, tickets to a dance or concert or movie. The license plates are picked by what they called "The Mystery Spotter." That was me, The Mystery Spotter. It sounds pretty important but all it meant was that when I was driving to work, or at lunch, or whatever, I'd pick four or five cars with KROM bumper-stickers and write down the license numbers and then turn them over to the manager. I was fair, too. I tried to be random, and it didn't matter if it was a new car or old one or who was driving.

'But what happened was *none* of the numbers I'd collected *ever* called in. The whole idea of the promotion is to make people listen to the station to hear their number called – plus the advertising from the bumper-stickers themselves. So after three days of no winners, nobody calling in, it got horribly embarrassing because it was like nobody was listening. The deejays started joking on the air that maybe The Mystery Spotter needed glasses. Then the station manager said, "Hey, bring in ten numbers; we'll go till we get a winner." And still nobody called. So the manager wanted twenty numbers. He told Evans, the night security guy, to bring in ten and me ten. None of my ten called. Eight of Evans's did.

'You understand what I'm getting at? It's like I wasn't connected. So I started cheating. I'd *tell* people I was The Mystery Spotter and that if they listened at eight o'clock or whenever, their number would be called and they'd win something. And they'd go, "Oh great! Hey, all right!" But they never called. And these were people who *put* those dumb stickers on their cars. It's like I wasn't real to them. Evans's numbers? At least seventy percent of the time.

'It seems dumb, but it really got to me. The Mystery Spotter who couldn't spot anything. I could stand there telling someone I was the KROM Mystery Spotter and feel my voice go right through them without touching, and they'd smile back right through me, and I'd go back to my apartment and open the door and walk in and wonder who lived there. Go look in her closet and touch her clothes and my hand would pass through them like air.

'You can't live like that, without any substance. I had this dream where I cut my wrists. Took a razor blade and sliced in deep, waiting for the blood to spurt. But there was no blood. I cut deeper and deeper till my hand flopped back and I could look right down into my wrist and there was nothing there – no muscles, no arteries, no blood. I think I would've actually tried to kill myself if I wasn't so terrified nobody was there to die.

'The only thing I could think to do was to get away. I took my sleeping bag, some blankets, borrowed a fishing pole, stole a knife, and eventually ended up here. I like it, but it's getting cold and I don't think I'll stay when the snows come. But maybe I'll try. I'm doing better now, trying to make myself real again. At first I was like a little baby – not learning the *names*, that was just confusing – but touching the water, trying to feel the light on my skin, the texture and color of this stone, that stone, the leaves and the trees, with nothing in the way. Going back to nothing and starting over. And I'm doing all right. It's slow. I'm not ready for people yet is all.'

'Mira,' I said, resisting the impulse to take her in my arms, 'I want you to spot me.'

She tilted her head. 'What?'

'You're a Mystery Spotter and I desperately need to be spotted. So please spot me. We need each other.'

She shook her head. 'Maybe you're *too* crazy.'

'And you're not? You're crawling around touching things you're afraid to name, licking rocks, going to extraordinary lengths to comprehend the most obvious things, and *you* call *me* nuts? Hey, the crazy have to help each other; nobody else knows how. My license number is BOP three-three-three. Call it in. I'll be listening for it.'

She shrugged her shoulders under the poncho. 'I can't. There's no phone. I don't even work there anymore.'

'You're so *literal*, Mira; that's part of your problem, I think. And maybe mine. Probably the opposite is true. But I don't know.' I picked up a small chunk of firewood and handed it to her. 'Here's a phone. Or use that rock over there. Use one of those hands you keep staring at – they'll work. Or you can do it in your mind without props, even without words, certainly without reason.'

'It'd just make it worse.'

There was an abject finality in her tone that freshened my determination, but I took a different tack. 'Do you ever see ravens around here?'

'Sure.' She looked puzzled.

'That guy I told you about that played the train recording? Joshua Springfield? Well, when Josh was a kid he heard a raven flying over calling "Ark, Ark" and he was sure it was the raven Noah'd sent out in the flood to look for land, the one that never came back, and Joshua figured it was still looking for the Ark. So you know what Joshua did? He went out in his backyard and built an ark so the raven would have a place to land. Joshua refused to leave his ark, to give up his vigil. Finally his parents had him committed. Does that make it worse?'

'I'm not Joshua,' she said, some fire in her voice.

'No, you're not Joshua. I'm not Joshua. Even Joshua knows he's not Joshua. We're ravens. That's why we build arks.'

'I guess I'm too dumb to understand. It's just words to me, George.'

My ghost appeared beside her, looking down consolingly. 'Don't worry,' he told her, 'he doesn't understand either.'

'Did you hear that?' I said sharply.

'No.' Mira was startled. 'What?'

'My ghost. He's right beside you. He said I didn't understand it either, so not to worry about it.'

'George,' my ghost said with irritated disgust, 'leave this woman alone. She seems to know what her problem is, and what to do about it, which is more than can be said for you, and she undoubtedly has better things to do than listen to your bullshit. She wisely asked you to leave a couple of times already, so why don't you lay off? If you need some miraculous conversion to bolster yourself, preach your madness at me.'

I repeated his speech verbatim, and Mira simply nodded – in terror or agreement, I wasn't sure which. My ghost had disappeared, looking sorely annoyed, as I repeated his words. I waited a moment for Mira to comment. When she didn't I went on. 'There seems to be a general agreement that this fool should leave, so that's what I'm going to do. I should get on with the night's work anyway. I've enjoyed talking to you, Mira, and I'm inspired by your faith. Excuse my preaching when I should've been listening – it's one of my larger faults. And please' – I smiled warmly – 'do accept this small gift I braved the river to bring you, a gift I hope will be the first of two I'll deliver tonight.' I picked up the Divinity Confections from where I'd set it down behind the rock and presented it to her with a small bow. 'It's candy, for a sweetheart.'

She smiled as she accepted it with both hands. 'Thank you.'

Her smile almost made me cry. 'You have a lovely smile, Mira. Under different circumstances it would be easy for me to hang around and fall in love.' I pointed at the can. 'I hope you like sweets. They make an excellent dessert for twig soup, tossed moss salad, and grubs in willow sauce.'

I was embarrassing her, and she looked at the can for something to do. 'You know,' she said, 'this looks like one of those things you buy in joke shops, where something leaps out.'

'A practical joke is one that makes you laugh,' I quoted. 'And no doubt there's both sweetness and nutrition in humor, but it would be in the poorest of taste considering the situation, don't you think?'

Before she could answer I took my leave, thanking her for her warm hospitality on a cold night.

'Good luck, George,' she said. 'I mean it.'

'Ah, you're not *real* enough to mean it.'

She smiled again. 'Maybe so, but you deserve the effort.'

'Then put some effort into spotting me.' I waved and walked into the dark thicket of willows. I loved her smile but wanted to hear her laugh.

I was about forty feet from her camp when I heard the springing *whooosh* of the snake uncoiling, and then her quick, piercing shriek. There was a faint, flat *whump!* followed instantly by a flare of light so intense I could make out veins in the willow leaves: the snake had evidently landed in the fire. As the burst of light faded, her laughter began – warm, full-throated, belly-rich laughter that rang against the stone bluffs and swelled down the river canyon.

I turned around and yelled through cupped hands: 'That's right, you idiot: *laugh!*'

'You're fucking hopeless, George,' my ghost said at my shoulder.

'Oh yeah? I *feel* like I'm *brimming* with hope.' I stepped out of the willows at the river's edge. 'So you don't think I'm one of the ravens, huh?' There was no answer. Though it was to dark to tell for sure, I assumed he'd vanished. 'Well, my ghost, just watch me – I'm going to *fly* across this river here and not wet a pinkie.'

I walked downstream till the bank widened. I concentrated fiercely, trying to let Mira's laughter lighten my bones and feather my flesh, and then I ran for the river, flapping for lift, vaulting into the air. I flew seven or eight feet before I belly-flopped into the icy water. I'd flailed halfway across before I managed my first breath. The current was stronger than I remembered, but swimming was easier without the burden of a gift.

When I finally pulled myself up on the opposite shore, hunching out on all fours, panting and shivering like a sick dog, my ghost was waiting for me. 'That was a spectacular flight,' he said, 'maybe a foot, fourteen inches.'

I trembled to my feet, jerkily stripped off my water-logged shorts, and swung them at his face. They passed right through it. Gasping, I said, 'You haven't seen anything. Foot's a good start. Like seeing a leaf. Mira's inspired me.' I turned and flung my jockey shorts out in the river, then scrabbled around in the dark till I found my pile of clothes. I put them on gratefully, topping the outfit with my flamingo hat. I imagined it glowing like a beacon. The gods knew where to find me, if they were looking. As I walked back to the car I looked for a raven's feather to stick in the band. I didn't find any.

I started the Caddy and cranked up the heat, then gathered my bag from the trunk and five or six records that had already played. I stopped and retrieved the bottle of liquid benzedrine, reshouldered my duffle bag, and took it all down to the river.

I threw the records at the stars, missing by a couple jillion miles. I unzipped the duffle, took out my bankroll, added the two grand still wadded in my pocket, peeled off $500 for expenses, and hurled the rest toward the river. The unwieldy was fluttered apart into rectangular leaves, dropping silently on the water, whirling away. I stuffed several good-sized stones into the duffle bag and zipped it shut. I grabbed a strap, braced myself for an Olympian effort, spun once, twice, thrice, and cut loose. It hit halfway across in a tremendous splash, and sank. I unscrewed the cap on the bottle of crank and sidearmed it across the water like a skipping stone, lifted the bottle in a salute to the night sky, took a couple of farewell glugs, then whipped it out there as far as I could.

I trotted back up to the Eldorado's heat, absently working my tongue around teeth and gums to cleanse the bitter chalk residue of the benzedrine. I smiled as I imagined some fisherman hooking into a trout full of speed, the pole nearly ripped from his hands, line smoking off the reel as he stumbled downstream howling to his buddy, 'Holy fuck, Ted!' just as the backing ran out on his reel and his $200 split-bamboo rod shattered in his hands. And Ted yelling back, 'Hey, piss on the rod. I'll buy you a new one. I'm wading in twenty-dollar bills here.' Even if this wouldn't happen, the possibility made me happy.

My ghost was sitting in the driver's seat when I opened the Caddy's door. 'I better drive,' he said.

'Move your ass over.'

He glared at me; I glared back. 'All right,' he said. 'Why should I care if you continue to wildly overestimate your capabilities and underestimate mine. But if it's going to be like that, let's fucking *do* it. No little lost raven-poo going "ark, ark, ark." Burn the goddamn Ark! Let's have some spirit, George. Let's scream through the night like eagles. Let's do it right.' And he was gone.

Fuck him and his eagles. I took it extra easy pulling up the embankment back onto the frontage road, not wanting to bottom out. I'd been abusing the Caddy lately, and it was built for cruising, not off-road racing. I approached I–80 with caution, then hung a right. No sign of official forces or black Oldsmobiles. We needed gas pronto, and a new battery for Joshua's solid-drive master blaster. I snapped on the radio, but KROM was gone – must cut back their signal, I figured. Or maybe this was some topographical anomaly, because I couldn't seem to find anything at all: just a blur of static from one end of the band to the other. *Or perhaps a little electronic interference*, I thought to myself, *like radar*. I went back through the dial and at 1400, crisp and clear, I heard a man talking to me:

'Awww*riiiight*, brothers and sisters! If you're twisting one up, keep right on it; but if you're twisting the dial, *stop* right there, 'cause you got KRZE, one billion megawatts of pure blow hammering your skull from our studio *high* atop the Wind River Range. Coming up in tonight's lifetime we got you some tricks and treats, some goblin chuckles and that monster beat, plus tons more good stuff than you'll be able to believe, so dig it like a grave while I whisper some sweet nothings in your ear. That's right, relax. This is Captain Midnight at the controls, if there are any; I want you to enjoy your flight.

'Now did I say treats? You might be worrying where you're gonna find a bag big enough to bring back all your goodies tonight, one that's big enough to truck the whole load home. No sweat, 'cause here's Mr James Brown and I do believe he's got a bag you can borrow, a brand new one at that.'

'Hey ghost,' I yelled as James Brown worked out, 'how do you like this station?' But ghost wasn't talking.

To save on gas, and because I was still jittery about troopers, I kept it at an even 65. 'Papa's Got a Brand New Bag' segued into Bobby 'Boris' Pickett and the Crypt Kickers doing 'Monster Mash,' which in turn slid without pause into Frankie Laine's 'Ghost Riders in the Sky.'

Then back to Captain Midnight, who was hopping with excitement: '*Did you dig* that message? Cowboys you *better* change your ways or it looks like eternity for sure busting ass, chasing them fire-eyed longhorns through the clouds. Yiiiiiippeeee-i-o, that's *hard*. And you little cowgirls better be good, too, or they won't let you ride horsies in Heaven, little britches, and you *know* that's hell on a girl. Hey, but enough cheap Christian morality, *right?* Tonight belongs to the beasties and demons, vamping vampires and the living dead. Yes, it's All Hallow's Eve, and something darkly stalks the land and the furthermost recesses of the human brain, which has always loved recess. But something good stalks it, too, because our Mystery Spotter is out there spotting mysteries left and right, as well as a few well-chosen license plates, and maybe tonight's the night your number comes up. That's right, hot dog: you may already be a wiener. So stay tuned and you might pick up a couple of tickets to the dance. And while you're waiting, we flat *guarantee* we'll have a few other numbers that will both elucidate and amuse. How's that grab your happy ass, fool? You got Captain Midnight in your ear, KRZE, where you find it is where it's at, so *high up* we're underground. Now catch a listen to this monstrosity.'

'Purple People Eater' came tooting on, but I'd just spotted a Sinclair station in some strange tourist trap called Miniature America and was already pulling into the pumps. The attendant, a sawed-off geezer in red, white, and blue overalls, was curious about the car and the big silver box in the back seat, not to mention the fried-eyed idiot in the pink hat. Too curious. He craned to watch me through the back window as he topped the tank and I hooked up the new battery. I don't know if it was his oppressive attention, the raw Wyoming cold, or a case of speed-jangles, but my hands were shaking so bad I damn near couldn't get the clamps cinched down.

The battery and gas came to $34. I gave the old geezer two twenties and told him to keep the change. He shook his head in disbelief, then grinned. 'Mister, if I had your money I'd throw mine away.'

'Throw it away anyway,' I advised him. 'It feels good.'

I rolled back onto I–80 and aimed at Salt Lake City, holding it at a solid 80. If I got stopped I could always argue I'd mistaken the highway number for the speed limit. I listened to the radio instead of records on Joshua's revived system, just in case my license number was called. But first got an earful of Captain Midnight:

'Now you might have thought your soul pilot, Captain Midnight here, was just flapping his lips when he said there was going to be some boss tricks and big treats on tonight's special show. Maybe you've got us pegged as some no-class outfit jiving in the sagebrush, don't know get-along-little-doggie from dactylic hexameter, so dumb we think Grape Nuts Flakes is a venereal disease. Well, how's this for some air-you-fucking-dition: we got America's main expert on poetry, history, and everything else to do us some short spots on the historical-emotional background of trick-or-treat. I mean this guy's got *fifteen* – count 'em – Ph.D. on his wall. We're talking words like *foremost* and *intellectual* and *anagogic insights into symbolic expressions of metaphorical parallels*, and when you're talking that sort of stuff, only one man rises with the cream: that's the poet John Seasons. He works out of Baghdad-by-the-Bay, but his spirit abounds. Hey, when you want the tops you go to the top. So let me introduce John Seasons with Part One of a KRZE exclusive, "A Social Demonology of the Hollow Weenie."'

There was a brief pause, then, no doubt about it, John's voice, his fake professorial tone resonant with five scotches: 'Good evening, ladies and gentlemen. My name is Christopher Columbus and you're a dead Indian.'

That was it.

Captain Midnight jumped back in: 'Didn't I *tell you* the man knows his shit? We're gonna hear more from him, just hang on, but first a little paean to his name, and another man you might wisely have for company on this night of wandering zombies and rabid werewolves, ain't that right, Jimmy Dean? Who're we talking about? Who else but "Big Bad John."'

I only half-listened to the song. The John I knew was neither big nor bad. Sharp tongued and a bit severe, like most poets, but sweet at heart. If he was self-destructive, it was only because he'd rather hurt himself than someone else. I was perplexed he hadn't mentioned the KRZE gig to me; John's only deep vanity was as an historian. He claimed to be a Metasexual Marxist, a school of historical scholarship where, according to John, one arrived at the dialectical truth by kissing tears from the eyes of victims. Maybe his KRZE series had come up after I left, or he'd neglected to tell me in the frenzy of my departure. But if all went right I'd probably see him in a day or so, and I could tell him he'd kept me company through a wild night. And maybe I could get a line on this weird radio station out of the Wind River Range.

'And speaking of the man,' Captain Midnight came in at the end of the song, 'here he is with Part Two in our public service series, "A Social Demonology of the Ol' Hollow Weenie." This time we're going to hear from a famous seventeenth-century religious leader, an old-fashioned, honest-to-God, down-home preacher man.'

John's voice came on: 'The Reverend Cotton Mather at your service. In 1691, one of the female members of my congregation at North Church came to me with the sad admission that she could not open her mouth to pray. I, of course, made every effort to help her. I tried physical manipulation, prayer, admonitions . . . all without success – though, in a noble effort to save her soul, I refused to admit failure. A few nights later I had a dream in which an angel appeared to me and urged me to kiss the unfortunate woman and thereby unlock her mouth to offer her prayers to God for the redemption of her soul. A less experienced theologian might have been fooled. In the past, you see, I had always been visited by angels in my *study*, not my sleeping quarters, and while *awake*, not in the vulnerable state of dreams. It was obviously a false visitation, the devil in the guise of an angel, and a devil plainly manifested through the woman who would not open her mouth to pray. I denounced her as a witch. Following a proper trial, she was burned at the stake, and so completely had Satan inhabited her that even under the scourge of fire she refused to open her mouth except to scream.'

'My *oh my*,' Captain Midnight cut back in, 'Reverend Mather don't seem too kindly disposed toward womenfolk. But don't you get blue behind it, honey. You give the Captain here a jingle on this Satanic night – he'd *like* to bob for your apples, know what I mean? While I'm waiting for the switchboard to light up, let's pin an ear to men of more modern understanding – Sam Cooke, say, with "Bring It on Home to Me" and Roy Orbison's "O Pretty Woman."'

It had been John Seasons for sure. The supercilious, righteous whine, the smug, zealous certainty of the conclusions – I'd heard his Mather imitation many nights in North Beach bars.

'This John Seasons is a good buddy of mine, you know,' I told my ghost. Evidently he wasn't impressed.

I honked the horn for the hell of it and bored on deeper into the night. It was all in my imagination, of course, but I could clearly hear the Pacific Ocean breaking on the edge of the continent.

About fifteen minutes later, John came on again, manifesting one of those inexplicable congruencies we call coincidence. At the same instant I saw the highway sign for Fort Bridger, John's voice began:

'Jim Bridger's the name. I trapped beaver in these mountains nigh onto a century ago. Traded the pelts for provisions and possibles, and pretty much went wherever my stick floated. Now what I wanna know, the thing that plagues on me, is what have you ignorant dung-heads done with the buffalo? I used to traipse this country all over and it weren't nothing to eyeball thousands of them critters at the same time. Now I don't see hide nor ha'r. You got 'em on reservations like the Injuns?'

All right, John! Maybe needed a little work on the mountain man accent, but it was nice to hear a whack for the natural world. Not that I remember John *personally* caring much for the wilds. I'd once tried to get him to go backpacking with me and Kacy, but he'd declined with the explanation that every time he saw a blade of grass he wanted to jump on the nearest cable car. His heart knew better, though.

I was just outside Evanston, moving right along, when his next lick hit: a lugubrious blackface, the parody of a parody: 'Mah name's John. John Henry. Ahm a steel-drivin' man. Whup tha steel. Whup the steel on down, Lawd Lawd. An' now them Southe'n Pacific muthafucks own half the Sierra Nevada.'

I couldn't help myself. I had to stop in Evanston and call him, tell him how good it was to hear his voice, let him know there were listeners in the night. I figured the program was taped, so I called him at home from a Standard station. There was no answer but I let it ring; maybe he was in the basement printing.

About the fourteenth buzz someone answered, either out of breath or patience. 'My *God*, all right, *who* is it?'

'My name's George Gastin,' I said, thinking this was one of his boyfriends and maybe I'd interrupted something. 'I'm calling John Seasons. We're old friends.'

There was a breathy pause on the other end, then: 'Well. I don't *like* bearing bad news, but John's in the hospital.'

I sagged. 'Is he all right?'

'They *think* so. All the tests are *good*. But for heavenssakes, he's been *unconscious* for *three* days.'

'What happened?'

'It's . . . *unclear*.'

'Hey, pal – fuck that shit. I told you he was an old *friend*. I've taken him to the Emergency Room more times than I care to remember.'

'Well don't get mad at *me* about it! *I* don't know you.'

'Okay. You're right. I'm sorry. But I don't know you either, though you're answering his phone.'

'I'm Steven.'

Steven? *Steven?* I racked my brain. 'You work at the Federal Building, right?'

'Yes, I do.'

'I haven't met you, Steven, but I know from John he holds you in high regard. You looking after his place? The manuscripts and presses?'

'Yes. Larry asked if I would.'

'I'm sure they're in good hands. Now tell me what happened. He get those Percodans mixed up with some Scotch?'

'Well, that's what the doctors are saying. Or he got drunk and forgot how many pills he was taking.'

'Did he try to kill himself, Steven?' I made this as direct as I could.

'No one *really* knows. Larry found him on the kitchen floor unconscious. It could've been a mistake.'

'No note?'

'No, nothing like *that*.'

'And this was three days ago, right?'

'Yes.'

'And he's in a coma?'

'Yes. But as I said, all the signs are good. The brain waves are absolutely *normal*. The liver function isn't *great*, but with the amount he drinks that's to be expected. The doctors say it isn't really a coma. I ask if he's still in a coma and they say, "No, he just hasn't regained consciousness yet." Good Lord, you know how *technical* doctors are.'

'What hospital is he in?'

'General.'

'Well, listen. I'll be there as soon as I can. I'm on my way now, but I'm coming from Wyoming and there's some business first.'

'I go by the hospital every morning before work. If he's awake I'll tell him to expect you.'

'Did you know he's on the radio here tonight in Wyoming? A special series called "A Social Demonology of the Hollow Weenie."'

'*Really?* He never mentioned it to me, and we discuss his work all the time. I think he's a *fabulous* writer, but you know he's so hard on himself. It must be taped, of course, but I just can't believe he wouldn't have mentioned it. Are you sure it's John? The title sounds . . . well, *tacky*.'

'It's his name, it sounds just like him, and he lives in San Francisco.'

'How odd.'

'Yeah,' I agreed, 'and getting odder all the time.'

'That's *so* true. You should see Haight Street these days.'

I wanted to avoid the sociological at all costs. 'Steven, listen, my time's up. Thanks, and sorry I jumped on you. I felt I had a right to know.'

'I understand,' Steven said. 'I can appreciate your concern.'

When I pulled out of the gas station I was so preoccupied I didn't realize for six blocks that I was heading downtown instead of out to I-80. I hung a U and had just straightened out the wheels when I saw three small skeletons dancing across the street about a block away, their bones shining with a pale green luminescence in the headlights. I wasn't frightened by their appearance – they obviously were kids dressed up in five-and-dime Halloween costumes – but I was terrified by my desire to stomp on the gas and run them down.

I didn't. I didn't even come close, not really. I hit the brakes instead and immediately pulled over and turned off the car, jamming on the emergency brake as hard as I could. I sat there watching the three little skeletons continue their skipping dance across the pavement and then disappear down a cross street, happily unaware that a man with an impulse to murder them sat watching from a car parked down the block.

After Eddie, how could the impulse even have entered my mind? I felt my exhaustion collapsing on its empty center, my point and purpose caving in to an oblivion of regrets I could neither shape nor salvage, an oblivion I was clearly seeking with a twisted vengeance, trying to destroy what I couldn't redeem, the gift I could neither deliver nor accept.

Yet it was also true that I hadn't even come close; I'd smothered the desire the moment it seized me. But would I again? I raised my fists and hammered them down on the steering wheel, hoping the wheel would break or the bones in my hands shatter or both: any reason to get out of that sleek white Cadillac and walk away. But with each blow all I felt was the congealing certainty that the only choice left was forward and my only chance was fast. I understood too late that it was too late to stop. So, with the rush of freedom that is doom's honey spilling in the heart, I got on it.

As I hit the on-ramp my ghost appeared, in the backseat this time, leaning forward to whisper, 'George, oooh George, you almost did it back there. You better let me drive. You can't trust yourself anymore.'

'Why don't you vanish for good,' I said. 'You're no help.'

He laughed. 'Okay, George. Sure thing. You bet.' And he was gone, leaving an unnerving silence.

Five minutes and ten miles later, when I thought to turn the radio back on, Captain Midnight was doling out the encouragement: 'Yup, the Captain's back from that trip down the voodoo track, and hey!, ain't we got fun? How are *you* doing on this night when the insane rip their chains from the walls and roam the night to play with the dead and plague the innocent? You still getting where you're going? Keeping on *keeping on?* I hope so, friend.

'cause if life ain't right with you, you better get right with life. Whatever *that* is on this ghoul-ridden night. You just tell 'em Captain Midnight, patron deejay of fool dreamers, prays nightly for your soul and twice on Halloween and Easter. *Lapidem esse aquam fontis vivi. Obscurum per obscurius, ignotum per ignotius.* Yes. And may the gods go with you, child.

'And now, because KRZE is dedicated to giving you heart for the path, or some path for the heart, whatever it is you think you need, here's John Seasons again with some more insightful demonology.'

'My name's Black Bart. A lot of people asked me why I only robbed Wells Fargo stages . . . if it was something *personal* against Mr Wells or Mr Fargo or both. Well, not really. I just sorta figured anybody with that much money should be robbed.'

'*OW!* Captain Midnight shouted, 'now there's a jack-o-lantern with a fuse. But your Captain's forced to concur that large piles of money are dangerous, so send me some if it's piling up on you and save yourself the grief. While you're getting it together, I got to attend to a couple of personal gigs. I could slap on a stack of platters and hope they didn't stick, but since it's Halloween I thought it might be a touch of class to leave you with some dead air. But to make it right by you, I'll bring back goodies that'll make you *drool*. Not just more boss sounds and John Seasons's exclusive demonology, but things you can't even imagine. But go ahead and wonder while yours truly visits the Lizard King and throws a few snowballs at the moon. Back in a flash, Jack – I'll make it up to you, and that's a promise.'

The air went dead. I would've turned it off and listened to Donna's collection if it hadn't been for John's social commentaries. I didn't want to miss one. They connected me to someone real, and I was convinced beyond reason that John would live so long as I kept listening. I thought of him drifting in his coma and wondered if, like Elmer, he had a smile on his face.

I slipped into something of a coma myself, my mind blurred

as the night blurred with speed, shadows whipping around me
like torn sails, waves breaking in my mind, a mind I'd maybe
gone out of, long gone, blooey, nobody home on the range, but I
was taking it on home anyway. I flew down the west slope of the
Rockies into Salt Lake City before I knew I was there. The lights
snapped me out of my trance. I started looking for my buddy,
the green dinosaur, and, when I didn't see him, felt like I'd lost a
piece of magic. I settled for a Conoco next to an interchange. My
bladder was a drop from bursting, but I stayed in the car with the
windows up tight, cracking mine only a quick inch to tell the pump
jockey to fill it with supreme. I was certain if I started talking the
way I was thinking I'd be surrounded by squad cars faster than
you could say, 'Up against the wall, motherfucker.' I didn't want
to fly apart when my only hope was to fly, to freeze my bead on
the Pacific shore and stand on the juice. I gave the kid a twenty for
the gas and told him he could keep the change whether he prayed
for my doomed ass or not. I came off the on-ramp running.

When you have to piss so bad your tonsils are under water,
it's as hard to fly as it is to stand still, so at the beginning of
the long desolate run across the saltflats between Salt Lake and
Wendover, I cracked my momentum to pull over and piss, doing
so with the profound appreciation that much of pleasure is mere
relief. The night was so cold that my piss steamed as it soaked
into the moonlit salt. There's nothing like a good, basic piss
to clear the mind, and by volume I should've become lucid,
but perhaps I was just giddy, because I asked my ghost as if
he were present, 'Are saltflats the ghosts of old oceans? Feel
like the seashore? Can we count it as the Pacific if we come
up short?'

No ghost. No answers. But I could feel him then, feel him as
he waited for his moment, waited with the massive patience of a
boulder that knows it will someday be sand for the hourglass. That
was his presence, but underneath I felt his essence, and his essence
was wind. I stood there with my dick in my hand – suddenly

alive in a memory when I was ten and a hurricane had hit out of nowhere and I'd watched, awed, as the wind ripped petals from the rose garden and flung them against the windows, pressing their colors against the quivering glass. The next morning, as he looked at his stripped and ravaged roses, was the only time I'd ever seen my father cry. The memory of it made me start crying, too. 'Help me, ghost,' I asked, not sure whether I was talking to my father's or my own – both, I decided, since I needed all the help I could get. If ghosts help. No ghosts. No answers. I got back in the Cadillac and burned on down the line.

The best thing about saltflats is the flat: a straight, level shot to the horizon, the meeting of heaven and earth, the limit of sight. If you can go fast enough, you can see over the edge. The road was two-lane blacktop, and I opened it up all the way, straddling the white line unless the rare oncoming car sent me back to my lane.

The silence and distance were eating me up. I was just about to shut off Captain Midnight and spin a few records myself when there was an explosion of static on the radio and my Captain said, Ah, back alive; proof against the demons so far, and so far, so good. "But who can tell on this witch's flight/the true darkness from the dancing light?" Them fuckin' demons are tricky. That's why we asked troubadour John Seasons to offer us some insights into the dark. Oh John, *way up* there in your shaman trance, come in please.'

'Good evening,' John said mildly. 'My name, if you don't know it, is J.P. Morgan, and I'm here tonight to reveal the secret to success in American business. I think you'll be surprised how simple it is. First, buy a steel mill. Secondly, buy workers. Buy them for as little as possible, but pay just enough to keep them going. Lastly, buy Congressmen, and pay them to enact tariff laws to keep out foreign steel. Politicians can be purchased cheaply, so buy in quantity. The goal, you see, is stability, and nothing destabilizes like competition. So remember: high prices,

low wages, and a lock on the market. Because when you scrap
off all the sentiment and rhetoric, spirit is for idiots and poetr
for fools. Money is power. And, put bluntly, power rules.'

Captain Midnight was right behind him. 'Right on, Brothe
John! Time to get real out there. Get your nose to the stone. Bea
down and deliver. You've got to be at least as real as the demons
and that's just to break even, Jack, hold your own ground. You go
to get up over it or slide down under it or slip away in betweer
Think that over if you've got a mind, and in the meanwhile I'
make more than good on my promise to make it right by yo
for that dead air. You think I'm jiving? Well, eat shit and craw
under a rock, because sitting right beside me live in the studio i
that legendary street prophet and avatar of the damaged, the on
and only Fourth Wiseman. You've probably heard the mantr
he chants every day, all day, for your edification and mayb
salvation: "The Fourth Wiseman delivered his gift and slippe
away." That *one* sentence, that single expression of holy being, i
all his priestly vows allow him. But what you might *not* know i
that he permits himself to answer *one* question every Hallowee
eve, and tonight it's my privilege, and yours, to have him her
in the studio with us, and I blush with the honor of having bee
chosen to ask him his question for the year. Welcome to KRZF
sir. He's nodding his head and winging his yo-yo.'

'Ask him what the gift was,' I begged.

'We understand, sir,' Captain Midnight went on, 'that you ca
only answer your one question and not engage in conversationa
pleasantries, so let me get right to it. Will you tell us, pleas
what was the Fourth Wiseman's gift?'

I cheered.

'No one knows,' the Fourth Wiseman said, and hearing hi
voice I knew this was either the Fourth Wiseman or an excep
tional mimic. 'Scholars generally recognize three possibilities, fo
which the evidence is about equal. The three most supportabl
possibilities for the Fourth Wiseman's gift are a song, a whi

rose, and a bow – the gesture of acknowledgment and respect, not the bough of a tree. But again, no one really knows.'

'And which of the three do you favor,' the Captain asked politely.

Silence. I heard my mother crying softly and my father, confused, saying, 'Hey, it was a *great* dream: my brain turned into a white rose.' I saw the rose petal kaleidoscope of colors smeared against the buckling glass as the wind milked their essence and infused the storm. I needed the names of the roses. I needed their protection.

'I beg your pardon, sir,' Captain Midnight apologized. 'I see the rules are strict – one question only. Thank you for being with us, you burned-out old speed freak, and please feel welcome to stay.'

The Fourth Wiseman said, 'The Fourth Wiseman delivered his gift and slipped away.'

'Well, slip away if you want, but you listeners out there rocketing through the dark better stay glued to the groove and be ready to move because *here it is*, a lucky license plate number picked by our own Mystery Spotter, plucked from the random churn of things like a speck of gold from the cosmic froth, and if it's *your* number that's up and you call and identify yourself within *fifteen* minutes, you're gonna win two tickets to the dance. *The* dance, you dig what I'm saying?'

I looked down the road into my parents' rose garden and tried to remember the names of all the roses while Captain Midnight paused for a thunderous drumroll before announcing, 'Well, well, well, we got a California plate – just goes to show our Mystery Spotter is everywhere you are, and you never know when her wild eyes may fall on you. Could be never. Could be your next heartbeat. Could be, ooooh, couldie be. But tonight's number could only be this one: BOP three-three-three. That's B as in Boo, O as in Overboard; P as in Psalm; three as in treys; three as in blind mice; three as in tri – be it trilogy, trident, trial and error, trick, or just a little bit harder. So okay, BOP three-three-three, California dreamer, whoever you are out there raving in the dark, you got fifteen minutes to call me at Beechwood 4–5789. But hey, Captain Midnight's gonna cut you some slack, Jack – I'm gonna give you twenty minutes to call in. Not only because I'm a righteous fool myself, but because the next side I'm gonna drop on you is so *rare* and so *fine* I don't want it interrupted by some crass promotional gimmick. This side just happens to be twenty minutes long. It's the only recording of this tune in *existence*, and the moment it's over I'm gonna burn it. That's right, you heard it straight: I'm laying on the flame the instant it's finished. So listen well, because the next time you hear it you'll be listening to your memory. And while the Captain isn't one to pass judgment on the musical sensibilities of his listeners, if this don't touch the living spirit in your poor, ragged heart, you best call a mortuary and make an appointment. I'll tell you the name of the man who made this music when it's done and burning.'

I didn't have to wait long on the knowledge. The exhausted keening of the opening passage was already etched in my memory: Big Red playing my birthday song, 'Mercury Falling.'

I felt like everything at once and nothing forever. I felt triumphant my license number had been called, joyous that I'd connected with Mira, who I was sure had spotted me. But I was crushed by the realization that there wasn't a phone within a half-hour in any direction, and moved to tears by the first bars of Big Red's sax calling to the ghosts across the water as we pushed the glossy Merc coupe over the cliffs and stood at the windswept edge waiting for it to hit. I was stunned, confused, possessed, lost, found, confirmed in my faith and strangely bereft. You can't be moved in that many directions at once without tearing apart.

My ghost was there beside me on the front seat. 'You worthless jerk-off, *I want to dance*. You think when he said *the* dance he meant some fucking sock-hop in a crepe-festooned gym smelling of fifty-thousand P.E. classes? No, *you* make sure we're in the middle of absolutely nowhere, a thousand light-years from a phone, so we can't win the tickets. Screw your dumb moral victories. I'm sick of being cooped up in your cloying romance. If we make it to the ocean, you'll probably want to pave it so you don't have to finish and admit your failure. You've gone crazy, George. That's what I'm stuck to, a crazy fuck-up. But we'll just see about that—'

'Shut up!' I bellowed. 'I want to listen to the music.'

'Well, *I* want to dance. You too proud to dance with your ghost? Afraid people will point and giggle? What do you think they're doing now? Come on, George, if you're not going to do anything with your body but abuse it, give it to me. I could use one. Just don't include your mind in the deal, all right?'

'Shut the fuck up!' I screamed again, 'this is my *birthday* song!' I reached over and twisted the volume all the way up.

But you can't drown out your ghost. He began singing, relentlessly off-key:

> *Happy birthday to you,*
> *Happy birthday to you,*
> *Happy birthday, mad George,*
> *Happy birthday toooo youuuu . . .*

Birthday Bow, I remembered. That was a name of one of the roses in the garden. My father was crying in the silence that Big Red had created. I could feel Kacy moving with me like a wave. A small blue rectangular miracle appeared before my eyes, a road sign:

EMERGENCY PHONE
1 MILE

came off the gas and told my ghost, 'Go get your dancing shoes, asshole.' He laughed as he vanished.

The light above the phone box was broken so I used one of

the birthday candles that couldn't be blown out for light as I carefully dialed BE4–5789.

Be-beep; be-beep; be-beep; be-beep; be-beep. The sound like an auger up my spinal cord. Busy.

I hung up and tried again. Still busy. I figured I had a minute left. I called the operator, hoping she'd believe my claim of emergency and cut in. I couldn't get the operator, not even a ring. Not even a hum. I tried BE4–5789 again and got nothing at all. The line was dead.

My ghost was standing beside me. 'Irony eating you up is it George? I'm afraid you're gonna become mutilated, just like that old con salesman warned you about. But that's *your* problem buddy. *Me*, I'm going to dance.'

'Be home early,' I snarled at him as he disappeared.

Back in the Caddy and on the road, I caught the last notes of 'Mercury Falling.' '*Burn it*,' I urged Captain Midnight, seeing the brilliant red petals in my mind. 'Gypsy Fire,' I remembered aloud. 'Borderflame. My Valentine.'

Captain Midnight whispered, 'Let's let his ghost go now.' I heard him strike a match. 'Whooooosh!' He laughed. 'Memory.'

The room growing darker as the petals clotted against the window. The yellow and orange was Carnival Glass. 'Carnival Glass,' I said it aloud. The orange and pink was Puppy Love. 'Puppy Love, Kacy, isn't that a wonderful name for a rose?'

'Ashes to ashes,' Captain Midnight intoned, 'dust to dust. Round and round the music goes, here in the majesty of bloom, gone in the voluptuous exhilarations of decay. Purchase for the roots, food for its green flesh, and where it stops nobody knows. But don't you worry. The whole is perfect. It's just never the same. For example, stick an ear on these new kids from England doing good-ol'-boy Buddy Holly's tune from six years back – that's right, brighten up for some truth, grab some stash and hang *on* to your ass, because you got the Rolling Stones and "Not Fade Away."'

Tell me it still couldn't come up roses. I joined in on the second chorus, singing it with rock-solid, gospel-light joy,

Love for real not fade away!

And my ghost, suddenly appearing sitting cross-legged on the hood, pressed his face against the windshield and roared,

Doo-wop; doo-wop; doo-wop-bop.

He smiled sweetly and then reached down and tore off the windshield wipers like a baby giant tearing the wings off a fly. I was so shocked it took me a second to realize I couldn't see the road. He'd turned solid. My hands froze the wheel in position as I came down easy on the brakes, craning to see around him, my heart lurching against my ribs.

'Better let me drive now, George,' my ghost said. 'You're so fucked-up you can't see through me.'

'Nova Red!' I yelled in his grinning face. 'Warwhoop! Sun Maid! Candleflame! Trinket! Seabreeze!' I was under 50 and still on the road. As I strained to see around him he moved with me, but I caught a glimpse off to the right of a low shoulder and open saltflats beyond, and that was all I needed. I cranked the wheel to the right, bottomed out in the drainage swale, then shot out clear and clean, mashing the gas.

My ghost was still hanging on, still sitting calmly and cross-legged on the hood, grinning madly as foam drooled from his mouth and flecked the windshield. I glanced at the floorboards. Both packages of Rabi-Tabs were gone. It no longer mattered what was possible.

My ghost lifted a hand to his foamy mouth, wiped off a viscous gob, smeared it across the windshield.

'The Hokey-Pokey,' I cried, 'is raw orange with a yellow center. You put your whole self in and take your whole self out.

The Bo Peep is light pink, white compared to my hat.' I whipped off my stingy-brim and waved it in front of his foam-blurred face to blind him, then suddenly cranked the wheel hard-left and spun the Caddy through a full 360°, your classic brodie, and then punched the gas and snapped one off to the right.

To see through the opaque Rabi-Tab film on the glass was difficult, but it looked like I'd thrown him off. My spirit broke with his first jarring stomp on the roof, dancing as he merrily sang:

> *The kids in Bristol are as sharp as a pistol*
> *When they do the Bristol Stomp.*

STOMP. STOMP. The headliner rippling as the roof buckled.

> *It's really sumpin' when the joint is jumping*
> *When they do the Bristol Stomp.*

STOMP. STOMP. Stomping on the roof.

My eardrums ached as I fishtailed to a stop, slammed it into reverse, punched it, and then did some stomping myself, down hard on the brakes. Nothing could budge him.

'Who am I?' he screamed. '*Who am I?*' He started singing again, to the tune of 'Popeye,'

> *I'm Ahab the Sailor Man — toot! toot!*
> *I stay as obsessed as I can — toot! toot!*
> *When weirdness starts swarming*
> *It's too late for warning*
> *Because things have got way out of hand.*

'And you, George,' he murmured, 'you're the innocent heart of the whale.'

The tip of a harpoon plunged through the roof, the barbed

head burying itself in the seat about a half-inch from my head, so close it nicked the brim of my hat. A harpoon. How can you even think about something like that?

'Let me drive,' he demanded. 'You're wasted. It's over.'

I drove. Rammed it in low, tached it up, popped the clutch. The nose of the Caddy lifted like it was some supercharged, nitro-snorting dragster getting off the mark. My ghost jumped back down on the hood and started tap dancing, stopping abruptly to say, 'Let me drive. I *know* what you want; *I* know what you're looking for.' And *tappidy-tappidy-dappity-tap* he started dancing again, not even swaying as I hit second and wound it out.

Over the engine scream and my dancing ghost and the blood pounding in my skull, a voice spoke clearly from the radio, a voice I'd only heard once in my life, four words in mimicry of his mother: 'Come on . . . we're *late.*' Eddie. I hit the brakes so hard I whacked my head on the steering wheel.

My ghost, unmoved on the hood, was lip-synching with great exaggeration as Eddie's voice explained through the radio, 'It was my favorite drawing. The horses are really deer who can pick up signals from ghosts with their horns like they were TV antennas or something. The big red flower can pick up signals from the sun and aim them at the deer. It's just a big red flower, I don't know what kind. The long green car is to go look for the flower and the deers. It needs big, tough wheels because it's a long way and the flower is hidden and the deer can run like the wind. And the sun's just there in the middle, you know, so you can see things. I didn't want to lose it.'

I got the Caddy stopped, brought my knees out from under the wheel and up to my chest, and uncoiled a savage two-heeled kick at the radio. A woman screamed as the glass shattered. 'It's done, George,' my ghost said softly, his voice coming through the radio. I kicked it again and again, and with every blow a woman screamed through the speaker and my ghost told me it was over, to let go. I was reaching for the battery out of Joshua's music box to knock out the radio when I caught the glint off the gallon can of white gas on the backseat floor. In one motion I picked it up, swung it over the seat back, and bashed it against the radio. A woman screamed. I was swinging the can for another blow when I understood she was Kacy. I'd never heard her scream before, but I knew it was her. I dropped the can on the front seat. The blow had cracked a seam in the thin metal. The gas leaked in erratic dribbles, soaking into the seat. My sinuses burned from the fumes, tears spilling down my cheeks. I sagged back against the seat. My ghost grinned down triumphantly.

'You drive,' I said.

I swabbed my jacket sleeve across my face to wipe the tears, and when I blinked them open a moment later I was lying on the Caddy's hood, my face pressed to the windshield, staring into the empty eyes of my ghost.

'George,' he said sweetly, 'if you want to live you must throw yourself to death like a handful of pennies into a wishing well.'

He pivoted from the waist and reached over into the backseat. He was putting a record on the turntable. I knew he was going to mock me by playing 'Chantilly Lace,' so I was stunned by the sound of an approaching train, its distant wail slicing the dark. For a spinning instant I thought we were parked on railroad tracks and would have leaped if I hadn't been hurled against the windshield as my ghost popped the clutch and smoked it through first into second as the train bore down and my brain bloomed with white roses. I shouted their names as he ripped it into high, wind tearing the petals away, flinging them to darkness and salt: 'Cinderella! White King, White Madonna, White Feather, White Angel! Misty Dawn! Careless Moment!'

'"Careless Moment?"' My ghost roared with laughter. He thought it was so funny he turned off the headlights. I was going to die. Meal for the roses, meat for the dream. 'It's such a beautiful dream,' my mother told me as the garden burned and the train screamed through my skull, obliterating every name I knew. I looked down at my body and only the skeleton remained. Then, taken by an undreamable serenity, I calmly stood up on the hood of the Caddy. I bowed to my ghost and then leapt lightly up on the roof. The wind sang through my bones. I could feel the exact pressure against every bone in my hands as I wrapped them around the jutting shaft of the harpoon and in one concerted movement snapped it off. I jumped back down on the hood, pivoting neatly as I swung the wooden shaft and smashed it through the windshield with all my might.

My ghost smiled up at me. 'Took you long enough, George. I thought I was going to have to do it by myself.'

I dove through the smashed-out window and went for his throat.

My flesh and blood hands were locked on the wheel where his had been, 130 mph straight ahead into the salt-glittering dark. I could have gone on forever if the engine hadn't blown.

The instant it blew I lost control. I tried to correct as it started sideways; a useless reflex. I was gone, and all I could do was hold on helpless and terrified as the Caddy slewed across the saltflats and finally went over, flipping three times bang-bang-bang, then skidding driver's side down, my cheek pressed against the window, greenish sparks shooting past as if I was being hurled through the stars. Then, violently, the Caddy flipped again, end over end, twisting, then again on its side in a wild twirl, and as it was slowing I felt like I was inside the milk bottle we'd used in our first, nervous game of spin-the-bottle. My first spin stopped on Mary Ann Meyers. I felt her lips touch nine, the jelly-tremor roll through my loins. I felt Kacy's arms slip around me naked in the sunlight. The whirling stopped. It was utterly still.

I took Harriet's letter from the glovebox and kicked out the mashed door. As I slid through the twisted frame I instinctively reached up to protect my hat, deeply pleased to find it still in place.

The cold night air was luxurious. I breathed deeply and looked around me. Not a thing for as far as I could see, just the totaled Eldorado against the salt, gleaming white-on-white. I thought about what I wanted to say as I struck a match to the box of candles you can't blow out, using their steady flame to ignite Harriet's letter, which burned with the scent of Shalimar.

I had run out of grand statements. I kept it so simple I didn't even say it aloud: *To the Big Bopper, Ritchie Valens, Buddy Holly, and the possibilities of love and music. And to the Holy Spirit.* I tossed Harriet's letter through a shattered window. The spilled gas detonated, flames billowing through the twisted metal, white paint bubbling as it charred, then the gas tank blew and it all roared upward. I stood there and watched it burn.

I had no idea where the highway was, so I started walking with the wind. I hadn't gone a mile when I saw a bloodstain spreading across the salt. Eddie's mother appeared before me, pointing at the bloodstain, her voice trembling like her finger: 'It's just *not* right,' she said. '*It is not right.*'

'Yes it is,' I told her. I kept walking.

The spreading bloodstain began to contract, rushing back to its center, spiraling downward into itself. As it vanished, a great whirlwind rose in its place. Blinded by flying salt, I knelt into a tight ball and covered my eyes. I awaited my judgment. But there were no words in the wind, no sound but it's own wild howl, nothing but itself. Within minutes it died away.

I'd walked another mile before realizing my hat was gone. I hoped it had blown all the way to Houston and landed on Double-Gone's head in a gospel stroke of glory.

In the distance I saw headlights on I-80 and took the shortest angle to the freeway. I was still a long ways out when I saw Kacy waiting in a cloud of light. I ran up, close enough to touch her before I understood she was a ghost.

'Oh, George,' she said, her voice breaking, 'we were on a dir road in the mountains out of La Paz. It was pouring rain. A hug lide came down and swept the van away. I was in the back. I ardly had time to scream. Nobody knows, George. It happened n late September and nobody even knows we're dead.'

'Kacy,' I cried, reaching for her. And I held her a moment real n my arms before she disappeared.

EPILOGUE

The significant problems we face
cannot be solved at the same
level of thinking we were at when
we created them.'

—Albert Einstein

THAT WAS THE END of George Gastin's story. If there was more, I heard it in my dreams, because I was asleep – or, more accurately, given the combination of doom flu, car wreck, codeine, the root soup (which I don't think was an entirely innocent brew), and George himself, I lost consciousness at that point in the narrative. But I *was* there, and heard a sense of conclusion in his voice that left little doubt I was free to go.

When I awoke the next morning, I felt much better. Not hale and hearty, but human. The first thing I noticed was that George was gone. I checked out the window for his tow truck, but the lot was empty. I got dressed and walked over to the motel office. A note from Dorie and Bill, tacked on the door, explained they'd gone bird watching and would be back by nightfall; I was welcome to stay as long as I needed, pay when I was able. I decided I might as well take care of business while I could, in case I suffered relapse.

I walked the four blocks to Itchman's to check on my truck. I caught Gus on his way to lunch.

'Well,' he said in greeting, 'I heard you've got so goddamned lazy you been trying to breed your truck to a redwood stump, hoping to produce some firewood. Seems to me it might be easier on the equipment to just go out and cut it regular.'

'Gus, there's no need to run your lunch hour short just to abuse me. Give me the damages and the date I can pick it up.'

'Six bills should cover it and four days ought to get it done. We

got to order the steering knuckle out of Oxnard; they'll greydog
it up tomorrow. There's terms if you need 'em.'

'Six hundred.' I sighed. 'That's just what George said. Guy
seems to know his shit. He bring you a lot of business?'

Gus shrugged. 'When he's around and if he's in the mood.
George sort of dances to his own music, know what I mean?'

'I know what you mean,' I said in full agreement.

Gus smiled. 'He bend your ear, did he?'

'Some.'

'Yup, George can sling the shit. Did he tell you how he and
some congressman's sixteen-year-old nympho daughter aced the
CIA out a million-and-a-half in gold down in one of them South
American countries, Peru or Bolivia or one of them? How he set
it up so the CIA couldn't touch 'em?'

'No, but he said he had some money. He didn't charge me,
did he tell you that?'

'Hell, he never charges anybody. But for all I know he lives
on Welfare. Different music, like I said.'

'Still music.'

'Did he tell you about his rose garden? He's trying to produce
a black rose.'

'No, but that'd make sense. What he told me about was his
pilgrimage in the Big Bopper's Cadillac.'

'That's one I haven't heard,' Gus said.

'He sure did right by me.'

'I'm not saying George ain't a good one. I'm just saying he's
something else.'

'He sure is,' I agreed.

And as I walked up the street a few minutes later, passing jack-
o-lanterns and paper skeletons in the store windows, I thought to
myself, *Yeah, he's something else all right: He's a ghost.*

And two years later I still think he's a ghost. His own, maybe,
mine, yours in disguise, a random shade. But a ghost for real

and in fact, holy or otherwise. The ghost spun from the silver thread the white lines thin to when you're running on the edge. A ghost loosed with the bands of Orion and squeezed from the sweet influences of Pleiades bound. A ghost risen on the river mist or released in the coil of flames. A rogue ghost. Spirit. A white rose. Rain for the flower in the spiraling root of the dream.

I don't know, and make no claims. But he was at least the ghost of what his journey honored: the love and music already made; the love and music yet possible for making. A ghost of a chance. A ghost of the honest gospel light and wild joy shaking our bones. The ghost in all of us who would dance at the wedding of the sun and moon.

Wop-bop-a-loop-bop-a-wham-bam-boom.

Also available from Canongate

STONE JUNCTION
By Jim Dodge

Stone Junction is a modern odyssey of one man's quest for knowledge and understanding in a world where revenge, betrayal, revolution, mind-bending chemicals, magic and murder are the norm.

With a genuinely awesome scope, a stiletto-sharp wit and an array of bizarre characters, Jim Dodge has woven a mesmerising and age-defining tale. *Stone Junction* is both hilarious and heart-rendingly sad but always utterly compelling.

"A book I put my life on hold for. It is an extraordinary, magical odyssey describing one man's quest for self-understanding in a world filled with bizarre characters, believable impossibilities and spiritual terrorism." *Sunday Herald*

"Reading *Stone Junction* is like being at a non-stop party in celebration of everything that matters." *Thomas Pynchon*

ISBN 1 84195 488 8
£7.99/pbk

You can buy direct from:
Canongate Books, 14 High Street, Edinburgh, EH1 1TE
Tel (0131) 557 5111 Fax (0131) 557 5211